SEVERANCE

A FALTERING SOULS NOVEL

BOOK 2

BY

HAVEN CAGE

I dedicate this book to those who have walked the blade's edge and felt the severing pain of being cut in two by fear, doubt, and uncertainty,

To the poor souls who've danced with the devil on more than one occasion, willingly and unwillingly, and fell victim to temptation,

To those that chose freedom over conformity and wandered the difficult, lonely roads, never looking back to the easier lives that could have brought them to a far worse end,

To the outcasts and misfits. May you, one day, find strength enough to have faith in yourselves and bask in a peace that can only be attained outside the box society tries to stuff us in,

And to those minds that question everything, for it is you who help us grow in all aspects of life.

In loving memory of the father who watches over me from above. I know you're in a better place now, but my selfish love wishes I could steal you back for just a little more time.

ACKNOWLEDGMENTS

No one will ever know how much love I have for my readers. I hold each and every one of you dear to my heart. Y'all are the ones who keep me going on this crazy journey. Without you, I would have given up long ago...and would have certainly pulled out all my hair by now.

Thanks to all the awesome authors who've helped me along the way, especially Renea Mason and Rissa Blakeley. You are truly inspiring!

Now, to those wonderful beings directly connected to my writing, I owe you the biggest thanks. Jaclyn Lee, you might be the one who criticizes me the most, but I love the way you edit my work. I couldn't trust just anyone to point out my flaws in a way that gives me confidence and molds me into a better writer. Diana Quiett, Dina Alexander, Michelle Hughes, Elizabeth Robbins, Amy Padgett, and Tammy Becraft—thanks for your time, honesty, and support. You, beautiful souls, give me hope that I can succeed as an author.

And where would I be without the amazing support system I have at home?

Thanks to:

my loving husband, who stands by my obsessive need to be a part of the writing world,

my sweet son, who loves me even when I'm a little too busy with book stuff,

my mother, who hands out my business cards to little old women in movie theater lines because she'll do anything to get my name out there and loves me that damn much,

my grandmother, who wanted to share my work with the ladies at church despite the darker side of my writing,

my best friend, who always believes in me,

my mother-in-law and sister-in-law, who continuously fight over which one's my biggest fan,

my many other relatives and friends who've bought my book, had kind words of encouragement, or share my posts on social media to help spread the word,

and my co-workers for always asking how things are coming along.

Let the light within burn, wild and ravenous, until it consumes all doubt and fear, rendering your soul a fierce beast for the devil to contend.
— Haven Cage —

Archard

THEN...

I crept through the shadows, squinting into the veil of dust swirling in the thick, balmy air. Invisible, hot tension squeezed my bunching muscles like restraints hindering my every move. The faint scent of humans and mold drifted around the crumbling cathedral. We chose our battleground well. It was quiet, open, and miles away from civilization. We had a clear advantage over the putrid demons while keeping the innocent away from harm.

Are you in? I thought to Nevaeh. My eyes combed over the church, searching for candles and traces of her presence within the sacred walls.

Yeah, can you hear me? Her sweet voice chimed in my mind, warming the cold places in my heart, yet the fear radiating from her shattered my core. I'd already caused her so much pain. How could I ask her to fight

1

in a war she was still too fragile for?

I shook my head to rid myself of the thoughts of regret creeping in and focused on the task at hand. *Yeah. I need you to stay there. The demons aren't far. We are getting into position now. Keep hidden until I tell you. I'll be able to see them from where I am.*

I didn't want to be so forceful with her, but I needed to make the urgency of the situation clear. Nevaeh had always been a stubborn girl. I hoped such strength would carry her through this trial, but my absence had affected her more than I thought.

Where are you? I need to see you. Her voice rushed through my thoughts in a panic, her tone laced with anxiety and fear.

Hold on a sec.

I glided toward a glass lantern perched on a small iron table and lit the wick. Rustling wings whispered behind me. I glanced over my shoulder and saw my brothers on the other side of the pews, igniting their own flame and lighting the remaining lanterns. The broken church filled with a dim glow, softening the harshness of the old building.

I looked down at my lantern again and smiled. The flickering light illuminated a canister of incense sticks lying on its side, caked under decades of dust. I plucked a few sticks from the tin and lit them. Waving the smoldering sticks in wide arcs, I prayed the thin tendrils of smoke curling into the air were enough to conceal our odor.

I closed my eyes for a moment and inhaled deeply, drowning in the scent of spice and sweetness evoking painful memories of my true home. My bones ached for the welcoming arms of Heaven, but I made my choice long ago. I accepted the responsibility of my actions with Nevaeh. A Guardian should never get so close. I'd broken the rules and risked her life at an innocent age. I carried that burden of guilt every day, yet there are times I'm thankful that she knows me now. I yearn for her attention and love her more than the graces of the God I abandoned.

My focus snapped back with another frightened call from Nevaeh.

What is that? What are you doing out there? Hysteria crept around the edges of her mind. I heard muffled sounds of fidgety movements sounding from her hiding place in the confessional. With a deep breath,

I focused my energy and stretched it toward her like an invisible arm, reaching out to comfort her emotions.

Something was wrong. She was a bundle of tight, fiery, nerves.

It's okay, we just lit some lanterns and incense. It'll make it harder for them to detect us. Are you still okay?

She didn't respond.

The silence in my head knotted my stomach. I searched her thoughts for an explanation for her distraction, but they were a jumble of flashing images and disconcerted feelings.

This was a bad idea. She wasn't ready. I couldn't let her do this. I had to save her. I had to fly us out of here.

I crouched between the pews, readying to push off in a sprint toward Nevaeh's chamber. I grabbed the back of the bench for leverage, planted my foot, then froze. It was too late. Like a slow fog clinging close to the ground, the stench of Hell rolled in, devouring the church from one end to the other.

My wings flexed instinctively and launched me into the air mid-step. The flesh on my back extended and pulled with the powerful extremities working to lift me upward to the shadowy rafters.

Nevaeh's mind was too chaotic for me to breach, but I knew when I saw the glint of her violet-blue eyes staring at me from a sliver of opening around her door, things were not going to go as planned. She'd made a resolution of some sort—the inevitability in her eyes was concrete.

This whole time, we tried to convince her of the destiny she was meant to fulfill. She was the Clavis. She was the key to changing the war between Heaven, Hell, and Celatum. I showed her a glimpse of the monster she could become if the darkness took over. All she had to do was have faith...and trust me.

It was not trust I saw in her eyes now, though.

During all her trials and experiences, there was never such an absolute certainty. She had somehow, in these last fleeting moments, discovered the will to make her claim, and it was not the fate I hoped she'd choose.

I choked back her name, fighting the urge to call out to her. This was all my fault. If I'd just been honest from the beginning, maybe she would have trusted me.

Archard, I can't do this. I know how this ends, she screamed in my head.

I exhaled, thankful to hear her words again, but the pit of my stomach soured with her admission. *What are you talking about, Nevaeh? Just stick to the plan. We'll keep you safe. I promise.*

We can win this battle. Please just stick to the plan, I begged to myself silently.

There's another way. I have no choice. I'm so sorry.

Her energy was pulling away from me. The steel-strong bond between us was quickly shredding to ethereal pieces, severing the fragile, heavenly fabric holding us together.

I shoved my influence upon her, attempting to reign in her panic, but she only became more and more distant. A sharp pain knifed through my heart. I clutched my chest and gasped. Even after years of our separation, nothing felt more crippling than the destruction she was causing our souls right now.

I was losing her.

Wait, what are you going to do? Nevaeh, don't do anything stupid.

Suddenly, a mass of images and voices flashed into my mind. The vividness of the pictures added to my disorientation. Gritting my teeth and squeezing my eyes shut tight, I watched Nevaeh's mind render visions of the ruined cathedral, the demons beating and tearing at her body, and her fatal ending.

As the scene played in my head, my legs grew too weak to hold my weight. I slumped to my knees, nearly falling off the rafter beneath me, and waited for the horrid memory to stop. Watching the moment of her defeat, her eyes slowly closing as she struggled to keep me in her sight, was unbearable.

The visions stopped abruptly. My eyes popped open, eager to gain a more tangible connection with her. *No! Nevaeh!* I pleaded within her mind, panting and righting myself amidst the shadows of the ceiling.

I swallowed the lump of loss and doom forming in my throat and wiped away the tears spilling down my cheeks.

The church doors creaked open, momentarily taking my attention from Nevaeh. A horde of demons filed into the church and stopped at the entrance, scanning over the building. A muscle ticked in my jaw as I considered my options. If I moved now, we'd be exposed. I couldn't risk our advantage, nor could I put my angelic brothers in jeopardy. I refused to lose her, though. She was mine to protect. I couldn't fail her again.

Devastatingly distant words rifled into my thoughts, a mere whisper compared to the definitive tone I was used to.

I'm so sorry. I'll come back to you. Please forgive me, she echoed.

My eyes darted to her hiding spot, to the demons, then back to the small room harboring her from the fiends. Nevaeh's beautiful eyes settled on me from the crack of space surrounding her chamber door once again as she said goodbye.

The Hell-monsters lurked dangerously close to Nevaeh. I lowered into a squat and stretched heavy wings behind my rigid body. Balancing on the rotted beam, I searched the shadows for the other angels while suppressing swells of anger, pain, and the need to rush to my ward. Shimmers of their heavenly eyes gleamed back at me. We were all on the same page. I only had to give the signal.

"Please don't let her choose them," I whispered to God, knowing my prayer would go unanswered. That was not how He worked; He would not force her to take His side.

Quiet mumbles resonated from the confessional. I didn't need to hear what was being said—I knew the words leaving her perfectly bowed lips by the complete emptiness that met me when I reached for her.

The demons paused, craning their heads toward Nevaeh's voice, then began their slow, deliberate trek toward the sound.

Nevaeh! Nevaeh! Answer me. Please. Answer me. I tried to break through the barrier steadily building inside her, but there was only silence. Laying brick by evil brick, she recessed to the dark unreachable shadows of her mind.

Seconds later, the walls around Nevaeh rumbled and shook. The final frayed strands of our connection severed as they had when I took her to the depths of the spirit world.

I balled my shaking hands into fists, digging my nails into my palms. Gnashing my teeth together, I bit back the roar of grief and desolation building in my chest.

I showed her the outcome of the decision to give into the dark temptations. Why would she do this?

Shouting at her verbally would do no good, let alone shouting to her thoughts. She was too far gone from my grasp. My heart pounded against my ribs, transforming from the steady heartbeat that throbbed for her into a treacherous, hollow thump of emptiness that would act as a constant reminder of her severance.

Demons hurried toward the little room, eager to overpower the body inside. Nevaeh's blood-curdling screams echoed over the boom of collapsing structures around the cathedral. The building couldn't bear its own weight, never mind whatever power Nevaeh had unleashed.

I couldn't wait any longer.

Without thinking, I dove off my perch, cursing the rush of wind gliding under my wings and lifting me upwards. If not for her, I would have let myself plummet. Instead, I allowed the force of air to carry me above the pews. The other angels emerged from their corners and joined in sieging the demons.

We set eyes on our targets and adjusted our flight patterns in unison, as we were trained to do for battles in the past. Each angel moved with focus and precision—a well-oiled machine gathering to entrap the monsters surrounding Nevaeh.

A rift of wind flicked against my feathers, foretelling a change in the atmospheric pressure, and forced me to deviate from my path. I braced myself just before an explosion of energy rippled throughout the weakening cathedral. My body hurled backward from the blow, slamming me into a marble pillar struggling to uphold its load of the remaining roof. I thrust out my wings to keep me aloft and sucked in a loud breath to replace the oxygen I'd expelled during the hit.

She renounced Him.

It was final.

I squinted beyond falling shards of marble and plaster to scan over my brothers' bodies flung all over the church and the demons that littered the floor. My gaze landed on a glowing red light seeping from the cracks and rubble of Nevaeh's confessional. The walls left standing were crumbling to the ground fast.

Hell-fiends pulled themselves out from under the broken fragments of cement and wood. Using the carnage of fallen bodies, they propelled themselves toward Nevaeh. They trampled over whatever obstacle lay in their way—flesh and bone or not—wrestling with one another and scratching at the remaining splinters of wall in a fight to be the first to reach Nevaeh.

Gliding closer, I noticed Arkin's arm reaching up through a pile of crushed bricks, shoving them off his buried body. Once he had a large enough opening, he latched onto a slab of ceiling next to him and drudged himself out of the mound of broken church. He stood up, wavering in his stance for a moment, before focusing his eyes on the demons mere feet away. He jumped into the air, a roar bursting from his throat, and plunged toward the fiends. Centuries of warrior's experience as my right-hand man made him cunning and skilled. He tackled the nearest demon, yanked it off the ground, and flew a good thirty feet into the air before releasing his grip and letting it fall. Arkin watched it slam against the marble floor with satisfaction in his eyes and a grin curling his lips. He moved onto the next.

Angel after angel swooped and arched through the air, disabling any enemy they could get their hands on.

I snatched up the demon close to me and pounded it with my fists, relishing in the satisfying sting tearing through my fingers. Capturing whatever ugly form I could get my hands on, I demolished one mutilated face after another, smashing their rotten bones into unrecognizable holes and lumps until chunks of skin were missing from my bloody knuckles. I refused to let them have her.

The barricade of demons was beginning to dwindle away when I finally caught a glimpse of Nevaeh, red light saturating her beautiful olive skin. Agony and wickedness contorted her fragile features. She was transitioning.

She squealed, stumbled to the floor, and homed her eyes on a spot at her ankle. I slowed my flapping wings, bracing my joints for a quick landing. Once my feet hit the floor, I sprinted in her direction.

Beyond the planks of wood splintering out from the confessional walls, a hulking body crawled along the floor into my line of sight, its claws digging into her leg. Nevaeh tried to shake the creature but paused the second she glanced up and noticed me barreling toward her. Our gazes locked; behind the regret in her eyes, she silently begged me to let her go. That look robbed the last ounce of breath—and hope—from my body.

"Nevaeh," I yelled, covering the last bit of distance between us. If I could just put my hands on her, if I could only wrap her in my arms and kiss her, she'd come back to me.

She kicked the demon off her leg and jumped upright. "See you in Hell," she promised to the monster.

In the blink of a second, Nevaeh disappeared, her body gulped up by the fiery opening in the wall behind her.

I didn't have a chance at saving her now. It was forbidden for me to follow into the depths of Hell. I would find her somehow though. I would bring her back.

Anger overpowered my grief, and with my brothers, I leveled the damned left behind.

We won the battle. We accomplished our mission of bringing the Celestial war to Earth.

Despite achieving success for the greater good, I would mourn my sacrifice until the day I could hold her in my arms again.

Orchard

CHAPTER ONE

Now

I peered down at the cracked gravestone jutting up at my feet, my eyes studying the simple but love-filled message barely readable under the owner's name: Gracie Caldwell, 1932-1939, *Your sweet giggles will echo in our hearts forever.*

I had no idea who this little girl was or how she died, but the mere sight of her chipped marker stirred all kinds of emotions in me. The anger and hate — the grief and love — I kept pushing down in my gut for the past few months refused to stay where I put it.

I huffed out a frustrated breath. I didn't know why, but this little girl disturbed me. I backed away from the child's grave and plopped down in front of the hunk of limestone at her feet. My gaze roamed over the faded etchings of two swallows carrying a wreath of flowers and pine to place at Gracie's head.

The sun was dawning. A glow of yellow and pink hues bathed the girl's stone in more and more light as the morning set in. I took the last swig of whiskey from the bottle I'd toted around with me all night, inhaling sharply when the burn settled in my throat. My eyelids were heavy, my bones weary. I'd walked the city the entire night without any luck and ended my search here — the last place I saw her.

A bobbing movement breached the crest of a slight hill in the distance, catching my attention. I squinted, struggling to make out the form heading my direction. Once the figure was close enough, I recognized exactly who it was. I rolled my eyes and lowered them back down to poor Gracie, wanting nothing more than to wallow at her feet, alone. From the look on Arkin's face, that wouldn't be happening anytime soon.

Arkin hiked between the gravestones as if they were nothing more than rocks along a sidewalk, then stopped when he stood at my side. "I figured you'd be here," he said, his gaze roaming over the same headstone that I'd been focused on for the last twenty minutes. His lips tightened into a thin line for a moment, seeming to pity the young girl, then he returned his attention to a spot at the crown of my head.

I knew he was staring a hole into my skull — I could feel it — but I wasn't going to give him the satisfaction of looking up at him. I didn't invite him here, so why should I appease his need for bonding? I just wanted him to leave me alone.

His fingers tapped the white, paper cup he held out toward me. "Coffee. You should try it sometime. It's better than that shit you've been poisoning yourself with lately."

My brows shot up, and I glared at him. He had no business saying that to me; I was in constant remorse, and a little alcohol to soothe my aching heart wasn't too much to ask for.

Rolling my eyes, I snatched the cup from him and popped the plastic lid off. Steam rolled off the coffee and hit me in the face, forcing me to swipe the back of my hand across the thin sheen of sweat building on my forehead. The sun had fully emerged from the horizon, making it hot, and having to wear a long ass coat during the middle of summer was already torture enough in the southern heat; why in the Hell did he think scalding, bitter liquid would make me feel better?

I sucked it up and took a sip anyway, hoping the caffeine would help clear the constant fog in my head.

Arkin lowered himself beside me, face turned up to the sky, ankles crossed out in front of him, soaking in the sunlight beaming down on us.

"What the fuck do you want?" I snarled, taking another sip.

His eyes darted over at me and narrowed. "We might have a hit on her," he answered in a slow, measured tone. His nostrils flared, and his jaw tensed. The hint of pent up tension in his eyes told me he was trying his damnedest not to pound me, right here and now, in the middle of this cemetery.

My hazy thoughts sobered a bit. I stared at him, assessing his annoyed expression, then felt like a jerk. I'd perfected my skills in taking my anger and sorrow out on those around me over the last few months, but I failed to remember that Arkin had changed that night at the cathedral too. His usual jovial and sarcastic manner took a backseat to a gloomier mood. He had nearly as many sullen days as I did. Her absence constantly reminded us of our failure.

Clearing my throat, I settled the cup of coffee against the stone behind me and adjusted my tone so as not to sound like a complete douche. I raked my fingers through my hair, and then down my face, trying to wipe away the premature disappointment weighing in on me. "What kind of a hit?"

I found it hard to get my hopes up anymore. In the early days after she surrendered to the Dark, we'd tracked her to various spots around the city only to come up short. Each time we lost her trail, it was another kick in the gut. The Light Celatum helped when they could, and we probably wouldn't have gotten half as far as we had without them, but it was never enough. It had been three months since she claimed sides, and thirteen days since there was any sign of her in the human realm.

"Maggie saw her leaving that old warehouse on 5th this morning," he responded, easing back into a relaxed sunbathing position. The last traces of his urge to deal me a beating quickly erased from his face when he mentioned the woman's name.

Maggie was a reliable source. She came to us as a Celata offering help after word got out about her kind's new involvement in the war against Hell and hearing that parts of the Heavenly battle were becoming more apparent to the humans. With the useful gift of energy tracing, she volunteered to help us track Nevaeh. She knew what happened in the cathedral bent the laws that maintained some sense of boundaries between worlds, and she didn't understand how or why Nevaeh had impacted those laws, or what the repercussions were yet; regardless, Maggie offered her loyalty to us, relying solely on her faith that we would win in the end.

Unfortunately, there weren't many Celatum who shared Maggie's trust. Hell, the majority of us were in the same boat. We hadn't found a damn thing about Nevaeh's past that could explain anything other than her possibly being half human and half demon since she could traverse portals to Hell — which we discovered was at will now, whereas before it occurred by accident or with the help of others. That made it impossible to nab her, or even confront her, if we did catch up to Nevaeh. We hadn't gotten close enough to figure out her other powers, but whatever they were inspired fear in those who have crossed her path.

What that all meant? We had no fucking clue, but many of us still held onto the idea of Nevaeh being the Clavis. It was the only bit of hope we had left. If she was, then maybe she'd be strong enough to pull out of this and turn the odds around.

There was also the prophecy we couldn't find, written in a book that no one seems to know much about. Then there's the fact that something shady happened to her mom, Arianna, and Arianna's rogue Guardian Angel, Rhett, which, again, no one seemed to know shit about.

Dead-ends everywhere.

But, hey, we did learn that the Dark Celatum were training her to recruit Light Celatum. That's a plus, right?

Yeah, right. I balled my fists and pushed them into the ground to keep from destroying my surroundings.

"She went in to check it out after Nev left," he continued, dragging me away from my darkening thoughts. Arkin shifted his weight to readjust the wings pinned behind him, and perhaps to procrastinate furthering the conversation. Judging by the thin line of his lips and furrowed brow, the results weren't good. "She found Vinney. He was dead."

"So, maybe she heard he was dead and went to show her respect," I retorted, knowing that Vinney was an old friend of George and hers.

Arkin's voice lowered the way it did when he was about to say something he knew I wouldn't like. He knew me too well at times. "Yeah, or maybe she killed him."

"We don't know that. Do we?" I spat, shoving off the ground. My shoulders stiffened, and suddenly my coat felt too restrictive. I needed to free my wings, to taste the relief of flying and escaping this reality. The burdensome appendages spasmed under my duster, itching for release. I repressed my feelings, yet again, and pulled them tight to my back.

A single feather swirled out from under my coat, drifting upward on a warm breeze before lazily falling to the ground. The bold purple tip contrasting with the cream color reminded me of how lost I really was. I forced my gaze away from it and stepped over the frail feather, ignoring the sadness and shame it brought as I headed toward the cemetery gates.

"Archard, I just want you to keep an open mind about this. I know you miss her, man. Hell, we all do," Arkin said, jumping up and rushing to match my pace, "but you have to see her for what she might be now." He grabbed my forearm with a comforting hand, determined to make sure I heard him. "She's not the same Nev we knew."

I jerked my arm from his grasp. "You don't know her like I know her. You didn't see the regret in her eyes. She promised she would come back to me." I stifled tears of denial back long enough to turn away from my brother. I couldn't let him see how weak I'd become.

"I'm sorry," he whispered before backing away, allowing me space to regroup.

"We will go to the warehouse and search it ourselves. We can't afford to miss anything." I tugged back the collar of my duster and pulled out a crumpled map of the city from the inner pocket. The worn paper made crackling noises as I flattened it atop an exposed tomb.

"What exactly do you expect to find at the warehouse?"

"Nothing," I answered. He stared at me, confused. I retrieved a pen from the pocket where I kept the map. My hand lowered over the dozens of squiggly lines representing our city roads and made a red dot at the same location I'd watched Nevaeh come out of her first portal—Vinney's warehouse. "Get Maggie."

"Alright. But, just so you know, I'd rather be spending my time watching the game than tailing along with you. It's out of the goodness of my heart that I will accompany you on your trip to disappointment." His fist jabbed my shoulder. My heart softened when a low chuckle rumbled through my brother's chest.

"Thanks for being so selfless," I joked back. While Arkin made a call to Maggie, I traced my finger over every red dot blotting the paper. There was one for each time Nev was sighted.

"The feisty little devil-tracker is on her way there," he said with a smirk. He crossed his arms, and the glint of happiness in his expression vanished when he approached the other side of the tomb. "She seems to stay pretty close to home, huh?" I glanced up to see his eyes hovering over the multitude of spots scattered within the city boundaries.

"Yeah." I sighed, irritated that she was so near, yet so far from my arms. "Shall we go?"

"Sure. Let's see if our Nev left us anything this time." Arkin slapped at my back and headed toward the exit.

Death had spoiled the air by the time we got there. The scent was so strong it assaulted our senses as soon as we flew over the lot. Maggie had called the authorities after finding Vinney's body. They extracted his corpse quickly, but the stubborn effects of a snuffed life remained longer than any human could detect. Their imprint on this world lingered, clutching onto what they once knew — regardless of where their soul ended up.

"It's about damn time you butterflies showed up," Maggie greeted with her usual smart-ass commentary. "I've been waiting here long enough to watch mold grow."

She was twenty-one, short, and thin with black hair that gradually shifted to the color of orange flames at the end. Her attitude matched the fiery tips. I learned early on that she was as meek as a lamb under the leather midriff, punky spiked locks, and tattoos.

"Hey now, you should respect your superiors," Arkin teased as we soared in a low circle around her. She coughed and swatted at the small dust funnels lifting from the ground just before we laid feet on the loose gravel.

"I will when I see 'em," Maggie piped up. The little pixie breathed in a long draw off her cigarette, then bent over to snuff it out on her black jump-boots. She searched my eyes for a moment, kindness betraying her tough act. "You ready?"

I nodded, then followed her farther onto the warehouse grounds. Miles of yellow tape wrapped around the building, but that meant nothing to us. The closer we got, the stronger the scent of blood and mortality became.

"Recap what you saw, Mags," Arkin said, dipping under a strand of yellow plastic and holding it up for Maggie.

"I was just patrolling her usual spots like you told me. When I got here, I saw a light waving past that crack," she pointed to a loose board on the warehouse front. "I skirted the entrance and snuck a peek." She paused and looked at me, "I saw her plain as day at first. Then, they were surrounded by dense midnight. I've never seen anything like that before. It's like the dark emitted the light, or deflected it...or something like that. It was just...wrong."

Arkin and I glanced at each other, unsure what she meant.

"Don't do that shit," Maggie demanded, stomping her foot and shoving her hands down by her side.

"What?" Arkin held up his hands defensively as the little pixie swatted at him.

"I know what I saw. Don't do that thing where you guys act like I don't know what I'm talking about." She turned and marched away.

The muscular angel to my right jogged forward and grabbed a belt loop on Maggie's baggy jeans, yanking her to a sudden stop. She slapped and punched at Arkin. He laughed, playfully ducking away from each blow. I watched the two dance around each other, smiling when the cocky beauty unsuccessfully resisted the grin of happiness brightening her eyes.

Wood creaked and moaned under the pressure of my prying hands. The police department boarded up the opening after they took Vinney, but it was easy enough to remove. Three swift yanks and the nails gladly gave into my grip.

Arkin and I coughed, covering our noses at the same time. Vinney's foul odor rushed out from the opening, smacking us in the faces.

"Man, you guys sure are pussies." Maggie shook her head as she traipsed into the dusty, old building.

"Hey, we just have sensitive olfactory systems," Arkin yelled, forcing his hand to uncover his nose. He followed Maggie in, unable to wipe the grimace from his face.

I tagged behind them, remembering the night I saw Nevaeh return from the portal. The night we kissed. The night I, yet again, gave into my own selfish need to feel her, instead of doing what was best for Nevaeh.

"So, this is where I saw the ink cloud swallow them." Maggie pointed to a small red smudge in the dirt next to an old assembly machine. "I saw her standing next to the old man here. There was a little light from the flashlight Vinney dropped there." She motioned to the black wand with a cracked lens laying four feet away. "I couldn't see anyone with Nevaeh, but she was talking to someone." Maggie tugged at a crumpled pack of cigarettes in her pocket and fished out a stick.

"How do you know she wasn't talking to Vinney?" I questioned, watching her lift a lighter in front of her face. The small flame threw a yellow glow across her porcelain skin, bringing out the softness of her features. Her mixed Asian-American descent allowed her just enough ethnic features to make her almond-shaped eyes and high cheek bones exotic and beautiful. I believed that was what drew Arkin in at first.

"I just know. This is what I do, remember?" She gently dragged her shoe in the dirt, respectfully covering Vinney's blood spot. The petite sprite drew in a puff and grabbed a silver crucifix hanging from her neck. She stood still, silent in concentration for a brief time, then made the sign of the cross. She sobered from her moment of prayer quickly when she realized Arkin was staring at her with a huge grin. She kicked a small patch of dirt in his direction. "What? *Someone* had to do it."

Arkin finally pried his eyes from Maggie and scanned the area for anything that might lead us to Nevaeh. "It'd be easier smelling roses in a shit-storm than finding traces of her in here."

I shook my head at his ridiculous comment, then surveyed the room myself. "This is hopeless. You were right. There is nothing here besides rust and dust." I rubbed my hand down my face to loosen the stress from my skin.

"Slow your roll, ladies. I wasn't finished." Maggie perched her fists on her hips. Raising my eyebrows, surprised that she hadn't already given us every detail, I cocked my head to the side and waved my hand between us, motioning for her to get on with it. "Whenever you're ready Maggie. Hanging on every word here."

"Okay. So, before the ink cloud swallowed Nevaeh and Vinney, I saw her cast-bubble."

"You really do need to get a better name for that, Maggie," I advised.

"What do you suggest for a big ball of colored energy that surrounds everything and everyone?"

"Well…" Honestly, I had no idea what I would call it. Maggie was a rarity, so it wasn't like we had a lot to go on for Celatum that could read and track remnants of energies. "How about energy ball?"

"Hell no! I like mine better." She hopped up backwards and settled on the old hunk of metal behind her. "Any-who, Nevaeh's bubble was swirls of red and blue, but there were streaks of black and white fighting against each other like snakes too."

"What's that mean? That's good, right?" Arkin shifted his gaze back and forth between me and Maggie.

"More like it's not completely bad. She still has some good in her," I verified, eyeing Maggie to make sure she agreed.

With a nod of her head, she confirmed my conclusion. "If she was Dark, her bubble would look like tar. The sucky thing about it, though? Her bubble got real messy right before the ink cloud came."

"What are you saying, Maggie?" I glared at her, my tone harshening from her accusation.

"I don't know. Everything blurred, and it became one big mush of color, instead of the pretty marbling I normally see. She's shifting, maybe?" Her shoulders lifted in a slight shrug, and her emerald eyes lowered to her boots. She didn't like the possibility any more than I did, and she especially didn't like giving me the bad news that my ward may be switching sides for the long haul.

We all stayed silent for a moment, thinking about the repercussions of Nevaeh submitting to the Dark completely. I have to think that, even though she renounced our maker, she is holding out on the Dark One from the other side.

"Maggie?" I said softly, glowering down at the place Vinney had breathed his last breath.

Her gaze raised to mine. "Yeah, Archie?"

"Was Vinney dead before Nev visited him?" I didn't want to know the answer, but the question had to be asked.

She dropped her head, reluctant to respond. "Well...I'm not sure."

I punched the machine she sat on, denting the metal where my fist landed. "You know, Maggie. Tell me the truth, dammit!"

She slowly ground the cherry of her smoke into the worn treads of her boot and sighed. "I couldn't see him very well, but his cast was still vibrant blue with white swirls before the ink cloud gulped them up. Afterwards, it was muted."

"So, he died after." I raked my hands through my hair. "But, you didn't see her kill him, right?"

Maggie shook her head. "No."

I let out a sigh of relief. I couldn't accept the idea of her taking human lives. There had to be another explanation.

"C'mon, man." Arkin draped one arm around my neck and patted my cheek with his other hand, "We won't find anything else here."

He was distracting me from my thoughts of Nevaeh, which made me angry; but, at the same time, in his distraction from my thoughts of Nevaeh, I was grateful.

CHAPTER TWO

Unwanted Developments

I followed the Crucio demon as it led me to my chamber. Its slow, shuttering movements made the trek seem to take forever. Every few steps, the Hell-fiend jerked its heavy head around to make sure I was close.

I've been under lock and key for three months now. My only time out of the tunnels of Hell consisted of training and doing biddings. I was sick of this place. Literally. I felt physically ill every time I had to return to this fuckin' sinner's cage. On the plus side, if there was such a thing here, I was thankful that they hadn't offered me the luxury tour of the deeper parts. Listening to the groans and cries that echoed to my chamber was enough to make a person mad. I couldn't imagine staying in the sections where the punished resided.

Layla sauntered down the corridor next to me, her overly saccharine voice reminding me of nails on a chalkboard when she spoke. "Nevaeh, it'll get easier. You just have to accept the power that comes with the choice you made. You are the only one hurting from it." She offered an emotionless smile and placed her hand on my shoulder.

"I don't need your advice, nor do I want it," I said, jerking away from her touch. Nothing about what I was becoming would get any easier for me to swallow. Even if the power was exhilarating. Even if it called to me louder and louder every day.

"Well, hon, I hate to be the bearer of bad news," she grinned, "but, until you fully develop, I'm your superior." Her shoulders broadened as she spoke, displaying her sense of control over me.

"Layla, let's get something straight. You will never be my superior," I spat. The thought of succumbing to her orders, knowing her true nature, made me cringe.

"Whatever you want to tell yourself, dearie. Just remember who's walkin' free and who's on their way to a cell, though." She shoved a manicured hand into my back and forced me to catch up with the demon ahead. "Oh, and that little stunt you pulled tonight? You better watch that shit. Next time, father might not be so willing to overlook it."

"How about *you* watch *your* shit. Don't worry about me," I snarled.

I snuck away from a recruiting mission to see Vinney. I'd over-heard from a few of the new street kids that he was dying. I didn't want him to die alone, so I wandered back to his warehouse. It was something good I could do to counteract my growing list of bad. All the lying, convincing, and judging I'd done these last few months weighed heavily on my shoulders. My will to fight the evil blossoming in my soul was weakening. I had needed to repent somehow. Vinney, I thought, was a good place to start.

I was wrong.

"Your Ater said he felt a rift in your powers today." Curiosity piqued in her cold, crystal-blue eyes.

"Is that a question or a fact?" I wasn't about to give her any more information than I had to.

The demons jerked to an abrupt stop and turned, their soulless eyes boring into me. "Into the cage, swine," one of the Crucios screeched out. Since my transition, I could understand the mind-numbing screeches of the Hellions. Lucky me.

Layla smirked at the demon's command, "I guess we'll discuss this more later." She waved at me with wiggly fingers. "Sweet dreams, Nevaeh." The clacking of her high-heels faded off into a tunnel to the right.

I was happy to finally get away from her, but that meant I was alone with the torture demons. His soulless eyes burned into my back as I pushed open the heavy, carved door. It never failed; every time I stepped into my starry room, my stomach leaped. The mirrored floor was hard to get used to.

It was *all* hard to get used to.

"Fucking move," the Crucio's rotted lips forced out. He bent, quivering as he reached for the door handle, and kicked me inside. The wooden corner scraped along my leg as it slammed shut.

Pain throbbed in my back from the Crucio's blow. I lay on the floor and stared at the tiny orbs of light reflecting from above me, trying to regain the breath knocked out of me. Tears spilled from my eyes while I contemplated giving in. How could I have ever thought I could beat the evil seeded in my heart? Let alone the evil surrounding me in this God-forsaken place.

As I wallowed in self-pity, his familiar scent swirled around the room, the spiced, woodsy odor calming my sadness. "Where are you? I know you're there. I can smell you." I closed my eyes and inhaled deeply. Seductive chills puckered my skin. He had a way of making me drunk from his presence.

"I am beside you, my love," he whispered in my ear, then materialized at my side. His forceful hands lifted me across his lap. "Why are you crying?" Long, thin fingers brushed away the wetness from my cheek.

"When can I see him? You promised me," I whimpered against his chest.

I couldn't let him know I was fighting the change. He was the only one that could truly control me here—other than their father. This being, my Ater, held all my fears. He was stealing all the love I had left in my heart and replacing it with an unstoppable dark need. I was defenseless when it came to him.

"Soon, my love. You are not ready. We must purify you before we can allow you to see George. Otherwise, you won't understand why we've done the things we've done."

I bit my tongue and nodded. "I just thought...It's been three months." My gaze lowered from his featureless face.

"I know how long it's been, Nevaeh. Don't you trust me?" A disembodied voice portrayed the stern intentions that the blank skin stretching over his absent eyes, nose, and mouth could not.

He could enter my thoughts, but not the way Archard had. It would never be the same with *this* guardian angel. Bron's way was not from love, but pure possession that claimed my clouded soul. He projected what he wanted me to see and hear so convincingly that it overtook me. Archard showed me truths that were already within my heart and allowed me to react at my will.

I didn't trust him. I didn't trust anyone in Hell. Unfortunately, I had to play nice in order to rescue George with some tactfulness.

I reached up and traced his sharp jaw, feeling it twitch beneath my touch. "Why won't you show me your face?" My hand slid down the raven strands of long, silky hair draping over his shoulder. "It's hard to talk to you like this. Don't you trust *me*?"

His fingers grazed over what would be his mouth as he considered my request, then snapped down and wrapped around my wrist. "I can't, my love. You have no idea what you ask of me. If you know what's good for you, you'll never ask again."

I tugged at my hand, but he held it tight, so I stopped struggling and smiled innocently. It was never a good idea to piss Bron off, so I constantly walked on eggshells, biting back the urge to let my rage override my focus, no matter the cost. Sometimes I felt like I was gaining a foot in our battle of power, but it didn't take long for him to remind me who had the upper hand.

"Layla told me you felt a rift today. What does that mean?" I asked sweetly.

Bron's hand relaxed and released me. "It means that you are growing stronger."

I pushed up from his lap and walked to a polished, intricately designed buffet table on the other side of the room. It was a lie, though. It was *all* a lie. I knew that under that antique beauty was probably a decaying wooden slab, held together by rusted nails. I frowned at the knowledge that nothing, *absolutely nothing*, was what it seemed here. Everything and everyone was just shiny and pristine on the outside, but inside, we were all damaged and rotting away.

"I don't feel any different." I picked a grape from the cluster laying on the gold tray and popped it in my mouth. As I chewed, I worked to keep my thoughts cloaked from him. Something did happen while I was at Vinney's, but I didn't know what. Until I did, whatever it was had to be kept a secret.

Heavy footsteps approached behind me. His demanding hands dug into the flesh on my shoulders. I leaned back into him, succumbing to the drunk dizziness he induced. My knees weakened, and a pool of silky fluid gathered between my thighs. His soft cheek brushed aside my hair and rubbed along my neck.

"Why are you lying to me, Nevaeh?" he whispered.

A subtle moan escaped my lips. "I'm not lying." Waves of ecstasy rolled over my body. He was seducing me into surrendering. There was no telling how long I could keep my walls up, but knowing what my Ater could do made it so much harder to deny him the truth.

"Why are you hiding?" Skilled fingers roamed down my arms, over my quivering stomach, and across my hips, heading straight for my sweet spot.

"I'm right here, dark lover." My words were only aroused breaths now.

Damn his control over me.

Any minute I would give in. "I should get some rest," I said, hoping to deter him. My fingers found his and slowed them to a halt just under the rim of my jeans.

He spun me so fast I nearly tripped on my own feet. Wide-eyed, I peered up into his non-existent face and waited for the lashing I was sure would follow.

Tattered wings the color of his hair sprung from Bron's back and bound me against him. I cried out as a bone-white talon from the apex of each wing pressed into my shoulder blades.

"Please, don't do this," I begged.

Anger spread from his body like warmth from a furnace. Once he got to this point, there was no stopping him. The malice inside controlled his every move.

I pushed against his chest in protest, but the sharp talons digging farther into my skin countered my attempts to escape. Hot trickles of blood soaked into my shirt. He had me stuck in his grasp, and he knew I was his.

"Nevaeh, if you'd just been honest with me, you wouldn't need punishment. Now, you have to learn. I am the only one who can save you down here. I am your master." His voice deepened and, from the corner of my eyes, I watched his veins turn black like poisonous vines climbing to cover every part of him. The dark malicious threads wound their way up his body, fueling his cruel intentions.

"Bron, please. I'm begging you." Tears fell down my cheek in rivers of helplessness. I cried because I knew what was coming. I cried, not because of the impending pain — I'd learned to handle that — but because I would lose another piece of my withering self. I would be one more step away from the woman I used to be. My hatred and hunger for revenge would flare again, making it that much more difficult to fight the change.

I finally submitted to his demands and relaxed my body against his pulling and yanking. The rip of fabric rang in my ears as he tore at my shirt. My breasts stung under his rough groping. A faint plunk of my button hitting the floor sounded just beyond the ghostly echoes of Bron's heavy breathing and animalistic groans. He shoved my jeans down, scraping the denim against my legs until they were on the floor.

"I knew you'd give in, my love. There is only you and me. Don't ever forget that." A poison-lined hand slid over my neck and another fisted a chunk of hair, jerking my head back.

I peered into the expressionless face before me and secretly wished for a saving grace. I didn't dare say a word. This is what my life had become. Fleeting moments of feeling like I belonged, followed by timeless periods of rape, beatings, commands, and oppression.

Bron pressed into my body, releasing the constrained chaotic yearning that always lurked beneath his surface. Engorged flesh dug into my lower stomach, and the dread built. He wasn't human, and I wasn't made to accommodate the girth he would soon give me. Regardless, my sensitive flesh tingled and slickened with a need to be filled in a way only he could.

I bit back a scream as his talons retracted from my back. He nabbed me up by my ribcage like I was weightless. Suddenly, I flew through the air and bounced, belly-down, onto the bed. The crimson, silk sheets gave beneath my grip as I grabbed handfuls and fought to hoist myself to the other side. There was no getting away though.

Two gusts of air ruffled my hair while my dark angel flapped his wings, covering the distance between us. "Where do you think you're going?" He dragged me toward him, a lake of red silk flowing across the bed when I pulled it with me.

"Bron, you don't have to do this," I whimpered. My hips hinged around the edge of the mattress, and I struggled to find something—anything—to hang onto. I forced my tears to stop and prepared for the actions about to take place.

"Oh, but I do, my sweet." My stomach twisted at the false tenderness in his words.

I took a deep breath, then slackened my body into his vice-like hold. As my flesh relaxed, the rage within unfurled. Power surged through my bones, pleading for freedom. The pressure pushed outwards from my core.

"Go ahead, Nevaeh. Let it out. Come out and play with me," the

Ater cooed in my ear.

Most fear what now hides behind the fortress I've constructed out of my body. I can bring the epitome of evil to their knees with the web of deviance I spin. I show them the depravity of their ways and make them feel the agony they've caused. You could say I'm the bringer of judgment and pain. The reminder of sins. Bron was different though. He reveled in the misery I dealt.

"C'mon. Give it to me. NOW, Nevaeh," he demanded, spreading my legs. Long, raven wings flanked us, the spicy scent wafting from them confusing my contrasting emotions of need for him and pure disgust. Again, the sharp tips of his claws disappeared into my body, sinking deep into my shoulders.

I hissed at the pain but held back my scream. The rope finally snapped under the tension of my power. I let out a guttural yell. Bron thrust into me, and the shadow burst out of me. The stinging pain of feeling too full throbbed in my bottom. Tangible waves of malevolence poured from my fingers and out of my mouth like smoke rolling from a pyre, wandering up and out through the room until it surrounded us in a cage of my darkest imagination.

Bron pushed and pulled, working me the way he wanted. Groans of pain and pleasure lingered in the air. He soaked in the brutal visions of murder and torment I spun for him. I knew what he liked. The faster I gave it to him, the quicker he'd finish.

Bruises were already forming on my hips under his clenched fists. My knees trembled, and a poisoned soul cackled from inside my hardening heart. Too much of me was enjoying this more and more as the moments passed. Yet, a small piece of me—very small—strived to deny the full transition that was just a matter of time.

My shadow of doom hung dense and black around me. The bitter taste of wickedness dried my tongue. Closing my eyes tight, I searched for a place of solace in the back of my mind. A section of sheet covered my mouth and nose as I buried my face into the bed and sucked in deeply. The lack of breath fogged my mind. *Maybe I could make myself pass out so I wouldn't have to endure any more of this.* My Ater would only wake me up to do it all over again.

With my face planted into the bed, I prayed for death by asphyxiation. But if I died, where would I go now? I was already in Hell.

My dark lover rode me until the sheets were soaked in sweat and tears. It seemed like hours before I felt him spurt into me. He slid out of me and retracted his talons, then gently lifted my body and laid me on the bed. Our little episodes always left me completely depleted, mentally and physically. One minute, Bron made me feel loved—wanted—and the next, I was fearing for my life.

The weight of a heavy blanket dragging from my feet to my shoulders comforted me. He laid down and spooned my quivering shell. "Please forgive me, my love." His fingers smoothed the sticky hair out of my face. "You know I can't help myself. I love you so much." The empty, possessive words echoed in my ears.

I closed my eyes, fighting the urge to turn and kiss him—to forgive him. Instead, I pretended to fall asleep and waited for my Ater to do the same. Soon, the rise and fall of his chest evened, and I let my mind wander to Vinney.

His smiling face beamed when I showed up at the warehouse. We wasted hours catching up and escaping our troubles with memories that made us laugh. But, eventually, it was time to leave. I'd already stayed too long.

"I have to go, Vinney." I smiled and patted his back.

"Naw. C'mon, you can stay just a bit longer. You rarely get around to seein' this ol' bag a'bones." His milky eyes glossed over as he stood and gave me a hug, accepting my departure. "It was good to see ya, kid." Shaky hands reached for the cane leaning against his cot. "I'll walk ya out."

"No, Vinney. That's not necessary," I protested.

"Pish." He swiped his hand through the air and shook his head, dismissing my objections.

I scanned over his trembling form and yellowed skin. His time was coming soon, so I walked beside him in a silent goodbye. We slowed just before the door, and I turned to give one last hug, but he didn't hug me back. His peaceful face tightened in fear and pain.

"Vinney?" I clutched his thin arms. He wavered before me, then fell to the floor. "Vinney!" I yelled. His feeble breath caught in a gasp, and he grabbed at his chest. I dropped the flashlight and lowered to his side, trying to comfort the man drifting away fast. I stared into his shocked eyes, uncertain of what to do. "I'll be right back. I'm gonna get help." I moved to leave.

Vinney strained a hand out to me and shook his head. "Don't," he rasped.

He was ready to leave this life.

As he dwindled, I moved in closer to hug him, the nearness triggering a deluge of colorful flashes from his life to enter my mind. I jumped back, surprised that I could see his past without my usual routine of calling it forth.

He'd led a long, mistake ridden life; however, the good he'd done far outshined the bad. This was a humble man, caring and generous with what little he had. A sense of calm settled over the most recent memories as they trailed to the seconds we'd just shared together.

This was the first time I'd seen the life of a "good" man since my gifts started to develop. The joy was overwhelming. Anytime I used my talents before, I witnessed only the filth that tainted my victim's prior years, and only when I allowed my monster to take over.

A tear trailed down my cheek. I smiled and said, "Go ahead, Vinney. Go home. They're waiting for you."

Suddenly, the impatience and ill-intent of my dark power quaked along my bones. It sensed death was near. I fought back the itch awaiting release. "I will not reveal his wrongs in his last breaths," I argued against the darkness through gritted teeth. The vicious waves of chaos ebbed and flowed within me, making their way to the surface.

Vinney's face contorted with fear when his eyes focused on me. I couldn't fight it any longer. "No!" I screamed as the black velvet cloud sprang from my mouth and fingers. It billowed from me. All the sins I'd watched Vinney commit just moments ago amplified in the shroud of darkness I layered around him.

I'd lost control of the shadow. Vinney, I'm so sorry, I thought. I scrambled to find the old man's hand and held on while the stormy cloud continued to spill from me and unfurl, his cries of shame and despair lost on the horrid beast escaping my depths.

Minutes of retracing his hideous faults, which would seem like an eternity to him, finally came to a merciful end. The punishing shadow retracted back to the dark crevices of my soul. Sated by the destruction it caused, it plunged inside my mouth, under my fingernails, along my veins and behind my eyes.

Light flooded the space around Vinney's convulsing body with the dark's retreat. I hunched over him. "I'm so sorry, Vinney. Please forgive me."

His skin paled. His breath stilled. His empty eyes closed.

I sobbed next to the corpse, hanging onto its lifeless hand while wishing he'd return, waiting for him to absolve the wrong I'd just done. Leaning in to kiss Vinney on the cheek, my chest tightened. Something pulled deep inside me, from my diaphragm maybe, like a vacuum sucking from my gut. I neared his lax face, gasping from the strange sensation.

Gravel cut into my palm as I tried to push away from Vinney. An invisible rope held me close to his shuddering corpse. The contraction in my torso grew stronger. I gasped again. The dead body shivered beneath me. I pushed against the rope tugging me toward his head. With my next swallow of air, a thin swirling material stretched from Vinney's mouth and licked at my lips, then curled up into my throat.

Oh, my God, oh my God, NO!

I choked on the fluttering sensation traveling down to my lungs. The strange suction in my diaphragm forced me to siphon another unwanted breath. Another glorious strand of vapor tickled my throat and filled my chest as if it were all I needed to live.

Stop. I can't do this, I screamed inside my head, unable to call out for help.

I dragged my bloody hands onto Vinney's belly, squeezed my eyes shut, and shoved at him. As the next translucent tendril danced up toward his teeth, something gave. I tumbled backwards, finally free of the rope, and slid myself away from Vinney.

The tingling in my lungs ceased, and I could control my body again. Hot tears streamed down my cheeks as I stared at the quiet shell of a man.

What in the hell just happened?

CHAPTER THREE

THROW ME A BONE

The chill of a cool breeze ruffled my feathers. Wisps of gray wandered in front of the yellow moon on and off throughout the night, yet thousands of glittering stars refused to let the roaming clouds hide their shine.

Up here, I could see it all. Up here, I was closer to home than I'd ever be again.

"Father, please let her make it through this," I whispered to the God I knew heard my every thought.

Leaning back on the ledge I was crouched on, I lifted my face to the sky and closed my eyes, enjoying the sense of peace and solitude above the city.

A distant sound cried out for my attention. It echoed from a few blocks to the east. Humans wouldn't be able to hear such a low whimper, but, lucky for them, I could. I stepped off the roof, my heavy wings raising and angling upward. Wind sifted through my hair and glided across my skin, allowing me to fall faster. Seconds later, my feathery limbs bowed by my side like the flared sails on a boat and slowed the drop just before my feet stomped on the concrete below.

The whimper called out again. I gritted my teeth, preparing myself for the discomfort I was about to endure. Without my duster, there was no way I could walk among the humans like this.

Searing pain commenced as I willed the crests of my wings to melt into the muscles of my back. A groan escaped my throat when I commanded the remaining length of feathers and flesh to enter the cage of my body. The solid appendages obeyed, transforming to a white and purple tar-like substance that reluctantly wrapped its way around my torso, sticking to me as if they were hot wax trailing over my skin. Fingers of the thick goo reached over my chest, shoulders, and back, creating a scraping sensation wherever it touched. I grunted as the last of the substance melted into me, leaving behind the faintest glow just under my surface. If I stuck to well-lit areas of the city, no one would notice.

I arched my back and stretched my cramped muscles, always feeling a little too tight, my body a little too overfilled, when I forced that part of myself into hiding.

I exited the alley, keeping my head down, and walked through the marketplace. I passed by a clothing vendor and snagged a green t-shirt from the rack on the sidewalk.

Everyone was too busy to notice—except for the man that brushed against my arm going the opposite direction. He looked over his shoulder, his wide, curious eyes focused on my movements. He slowed and almost turned to follow me. The yearning in his gaze warned me to dampen my graces a little more than I had already.

Though it was a struggle to control my pull over the humans *and* keep my wings from exploding out from under my skin, I did my best. The man shook his head, seeming confused, then continued on his way.

I set into a jog, dodging the people clambering from one merchandise table to another. When the end of the vendors came into sight, I picked up the pace.

A loud bang, followed by a screech, sounded from four buildings down. I sprinted across the road, running until I approached a gun shop near where the sound seemed to come from. The barred windows couldn't contain the stench of sulfur and burnt flesh polluting the air. Sections of my skin rippled, my wings threatening to break free, as my natural — though inconvenient — angelic instincts reacted to a demon in the vicinity. I pressed on the protruding areas until the tension subsided.

Another bang resonated from the building. I kicked the door in. A bell dropped from above the entryway, its musical ring falling flat when the brass clanked to the floor. The door slammed into the gun case behind it. Clear shards of glass burst into the aisle leading through the shop. I'd have to pay for that later.

"Hello?" I called, casing the shop for movement.

"Get the fuck out of here!" a woman yelled from another room. Shots fired, blasting a plate-sized hole clean through the wall to my right.

"Well, that's welcoming." I grabbed the dagger holstered behind my belt. The scrolled blade gleamed under the florescent lights. I inched closer to a doorway behind the counter, the broken glass crunching with each step.

"What do you assholes want? I told you I'm not coming with you." High-pitched screeching answered the woman. Another shot blasted through the wall, hurling a piece of drywall past my face.

I entered the next room. It was a battlefield. Bar lights sparked, dangling from the ceiling. Large holes peppered the walls, smoke still billowing from them. Blood and ash smudges speckled the floor.

My gaze roamed around the room assessing the damage, until I saw an elderly man slouched in the far corner. His head drooped to his chest. A tall woman with a trucker's hat, plaid sleeveless shirt, and jeans with as many holes as the walls, trapped a demon against a steel vault door.

"What the...?" I guess I expected to see a damsel in distress, but she appeared to have everything under control.

"I'll never betray my God. You tell them that when you get back to Hell." A bright light stemmed from her fingers as she held them to the Animus demon's mouthless face. Suddenly, a ball of pure blue energy sprang from the woman's hand and engulfed the demon from head to toe. The only thing left was a blackened smudge and smoke drifting into the air duct above.

"So, I suppose you don't need my help after all?" I ask.

She dusted the ash from her hands and turned to stare at me. "Who the fuck are you?"

"I'm Archard." My gaze found the nametag on her shirt pocket.

"Yeah, well, I'm fine." Defined muscles clenched as she plucked a piece of gum from her mouth. She marched toward the old man in the corner, extending her hand out to press the wad of gum under the edge of a table when she passed.

"Look, Sally, I heard the scuffle and thought you might need help."

"As you can see, I don't." Her hand gently touched the old man's neck and rested there for a few seconds. Sally's head dropped with disappointment, then her hand fell too.

"Is he gone?" I asked. I've always felt sorry for those losing their loved ones to this messy war.

"What does it look like to you, genius?" She pushed back on her heels, then stood. Sally grabbed a tarp laying over some gun boxes next to them and covered the body.

"I'm sorry, I know how —"

"You don't know shit." She spun and stepped my way. "You think I don't know who you are?" Her ash-covered fingertip poked into my chest. "The angels threw this on us. Ever since you idiots engaged those bastards with a Celata, we've had to fight even harder to stay alive — to stay good. This is all your fault."

I encircled her angry hand within mine. "I realize we've brought this on you all, but the war was not just ours. We've been fighting for humans all along. It's time we had some help from those that are able to actually do something," I retorted through gritted teeth.

Sally yanked her hand from my grip. "Some of us just wanted to be left alone. Now, we're being attacked. Not only by Dark Celatum but demons too." Her eyes traced back to the dead body under the tarp. "How are we supposed to make it out alive like this?"

"Honestly? I don't know. The one advantage we were counting on backfired." A flash of Nevaeh entering the portal in the cathedral entered my thoughts. I rubbed the heels of my palms into my eyes, attempting to blot out the memory. "All we can do now is rely on each other and have faith that there is a way to beat them."

How can I tell her that, when I didn't even believe we had a chance?

"Sorry, but my faith in your kind ran out the door long ago. I'll take my chances on my own." She rested her hands on her boyish hips and scanned the room. "Just leave me alone," she commanded under her breath. She crouched down to pick up a broken picture frame from the floor. "Just leave me the hell alone, angel. Go help some *poor* Celata that might actually give a damn."

I left the gun shop without another word. There was no use in trying to convince someone to trust an angel that barely had faith himself.

I rounded into a narrow passage between two businesses. Jumping into the air, I spread my legs and planted a foot on the side of each building, straddling the alleyway. My expression hardened from focused concentration. I shoved off the wall with one boot then lodged the other higher on the opposite brick façade. I pushed off again. Gaining momentum, I nimbly hoisted myself upward between the two structures.

With my eyes homed on the rooftops, I freed the appendages itching to escape my body. A grunt exploded from my throat as they ripped from the pores of my flesh in pearls of goo and solidified into the hated reminders of what I used to be.

Once I cleared the narrow passageway by foot, my feathers sensed a current, and I gave in. Flexing my muscles, I leaped into the sky and rode the draft higher and higher, rising above the roofs of both buildings. The night sky, low clouds, and bright lights kept me well camouflaged as I traveled home.

Breath raced in and out of my lungs while I glided over hordes of people ignorant to the truth. Human shouts and demon screeches reached out to my ears from dark corners, unfortunate homes, and random sites of the city—signals of the battles corrupting the area more and more every day. Random glimpses of demons and Celatum fighting below heightened my concern, but I flew on. I must have counted six fights before reaching my destination, but I couldn't help them anymore. There was only one being that I cared to save, and she was long gone.

A single deep-purple plume floated away on the gust of wind swirling below me. Leaving it behind to disintegrate—just like my hope—I pushed on.

I stumbled into my room and fell against the door, slamming it shut. I slid down to the floor and gulped back another swig of the vodka I'd procured from Arkin's stash. The slow burn coaxed the fog over my thoughts to inch in. The bottle slipped from my fingers and thudded to the floor, splashing clear fluid out of the opening and onto my hand. I grabbed the glass spout and tilted the half-empty bottle against my leg.

I'll never get her back. I've failed her every second of her life.

My heavy eyes fell under the spell of a candle flame whipping in the air across the room. The tiny fire flickered violently for a few seconds, then bent horizontally, reaching out to the wall behind it. I watched suspiciously as it poured from the wick, working its way up the plaster like molten lava refusing to obey the laws of gravity. The liquid flame stopped halfway up the wall, then gathered into a spinning puddle. Its edges began a slow spread outward, stretching the puddle's surface into a glowing, red disk the size of a large mirror. The fire continued to spin, flinging hot droplets to the floor. My eyes darted to the specks of sizzling embers, expecting to see holes burned into my room, but nothing caught fire. The droplets cooled then dissipated like they were nothing more than steam on the hot pavement.

I left my bottle of liquid pain killer on the floor and crawled closer to the hovering fire. The flames danced with one another, spinning, waiting for me to fall under their hypnosis. As I crawled to the other side of the room, the center of the burning pool began to form a point and extend toward me.

I shoved myself off the floor and stared into the twirling cone of heat. *What a peculiar thing.* My fingers hesitated just before touching the red-hot tip. *It wasn't burning the wall, so maybe it wouldn't burn me.*

A hand thrust out from the middle of the blazing loop. I stumbled backward, landing on my ass. Another hand pushed out, and the pair of them worked to make an opening. After a minute of coaxing the fire to the edge of the ring, one finger pointed at me then curled, motioning for me to approach.

"Who are you?" I asked, slurring through my drunkenness.

"Come here, Archard," it beckoned.

Too curious to refuse, I stood and stepped forward. In the middle of the flaming ring, an older man peered back at me. The darkness on the other side shadowed most of his face; however, light from the flickering opening around him accentuated the silver in his salt and pepper hair. Faint violet-blue eyes measured me up and down as I did him.

I grimaced, smelling the bitter undertones of sulfur wafting towards me. "What do you want, demon?"

"I want the same thing you want. To save Nevaeh." Remorse and guilt underlined his words.

I crossed my arms over my chest, doubtful that he spoke the truth. "And who are you to think I would listen to anything you have to say?" I stepped closer and leaned in, only inches from the blazing loop. "The pain of crossing this ring of protection you have would be worth it just to drag your ass out here and beat you to ashes." My knuckles were going numb from balling such tight fists, and I couldn't stop the twitch in my clenched jaw.

He jerked his head to the right as if he heard something on his side of the portal. Furrowing his strong brow, he continued, "Look, we don't have time for this foolishness. Pull me out, beat me, I don't care. But realize, I'm the only one that can help you get Nevaeh back." The demon grew more anxious and scanned the pitch-black around him again.

"I'm listening."

"My name is Kenet. I'm in charge of George's soul, but I'm also the one who helped Nevaeh get out of Hell before she made her declaration. I've been keeping an eye on her, but I can't get too close."

A distant screeching echoed beyond the window. The worry lines on Kenet's face deepened.

"You know where she is?" I held my breath, knowing that getting Nevaeh back wouldn't be that easy.

"Yes. She is as safe as she can be for now, but I can't get to her. It's too dangerous for both of us."

"Is she okay?" I braced myself with one hand on the wall, eager to hear his answer. My wrist stung from the rogue flames licking at my skin. A silence too long for my patience passed. "Well? Is Nevaeh okay or not?" I needed to know.

"She is strong. She can handle herself for now." Another screech rang through the air, closer this time. "I have to go," panic shook his voice. "I'll try to contact you as soon as possible."

The ring of fire contracted for a beat, then flared open again. Puffs of smoke from the extinguishing halo of flames whirled into my room. The heat sputtered and sizzled before reigniting in its struggle to stay alive.

"Wait, don't go. I need to know more about her. What am I supposed to do to help?" I yelled, banging my fist against the drywall. Without thinking, I grabbed for the man to keep him from leaving. A jolt of electricity sent a shock through my body the second I got too close. I pulled back, cradling my stinging right hand in my left. "Kenet, what do I do to get her back?" I growled.

His head jerked over his right shoulder, then his left, frantically watching his surroundings. "I don't know, but we'll figure it out. Just...Just keep searching for her. And, whatever you do, don't let her get a hold of this...," his whispers trailed off.

The ring contracted one last time then closed in on itself with a puff of sulfur infused smoke, but not before something heavy thumped the ground at my feet.

I wiped the small remnants of ash from the wall—the only proof a portal had opened—and dusted it off on my pant-leg. I rested white-knuckled fists on my hips and stared down at the object between my feet.

The hard floor didn't give an inch as I fell to my knees in disbelief. Soft velvet tickled my fingertips when I traced over bold scrolling.

C-L-A-V-I-S.

HAVEN CAGE

Nevaeh

CHAPTER FOUR

WHO AM I TO JUDGE?

"Honestly, I don't know what your problem is. This would be so much easier if you just played along like a good little girl." Layla yelled over the music thumping in the background. She took a sip of her martini and laid a sly hand on Gavyn's lap. Her eyes bore into mine, a wide grin spreading across her face as she waited for a response.

This was all a game to her. How could she bring him along on a mission with me? Dangling Gavyn in front of me, knowing there was nothing I could do to save him, was low. She was doing everything possible to get under my skin, but I had to keep my anger in check. I couldn't risk letting my darkness loose in public.

Glaring at her, I picked up a shot of whiskey from the highboy table and gulped it down instead of doing what I really wanted to do—punch her in the fuckin' face. The swallow of amber liquid burned its way to the pit of my stomach where my disgust for the catty blonde was most prominent.

"What is so damn hard to understand? *You* are my problem." Pressure from my new gift bubbled just below the surface, begging for a chance to show Layla the torture she deserved.

"He's on the move," Gavyn interrupted, watching the man in a pristine Armani suit stride across the dance floor and exit the bar. "Let's go."

Layla slid off her stool, straightened her skin-tight dress, and picked up her glass to finish the rest of her drink. Before it reached her perfectly red lips, I snatched it from her hand and gulped down the remaining liquid. "Let's go then," I agreed, grinning while Layla eyed me, aggravated.

"We don't have time for this shit, ladies." Gavyn's olive-green eyes darted between us, reprimanding our childish behavior. I missed those eyes. I used to find safety in them. Now, all I found was ice.

Layla latched onto his hand, tugging him around the high table. I smacked the martini glass against the edge of the table, breaking the cup from the stem. Visions of me stabbing the long shard into Layla's jugular danced through my mind. *Oh, how sweet it would be.*

I followed the couple past the bouncer and out the door.

The street was quiet and dark except for the few street lamps lining the sidewalk. Somewhere in the near distance, a car alarm disengaged, and a trunk popped open.

Layla giggled, giddy as a school girl. She got off on this. Unfortunately, after I finished a few missions, my own excitement began to pique during these times—just before I brought someone to terms with who they really were. It was getting harder to fight the desire to free my true self.

Gavyn swung his and Layla's hands between them as they all but skipped towards the man in Armani. He didn't notice us closing in. He was too busy laying the expensive jacket neatly in his trunk.

"Hey there," Gavyn greeted, settling a hip against the car. "I was wondering if you could help us out?" His green eyes appeared friendly, but I knew better.

"I'm not from around here. Not sure how much help I could be," the man said nervously and closed his trunk.

"Oh, don't be so modest, Ray." Gavyn leaned towards the man and locked a hand onto his shoulder. The more fear Ray showed, the harder Gavyn squeezed.

"Who are you?" Ray asked, gaining the courage to smack Gavyn's hand away. His eyes jumped between the three of us, probably noting every visible detail about us so he could report to the police. He wouldn't make it that far.

I hadn't seen Gavyn for months. Tunnel after tunnel, dungeon after dungeon, I'd searched for him. They'd had him hidden well. Now, Layla decides to bring him along? I couldn't figure out her angle—and there was definitely an angle.

"We're just some friends asking for help, Ray. There's no reason to be scared. You have great potential, darlin'. We'd like to show you how to hone it. All you have to do is join us." Layla held her arms out, offering a sense of surrender. Under that fake sweetness, she was rotten to the core.

She and Gavyn stepped toward Ray, like hyenas surrounding their prey. "What have you got to lose, Ray?" Layla purred. "You don't have a family anymore. *We* could be your family. *We* could offer you more than they ever did."

Ray's eyes glossed over and lowered to the pavement. The pain lining his face was fresh. His loss was recent. A dull stab in my darkened heart reminded me of my own loss. That's what I did this for, wasn't it? To save those dear to me.

My gaze drifted to Gavyn's back and, in my mind, I screamed at him— to the soul that was drowning within his hollowing shell. I yelled for his attention. Maybe, if he looked deep into my eyes, he could see the good I was struggling to hold onto and find his will to hold on.

Gavyn's frame tensed, and Layla draped her arm around his neck.

He never looked back.

"So, what's the verdict, Ray? We haven't got all night," she huffed, sounding bored as she tousled a section of flawless hair with her free hand.

"C'mon man, we can give you unbelievable power. Take the easy road. You don't want to see what happens if you don't." I couldn't see his face, but I could hear the devilish grin behind Gavyn's words. He stepped closer to Ray, ready to pounce.

Ray stood silent for a moment, looking at his hands and then to the sky.

Was he praying? *Good for you, Ray. You'll need to with us coming at you.* What had this poor S.O.B done to get the demons' attention?

"I think I'll take my chances without you," the man in Armani growled. He lifted his hands and splayed them out in our direction.

Suddenly, a heavy weight bashed into my stomach, knocking me on my ass. Stunned, I sucked in a sharp breath from the surprise blow. *What the hell?*

Groaning through the throbbing pain in my abdomen, I scowled down at an uprooted parking meter pinning my legs to the ground. I shoved the bent post over my thighs, rolling it off my lap until it pinged against the ground. I wrapped my arm around my midsection and surveyed the area.

Gavyn slumped back on one elbow near my feet, grunting and picking chunks of broken concrete off his body. There was a gaping hole in the sidewalk next to Ray's front bumper. I stared up at Ray, wide-eyed.

Apparently, he could move objects with his mind because I sure as shit didn't see him move a muscle, and none of us had the power to yank the meter out of the ground without touching it. Ray was the only logical answer.

Layla yelled at her partner, "Get up and get your shit together, Gavyn. This is your show. You better perform well."

Her eyes never left Ray. That tell-tale red ring blazed around her irises—the one I noticed always preceded one of her bat-shit crazy episodes. She was nearly losing control. Balled fists rested tight against her sides, reigning back the Aether demons under her spell. We couldn't see them now, but soon they would swirl around us like a storm. One word from her poisonous mouth and they could destroy us all.

Gavyn shoved himself from the dirty cement and marched towards Ray, his heavy breaths creating puffs of white in the cool night air. Ray stiffened as if he considered running, then, a moment later, slouched. Defeat clouded his glossy eyes. He knew it was too late.

"That wasn't very nice," Gavyn taunted through gritted teeth. His tense body relaxed, stopping inches from the helpless soul we came to win over. "Looks like you prefer the hard road." Gavyn didn't move or do any kind of gesture warning the unclaimed Celata of his coming power. It was just there, taking over Ray.

My senses tingled as Gavyn swayed Ray to our side. Even Layla's body wavered to the haze of influence drifting from Gavyn. A numbing calm brushed over my raw hate and suffering. And, for a second, I forgot that he wasn't the Gavyn I knew before all this.

The false numbness fizzled when Layla commanded us to follow her behind the bar. Ray was the first to fall in line. He glided in slow movements toward the shadowy end of good in his life. His eyes fixed on Layla, his face slack and lifeless like a zombie.

Gavyn had swayed him into mindless submission.

That's new.

His gift wasn't a nudge in the right direction anymore; it was a curse of complete mind control.

I followed Layla and the men into the alley, checking the parking lot for innocent bystanders. Thankfully, we wouldn't have to damage anyone else tonight.

"Alright, Nevaeh. It's your turn, darlin'." Layla's phony charm made me want to punch a hole in her pristine face.

Gavyn gently guided Ray to sit on the ground and lean against the brick wall. Like a puppet, Ray abided. Gavyn retreated to a spot next to the dumpster behind me, finished with his part. I could feel his eyes lingering over my frame as I hesitated to approach Ray.

"Chop-chop, honey," Layla snapped, still caging the demonic army she led.

My job during these recruitment missions was old news now. I'd forced my fair share of evil souls into our ranks. Some, I'd punished into resignation and enjoyed it. Others turned to mush under my judgment. But, this…this was different. It was too personal with Gavyn here.

I glanced at Gavyn propped against the scuffed metal box, his handsome face hiding in the shadow.

"What the fuck are you waiting for? Christmas?" Layla's impatience was becoming intolerable. I thought about prolonging a little more just for spite, but the ring around her eyes was growing more wild by the second.

I lowered down, straddling the zombified man awaiting my doom. My hands rested on Ray's chest, and I sat back on his lap, taking in every feature of his face. His gray eyes shifted from Gavyn to me, catching me off guard. *Did he know what was coming?*

His relaxed facial muscles couldn't erase the deep worry creases on his forehead and around his eyes. There wasn't a need to wonder what caused them, I was about to find out. By the time I finished with this successful, middle-aged man, the last bit of light would be extinguished from his soul. I will have forced him to relive every dirty deed in his life.

I slid my fingers to the back of his neck and laid my forehead against his. Our eyes locked. There was nowhere for him to hide. When I linked with my victim this way, it was more intimate than two lovers. They were more vulnerable. I would know things they wouldn't dare tell another soul.

My heart pounded faster and faster inside my chest. The breath leaving my lungs quickened. Shivers worked their way up my spine as I loosened my grasp on the darkness within.

Ray flinched, the slightest quiver moving his lips like he was about to say something. I peered into the eyes staring back at me and saw a reflection. The mirrored image of Vinney dying—his soul invading me against my wishes—played in his pupils as if I were looking through a keyhole and watching my own wrong-doings. I faltered and sat back on

Ray's thighs, breathless.

"What is your deal? If he won't submit, then it's your job to convince him." Layla's voice was low and multiplied. She was at her brink. "Do your thing already," she hissed.

Gavyn shuffled behind me. "What is it, Nevaeh?"

"Nothing." I ignored the vision and locked eyes with Ray once more.

The pressure building in my gut bounced upwards through my chest, aiming to escape. I fisted Ray's black tufts of hair and held on for dear life. My body trembled. My mind darkened.

The midnight cloud billowed out of my mouth the second I opened my fortress doors. A deafening scream pushed out from my gut.

Oh, how sweet the pain.

Ray's body convulsed beneath me. He groaned at the darkness brewing around us. I reached deep into the windows of his soul and scoured it for what I needed. I searched for the right times in his past which would allow me to manifest the most effective experience—just for him.

Countless memories bombarded me. This man loved his family. He took care of them and did everything within his power to keep them safe and happy. They went to church, picnicked, and had family game night. It was almost sickening how perfect they were.

And then, there it was, deep in the blackest corner of his soul. A blip really, compared to the good deeds this man had done. He'd murdered someone. He'd enjoyed it. Every detail was planned and acted out exactly.

As I pulled the memory to the forefront of his mind, snapshots of a bloody scene flashed in and out of my vision. A little girl lay wrapped in a trash bag. Creek water flowed against her body, failing to wash away the blood and dirt smeared on the black plastic. Such a sweet face to be so lifeless. Sweat dripped from Ray's brow, his forehead wrinkled in sorrow.

Ray's convulsing stopped. He was giving in as he relived the brutal memory of what I could only imagine was his daughter. For a second, I thought it was Ray who'd killed the child, but the rage and anger that surrounded *this* sight was different from the murder he'd committed.

I quickly shoved back the flashes of his poor daughter and yanked forward the other murder. Ray stood over a man bound on a soiled floor. I was a visitor, able to feel and know Ray's mind, during his crime of revenge — so I sat back and watched.

The stench of blood and urine filled my nostrils. Dark, thick liquid dripped from my host's right hand, trailing down a pair of hedge clippers before pattering to the ground.

"What did you do to her?" Ray yelled at the frightened hostage. His jaw ticked. His teeth ached from grinding them too hard, but he didn't care; it was nothing compared to the aching void this man had left in Ray's life. Ray just wanted to know what happened to his darling Ava. He would not rest until he knew every last detail.

"What did you do, bastard?"

The man on the floor didn't answer. A steel-toed boot kicked at the bound man's side, forcing him to curl into a ball to ease the pain. Short wiry hair stuck to the captive's face. His tattered clothes were soaked in his own body's waste. He'd likely been there, like this, for days.

"Wouldn't you like to know?" he spat back at Ray, chuckling. "You think you got me. You think I'm gonna turn myself in, don't ya? Well, I got news for ya, daddy. If the pigs couldn't get to me, there ain't nothing you can do." The crazy eyes beaming up at Ray was all I needed to know that he was guilty of Ava's murder.

"That's where you're wrong, Jones. I *am* doing something about it." Ray lifted the hedge cutters and leaned down towards Jones. "You're going to pay, one way or another." He grinned in the sincerest way.

Jones wrestled with his bindings but couldn't get free. His hands were securely fastened behind his back, his feet tied at the ankles. I hadn't noticed before, but several of his fingers were missing. Clots of blood worked hard at sealing the nubs, but they still oozed, leaving a trail of red wherever Jones's fingers grazed. "You ain't no killer. You wouldn't harm a fly." An uncertain laugh rumbled from Jones's throat as he squirmed. "That's why I got to your sweet little peach and used her until she had her fill. Ya know, she called *me* daddy too." His cracked lips spread into a deviant smirk.

Ray's hand tightened around the shears, his lips turning up into a smile. "I think I've proven you wrong already. And I have no problem giving you more proof." He kneeled on the floor next to Jones and looked down upon him with a peace that only comes with finding justice when you've been wronged. "This is for my Ava." His hands hoisted the cutters above his head and speared downward into Jones's chest.

Crimson pumped out of Jones's body, fast at first, then slowing to the fading beat of his murderous heart. Ray rested his forehead on the clippers and wept. He wept for the life he'd just taken—no matter how vile—and for the beautiful daughter he'd lost. That moment of peace was fleeting. He still carried the guilt of both murders on his shoulders, punishing himself more than I ever could.

I broke ties with Ray and leaned back to ponder my next move. He didn't deserve this. As much as I loved the freedom of dealing someone's hand, I couldn't do this to Ray.

The black storm of judgment churned around us, shielding us from Layla and Gavyn. I scanned over the rattled face before me and gently touched his cheek. "I'm gonna get you through this. Trust me?"

His drained eyes glossed over, and he managed a weary smile. Ray worked to tip his head up and glance at the sky. A soft whisper escaped his lips. "Please forgive me," he said.

I smiled and began to swallow my cloud of doom. One deep inhale, and the dark substance unwillingly fled back into my body. It didn't want to be inside me any more than I wanted it to, and I'd just taken away its chance to punish. It was not happy.

Fat ropes of the menacing cloud rushed into my throat and nose nearly making me suffocate. After a minute, the ropes thinned. I could feel the air returning to my lungs, again. My eyes were beginning to see my surroundings, instead of the pitch black that blotted them out moments earlier.

There was a commotion at the end of the alley. "Stop, Nevaeh," I heard a female squeal. "Stop," she yelled over and over, sprinting towards us.

I tried to right myself and waited for the last of the darkness to slink back into my fortress. Ray's body tensed beneath me. His head slowly swiveled around to Layla. *Oh, no...no, no, no.* Layla would have no mercy on a stranger imposing on our recruitment session.

My wobbly legs pushed me up. I looked down at Ray, helpless between my feet. The last bit of dark tendrils dissipated with my breath, and I stumbled to the wall. Being undone for so long took a lot out of me, especially when the cloud of doom and I don't work together.

"Layla, don't," Gavyn pleaded from behind me.

When I turned around, I saw Gavyn shaking Layla. He fought to get her attention, but she was too focused on the stranger barreling towards us.

The red rings bled into the whites of Layla's eyes, and her chest heaved. In between each heavy breath, she exhaled a foreign command. Shadows scurried around us, gathering by the dozens. She was calling them.

"Stop her, Gavyn." I stepped away from the brick and fell to my knees. "You have to get the girl to leave."

Gavyn paused, understanding what I meant. He hurried toward the stranger with short, flaming-red hair. The flux in power was almost visible as he gathered all his strength to sway the girl into retreating.

The inevitable nausea boiled in my gut, and the smell of demons spoiled the air. The shadows peeled off the walls and took on their smoke- like forms, diving and jetting through the atmosphere. They waited on their master to give the orders.

My disorientation finally subsiding, I ran to the wall next to Layla and placed a hand on the stone. The hot tingling stirred in my fingertips then crawled up my arm. Dull, pulsating electricity vibrated through my bones, increasing as the portal grew beneath my touch. The fiery opening would soon give way, and I could drag Layla back to Hell with me.

Just as the brick started to melt away, a blood-curdling scream echoed down the alley. Layla thrust her hands outward, and the Aether demons followed. The smoky beings shot through Ray's paralyzed body like arrows.

"No. Layla, call them back," I begged. I ran and skid to Ray's side. He was barely grunting from the pain anymore. The demons continued to snake around him, taking turns piercing his body. They'd ripped his insides to shreds by then.

"C'mon, Ray. Stay with me." I grabbed his limp face and forced his dying eyes to look at me. Seconds later, he was gone. The Aether demons dodged me then zoomed down the alley.

Gavyn stood in front of the petite girl with a hand on each of her shoulders. She stared at him blankly until he let go. The tension in his body relaxed as she turned and jogged in the opposite direction. It was too late, though. The shadows were closing in on her. Gavyn stiffened when the demons blew by him in a gale of evil.

Layla chanted relentlessly next to me. Gavyn dropped to his knees, knowing what would happen when the Aethers caught up to the girl. I cradled Ray's hand to my chest, not wanting to let him go. I wanted to do something good. I *needed* to save him, but the chance had slipped by faster than a blink.

Suddenly, my lungs tingled, and that familiar tug in my diaphragm stirred to life. I glanced at Ray. The tiny string of his soul lazily danced its way across his lips. I gasped, and the ethereal coil lunged closer to me. I held my breath, dropping Ray's hand, and scooted back.

My gaze darted to Layla. Thankfully, she was too focused on her task to notice Ray's soul hunting me down. I crawled to the wall and slapped my palm up to the brick, reconnecting with the dormant portal. The brick began to crackle and burn, then melted away from my hand.

"Gavyn, get her, and let's go," I called over Layla's incessant chanting and the whirring storm of demons. "Gavyn!"

He turned his defeated face my way. Sprinting back to us, he yanked Layla by the arm and pulled her along. I locked hands with him. "Hold onto her," I urged. For whatever reason, no one had ever made it through the portals without Layla touching them. I could open the damn things and make it through myself, but I hadn't mastered the art of crossing people with me yet. "This is gonna hurt," I warned, shoving Gavyn and Layla into the crackling, burning hole. The pain was already searing my insides, even though I was made for realm-jumping.

Gavyn held in his scream until he couldn't handle it any longer. Layla's chanting ceased, and she squalled like a little bitch. Even through the mind-shattering agony of portal-jumping, her suffering brought a smile to my face.

The Aether demons dissolved back into the atmosphere with Layla's absence, but a dark lump remained under the street lamp at the end of the building.

I frowned. I couldn't help her now.

As I stepped through the opening, I took one last look at Ray and hoped he would be forgiven.

CHAPTER FIVE

WHAT'S THE DAMAGE?

I stared at the encased pages on the foot of my bed for hours. Kenet's visit had sobered most of my drunkenness, but I still couldn't find the courage to open the stupid book.

What if the words written doomed Nevaeh? What if there wasn't a good ending in sight? I couldn't let a glimpse of promise instill a false hope if darkness was her only fate.

I pushed my wings against the drywall behind me, rolling me forward onto my knees. I picked up the book and rested it on one forearm. The velvet cover looked as if it were bound yesterday, but I knew it was centuries old. Shiny, gold stitching embroidered the front with an understated title.

I slid my index finger down the edge of its vellum sheets, then slowly lifted the cover's corner. Cursive handwriting scrolled the title on a page by itself. When I flipped to the next, I recognized my home language. Line after line stretched elegantly across the leaf.

"I am The Guardian Rhett. This is my sworn testimony to the predictions and happenings shown to me by our most precious and almighty God," the text proclaimed.

"Archard," an urgent voice called from the door. Startled, I slammed the book closed, twisting around to see Arkin entering my room.

"What is it?" I quickly opened the drawer of my nightstand and placed the book inside, then focused on the angel rushing towards me with staggered breaths and a grim expression.

"It's Maggie. She's hurt, man." The pain in his eyes matched the torture I felt when I lost Nevaeh. I wasn't sure he'd realized the feelings he possessed for the spunky Celata until now.

"Where is she?" I threw my legs over the side of the bed, bending down to grab my duster off the floor before I stood.

Arkin took off toward the door, nearly sprinting out of the room as soon as he knew I was ready to follow. "Her Guardian came to us for help. She said Maggie had nowhere to go, no one else to save her, except us." He increased his pace as we traveled through the factory. "She's by that bar on Queens Avenue." Arkin froze and spun to face me, seeming to struggle with his thoughts. "The Guardian said demons got to her." A storm of anger and fear stirred in his eyes.

I placed an assuring hand on his shoulder. "She'll be alright." The words sounded as sincere as I meant them, but I didn't have high hopes.

We burst through the exit doors and spread our wings. The heavy beats of our feathered appendages swirled dust and leaves beneath us while thrusting us higher.

Thousands of humans scurried below us like ants, completely unaware that our world continued to infringe on theirs. Screeches and cries rose into the starry sky from dark pockets of the city, but there was only one Celata that we worried about right now.

Arkin lowered, soaring between tall buildings. "We're getting close," he said in a breathless voice. I wondered if he was talking to me or convincing himself that we'd make it in time to save her.

Minutes later, we landed on the roof of a club. Music pounded against its ceiling. Pink neon shined onto the empty street in front of it.

I led Arkin to the side overshadowing the alley and searched for anybody wandering out of the club.

A bright yellow glow washed over Maggie's body like a spotlight, drawing my attention toward the street. She lay curled in a ball as if she were asleep on the cold cement.

"There she is," Arkin pointed out, leaning over the edge to see around me. Before I could give the order, he leaped over the side and threw out his wings to slow the descent.

"Arkin," I grumbled, jumping off the roof to chase him.

His massive silhouette blocked the body on the ground. "Arkin, put on your coat," I urged, scanning the area for onlookers, but he ignored me and approached the lit sidewalk.

I watched Arkin cautiously, biting back the sharp pain that came when retracting the crests of my wings. With the first six inches tightly melded under the flesh between my shoulder blades, I tucked the remaining wings against my backside and shuffled into the duster I'd brought.

Arkin lowered to his knees, staring at Maggie in an eerie silence. "Is she okay?" I asked, squatting down beside him.

Maggie's face was pale and hollow, but her scent still rode the wind, wild as ever. If she were gone, the stink of death and decay would've taken over by now.

"I don't know." His sullen gaze swept over the frail girl from head to toe, assessing the visible damage to her body. He reached out a hand to touch her but yanked it back before making contact. "What was she doing here?" He pinched the bridge of his nose and squeezed his eyes shut, mumbling a curse while he exhaled.

Drunk cackling carried into the street as the club door open and closed. A man steadied his woman against the wall, groping her breasts and kissing her neck.

"We have to get out of here," I advised.

He nodded once, then slumped over and lifted Maggie's small frame into his arms. I guarded him from being seen by the bar patrons until we entered the alley. "See you at home," I said.

Without a word, Arkin extended his wings and took flight in a blur of white and indigo. Shrugging off my coat, I released the caged bits of my wings and flexed them out at my sides. I inhaled, readying myself for flight, but stopped when an alarming breeze blew through the alley, keeping me grounded.

The faint odor of a soul departed swirled around me.

I paused, breathing in another lungful of the tainted air. It grew stronger as I moved toward the back of the buildings. Remnants of sulfur mixed with the unyielding smell of human remains.

Relaxing my pupils to soak in more light, the outline of a body became clear. I stood over the man slumped against the wall and wondered why his fate brought him to this alley. Maggie would likely know—if she made it through the damage, that is. Perhaps he was the reason for her current condition.

I hoisted the man onto my shoulder, then carried him closer to the street. Someone would find him there and notify the proper authorities. It was the best I could do right now.

I settled the body near the front corner of the club and angled his arm out onto the sidewalk. Kneeling over the poor vessel, I straightened his messy shirt and pulled at a piece of wrinkled paper peeking out of his pocket. The paper unfolded to a photo of a young blonde girl, maybe eight or nine years old. She dared the camera to catch her as she happily ran in a field of wildflowers.

I peered down at the man, feeling sorry for the family he'd left behind. "May God forgive your sins," I prayed, slipping the photo neatly back into his breast pocket. Another cool breeze ruffled his hair, carrying with it a rush of memories.

It was her.

Nevaeh's scent laced the draft with a sweetness I couldn't deny, inducing visions of her lying beside me in our bed—her laugh, her tears.

I leaned over and rifled through the man's clothes, breathless and desperate, searching for any sign that he came in contact with Nevaeh. The club door banged shut, and the voices of a small group moved closer to the alley.

"Oh my God. Is that...is that a hand?" someone asked on the verge of panic.

I left the body without any answers and retreated into the shadows.

Arkin hopped up from the office chair stationed next to Maggie's cot. "Where were you?" His eyes had acquired a few more creases just in the few hours he'd spent worrying about her.

"She was there," I responded gruffly, towering over Maggie's motionless body.

"Wait. Who was there?" He glanced between me and Maggie confused, then the light bulb switched on. "Nevaeh?"

"Yeah. Has she come to?" I smoothed down a lock of unruly red hair and noted how peaceful Maggie appeared.

"Not yet." Arkin returned to his chair and clasped hands with the sleeping beauty. "I called in one of the healing Celata. He put his hands on her and said some chants, then left. Said he'd be back to check on her later. The only thing to do now is wait, I guess." He sighed, clearly unhappy with the idea of leaving Maggie's fate up to time. He never did like the waiting game.

"So, how do you know Nev was there?"

"I found a dead man in the alley. Her scent was all over him." I turned to leave, not wanting to elaborate anymore. "Get me when she wakes."

"What are you going to do now?" Arkin asked.

"I have a book to study," I shouted, exiting the room without a glance back.

Nearing my lonely cage of solitude, I noticed the door was cracked. A dim glow wavered and flared from inside, casting shadows out into the hallway.

I gently tapped the door open and eased into the room. Eyal, the Archangel who'd told us about Rhett and Arianna going rogue, stood over a makeshift fire blazing from my trashcan. He held the red book — Nevaeh's book — at his side, its velvet sheen glinting against the black slacks he wore.

I walked to the middle of the room and crossed my arms. "What do you think you're doing?"

His majestic wings were so white that they almost outshined the fire. Heaven's glory seeped from his ebony pores, taunting me, throwing the guilt I carried for abandoning my father in my face. I raised my wings a minute amount to show Eyal that I wasn't intimidated. His troubled eyes slowly traced my crest of feathers down to the plum tips, then smiled.

"Relax, my friend." He returned to the fire and held his empty hand over the flames as if he were warming himself.

"Answer me, Eyal. What the fuck are you doing with the book?" I stepped closer, preparing to pounce if I had to.

His broad shoulders sagged, his wings drooping low on his back. The glow of fire rippled across his smooth, brown skin. Nothing about his stature indicated that he meant harm. In fact, he almost looked sad.

"It's too much risk, Archard." Eyal's fingers danced in and out of the flickering heat, testing its strength. "Now that we know this is real," he shook the bound pages in the air, emphasizing the book's physicality, then looked over his shoulder in my direction, "we have to do everything possible to keep it from her grasp." His empty hand lowered to his side as he hovered the book over the trashcan.

"Wait," I shouted, striding towards the Archangel. "Don't."

He circled the can to get a better view of me, but never retracted the object he held. "Do you think I want to do this? Do you think I want to destroy a product of God's vision? It must be done, Archard. If she gets this book," his dark eyes fell to the floor," there's no telling what will happen under the power she's obtained."

"Please, Eyal. I can get her back. But, I can't do it without the book. It has answers. I'm sure of it. Let me guard it. Please, brother." I inched closer to the can, my hands held out in caution.

"If I'd done my job, none of this would've happened." A tear rolled down the sharp angle of his cheek. "I didn't realize what was happening to Rhett. When I figured it out, I was too late."

Now close enough to feel the heat warming my knees, I watched Eyal and listened, ready to catch the book at any moment.

"C'mon, Eyal. Just hand it over. I can protect it."

The spark of anger and doubt gleamed beyond his glossy eyes. "You are no more a protector than I, brother," he forced through gritted teeth, relaxing his grip from around the velvet spine.

"No!" I leaped for the book, snatching it out of the fire.

Hissing, I shifted the book to my other hand and shook the fingers I'd pulled out of the flames, trying to rid the pain. Though my skin felt like it was still burning, the book hadn't suffered any damage. As I looked up in relief, Eyal vanished.

Nevaeh

CHAPTER SIX

BEYOND SINNER SEA

Layla's hand collided with my cheek, leaving behind one hell of a sting. I knew what I had done in the alley would bring consequences, but nothing got under my skin more than Layla being appointed my punisher. A bitter metallic taste mixed with the saliva in my mouth.

"How could you be so foolish?" Layla paced a circle in front of me as two Crucio demons restrained my arms. "Such a selfish little bitch. You made me look like a complete idiot out there." Her hands perched on her hips while she talked more to herself than to me.

"You don't need my help for that." I licked the blood from my cut lip and spat on the ground as close to her feet as I could manage.

Layla froze and glared at me. "This isn't a game, Nevaeh. If you don't comply, I won't get what I've worked so hard for." She lifted her six-inch heels over my spit and sauntered towards me, stopping a breath's span from my face. "You won't see George's soul ever again." I lifted my head, glaring back at her. A sly grin widened her ruby-red lips. She knew exactly what buttons to push.

The reality of her truth unsettled my already sour stomach. "Just what is your goal in all of this, Layla? You already have Gavyn. What more could you possibly want?" Iron flooded my mouth again, and I fought the urge to spit in her pretty face.

"You could never understand." Her grin faded as she pondered a distant thought. "Everyone has a price to pay." For the first time that I could remember, Layla faltered in her conviction. Her eyes dampened in a fleeting moment of sadness.

"Wow," I chuckled through a wave of nausea.

"What?" she scoffed, her face contorting with confusion.

"You almost had me feeling sorry for you."

Layla's knee jabbed my stomach, and I hunched over. I couldn't move far though. The hideous monsters holding me tightened their grasp as my knees buckled. I coughed and gasped, struggling to get the lungful of air that escaped me with her blow.

"You don't know the first thing about me. Don't think for a second that you are any better." Rage played behind her reddening eyes.

The mischievous entity dwelling within my soul whispered sweet promises of revenge as I considered letting it loose. I reigned it in, knowing that it wouldn't help my situation.

With crimson spreading into the whites of her eyes, Layla balled her fist and pulled it back. I winced, readying for the next hit.

"Layla. Her Ater wants her," a familiar voice said. I opened my eyelids to see Gavyn standing behind Layla with his hand firmly wrapped around her fist. The red quickly fled from her eyes—along with any pending satisfaction.

"Take Nevaeh back to her cage, boys," Layla commanded the Crucios. She spun on her heels and melted into Gavyn's chest, planting a long, sickening kiss on his lips.

The Crucio demons dragged me to my room at the end of the tunnel.

Bron was waiting in front of my chamber, his arms crossed over a rippling chest, and his featureless face homed on me.

Regardless of the pain and anger I was feeling right now, his strong body stirred the nasty attraction that always called to me when in his presence. It was hard to fight his demands when my flesh yearned for him every time I was within ten feet of him.

Bron snarled at the demons in his ominous voice. "Release her, filth."

The demons quaked and shuddered beside me, hesitating to submit. They lifted their large heads to the air, stressing the exposed vertebrae that held their skulls in place, and squealed in protest.

"I said, let her go," Bron snarled. Tiny black lines appeared at his wrists and began climbing the veins in his forearms. His bad side was surfacing.

The demons took note of my Ater's severe tone and released me. I fell to my knees. Propping myself up on wobbly arms, I gazed at a spatter of blood on the back of my hand. Another small drop dripped from my lip. I wiped my mouth with the sleeve of my shirt.

I angled my head up toward the dark angel, anticipating his next move.

"What did you do, Nevaeh?" he purred, turning on the charm that usually convinced me to give him what he wanted.

"Nothing. I...I just lost control of my cloud." I tried to sound as sincere as possible, praying that he couldn't sense the lie in my words.

His head cocked to the side, and a minute passed before his voice echoed around me again. "Don't you want to be here, Neveah?" Suspicion swirled in the energy flowing from his beautiful body. "Do I have to remind you which side you declared your soul to?"

I bowed my head, closing my eyes to the painful memory of that day. "No. I know very well which team I'm playing for. I want to be with you." My eyes trailed to his smooth face with feigned clarity and intention. "I want to be with you," I repeated with sweet innocence. My fingers reached for his leg and lazily made a path up his inner thigh.

"Liar," Bron hissed, kicking my hand away. "Where is it, Nevaeh?"

His bulging arms unwound from one another and rested on his knees as he squatted down in front of me.

I sat back on my feet and glared at him. "Where's what?"

Before I could blink, his hand was tangled in my hair. He yanked my head back and curled over me, nose to non-existent nose, forcing me to cower like a cat trapped in the jowls of a wolf.

"Where is the prophecy, whore?"

My insides clenched and tingled under his rough touch. This was a game we played often. He'd conditioned me to this treatment in such a short period of time. I could feel the dampness pooling between my thighs. My breath hitched. "I don't know what you're talking about?" I exhaled, drunk with lust.

"The book, love. What have you done with the book?" he whispered. His cheek caressed my ear. "I need it. If you are truly with us, prove it." His raven hair draped around my face as he positioned himself on his knees and bent me back, arching my chest into the curve of his body. I sucked in the delicious spiced odor he exuded, tasting it on my tongue.

"I don't know where it is. I lost it after chasing an Animus through a portal into this realm. I haven't seen it since." My words always sounded sleepy while under his spell.

His long fingers loosened from my hair. He shoved my head backward in a final act of dominance as he straightened and stood up. The distance eased my need.

"Take her to him. Let her watch while she thinks about her answer."

Puss covered hands yanked me from the ground. Each of the demons latched onto one of my elbows and stretched me between them, pulling my limbs until they were nearly dislocating from my shoulder joints. I groaned, fumbling to stand on my own feet. They lurched forward and hauled me lower into the tunnels of Hell.

The dampness in the air lessened as we descended farther into the depths of Hell. I'd never been this deep before. The thought of no one knowing my whereabouts in the maze of sinners brought a new fear: an eternity of failure and solitude. Flashes of my time in the spirit realm came to mind, reminding me what that felt like.

A chill bore into my body, forcing goose bumps to pucker along my skin. Rapid, short breaths left my lungs in puffs of white. The dirt floors and tunnels slowly shifted to icy corridors of hard stone. Streams of water trickled from openings in the walls, freezing before the moisture hit the floor.

The journey seemed to go on forever, considering how long it took Crucio demons to get anywhere. Anticipation was a bitch. Their constant stammering and shaking only made me want to reach our destination that much more. *A hell of solitude might be better than being stuck between these two jerking me in all directions.*

Gray light illuminated the tunnels like an underground moon. It brightened as we moved along. Whispers of screams drifted through the corridor, stopping short against a material that should have echoed them on for miles. The walls swallowed the sound before anyone could be certain they heard the souls crying for help and not just a draft whistling from the cracks.

We neared an opening, and the demons' shuffling slowed. They dragged me into an underground cavern with webs of long, slender stone stretching from ceiling to floor. Frost formed on the stone as it reached into a sea of tar-like water. Choppy waves crashed against the icy spindles. Plates of ice riding the surface broke from the impact then disappeared into the thick, inky substance creating the large body of fluid.

The demons released my arms, and I dropped to the ground, my knees slamming into the hard rock. The cold soaked through my pants and threatened to freeze the bones holding me together.

"Get the light," one demon squealed. The other obeyed, scuffling toward a pit of green fire erupting from the floor. Neon-lime streaks flew through the air in a shower of sparks, igniting a torch in the submissive fiend's hand. It lobbed the torch across the floor to the other monster, the frosty coating never once affecting the fire's will to burn.

The fire-starter lit a second torch and carried the light at its side like a club. Bits of the monster's flesh caught fire when brushing against the flame, but the demon paid no attention and continued its stuttered path back to us.

I let my eyes wander to the shiny, pitch-black water lapping at the shore ahead of me. Murmurs of "help" and "save me" floated from the waves.

Studying the ocean of tarry substance, I noticed that ice was not the only thing breaking the surface. "What is that?" I asked the demons, afraid of the answer they would give.

The fiend to my right held its torch out, casting the green light out over the liquid. Its crispy, retracted lips pulled back even farther. Onyx points lined up from one cheek to the other in its feeble attempt to smile. "That's Sinner Sea. And we're going to wade across."

"Heeelp m...," someone shouted.

A head and torso bobbled up from the insidious water. Dense, black tendrils thrust out of the substance and wrapped around the body like a net. An inky fist thrust into the sinner's crying mouth, stifling his request before it was finished, then yanked him under.

Bile churned in my stomach. Panic flourished, tightening my chest. "No fucking way," I protested, shaking my head emphatically.

The demons tugged me up to my feet, gargling a disturbed laugh. "Yes fucking way."

One of the Crucios nudged its pointed jaw toward the shoreline, urging me to get going.

Cautiously, I moved with them across the frozen shore, focusing my energy on tamping down the eager pressure clawing its way up the inside of my body. My bad side sensed the evil I approached. That familiar tingle vibrated through my limbs, begging for freedom to show the lost souls that undoubtedly lived here my version of punishment.

I slowed, dragging my feet, eyes locked on the edge of tarry substance creeping toward me. "There's seriously no other way to get across?" I asked the Crucios, knowing the answer already. They shoved me, forcing me to lurch forward.

One more step and the sticky liquid pooled around my feet. Its heaviness went far beyond the weight of water. Another step and tiny, liquid fingers seemed to latch onto my calves, reaching upward, eager to submerge the rest of me. Four steps later, only a third of my body was under, but I felt like I was damn near suffocating already. The frigid temperature seeped into my bones.

I lifted my leg and a sucking sensation plucked the shoe off my right foot. I stumbled and lost my other shoe. It was like swimming through honey in a freezer. The demons kept a tight grip on me, sloshing me through the ick between them.

When I got to chest level, I could hardly breathe. I felt as if I was trapped in a slab of concrete. The sea stretched beyond the green light's cast, and there was no end in sight.

Scanning the surface, cautious of any little change in the current, I noticed a swirl ahead of us. "What was that?" The demons slowed and shined their torches in all directions. "There it is again," I yelled, panic lacing my voice. Something bumped my leg. Depending on the demon's holding me to support my weight, I jerked my legs into my chest to escape whatever was lurking around us.

"Keep moving," the commanding Crucio demanded.

Before I could move, an icy hand wrapped around my ankle and yanked down. Black water splashed over my head and blotted out the green glow above me. My arms slipped free of the demons' grasp. And, for a moment, all was peaceful. I was free in the darkness.

Serenity didn't last long. The greasy water took on a solid state and dove into any orifice I had open. My nostrils and ears stretched to accommodate the harsh tendrils rushing into them. The substance forced its way down my throat, leaving behind an acidic taste on my tongue. It was hopeless; I couldn't evade this wickedness. Soon, I would drown or suffocate.

The muck shifted around me violently. My head emerged, green light flooding my murky vision. The demons lifted me out of the water, tearing the tendrils from my body. The fluid dripped down my neck and shoulders, draining from my ears until I could finally hear the demons chanting. The final strands of goop withdrew, and I gasped for air, clutching at the fiends' arms to hold myself upright.

As uncomfortable as my cloud of doom was, that was far worse.

The demons lowered me back into the water. "We're here," one said.

I raised my gaze, assessing the shoreline. My brow furrowed in confusion. "But…this is where we started," I panted. "Please, don't tell me I went through all of that for you morons to get us turned around, just to bring me right back to the beginning," I scoffed through chattering teeth.

The demons laughed deep, gargled laughs then carried me to the shore I thought we'd left behind. Every muscle in my body ached, but I couldn't allow myself to relax after that experience. I clutched the demons' arms until we were on solid ground then flopped to the hard surface.

I would have kissed the cold rock under me if I didn't think my lips would stick to it. I shivered as if I'd just been plucked from a glacial spring and thrown into a deep freezer. Every part of my body contracted and quaked, struggling to get warm.

The demons dropped the torches on the ground. I scrambled to get closer to the green fire, but soon found that the light didn't emit any kind of heat. I huffed, glaring up at the Crucios, who were watching me with the faint hint of satisfaction on their marred expressions.

"Get up," Thing One demanded, "You'll warm up when you move." Leaving the torches on the arctic floor, I clumsily lunged to my feet and followed them into the gray-tinged corridor leading out of the cavern. The humidity returned and the gray illumination faded.

Slowly, the terrain began to change and morph back to the dirt tunnels I had grown used to. My body whined with exhaustion, but I traipsed along with the monsters. "Where are we going?" I whispered, too tired to raise my voice.

"Quiet," the fiend to my left sneered as we veered into a side tunnel. *That wasn't there before.*

At the end of the tunnel, a single door stood looking out of place. Wrought iron bars swirled and angled into angry gargoyle faces, decorating the splintering wood like lace. An eerie silence filled the small dugout.

"Open it, bitch." The demons threw me at the foot of the door.

I searched the bars for a latch or handle, but didn't see one. "How?" I asked timidly, glancing over my shoulder at them.

A decayed, shuddering hand pointed to a medallion buried in the dirt wall. "The key."

I pushed myself up and approached the wall, wondering how to get the glittering hunk of metal out of the earth pocketing it. I lifted my hand and spread my fingers around its edges, digging my nails into the crevices surrounding the medallion, and pried it loose. The gold medal tumbled from its slot. I thrust my hand out, catching the circular plate before it hit the dirt.

Holding it in my palm, I studied the engraved details embellishing the surface. It was stamped with a tribal-looking pattern of lines and curves I couldn't decipher. I traced my hand along the raised shapes, wincing and yanking my fingers away when the sharp edges sliced into my skin. A single red drop of blood grew on my fingertip then slid off the side, landing on the shiny plate. The bright red droplet leached into the recessed spaces on the gilded piece, drinking it in like life-water. The lines began to shift and swirl into the center of the medallion, creating a vortex of sorts.

"Place it in the circle," one of the monsters screeched over my shoulder.

I followed the demon's directions and set the piece into an open ring fixed on the door's center. Stepping back, I watched the continuous morphing of gold swirl, bubble, and mold into an exact replica of my face. The miniature, metallic eyes stared back at me with the same bewildered gaze I was sure I wore.

Leaning forward, I examined every feature. As I moved forward, to my surprise, the golden face stretched from its ring out to meet me. The corners of my mouth turned down, and my brows pulled together. I spun around, searching for an answer in the monsters' expressions. They smiled their mutated smiles, offering no explanations.

Something's not right.

The moment I had the thought, hot bars entwined around my biceps and tugged me backwards. Impressions from the door pressed into my back, while the metal on my arms seared my skin. Unforgiving, angular gargoyle faces dug into my shoulder blades, threatening to split the flesh open. A scream built in my throat and exploded past my gritted teeth, unable to hide the pain anymore, as the door continued to squeeze my body.

When I thought the searing rods couldn't possibly squeeze me any tighter without threading completely through my body, the door flipped, end over end. Though I was upside down from where I started, the new world around me was right side up.

Archard

CHAPTER SEVEN

BLANK PAGES

"I've never seen anything like it," Maggie said weakly between sips of water. "She was there and then...the light just disappeared around her. Like a black hole opened in the alley, sucking up every glint of light in her immediate vicinity."

"Okay, just take it easy," Arkin insisted, taking the cup from her shaking hands. His worried eyes met mine. "Can't we do this later, Archard?"

"No. I'm sorry." I nodded for Maggie to continue.

She placed a hand on Arkin's forearm and smiled. "I'm fine. Really."

The demons had drained her considerably. Even her hair seemed a little less vibrant than usual.

"Give me anything you can remember." I was desperate to find clues that would lead me to Nevaeh.

Maggie rehashed every blurred detail of following Nevaeh, Gavyn, and Layla downtown, then losing their tracks only to catch them luring a man into the alley behind the club.

"That's when I saw Nevaeh straddle the man and do her thing. Her colors were still mixing, so I waited to see which way she would go. I'd hoped she would stop it all. There wasn't much I could do by myself." Her usually spiked hair lay flat against her head, softening her appearance. She hung her head thinking about what to say next. "I thought he was gonna die in her shadowy mess, but the man was alive when she swallowed the black stuff. His bubble kept flickering a dingy white with tinges of orange." Maggie looked down at her hands and began picking at a piece of skin at her nail bed. "He was an unsettled soul, but still a good man—a good Celata. What was she doing to him?" she whispered the last question more to herself than us. Her head shook, ridding a passing thought, then she raised her gaze to me again. "I yelled out. I didn't know what else to do. It's not like my gifts are very aggressive. I couldn't save him." She took the cup of water from Arkin and held it to her lips, but didn't drink. "Layla was pissed and released a horde of Aethers." Maggie shivered as she spoke. "They ran through me like a sieve. Then they attacked that poor man."

A single tear trickled down her cheek. Arkin reached to wipe it away and cradled her face in his hand. I looked away, fighting back the painful memories of touching Nev like that.

Maggie sniffled and went on, "That's all I remember before passing out."

"That's enough," Arkin assured. He swept her short locks from her forehead, and they shared a moment staring into each other's eyes. Maggie quickly averted her gaze, fiddling awkwardly with the blankets. "Uh...I think I should get some rest. I'll try to remember more details later." She lay down, rolling away from us. It was her way of escaping anymore conversation or eager looks from Arkin, I assumed.

Arkin reached out to touch her shoulder, but hesitated. His wings ruffled, and he pulled his hand back. I patted his shoulder, understanding the struggle of loving someone you shouldn't.

When I turned and headed for the door, Arkin stood and followed. "What's that?"

I was reminded of the burdensome book in my hand. "I hope it's the thing that will help us get Nevaeh back before she's beyond saving."

"You found the Clavis prophecy?" Arkin's steps sped up, bringing him to my side when I didn't answer. "Have you read it, yet?" he asked.

"No. But, I guess it's time I start." I entered my room and tossed the bound pages onto the bed. "Eyal was going to destroy it, but I managed to get it back."

His brows pulled together. "Why would he get rid of it?"

"I don't know. He said that Nev couldn't get ahold of it. The thing is...Eyal wasn't the only one to tell me that." I settled my fists on my hips and scowled at the taunting book. Arkin plopped down on the other side of the bed, keeping a distance as if the book would combust if he touched it. "A demon named Kenet visited me. He said he was trying to help, then gave me this and told me to keep it from Nev."

"Well...you won't know if it can help unless you actually open the damn thing, right?"

I took a deep breath. "Right." Kneeling beside the bed, I dragged the red velvet toward me. The pages crackled as I turned them, reading every word carefully.

Meticulously scrolled writing recounted the day God came to Rhett in a vision. The angel repeated the story of a love bridging Heaven and Hell. A child born of this doomed love would possess traits surpassing both worlds. New wars would be created by her hand and bleed into untouched territories. As I soaked in the words, I found that the rumors we'd heard were close to what was written on most accounts.

After twenty minutes of flicking cards from the playing deck on my nightstand across the room and keeping silent while I read, Arkin's impatience finally got the best of him. "So, what does it say?" he asked, hurling another card into the trashcan, making his goal.

"Nothing we don't already know so far. It talks about her coming from a parent on each side and having powerful gifts. It says something about her creating new wars."

My brother thought for a moment, then answered, "She did make it possible to bring the Celatum into the war. There's so many more battles here now." He plinked another card into the can.

"True." I read on. "It says she will cast judgment and yield damnation or redemption to her victims."

Arkin sat up and leaned over the book with me. "What in the hell is that supposed to mean?"

"I don't know. Maybe it has something to do with the new cloud she's spewing out."

Arkin grabbed the book and leaned back, laying it against his knees, his eyes roaming over the words. "'Once the Clavis awakens its key with original love's blood and the traitor's plume, it will possess the power to unlock doors to the gates of realms beyond its own and travel at will. Satan will gain control of the Clavis first. Tides may change, but not without great tribulation. Fire will purify what water cannot obtain. The breath of life will make holy what evil consumes.'"

I rose from the side of the bed and started pacing in a circle, waiting to hear more of the troubling prophecy. Arkin flipped to the next page and glanced up at me. His hand nervously advanced a few more pages.

I paused and scowled at him. "What is it?" I threw my hands up in frustration when he just peered down at the object in his hands, lips tight in a thin line. "Continue," I demanded.

"I can't."

He tossed the book down on the mattress, opened to the page he'd read on the left and a blank page on the right.

I stared at the bare parchment for a moment, trying to will words to appear. There had to be something that would tell me how to get Nevaeh back. "I don't understand." I grabbed the edge of the book and lifted it from the bed, cradling it in one hand while thumbing through the empty pages. "This can't be it," I exhaled as if I'd been kicked in the gut. "There has to be something about the key or what will change Nev's mind. Where's the key?" I yelled, glancing up at Arkin with wide, desperate eyes.

"It doesn't even give us a sure-fire 'yes, she'll come back to our side.'" Arkin raised his hands, surrendering to defeat. "I'm just as lost as you are, man. That was the worst written prophecy I've ever read."

With one flick of my wrist, the velvet binding flew from my hands and hit the wall with a loud thud. "What was so damn important she couldn't get her hands on it?" The muscle twitched along my jaw. I raked shaky hands through my hair. "Let's go," I said to my brother as I strode toward the door.

He jumped off the bed. "Where are we headed?" The angel stretched his wings, then folded them neatly behind him and trailed my steps.

"To talk to Malach. We have to find Rhett."

"So, you guys thought I knew where that traitor was?"

Malach sat on a barstool in Gavyn's kitchen, eating a bowl of cereal. He'd listened to me recap everything that had happened since I last saw him with indifference. Surprisingly, he took the lack of information offered by the book better than me.

"No. I *thought* you could help us find him," I corrected, watching the warrior and wondering if there was a bone in his body that wasn't completely arrogant.

Shoveling another spoonful of sugary flakes into his gullet, he chewed noisily, calm eyes focused on me. I couldn't tell if he was thinking about a response or just didn't hear me. He dropped his spoon into his bowl and set it on the counter, tongue working to get the remnants of food from his teeth. "And how do you propose I do that. I'm just as much in the dark as you."

"There has to be an angel from Eyal's group that knows what

happened."

"Maybe." He leaned back, eyeing me with arms folded across his chest.

I held back the slew of insults at the tip of my tongue and continued civilly. He had helped us in the past, but that didn't mean I had absolved him of his daily habit of being a chronic asshole. "Malach, you have access to the Heavens. You can contact the angels. Please, just ask around?"

"What are you going to do while I investigate the Holy Realm?" A smug grin formed around Malach's words.

"I'm going to find a way into Hell."

"What?" Arkin questioned jumping up from the futon. "No way!" he protested.

Malach's gaze traced over my expression, undoubtedly searching for a sign I was joking. "You're crazy, Archard." He shook his head, then reached for his spoon and shoved another loaded spoon in his mouth. "Alright. I'll ask around," he said, crunching on the cereal in his mouth, "but don't get killed before I can deliver on my end. Your little trip to Sinner's Paradise might not be necessary."

I nodded, agreeing to wait a little longer before exploring that dangerous avenue. "Start with Eyal. I think he knows more than he's letting on." My eyes wandered around Gavyn's abandoned apartment. "You know, we have room at the factory if you need a place to stay."

As much as Malach got beneath my skin with his smugness, he was still a brother. I knew what it was like to feel stuck between realms and not have a place to go. Torment of the failure to keep Gavyn under his wings darkened his features. Staying in his ward's empty home couldn't make it any easier.

Malach picked up the bowl and dipped it to his mouth, slurping the milk until it was gone, then looked at us with a forced smile. "I'm good here. He might come back one day...for socks or something." The Arch rose off the stool and wiped his lips on the back of his forearm. "I need to be here if that happens."

"Right," I responded, nodding with understanding. "The invitation is open if you change your mind." Floorboards creaked as I strolled over to the black leather chair I'd thrown my duster on. I shrugged my restrained wings into the coat and turned to leave.

Arkin was a few steps ahead and nearly to the door when Malach cleared his throat. He looked deep in thought. He clearly had something to say, but was going to make me ask for it.

"What is it?" I asked, rolling my eyes.

"I was just thinking…what kind of demon is nice enough to help a falling soul such as Nev? She said this Kenet had shown up before and assisted her in escaping Hell. Could it be that *he* is her father?"

I mulled over the possibility for a moment, then looked at Arkin. "How did we not see that?" He shrugged, avoiding a verbal response. He must've felt as stupid as I did.

"Don't fret over missing it. I *am* an Archangel after all," Malach boasted through his haughty smirk.

"That would explain their shared ability to open Hell portals," Arkin interjected.

"Son of a bitch." The curse erupted under my breath as I dragged my hands over the tension building in my face. "Why didn't he tell me? Seems like an important detail to omit when you're trying to save your daughter."

Malach strode to the other side of the bar, his brow cocked. "Maybe you should talk to him. Perhaps *he* knows more than he's letting on." Dishes clanked as Malach dropped his bowl in the sink.

His pristine feathers spread to his sides and thrust upwards. The Arch exploded into a whirlpool of water opening the ceiling. Together, Arkin and I watched him cross to the home we had abandoned; our hearts ached to follow the holy angel.

Nevaeh

CHAPTER EIGHT

SURVIVOR'S HELL

The branding bars untangled from my limbs and released me from the door. I fell into a crumpled heap on the ground. I was too worried about where I'd arrived, to consider the torn skin stinging on my back.

"Hello?" I called. No one answered.

As much as I loathed the demons, it made my senses prickle to know they had tricked me into this new world and hadn't follow. Was it that bad here that the monsters of Hell didn't want to enter, or was this place only meant for my eyes?

"Come on, Nev. Get it together," I whispered, surveying my surroundings. It was night. A streetlight towered over the lonely highway stretching under my feet. Tall trees bordered the road on either side of an otherwise remote patch of land.

I glanced at the door levitating behind me and wondered if it would stay there or disappear the moment I left its general vicinity. As I stood up and scrutinized the slab of wood hanging two feet off the pavement, the cool trickle of a raindrop dampened my face. Within seconds, the sky opened up. My hair was dripping wet and my clothes stuck to my frame as buckets of rain drenched everything in sight. Squinting into the darkness, I searched for somewhere to hide until the downpour passed.

I sprinted to a nearby tree with heavy foliage and took cover under its thick branches. The hard pattering of water against the leaves increased to a dull roar. The street light gleamed off the water gathering into a small stream on the road, highlighting the ripples grazing over rocks and leaves littering the blacktop.

I peered into the night sky. Not one star shined. There was nothing beyond a faint luminescence of the lamp across the street, not even a moon.

That's okay. I can just stay here and wait it out. How long could it last, I thought to myself, frowning as I took note of the rising level of water covering my toes.

Tires shrieked on the wet pavement some distance away, and I jerked, slinking around the tree trunk for cover. Two headlights bounced, jolting in an erratic path set in my direction like a derailed train. I dug my toes into the dirt and bolted for the other side of the street, water splashing onto my legs with each stomp.

The tires squealed, fighting to gain friction with the road, and a shifting engine howled. The nose of the car zig-zagged toward me, then the tree, then me once again. For a second, I wasn't sure if my move had been a good idea. I lunged for the grassy shoulder just as the vehicle took a last-minute veer toward the tree and maintained its course.

Spinning tires failed to grip the road. The car skidded across inches of water, spraying the windows with a fresh layer of moisture that the wipers couldn't keep up with. A loud bang, followed by the sound of glass breaking, sharp pops, and the hissing of steam rushing from the car's pipes rang through the air.

Then, everything was suddenly still again.

The rain vanished so quickly it was as if someone turned off the faucet. I trudged onto the pavement, my feet sloshing through the small creek left behind from the tsunami that just vanished. Red taillights beamed back at me. A thin streak of smoke escaped from under the car's hood. I approached the chunk of broken metal, noticing the splintered oak leaning on top of it.

"Hello?" I yelled.

A man grumbled from inside the vehicle.

I moved toward the voice, inspecting the crash site along the way. The rear seat was empty. Tiny glass shards were spread in a glittering blanket over the leather interior.

"Hello?" I repeated, making sure the man was still with me.

"Bonnie?" a raspy voice called. "Bonnie, you alright?" he slurred as I drew near his side of the car.

"Hey there," I greeted, looking through the broken window. "Just stay still," I instructed, assessing the damage. The man ignored me and tugged at the woman beside him. Her forehead rested against the dash, blonde hair falling in a bloody curtain around her face. "Sir, I need you to be still. You were in a car accident."

His red-stained hands struggled to release the seatbelt restraining him.

"I'll check on Bonnie. Please, just hold on."

The man stopped, jerking his head toward the backseat as if remembering something precious had been there.

I rushed around the trunk to the other side. I skid to a stop when I met the sad sight of a miniature body slouched with her back against the front wheel. Her head slowly lulled to the side, fixing her quiet eyes on me. "Hey, sweetie," I said, inching closer. She looked straight through me.

"Anna," the man cried out from inside the car, "Anna, baby, where are you?" Panic racked his voice as he realized she wasn't in the vehicle.

"She's right here. I've got her," I assured, bending over the little girl to examine her injuries. A soaked baby-doll dress clung to her fragile body. A bloody gash parted the side of her head. It was then that I realized she wasn't looking through me at all; she wasn't looking at anything anymore.

She was dead.

"Anna," a worried voice echoed out of the car again. The man grunted and whimpered over the sound of strained metal creaking. Finally, a thunderous pop and the high-pitched whining of the driver's door opening quieted his struggling noises.

No, he can't see her like this.

There wasn't anything to cover her up with. I stood up and spun around, blocking her tiny corpse with my body. The father stumbled around the rear of the crashed car, bumping into the trunk while trying to find his bearings. "Don't come any closer, sir," I warned, throwing my hands out in front of me.

Sweat and blood dripped from his short blonde hair. His suit jacket was barely hanging onto one arm and the other arm was missing completely. One shoed foot and one bare foot sunk into mud as he slid along the passenger side.

The man peered down at my legs, recognition twisting his expression into a jumble of pain and anger. He dropped to his knees. At first, he appeared too exhausted to react to what I hid behind me, but the slow deep rumble of protest erupted from his mouth just seconds later. The way he cried out in anguish caused my heart to skip a beat. A contagious imprint of his grief weighed my emotions down.

"Sir?" I whispered, battling to keep my own tears at bay.

Trembling fingers lifted to his mouth, slipping upward to mask his sullen face as he rocked back and forth on his knees. I reached out to comfort him, but thought better of it when he leaned away from me and settled back on his feet. He raked at his scalp, pulling at his matted hair in despair, unsatisfying breaths heaving in and out of his chest.

"Sir, we have to find help. We've gotta get you out of here," I urged.

The heartbroken father raised his eyes and met my gaze. In that fraction of a second, years of memories flooded me. I distorted the image of the man at my feet, adding gray to his hair, wrinkling his skin, and paling his skin color. With a few pounds added here and there, I realized I was face to face with the very reason I was in Hell.

"George!" I squealed, but my excitement soon dulled.

Why was I suddenly allowed to see him? Why would they bring me here for punishment, then give me exactly what I wanted?

George returned to his hysterical rocking without missing a beat. I knelt and placed a hand on each of his shoulders. But, when I touched him, my hands sifted through his body as easily as penetrating a cloud.

He continued in his grieving ritual and seemed to have no idea I was right in front of him.

"George, please look at me," I repeated over and over with tears streaming down my cheeks. The only time he lifted his gaze was to find his poor daughter, slumped lifelessly, behind me.

He suddenly stopped rocking, stood, and stumbled backwards to the other side of the car.

"Okay, then," I said, grimacing in confusion while I watched him back away.

He spoke, but his words were mumbled and senseless. Thunder cracked, drowning out my shouts to get his attention. Droplets of rain floated off the ground and ascended to their rightful place in the sky. I spun in a circle, wide-eyed, marveling over the fact that it was raining in reverse.

I rushed to the driver's side. "What's going on, George?"

He continued retracing every tragic step he had taken minutes ago. George slipped into the driver's seat and struggled to click the mangled seatbelt back in place. I braced myself on the door and peered into the window, glancing at George's dead wife when he turned to tug at her body. His gibberish and painful cries warred with the thunder vibrating through the atmosphere.

Crunching and scraping rang in my ears as the heap of metal began to shift. I yanked my hands from the window ledge and stepped back. "George," I screamed one more time, but he didn't even look at me.

Every dent unbuckled, and every scratch seamlessly disappeared. The bunched hood flattened and tires plumped up with air. Damage sustained from the crash worked relentlessly to mend itself.

George's cries silenced, but terror distorted his otherwise soft face. My eyes darted to Bonnie. The dried blood staining her head dissipated. Her golden hair swung back from her cheeks, tucking neatly behind her ears. She sat straight up, pressing her back into the car seat, the dash impression on her forehead smoothing into the beautiful, flawless face it was before. She turned to look at George, hands braced against the dash.

I retreated another step and watched the commotion in amazement. *This is good, right? They look okay.*

In the event of George's reversing misfortune, I'd forgotten about Anna. I ran to the other side of the car. Anna's sweet curls coiled and bounced to their proper place. The crimson streaks dying her clothes receded until the white of her dress was pure again.

Slowly, the tiny corpse raised from the ground as if a marionette controlled by invisible strings. Her thin legs stiffened while she performed an awkward flip in the air, smacking her left temple on the quarter-panel, then levitated back through the rear window, feet first. She settled comfortably onto the back seat while the shards of glass lifted into the air around her and gathered in the window opening, sealing her in the car. The seat belt crossed her little lap loosely, but the shoulder strap wound behind her, doing little to keep her safe. Anna's lips curved into a loving smile. She stared at her parents, oblivious of the gruesome fate she'd just experienced.

Dots of glass hastily filled the other windows and completed the car's miraculous repair, encasing the family once more. The splintered oak groaned, its branches pushing against the car like a giant trying to right itself after tripping over a pebble. Pieces of bark soared up from the car's roof and surrounding soil reattached to the tree's trunk. Leaves and wet dirt tamped into the ground, erasing tread tracks as the wheels rolled away from the tree.

Water seeped from the earth, puddling around my ankles. Tires sloshed over the road's shoulder. The car scrambled backward, then squealed against the road, zigzagging in the direction from which it came.

I squeezed my eyes shut and threw up my arm, shielding them from the blinding light. By the time I opened my eyes again, the vehicle was gone — and George with it.

I jogged toward the horizon, chasing after George, refusing to accept I'd lost him again. My darkened heart ached. I gasped for air, breathless from running, but more so from the fresh stabbing sensation in my chest.

Why did I get my hopes up? I should've known.

A cool gust of wind chilled my skin as the rain slowed, then stopped. I leaned over, bracing my hands on my thighs. The scene was quiet around me. I searched behind me for the door, but it dumped me in this place then vanished, leaving me without a way to leave.

I could continue to follow George, but there wasn't much of a chance that I'd actually find him in this strange world. I was certain neither direction — North toward George or South to the door — offered anything better than where I stood now, but I couldn't wait for the demons to come collect me.

The beast prowling beneath my surface yawned and stretched like a lazy cat disturbed from its sleep. It was always there, lingering in my depths, but sometimes I had a moment of peace or distraction that allowed me to forget about it. Swelling against my insides, it whispered a reminder of my power to open portals.

Maybe I could open my own doorway out of here.

I loosened the reigns on the darkness the tiniest bit and let the surge of energy sear a path to my fingers. Amethyst light ignited under my skin, burning brighter as I focused it on a spot just beyond my hand. An invisible hum of power pushed back, competing for control of the elements. I unleashed more of my darkness, attempting to increase the effect. Fizzling sparks and dull electric streaks snapped the air, but nothing opened.

Pressure flared against my ribcage. My throat filled with the cloud threatening to rip out of me. I clamped my jaw closed tight, hoping it would be enough to keep the beast captive. The line of fear and yearning was growing dangerously thin, but I couldn't remain in this Hell they created for George. I swallowed back the force and prayed for strength to contain my evil.

Taking a deep breath, I focused on opening my fortress only a little more. Sparks shot from my fingers and electricity zapped through the air like lightning. Thin, black ribbons fled my mouth and eyes as I fought the urge to give in.

A single raindrop fell from the sky, dampening my shirt. A second droplet of water landed on my forearm. The moisture hissed and rolled from my skin in a winding vine of steam.

"I wouldn't stoke your fires if I were you." The smell of smoldering flesh drifted on a soft breeze and filled my nostrils.

I turned in the direction of the familiar voice, severing the connection to the portal, and found violet-blue eyes watching me.

"Kenet." I yanked on the reigns of my darkness, barely maintaining control. "What are you doing here?" I shouted over the increasing roar of rain.

A blaring light flashed across his handsome face. His eyes darted to a spot behind my left shoulder. "You'd better move," he urged, stepping toward me.

Tires squealed. Kenet grabbed my bicep and dragged me to the side of the road. A car jerked across the flooded pavement, then rammed into the oak. Taillights shined from the crash site.

I waded through the water flowing down the road. The rain stopped.

Is the weather ever consistent around here?

George's voice grumbled and cried from inside the smashed vehicle. On the passenger side, I found Anna in death's slumber.

I sprinted to George's door and tried to pry the door open. "George, I'm here," I yelled breathlessly.

He repeated the same actions as last time, while I tugged and kicked at the crumpled door. I glanced at the seat next to him. Bonnie leaned her pretty head on the dash. It was an exact replica of their first horrific accident, right down to the tiny glass blanketing the floor boards and seats.

"Open, you piece of shit," I shouted, jamming my knee into the metal while I pulled on the door handle.

"It's no use, Nevaeh," Kenet said.

I glanced over my shoulder at him, still tugging on the metal separating me from my father. He looked at the car with pity in his eyes. "Help me, then," I grunted.

"There's nothing you can do to help him. This is his punishment."

I stopped struggling and slicked the wet hair out of my face. Sliding my hands back over my mouth, I held back the sobs of hopelessness about to break free. My line of vision homed on George's bloody hand pulling at the seatbelt. Tears slid over my lashes. He cried out for Bonnie and Anna, the misery in his voice stabbing another blade into my damaged heart.

I folded my hands together, as if I were holding something in my palms too precious to leave unprotected, and slid then down to my heart. This was killing me to watch.

"What do you mean punishment?" I asked with a shuddering voice. "I thought you were supposed to be his keeper." I stumbled back a step when the door lurched open, my gaze fixed on the suffering soul tumbling out of the car.

I wanted nothing more than to hug him and break free of our Hells. "How is he safe here?"

"I never said it was a pretty fate, but it's better than you think." Kenet followed George with weary eyes while he staggered drunkenly around the rear of the car and found Anna. "I've done my best to give him a prison he can live with. He created this torment himself. He's dealt with this memory for years." Steam trailed from Kenet's skin as he stepped closer to me, his eyes pleading for forgiveness. "What would you have me do, Nevaeh?"

Rage antagonized the dark cloud inside my gut, stirring the urge to serve Kenet punishment too. "I guess I pictured George captive in a room somewhere—not reliving the trauma of his mistakes." I bit back the desire to hurt Kenet and calmed the heightening heat within. I spread my arms in desperation. "So, what? He has to relive this over and over? Is that his eternity now?"

"For the moment, yes." Kenet searched the crash site to avoid looking me in the eye.

I dropped my hands to my sides and let his affirmation sink in for a second. "Why can't I touch him?" *If I could just grab him, I could open the portal and take him with me.*

"Only those from the worlds beyond yours can manipulate a soul. I'm sorry, Nevaeh. I'm just as much a pawn in their game as you are. Please believe that I want to help you. I just don't know how."

Memories of the ethereal tendrils leaving Vinney and Ray's corpses came to mind. It didn't happen with George when I tried to touch him, though. I couldn't control this thing enough to use it.

The line between using my curses to help George and becoming consumed by them was getting thinner by the day. The next time I used my powers could very well flush out the last of my goodness. *Then how would I help George?*

I closed the distance between me and Kenet, broadening my shoulders and straightening my spine. "I will find a way to get him out," I said with absolute conviction. There was no doubt in my mind that I would free George, though it may take time and every bit of my humanity to do it.

Kenet's thin lips pulled into a grin. "I know you will, my dear." Pride beamed from his violet-blues. "Now, let's work on getting you out." His steaming hand spread over the back door of the car, and a ring of fire ate away the metal beneath his fingertips. It widened, opening a hole to the city sidewalk beyond. I looked at George, hating that I couldn't just grab him and take him with me, then stepped through Kenet's portal.

CHAPTER NINE

DEMON WHISPERER

"Archard, we've been over this a bazillion times," Arkin reminded me. Exhaustion had created a dusty blue hue under his eyes hours ago, yet he continued to flip through the pages of aged vellum.

"I know," I grumbled. Defeat wasn't something I wanted to admit. There had to be clues in the writing that we missed. "Go back to Rhett describing the day he had the vision." I stood and extended the heavy wings creating tension on my back. The rich purple marking the end feathers appeared almost black in the dim light of my room.

"He talks about watching over his ward…" His eyes skimmed over the passage, then looked up lost in thought.

"What?"

"It says that his vision happened after he announced himself to his ward for the first time."

"And?"

"I was just thinking…why did you allow Nev to see you after all of those years?" The angel grinned knowingly.

My heart throbbed as I thought of the time I found her standing on Joe's steps. She was a little girl the last time I had seen her, but I knew the moment the sun shined into her periwinkle eyes, hues of violet streaking the iris like oil strokes from a paintbrush, she was mine.

She tripped on the uneven stones as I was about to announce myself. The smell of her lavender skin haunted me even now. I wanted to hold her in my arms and explain everything, but fear of losing her again squashed my plans.

The longer I stayed in the background spying on her, the stronger her gifts became. Opportunities for me to ease her into this world, of enlightening her in a way that wouldn't terrify her passed and my soul submitted to the longing I felt to be near her. Even so, I battled the obligation of telling her who she was — who I was. Instead, I waited until the right opportunity was gone, and my world had already latched onto the innocence I'd meant to protect.

"Well?" Arkin asked, waiting for my answer.

"Love," I whispered. "I let her see me because I loved her." My hands rubbed at the stinging in my eyes, hoping to push back the tears gathering there. "What's your point?"

"It's the reason I let Theora see me. It's the reason any Guardian allows their ward to see them. Our love of them as a child transforms into something undeniable as they get older." He huffed out a frustrated breath and scooted to the edge of the bed. His feathers spread over the mattress like a comforter. "What if Rhett had fallen in love with Arianna? Maybe that's why he left her."

"Okay. So, Rhett loved Arianna. Arianna falls for Kenet and has Nevaeh. Rhett figures out that Nevaeh is the Clavis and leaves?" I crossed my arms, annoyed that connecting what little dots we had wasn't giving me more useful information.

I walked over to the wall and pounded my fists against it. Dust floated to the concrete floor. "Kenet," I shouted. I knew it was a long shot, but I had to try.

Arkin's face twisted, his eyebrows raised. "What, on all that is holy, are you doing?"

I sighed, resting my forehead on the wall. "We've got to find the key. Surely Kenet knows where it is."

"And you think pounding on the wall will get his attention?"

"Not really, but it was worth a try," I mumbled. A moment passed, then I felt a hand cover my shoulder and squeeze.

"I know who can help us." I turned as Arkin threw a wadded-up duster at my chest. "You'll need this." He winced when the crests of his wings disappeared behind his shoulder blades before shoving into his own long coat.

"Who do you have in mind?" I retracted the peaks of my own wings, then tugged my duster on.

His lips curved into his familiar mischievous smile. "We need a demon-whisperer," he said with a glint of trouble in his eyes.

Frankincense and the smooth voices of a children's choir soared heavily through the chapel. Arkin and I sat in a pew near the back of the church, watching the priest swing a thurible between the rows. Parishioners knelt and took the sign of the cross, accepting the blessings offered when smoke from the smoldering incense wafted toward them.

I leaned over my brother's shoulder as he kneeled on the raised, carpet-covered plank at our ankles. "What are we doing here?" I whispered. I had avoided churches and the such since the cathedral. The memories of a home too far away and a love too far gone taunted me more than I could bear. The walls of these places felt like a prison of reminders, no matter how beautiful.

Arkin nudged his chin toward an older gentleman performing the mass.

"The priest is your demon-whisperer?" I sighed, leaning my forearms on the pew in front of me.

"No." He took the sign of the cross and pushed back onto the seat with the rest of the congregation. "Him."

A tall, lanky boy emerged from behind the clergyman. He couldn't have been older than fourteen or fifteen, but fine lines already aged his pale face. He carried a gold bowl and spoon, holding it out for the priest to get fresh incense when necessary.

"He's a Celata?" I asked, surprised that our world had touched such a young soul. That was rare.

"Since he was nine. His father shot his mother, then himself while the boy watched. That night he saw the first of many demons that would scar his life." Arkin studied the boy with a sympathetic expression. "His name's Dominic." Dominic dutifully followed three other boys back to the altar and prepared for Communion.

When mass ended, Arkin led me to a sacristy behind the confessionals.

We entered the modest clergy's quarters without knocking.

"Arkin. It's been a long time," the priest greeted, unaffected by our intrusion. "Not long enough, actually," he jabbed in a thick Hungarian accent while draping his vestments neatly on a hanger and placing them in an armoire.

"Nice to see you too, Father Varga." Arkin plopped down in a high-backed, velvet-trimmed chair across the room and stared at the man as he unrobed. "Where's Dominic?"

"What could you possibly want with Dominic?" The stocky man hooked the last hanger on a rod and turned to glare at Arkin, straightening his simple, black button-down shirt.

"Cut the shit, Father. I know he's around. I can smell him." The muscles in Arkin's body tensed.

"I told you and your kind to stay away from him. Dominic has enough trouble fighting demons without the Heavenly driving him into their arms." Burly forearms crossed over a thick chest as the priest scorned us.

"I wouldn't come here if it wasn't an emergency, Father, and you know it."

"Stop. That's enough," a dirty-blonde haired boy demanded from the doorway. "What do you want, Arkin?" Dominic limped into the room and situated himself on the chair next to my brother.

"We need to talk to a demon."

The priest gasped. "Those damned creatures of Hell may chase him— why, I'm not quite sure—," he mumbled the last words, "but he can't just call them at a moment's notice to serve your fancy and strike up a conversation." He shook his head, unease pinching a line between his brows.

"I can," Dominic said softly, correcting Father Varga. The boy's gaze lifted to the priest rushing to his side. "I'm sorry I didn't tell you sooner." Dominic's apologetic frown begged for forgiveness.

Father Varga settled on the end of the coffee table next to Dominic and anxiously clutched his knees. "You could have, you know." His concerned posture and tone regarded the boy as a father might a son. "You can't do this, though. Each time you use your abilities, they get closer to your whereabouts."

"I can't hide forever, Peter. Either I use this curse for good, or it's going to eat me alive." Dominic placed a calming hand on Father Varga's white- knuckled hand.

My curiosity piqued. It was strange Arkin had never told me about this boy. "What exactly can you do?"

His honest eyes hid a much darker intention, one that walked a thin line. "I have a connection to them. I can hear their thoughts. They unknowingly whisper to me all the time. Sometimes I can invade their psyche." He peered through me for a moment, perhaps hearing them as we spoke. "And, I can most certainly call upon them by name."

The temptation was buried deep, but his struggle with it was fierce.

When just a glimmer of the opportunity to let go sparked in his eyes, Dominic's sweet incense odor turned sour — spoiling the air with sulfur.

"Then you'll help?" Arkin rushed.

"Wait. If you can call them by name, can you call Nevaeh?" The air filling my lungs halted. I couldn't afford an ounce of hope to seed in my heart. I allowed myself to entertain fantasies of her safe in my arms too many times.

Dominic looked at Arkin, his thick brows cinching together. "You didn't tell him?"

Arkin's hand gripped the back of his neck as he opened his hesitant mouth to speak. "I...I didn't want to make it worse."

"What are you talking about?" I questioned, balling my fingers into fists at my sides.

"We already tried. He couldn't get a straight answer from the demons." His gaze fell to the floor like a child awaiting punishment.

I breathed again. "And you couldn't get her to answer either, right?" I prayed that she wasn't demon enough to be included in the vile beings the kid could communicate with.

Dominic shifted in his chair. "No, I didn't get an answer when I called. I did, however, hear some of her thoughts. Just echoes in the wind, really."

"What did you hear?" I searched Dominic's eyes for good news, but only found disappointment in his silence.

Arkin stood and ambled closer. "Archard, he didn't find anything useful to us. That's why I didn't tell you. I didn't want you to worry any more than you do now." He let out a long sigh and combed a hand through his auburn hair. "It was a lost cause."

I stared into Arkin's rueful eyes, then forgave him with a nod. "But there is a chance to get information now?"

"I can try to reach the devil you seek, yes."

The priest shoved off the table and paced toward a stand across the room. His unsteady hands clanked a crystal decanter against the tumbler at its side. Burgundy liquid spilled into the glass, and the good Father raised it to his lips then gulped down the contents. "But last time,

Dominic...," he rebutted after letting the wine coat his throat. He set the glass down on the table.

"I know what they ask of me, Peter, but I have to release it somehow. If it is to help them—I find that's better than allowing the demons to help themselves while they drive me to insanity."

Father Varga placed his fists on his waist, his shoulders slumping forward, then spun toward the boy. One of his cheeks had a wet path trailing from his blue eye to his chin. "I can't watch you do this, son."

"I understand." Dominic lifted from his seat and approached the weary man.

The light dusting of gray in his jet-black hair seemed to multiply in that second. The priest raised a hand and placed it on the back of the boy's head, pulling Dominic to his chest in an embrace. A whispered prayer left his lips, "May God keep his loving hand firmly on your spirit, my son, and a watchful eye on your body."

"I'll be fine," Dominic assured.

Father Varga released the boy and made his way to the door. Stopping just before, he turned. "I've kept his soul away from those savages this long. If it goes wrong...I hope you two suffer with the guilt for eternity." The blue in his eyes deepened. "Aldott legyen. Blessed be," he breathed while stepping out the door.

A moment of silence saturated the restive room. I turned to Dominic and Arkin, considering whether another soul was worth the small chance that we might gain information about Nevaeh.

Arkin clapped and stood with an eager wink. "I guess we better get started then?"

Dominic limped toward me, offering a smile that didn't reach his eyes. "Follow me."

Arkin filed behind him, then I joined in, mentally unraveling the tightening knot in my stomach.

We trailed the young Celata down into a large, dank wine cellar far below the bones of the cathedral. Water trickled from the ground surrounding the cellar through tiny holes in the rock walls, creating small dirt pools on the floor. Dusty wine bottles lined the shelves, reflecting our guide's flashlight in a rainbow of colors—an art-form of stained glass in their own right. The sweetness of incense couldn't reach the depths we'd walked; instead, the pungent odor of rot and death strengthened.

"Where are we headed?" I asked, my words echoing back to me.

Dominic stopped in the center of the cellar and pointed to a wood slat door held together by thick iron bands. "There." He pulled a ring of skeleton keys from his jeans and shuffled to the door. "St. Julia's Chapel was built on a labyrinth of tunnels more than two hundred years ago. Before then, they were a place to leave the dead soldiers and prisoners from wars that tainted the land."

Pitch black forced my angelic pupils to widen and adjust. My surroundings became clearer but held a soft blue haze. The sheen from Arkin's eyes glittered in the dim light. We could've seen into the tunnel without the flashlight's help, but I knew Dominic needed it.

The boy ducked and entered the passageway. Arkin and I tailed him, hunching our large frames down to fit. My wings ached to be released as they felt even more cramped in the narrow corridor. We stopped a few feet from the door.

Dominic spun in a slow circle, inspecting the mine-like shaft with his flashlight. "I guess this will do." He shined the light at my chest, so he could see my face without blinding me. "The name of your demon?"

"Kenet," I answered.

He lowered to his knees and sat the light down on its side next to his leg. Dominic's hands dug deep into his pockets and emptied them of their possessions: keys, a money clip with a few dollars pinched in its grip, and a cobalt-colored rosary. He lay the keys and money clip on the ground next to him. He held the beads tightly in his hand and traced a cross from his face to his chest then across each shoulder. With closed eyes, the boy expelled a jumble of words, each one racing from his lips with the hope of reaching mighty ears.

"You ready?" Arkin asked, lowering to the ground next to Dominic.

I nodded, scanning over our surroundings cautiously. Thick, aging boards created archways that held the crumbling, earthen walls in place.

"Why here?" My curiosity and unease were too much to deny.

"I can't technically leave the church without running the risk of getting attacked or interfering with normal people," Dominic answered, gathering a handful of dirt in one of his fists before tossing it into the beam of light at his knees. "Here I'm close enough to the church I can get there if I need to, but still on unholy territory. There's a fine geographical line with these things." His dirty-blonde bangs fell into haunted eyes that darkened like a hurricane brewing over a vast sea. "I can't play with the Devil in the house of the Lord, right?" His childlike lips curved into a deviant grin. He bent forward and placed the string of beads neatly on the ground just out of his reach.

Archard

CHAPTER TEN

Uncooperative Help

The earth trembled around us. Dominic's heavy breaths turned to panting. Sweat seeped from his forehead as he rocked back and forth on his knees. What began as low mumbling, increased to a roar of gibberish spewing from his mouth.

"Arkin," I growled, "what's going on?"

"He's doing his thing," the angel at my side answered, unable to take his eyes away from the commotion. He lifted his shoulder in a half shrug. "This is what he does…I think."

"We can't allow him to do this. There has to be another way." I lunged to shake the boy from his trance, but his words became distinguishable.

Dominic suddenly spat in my face, warning me to stay away. His eyes rolled back. He lurched forward, hands digging into the soil in front of him. I hesitated, trying to decide if we should let this play out or save the poor soul hunched on all fours like a dog. This didn't feel right.

The unnatural sound of bones cracking rang into the air. Dominic's head rotated over his left shoulder, the whites of his eyes locking on me. I settled onto one knee to keep him from straining. His eyes followed my movements, appearing to measure me as a potential threat. His lips peeled back into a snarl. "Kenet, Kenet, Kenet," he yelled over and over again in different tones and pitches like he was searching radio frequencies.

"Dominic, can you hear him?" Arkin interrupted the ugly chant.

The boy's head snapped toward my brother and growled. "I hear his mind," he confirmed. His expression relaxed while he listened to some distant voice we couldn't detect. "Ah, the sweet sorrow. He's steeped in guilt and anger, this one. What do you want to know?" His head whipped back toward me.

I stared into the blank whites of the boy's eyes. "Does he know where the angel Rhett is?"

The slender frame rocked to and fro. He hummed in pain, thrashing his head all around. Dominic stilled. "He knows not the whereabouts of this angel."

"What about Arianna? Does he know where she is?"

A menacing cackle shook the Celata's body. "He knows well where her soul roams. He is the demon that surrendered her there — wandering the In-between with those that await salvation."

His riddled words left me frustrated. "Alright. That's enough." I motioned for Arkin to help me take him back into the church's cellar. I picked up his belongings and reached for the rosary.

"I can see her," he squealed, drool stringing from his lips. "The half demon...Nevaeh."

I froze, afraid that if I moved he would lose his site on her. "What do you see?" I choked, desperate for a chance to find her.

Dominic's head thrashed again, his body convulsing on all fours. He grated his palms into the ground hard, smearing a trail of blood along the dirt. "She wanders the streets alone. The darkness within her screams to me." He cackled once more. "Free me, free me. She buries it, pushes it down. One tiny crack in the surface and it will all be over." His long index finger scratched at the floor like he was scratching an itch he couldn't reach.

"Where is she, Dominic?" My hands seized his shoulders, willing him to focus.

A fresh batch of spit hit my cheek, and he scurried backward out of my reach. "What is this?" Dominic's voice was replaced with another's. "Who are you?"

I recognized the gruff, worried tone. "Kenet?"

"Archard?"

"Kenet, where is Nevaeh?"

"She's in the city. They were punishing her, but I helped her escape for now." Dominic shook, then quieted. "Do you still have the book?"

"Yes. But there's nothing in there about how to save Nevaeh." A sigh of discouragement left my lungs. "Kenet, where is Arianna?"

"I can't tell you. It's for Nevaeh's safety. Please, trust me." Dominic's eyes fluttered, and he pounded a fist against the dirt, struggling against some unseen force.

"What about the key? We didn't find enough answers?" I inched closer to the possessed boy.

"The book *is* the answer. Make no mistake, though, it may hold a way to set her free, but it has a greater chance of causing more destruction than you could ever imagine." Kenet's voice began to fade.

"You have to give us more than that," I commanded.

"I'm sorry. It's just too dangerous now that she's declared herself to Hell. They are watching so closely. Just keep her away from the book, Archard."

The young Celata shoved his fingers through his sweaty hair, then pounded the walls with his fists. Now leaning back on his haunches, Dominic's voice returned.

"No, you can't have me," he argued. His eyelids squeezed tight, and he cupped his ears under shaky hands. "Leave me. I'm not yours," he yelled. The earth around us quaked angrily. The boy's cries echoed through the black tunnel.

Kenet was gone, and Dominic was being tortured by whatever evil he'd let invade his mind. "We have to get him into the church," I commanded.

Arkin tugged on Dominic's arm, dragging him up from the floor. I scooped up his belongings. The rosary beads dangled heavier between my fingers than I expected.

"Is he okay?" I asked, glancing back at Arkin as he struggled against Dominic's convulsing body. "Arkin? You got him?"

"Get the door!"

I sprang toward the church, scraping my shoulders along the rocky walls. Arkin barreled down the corridor behind me, Dominic pulling and shaking against his own will.

"They're coming," the poor kid warned.

A dense feeling of turmoil and hate filled the stale air. My senses sharpened, detecting the promise of the wicked force crawling its way into the young boy's soul. He reeked of sulfur.

"They're coming, they're coming." Arkin jolted forward, increasing his pace behind me.

I glanced back and saw Dominic raise a tremoring hand to the angel's nervous face. "Tell Peter that I loved him as my father."

A great howling rushed down the tunnel like a train. An invisible force bounced from one wall to the other, compromising the structure around us. Just one or two more feet and he'd be inside. Just one or two more seconds and the predator chasing us would be at their heels.

The howling sped closer, piercing our ears with shrill cries.

"Let's go," I bellowed over the noise. I reached for Arkin and yanked on his arm. Together, we tumbled over the threshold.

I'd never been more thankful to have the weight of two bodies piled on top of me.

The wailing and howling ceased as soon as we crossed back onto the church grounds. Only the sounds of our relieved breathing stirred in the cellar. Soon the sulfuric odor dissipated, and the sweetness of incense returned.

"Well, that was fun," Dominic panted, rolling off the dog-pile and slumping to the floor. "Remind me to never do that again."

I shoved Arkin off me and inhaled a deep, replenishing breath.

He scooted away from the door, resting his back against a wine shelf, and stared at Dominic with guilt in his eyes. "I'm sorry," he whispered.

"Sorry for what?" A worried voice questioned from the dimly lit stairwell across the room. The beam of a flashlight swept over us. "What happened?" the good Father asked impatiently, hurrying to Dominic's side.

"I thought you didn't want to be around this?" The boy hoisted himself off the dirt. Father Varga assisted until Dominic's weak frame was fully stable and upright.

"I didn't," the priest sighed, "but I couldn't bear not being here for you when you needed me." The dimness of the room veiled his expression but did little to hide the concern in his words. "What happened?"

"Nothing much. We just tripped over each other." Dominic faced Arkin and me. "Did you get what you needed?" His shadowy gaze begged us to keep his secret from the priest—for his sake.

"Yeah. You did well, kid. Thanks." I stood and dusted off my soiled coat, then offered a hand to my brother. He clasped his palm in mine and pulled himself up.

"What now?" The recovering Celata limped over and slammed the tunnel door shut. His trembling hands fumbled to push the keys into the lock, but he managed to secure the door, sealing the wickedness on the other side.

"Your part is over." I approached Dominic and held out my hand. He accepted it and shook. "Thank you," I said, noting by the new fear in his eyes that this incident had been more than he'd anticipated.

Father Varga opened his arms, beckoning for the boy. "Come, Dom. You look like you could use a nap."

Dominic shambled over, taking his safe place nestled against his father's side. Just before beginning their ascent up the stairs, he turned.

"What will you do?"

I glanced at Arkin then looked at the young man. "I'm going to look for Nevaeh downtown."

"And if you don't find her?" he asked.

"I'll be taking a trip." I grabbed the handrail and followed their slow steps out of the cellar.

Arkin tugged on my duster from behind. "What trip?"

"To the In-between," I exhaled, hoping I would find Nevaeh before having to suffer that consequence.

CHAPTER ELEVEN

TROUBLED SOULS

The misting of a late-night drizzle dampened my clothes and hair. I wandered through the city that used to be mine. It all felt so foreign now. Neon lights shined from business signs fixed to various shops and restaurants, reflecting on the wet pavement. Small puffs of white breath drifted from my lips, reminding me that I was cold but still alive.

Every corner I turned, I expected Bron or one of Hell's minions to greet me. With my nerves on edge, I suspiciously scanned everyone that passed. They wouldn't let me out of their reach for long. Thankfully, Bron didn't have the power to track me by thought up here.

A bell pinged above the door I pushed open.

"Welcome," a slender teenager chimed from behind a busy register.

She smiled then continued scanning and bagging items for the customer she was ringing up. I ignored her polite greeting and sifted through the racks with my head down. When the employee left her post to help a plump lady retrieve a shirt from the high wall display on the other side of the store, I nabbed a hoodie from the hanger next to me and darted for the door. The bell pinged behind me as I left the store unnoticed.

I bit the tag off and tugged the jacket on, continuing my trek downtown. Clutching the hood around my face, I finally felt the warmth my chilled bones needed.

Mindless bodies bumped into me left and right, oblivious to anything outside of their mundane lives. Occasionally, darkness would tingle and snap from behind my ribs like a caged dog ready to fight. I sensed the souls that didn't deserve their place among the others, but I couldn't afford to use my power right now. With everyone as a potential spy, it would only confirm that I was Celatum.

I had to find somewhere to hide for the time being. A few more blocks and I'd be at my destination. The massive, white pillars were already in view.

Nevaeh, my name carried on the wind.

My head jerked around, searching for the source.

Nevaeh, come back to us, it urged.

Shit, they knew I was missing already.

I picked up the pace. Bron could call to me all he wanted, I just prayed he wouldn't be able to locate me as easily.

I threaded through the crowd, making my way to the Banquet Hall. Spotlights shined on the impressive stairs leading up to the door. Though the lights were a security measure to keep intruders at bay from fear of getting noticed, they lit the old building in such a way that it looked like a monument of sorts. I veered onto the street next to the Hall and stalked toward the rear of the establishment.

The back lot was much darker, much less secure. I pulled out the pick and tension wrench that I kept in my pocket for instances like this. I inserted the tools into the lock and, after a moment of finding the right position, it clicked open. The Hall was pitch black except for the faint green glow of an alarm pad next to the door. I pressed a four-digit combination the guard, Dan, had given to George and me a few years ago in case we needed a place to hide.

The smell of antiques and polish reminded me of all the times George brought me here to get cleaned up or to stay out of the rain. We had been guests here without anyone knowing—aside from Dan—for many years. We were lucky to have a place to retreat to when we really needed it.

I skulked deeper into the building, keeping away from the windows and the beams of light reaching in from the outside. There was a small kitchen in the basement, so I made that my first stop. It seemed like days since my last meal.

A stale loaf of bread and a drainer with a few dishes sat on the counter. I ransacked the cabinets, finding happiness in a jar of peanut butter and a half sleeve of saltines. As I walked out of the kitchen with my loot, I grabbed a warm bottle of water from a pack on the counter and a spoon from the drainer for good measure. Nothing beat a giant spoonful of P.B.

I cracked open the jar of sweet goodness before I even finished climbing the steps. Strolling through the expansive lobby, I noted the rose- pink, tufted chaise summoning me from the other side. I fell backwards into the cushions and dipped a saltine into my peanut butter.

As I sat in the silence, my body tensed, my eyes chasing a shadow that skittered across the wall when a passing car's headlights beamed through the windows from outside. I relaxed back into the stuffed upholstery, realizing it was in fact just that…a passing shadow, not a demon sent to kill me. I reminded myself that the wickedness inside me was far more dangerous.

Once my growling stomach was satisfied, I peeled off the hoodie and rested my head against the chaise's velvety arm. It felt safe here in the memories of the life I had before my world flipped upside down. I closed my eyes, sinking deeper into the cushions.

Just as my consciousness reached the edges of deep sleep, echoes of a shutting door and heavy footsteps snapped me awake. I grabbed my jacket, sliding off the chaise and onto to the floor. The building was still dark, which would make for an easier escape.

Someone whistled "Mary had a little lamb" from a hallway on the opposite side of the lobby. They were getting closer, but I had time.

A beam of light swept over the chaise just as I crawled into the corridor leading to the exit. I stood and sprinted as quietly as I could toward the red, glowing letters indicating the way out. I reached for the knob, not quite close enough to turn it yet, but anticipating the motion. The moment my fingertips grazed the knob, it swung toward me, crashing into my hand then my face.

I dropped to all-fours. Blood trickled down my nose, coating my lips in the bitter-sweetness. I squinted upward and examined the large silhouette blocking my way out.

"Nevaeh," he called as I finished my descent to the ground and passed out.

The weight of bound pages spread over my hands felt right. A dim light spotlighted the book in my palms, casting a blue haze on the thing I coveted most. Blurry scrolling lined the parchment on one side; the other page lay blank.

Three single drops of deep-purplish liquid floated from somewhere above me and splashed onto the empty sheet.

Chanting commenced in the background, growing louder and louder. "With our trinity of blood, I accept my fate. With our trinity of blood, I accept my duty as the Clavis." Over and over, the mantra rang through the atmosphere.

Suddenly, the book disappeared, and I was left with my empty hands bathing in the sapphire glow. I flexed and extended my fingers carefully, studying how they looked like mine, but different somehow. The etched lines that created my unique identity were all wrong.

A slow burn snaked up my fingers, starting in the tender flesh hidden beneath my nails, writhing and spreading into a power that crept up my forearms, riding the ridges of my muscles and tendons in a relentless blaze beneath my skin. The fluid glow of reds and oranges rippled under my surface as if I had lava in my veins.

A scream bubbled up into my throat, but my mouth, I'd realized, was already busy. The chanting I'd heard streamed from my own lips, continuing to flow like a fountain against my will.

Inside, my soul trembled with fear and agony; outside, I was as steady as a rock, reciting phrases that seemed to mean much more than I understood.

The dim radiance of a bonfire flickered to life, then grew, brightening the pitch-black space around me. A soft warmth caressing my chilled limbs built into an intense, raging furnace encompassing my entire body. Flames slithered across the ground like an overflowing river, leaving wreckage in their paths until white-hot tongues licked at my feet threatening to climb my legs. I tried to step back, but I couldn't. Unable evade my cage of fire, or yell for help, I spewed my mantra repetitively and raised my gaze to search for anyone who might take pity on my poor soul.

I was on the edge of a cliff, high above a dry gorge. Trapped below, between the stony walls of my cliff and another, were thousands of frightened people. The blaze had swallowed them on its way up to torture me. Cries and helpless hands reached upward, clawing at the clumps of dirt entrapping them, begging for my help.

I stretched my glowing hand out over the poor souls, fearing that we'd all meet a terrible death too soon. I couldn't move to save them, let alone save myself.

The chant continued to tumble from my lips. The fire seemed to escalate with any small flick of my fingers. I prayed from the confines of my mind that God would give me the power to stop the terror below.

Instantly, my chanting ceased, and the wicked pressure I imprisoned within my body spewed from my mouth in place of the words. I convulsed and screamed as the black mass ripped from my soul, billowing up like a tower of poisonous gas before blanketing the burning people in the gorge.

The shrill cries ended in the blink of an eye.

Silence and darkness filled the landscape, leaving me to stand alone in my own receding flames. Tears poured down my cheeks. I had caused this somehow, though I couldn't control it.

A moment later, the dense cloud returned to me like a lost love, swirling around me with excitement as it consumed my body, rendering me to a pile of ash.

Only the echoes of my erratic breaths carried on the wind.

"Nev," someone called to me in a loud whisper.

The fog in my brain began to dissipate. Large hands jerked my shoulders.

"Nev, get up," the voice demanded.

My sleepy eyelids fluttered open. I winced, holding a hand up to the small cut stinging on my forehead.

"We have to move. It's not safe here."

I squinted into the dark, allowing my eyes to adjust and assess the figure kneeling beside me. "Gavyn?" I asked, swallowing the gravel in my throat. "What are you doing here?" I pushed myself up into an awkward sitting position. My hand landed in a small puddle of stagnant water on the ground by my leg. I wiped the sludge on my jeans then surveyed my surroundings with a muddled head.

"I came looking for you. You almost got caught in the Hall," he chuckled. "Knocked yourself out on the door when I opened it. Lucky for you, I dragged ya out before the guard came around the corner."

His warm hand rested on my shoulder while his other pushed the hair back from my forehead. I jerked away and slowly reached for the knife in my pocket. When he saw the slight movement of my hand, his gaze fell to the ground in regret, and his lips pressed together, sealing in something he was anxious to say.

I couldn't trust Gavyn right now. I saw what he was capable of at the club. In the end, he was still too loyal to Layla.

"How long was I out?"

"Pretty much all day. You looked like you needed the rest, so I let you sleep."

My eyes wandered to the spiraling row of quiet cars lined up around us. We were in a parking garage.

"How did you know I was at The Banquet Hall?" I leaned back against the wall behind me and massaged my throbbing forehead with one hand as the other worked to slide the small knife out of my pocket without Gavyn noticing. Hidden next to my thigh, I forced the small blade out with my thumbnail. I didn't want to hurt Gavyn, but I couldn't go back to the torture and demands of Hell just yet. Not until I had a better plan to get George out.

"George had mentioned that y'all went there sometimes. I thought it was worth a try." He reached behind his back and pulled around a book bag. As his hand shoved into the pack, I readied myself to attack at a moment's notice. Paper crinkled under his grasp, and he pulled out a gas station burrito. "Hungry?" he asked, holding it out to me with a half-smile.

My stomach growled, yearning to devour the cold, questionable wrap. "No," I lied, relaxing my grip on the blade in my hand just a bit.

"Come on, Nev. I know you haven't had much to eat. I know what it's like down there."

I almost felt sorry for him. Was he being tortured like me? What part of himself was he sacrificing to thrive in Hell?

"Thanks." I reached for the burrito timidly, then ripped the paper from it faster than I'd meant to. "Where's Layla?" I shoved the end into my mouth and took a large, glorious bite. Scanning the concrete lot, I gulped down the chewed ball of food in my mouth and shoved in another.

"She doesn't know I'm here." A hint of guilt underlined his words. "I wanted to find you before the others."

My body flooded with the sweet numbness I'd felt before when Gavyn was trying to dull my pain. I stopped chewing and glared at him. "What do you think you're doing?"

His brow creased as he stared at me, struggling to gauge my reaction. "I...I just sensed how uncomfortable you are around me. I thought, maybe, I could ease that for you."

"Well, don't," I demanded, keeping my eyes on him as I finished chewing and took another bite.

His gesture of comfort and concern should have melted my icy emotions, but it didn't. We were different now. There was nothing soft about my poisoned heart anymore, and I couldn't trust his intentions.

Gavyn leaned back against the wall beside me, resting an arm on his bent knee. "Ya know? I did this for you," he whispered, bowing his head. "I just wanted to save you, Nevaeh." He chuckled without humor. "They got you anyway." His hand reached for a small chunk of broken concrete next to my leg, held it tight in his fist and then threw it across the parking area. The sound bounced off the walls as it skipped along the floor to some dark corner several yards away. "Night after night, I sit in that cage they've dressed up as a bedroom and think about getting you out."

I stuffed the last bite of burrito into my mouth and gnawed it down to something I could swallow. As I forced it down, I pondered his words carefully. My eyes met his serious gaze and wished we could start over from the beginning—that we were just two people falling in love, oblivious like the rest of the world. "You're with Layla now, Gavyn. And there's nothing you can do to save me. You should worry about saving yourself."

His jaw tensed. He began biting on his dry upper lip and averted his glossy eyes. There was so much pain hidden there.

I bent my knee up and busied myself with tying a loosened shoelace, pretending not to notice how much my words affected him. "What are you going to do?"

"I'm going to kill Layla," Gavyn answered with surety. He pushed off the ground, his shoulders wide and his back straight as an arrow. His sorrowful, olive-green eyes peered down at me. He offered his hand to help me up. The admission had fallen from his lips so easily, like he was informing me how cold it was outside.

Taken back by his words, I gawked at him for a moment. "Uh, I meant now. What are you going to do right now? You know, for food and shelter while you're on the run?" I locked my fingers around his palm, using him to hoist myself up. I swiped the dust and dirt off my ass and looked at him, waiting for an explanation.

Gavyn laughed nervously. "Oh. I snagged some money when I pick-pocketed a man earlier. He looked like he could afford a little dent in his wallet." His fingers disappeared into his jacket and reappeared gripping a rather thick, leather billfold. "There's enough for us to get a few meals and, maybe, a hotel room for the night. We can't stay on the streets, Neveah. They'll find us." The hand he helped me up with was still wrapped around my palm, urging me closer without thought as he spoke.

I slid my hand from his grasp and stuffed it into my pocket. I missed his touch too much. I had forgotten how good it felt to be in his protective presence, but this was not the Gavyn I knew.

"Speak for yourself." I backed away from him, zipping up my hoodie as I moved. "I made it on the streets before. I can do it again." I turned to leave, but glanced over my shoulder at a lost Gavyn leaning his shoulder miserably into the wall where I left him. "Let them find me," I dared with a smirk before heading toward the street.

My feet couldn't march me down the exit ramp fast enough—out of the sight of a troubled soul still harboring hope for me. What was even worse was that part of me still wanted to run back to his arms.

CHAPTER TWELVE

CONVERGENCE PART 1

"Hey! What the hell, dude?" a man yelled when I shouldered passed him in a jog down Main Street. I couldn't bother myself to care, though. She was close. Even with the rain cleansing the city and shifting its odors, I could smell her. There was a hint of change in her fragrance, something fiery and frenzied, but the lavender I knew called out to me like a siren. It was undeniable.

Thoughts of her happiness to see me, of our reunion, played out in my mind as I ran. I would wrap her in my love and never let her go this time. If I could just find her. This was the closest I had been to her in months.

My feet slid against the wet sidewalk as I jerked to an abrupt stop. I spun in a slow circle with my nose to the air, pulling her fragrance into my lungs in deep inhales. I closed my eyes and allowed my other senses a chance to kick in.

I reached my mind out past the chattering humans surrounding me, their words growing muffled as I pictured them fading into a blank background of my psyche. The raindrops vibrated against the walls of my head, distracting me, creating ripples of watery energy that bounced through my thoughts. I concentrated harder, freezing the vibrations where they began. All earthly movement bustling over the city seemed to halt like time standing still. I stretched my spiritual sensors into the streets and alleys, searching for her.

My body started to quiver from the intense drainage of what little heavenly power I held. It was too much work for an Earth-bound vessel.

Come on, just a little farther.

"I know you're here," I whispered as if she could hear me.

My senses scoured the immediate area for some hint of Nevaeh, but her scent was diminishing at a rapid pace. She was moving away from me.

I shoved every bit of my ability out from my core, hoping it would be enough. My palms were sweating, my body shaking and tingling, and a black curtain of depletion was closing in around my mind's.

"Nevaeh," I cried out desperately.

Suddenly, my mental vision tunneled and sped like a train down three different streets, twisting and jerking as it went. Stores and restaurants blurred as my extra sense hurried past them, traveling two or three miles away from where my body remained. A haze settled on my thoughts, leaving me dizzy when the search came to an unexpected stop in front of a large parking deck on the outskirts of the city.

The image of Nevaeh stepping out of the garage appeared in my head. My heart beat quickened, my breath faltered, and a sharp pain traveled along my legs as I dropped to my knees in relief on the sidewalk. The vision was crystal clear in my mind, like I was just across the street, watching her walk back into my life.

"Nevaeh," I whispered.

Her violet-blue eyes darted up and looked into mine as if she was here with me, not miles away. She hesitated in front of the parking deck, her brow pinching together with confusion.

The metallic sound of a can scraping along cement echoed from somewhere outside of her line of sight, stealing her attention away from me. Nevaeh's face hardened once she found the source of the noise. She raced down the sidewalk, never looking back.

"No!" I cried out, scared to lose her again.

Suddenly, all I could see were humans throwing me sideway glances while they walked in a wide breadth around me. My wet palms rubbed frantically over my closed eyes, desperate to gain sight of her one more time.

I pounded my fists against my thighs then pushed myself up. I broke into a sprint. People, stores, and cars seemed to vanish as I ran, turning this way and that down the alleys and roads leading to the spot where I saw Nevaeh.

My chest heaved, my heart raced — not because I was running, but from fear of getting to the garage and having no evidence of which direction she went.

"Please be there, please be there," I recited over and over.

I slowed, turning right onto the street in front of the parking deck. Pulling my collar up around my neck and thrusting my chilled hands into the pockets of my duster, I advanced down the sidewalk. My cautious eyes scrutinized every subtle movement and shadow on the street.

Raindrops pummeled a tin can lying on its side on the walkway across the road. The familiar metal ting assured me that it was the can I heard during my vision. I walked to the spot where she'd stood, just beyond the dark exit of the deck, and closed my eyes, filling my lungs with the lingering lavender air.

"You won't find her," a voice echoed from the garage behind me.

I spun on my heels, tense and ready to fight. "What does it matter to you?" I asked, squinting into the darkness as my angelic vision adjusted. Standing behind the first car parked just beyond the cross-bar, the face and outline of a figure became clearer. His scent was as distinguishable to me as Nevaeh's. Cedar and soap.

119

"It *does* matter to me," Gavyn said, striding down the exit ramp, then emerging into the gray, stormy, evening light. "I love her too, Archard."

"So, you know who I am?" I stood a little taller, widening my shoulders with confidence.

Gavyn nodded then lowered his head wearily to peer at the ground in thought. "They've taught me who my enemies are." His eyes shot back up to meet mine. "I don't wanna be your enemy, but the struggle is so overwhelming." Pain and extreme restraint shadowed his gaze. His forehead wrinkled with despair. "I know how hard this is for me. I can only imagine how difficult it is for Nev." His fists balled at his sides, clutching the hemline of his jacket.

"What do you want, Gavyn? I don't have time to play games." I ground my teeth together, anger flourishing in my chest.

"I want to help you. I love her as much as you do."

I rushed forward, gripping the front of his jacket, and slammed him against the wall. "There's not a chance in Heaven or Hell that you love Nevaeh as much as I do." My tone was low and harsh from the rage working its way out of me.

Gavyn's brows raised, surprised by my outburst, and then his expression contorted to a fury that easily matched mine. His hands wrapped around my wrists, but instead of pushing me away, he held me close. His eyes bore into mine as a wily grin curled his lips. "Games? Who's playing games?"

My hands loosened around his coat, and I stepped back. My emotions jumbled together, settling on an urge to forget Nevaeh. I felt the need to go home and never look for her again. Gavyn's fingers dug into my skin, holding me at arm's length.

"Let go of me!" I grunted, stumbling backwards and snatching my hands out of his grasp. I shook my head, shaking the urge to abandon my responsibility — to abandon my love.

I glared at Gavyn, my warrior instincts bubbling just below the surface. It took all I had to refrain from pounding him to the ground. "I told you. I'm. Not. Playing. Your. Games."

Gavyn held his hands up in surrender, his grin turning to a frown.

"I'm not trying to. I…I can't help it." His sad eyes lowered. "The need to unleash the power in me heightens when I'm threatened."

"You're lucky I can fight it," I said, my fists unclenching at my sides.

"Actually…you're lucky you aren't human. You would have been putty in my hands, and it wouldn't have been pretty."

I nodded in agreement, admitting that he was stronger and more dangerous than he appeared. "You can't help me, Gavyn. You can't even control yourself."

Tears erupted from his eyes, blending with the droplets of rain trailing down his face. He leaned over and gripped his knees to brace himself. "I know. What do I do? Tell me what to do." The man choked out a desperate cry before sliding to the ground and covering his face with shaky hands.

"I'm not the one to ask," I whispered. I turned away and left Gavyn alone and broken at the Garage.

There was no time to spare in my search for Nevaeh, and I was the last being that could help him save his soul.

I put my sympathy for Gavyn aside and focused on the aroma that was faint at first but grew stronger as I traveled farther out of the city. I chased the scent down several back alleys and into an old neighborhood.

I entered the community, passing a distressed sign. Large painted flowers accented blue and white letters reading "Magnolia Downs."

Dogs yelped from a distance, inviting me to enter. Were they just restless, or was someone new, maybe Nevaeh, lurking around their territory?

I roamed down the main street, eyeing the knotted branches of live oak trees creating a bridge of twisted wood and leaves above me, reaching from one perfectly manicured lawn to another as they lined both sides of the road. I glanced up through the canopy of Spanish moss, glaring at the millions of tiny stars glittering in the sky. I bet they could see where my Nevaeh was, but they weren't telling.

Porch lights speckled the dark houses, guiding my path deeper into Magnolia Downs. I followed the scent about a mile down Confederate Street only to encounter a dead-end. The smell of lavender strengthened as the rain trickled to a stop.

I folded my arms over my chest and studied the two-story house at the end of the road. My eyes scanned over the roof of missing shingles, then slowly drifted down to the warped porch boards.

Years of weathering chipped paint off the siding and rusted the nails until they barely held the shutters on. The jungle of grass and weeds growing in the front yard added a sense of loneliness to the abandoned home.

I closed my eyes, lifting my nose toward the sky, and inhaled. The sweetness was dizzying, wafting on the faint currents of age floating from the house. I opened my eyes and tramped down the dirt path leading to the front door.

Movement in a window on the first floor caught my attention. A dingy, sheer curtain ruffled on a breeze entering the house through a broken pane of glass. My senses tingled as I approached the front porch.

I lifted one foot and carefully placed it on the first step, the wood creaking under my shifting weight. My other foot followed as I ventured onto the landing. Wide paddles of two outdoor ceiling fans twirled above me on a passing gust of wind.

I pulled open the screen door, and the tension spring whined from being stretched for the first time in years. The front door was already cracked open. I leaned to the left, searching for any sign of danger beyond the door's edge. Everything was quiet inside. I nudged the slat of wood open farther and crossed over the threshold, leery of what I might find inside.

The foyer was small with a rather plain staircase to my right. The three feet of railing guarding the steps vanished into the wall forming one side of the corridor directly in front of me. I squinted into the shadows, seeing that the hall spanned the length of the house and split the lower level of the home in half.

My eyes adapted to the dark, soaking up the silvery moonlight spilling through the open backdoor on the opposite end of the house. The dim light stretching over the better part of the dusty hardwoods shined bright under the power of my angelic pupils, enhancing my visibility tenfold.

I wandered down the hall, approaching the rooms on either side of me vigilantly. I peeked in each one, making sure they were empty before moving onto the next. As I entered the kitchen at the back of the structure, I noticed all the cupboard doors were open and all the shelves were empty. At some point, someone had raided it for food.

My eyes closed, and I took in a deep breath. Lavender filled my nostrils, so strong I could nearly taste the floral aroma on my tongue. I shrugged my duster off, bunching it in one hand as I stretched my wings and loosened them from the pockets of muscle on my back with a muffled grunt.

I turned in a slow circle, scrutinizing every detail of the home, searching for any sign of my love.

Come on, Nev. I can smell you. I know you're close.

My thoughts reverberated back to me without a response. The old house was as silent as death.

I opened the kitchen door and stepped out into the back yard. Wading through the unkempt yard, I moved toward a small building at the edge of the property. My hand swam through the reeds of silver-hued weeds and grass waving with the wind under the light of the moon.

The odor I was chasing seemed to get stronger the closer I got to the shed. My steps quickened. The slight hum of power charged the air. My heart raced. She was so close — if I could only lure her out.

"Nevaeh," I breathed, yanking the shed door open. I stepped inside, glowering at the rakes and shovels lining the wood-planked walls. A rusty tractor took up nearly every bit of the floor, leaving no space to hide, but I walked in a tight path around it anyway; I had to see for myself that she wasn't there.

I completed my investigation of the withering building and stopped next to the rear tire of the old tractor, staring out the door at the back of the house. Clenching my jaw, I ground my teeth together, biting back my growing anger. I raised my hand and commenced in beating a dent into the curved wheel cover on the back of the tractor. I stopped when pain throbbing through my knuckles distracted me from the fury clouding my mind.

I panted, glaring down at the dark spots of blood glistening in the dented pit I left and raked my hands through my hair, clasping them at the back of my tense neck.

"Nevaeh, I know you're here somewhere. Please, come out," I pleaded into the humid night air.

My wings dragged along the dirt behind me as I stomped back into the yard. I gazed out over the tall grass and into the black woods that marked the perimeter of the property. Everything was so quiet and serene. Only the rhythmic sound of crickets and frogs echoed into the evening along with the occasional gust of wind that rustled through the thick heat.

"I'm chasing a fucking ghost," I said to myself, shaking my head, wondering why I was even there.

I headed toward the front of the house, but stilled when I noticed cones of tiny, dark flowers mingled in with the weeds at the edge of the property.

"Son of a bitch!" I marched over to the stem of flowers and yanked it out of the ground, scowling at the plant in my hand. I held the cluster of petals to my nose and inhaled. "Lavender."

"I need you to stop looking for me, Archard."

My hand dropped to my side, letting go of the insignificant flower that dared to mimic her seductive aroma. I sucked in a deep breath of muggy air and turned slowly, my heart aching to have her in my arms again.

"I can't," I replied, watching my love emerge from the black line of trees.

I drank in every bit of her as she slinked toward me. Her body moved with a new confidence, smooth and fluid with undeniable power like waves crashing against a shore. A long, dark braid draped over her left shoulder while stray hairs framed her beautiful face. She was thinner since I last saw her. She crammed her hands into the pockets of a fitted hoodie as she headed straight for me.

She stopped five feet away—still too far to satisfy my need for her. Nevaeh's shadowy eyes stared back at me with indifference while her fiery essence twirled around me, calling me like a beacon.

I moved forward to close the gap between us.

"Stop. Don't come any closer," she commanded, holding a hand up in front of her.

"Why, Nevaeh?" My fingers clenched the duster held within it, channeling my frustration to the leather. "I found you. Come home. We can fix this." I took a step forward.

"I can't. You don't understand. I have to do this on my own. You can't fix me, Archard." Her voice was as certain as the night. "Stop searching for me. You'll only hurt yourself."

"No. There is nothing that can hurt me more than being separated from you." My legs lunged me forward before my brain had time to think about it—my body too eager to have her near. I wrapped her in my arms and held on for dear life as my lips crashed into hers.

That moment was all I needed. A ping in her armor. Our mouths moved relentlessly against one another. That connection of pure electricity sparked between us as our tongues danced. Hot, eager breaths escaped with helpless moans.

For a moment, it was as it should have been.

The smell of sulfur rolled in around us like a fog, stifling Nevaeh's sweet, floral aroma. I jerked my head from her, gripping her wrist to keep her from backing away as I scanned our surroundings. The air thickened, and my angelic senses piqued, forcing me to be acutely aware of my surroundings.

"Let go, Archard," she whispered.

I looked down to find her gaze knowingly searching the tree line.

She tugged her hands against my grip, slipping free and stumbling backward before I could secure her again.

"I can't stay," she said. Her sad, apologetic eyes roamed over me once and then she sprang into a sprint toward the front of the house.

"Wait," I shouted out, preparing to run after her, but the disturbing charge zapping through the air kept me planted where I was, trapped in a bubble of static.

"Shit!" Her defeated voice cut into the tense atmosphere. Nevaeh slid to a stop only a few paces from where she started. She struggled to take a step, but her feet were glued to the ground. She leaned forward, trying to break the connection with the dirt, her hands grasping handfuls of the knee-high grass and pulling for leverage.

"Nevaeh?" I asked when she straightened and acute alertness stiffened her body. She looked over her shoulder, peering past me.

"Archard!" she yelled, pointing to the trees.

I jerked my head back to where she was pointing and laid eyes on four Crucio demons shuddering in slow movements from under the concealing woods.

I threw my coat to the ground and tightened my back muscles, flexing my wings into a position of defense and control. I glanced back at Neveah. She twisted her torso back and forth in a semi-circle, her bottom half as stationary as a statue. She eyed the ground at her feet with an irrefutable fear lining her face.

"Hang on, love. Let me take care of these bastards, and I'll be right with you," I assured, returning my attention to the demons trampling through the grass.

Suddenly, the ground roiled beneath us, threatening to break and swallow us whole. Clouds blotted out the moon above, forcing my pupils to dilate further. Thunder boomed from the pitch-black sky, and the crackle of a sparking fire broke into the air behind me.

I focused back on Nevaeh and the silver blades of grass swaying around her. A flash of red electric current slithered past me and surrounded her in a circle of zapping heat and sparks, setting the dry meadow ablaze.

"No, no, no!" Nevaeh screamed, thrashing inside the flickering ring nipping at her flesh, unable to get out.

The soil ruptured into a web of cracks beside her.

She stiffened, preparing for what was to come. Her sad eyes hardened and peered at me with an indifference that chilled my heart.

Glaring back at the monsters that had come to a halt only feet from me, I measured each one as they groaned and squealed with anticipation. Their stout, rotted bodies quivered from a poison no one could save them from.

I assessed the various weapons at their sides, debating whether I could take them on by myself or not. One demon held a sickle high in the air, poised for attack, a yearning for destruction darkening its already blackened eyes. Another monster gripped a rusted machete in its jerky, outstretched hand, rocking back and forth on eager feet. My eyes shifted to the next fiend. Yards of chain with long, thin barbs spiking out from the large links draped in loops around its oozing shoulder. The fourth one focused a scowling face on me as it gripped a metal pole, five foot in length, in its claws. At the end was an open metal collar with silver points jutting toward the center of the ring.

I growled, determined to take every one of the Crucios down before they had a chance to get Nevaeh.

"Archard!" Nev screamed.

I looked back in time to see a figure with dark wings soar out of the wide split in the ground next to my love. It bolted up ten feet above her head then shot down to the spot at her side like it was snapped back by a short leash.

The being straightened from its crouched position and settled its raven wings behind each muscled arm. Tar-colored veins wound around each wrist and climbed to his shoulders, disappearing under a long, straight mane then reemerging along his bare chest.

As he lifted his head to look my direction, the black curtain of hair revealed his face and a thick band of sticky, dark red substance wrapping around his neck. A slack rope of the blood-like material extended from the winged man's neck and vanished into the crevice he flew from.

A low growl rumbled from my chest. I immediately recognized the faceless being as one of The Fallen—a brother that betrayed our God.

"Bron," Nevaeh breathed, staring up at the dark angel with heady eyes.

His head turned as if to look down at her. She fell to her knees, bowed her head, and locked her hands behind her back in submission at his feet. Swirls of her arousal mixed with the smoky tendrils drifting from their ring of fire, heightening my anger.

The disruption between realms and the invasion of this atmosphere allowed me to break free from the invisible tether shackling me to the ground. I ran toward them. "Get away from her, abomination!" I yelled.

Bron snaked one hand around Nevaeh's chin from behind, ready to snap her neck at any moment, and wagged an arrogant finger with the other.

I skidded to a stop just outside the flames and eyed my love, hoping that she would snap out of her trance and bolt into my arms. "Nevaeh," I barked, intending to pull her focus to me, but she continued to stare up at the disgrace towering over her with a confident grasp on her will. "Let her go!" I snarled at the Fallen being. My fists clenched, and I widened my shoulders in a silent challenge to the dark angel.

He turned his attention toward Nevaeh again.

Suddenly, the flames receded between us. As I was about to take a step closer, Bron's hand released her, and she shifted her gaze, hazy eyes fixing on me. She slowly stood and sauntered through the ring of flames like they were nothing more flowers bending to the breeze. Her hips swaying in a dangerous rhythm like a lioness on the prowl.

"Nevaeh," I exhaled as she approached me then leaned into my body.

Her hands slid up my chest, neck, and face and stopped at my temples. I closed my eyes, seduced by the intoxication of her intimacy. Breath after breath, I took her in until my lungs and nose were as full as possible with my love's fiery, sweet essence.

Her soft lips pressed into mine, and I melted into her. I opened my eyes while we kissed and peered into hers, hoping to see the soul I knew. She swallowed my gasp when I tried to pull away to break our kiss. She held me captive under her delicious mouth.

Her eyes were clouded with rage and judgment. I gazed into her depths, witnessing countless sins played out by all manner of people. Some criminals, some seeking revenge, others in the wrong place at the wrong time. Still, she carried each one within her. She had punished each soul, enjoying it in her own way, as they fell to the hands of The Devil himself.

The evil she unleashed with these people was a cancer consuming her spirit.

I gasped again, struggling to breathe under her hypnotizing power. My eyes stung, fighting back tears of despair and sadness. She rested her forehead against mine, keeping our connection, but allowed our lips to rest.

The warmth of her fast breaths rushed at me like lashings of lust and danger. "I told you to leave me alone. There is nothing you can do to save me," she whispered.

She opened her mouth inches from mine and sucked in a slow, deep breath. With her inhale, I was forced to exhale. My lungs resisted the pull, but lost. She breathed in again, and I helplessly surrendered all the oxygen I held. When she opened her lips the next time, she demanded something deeper. My body shuddered, unwilling to release what she wanted.

"Stop," I choked out. I grabbed her hands and tore them from my head. Gasping for air, I stumbled away and fell to my knees.

"Oh no! I'm so sorry." Nevaeh dropped to her knees beside me, her eyes wide with shock, and rocked back and forth with her fingers digging into her thighs. "I'm so sorry," she repeated.

When I glance back at her, almost too afraid to look her in the eye, I caught a glimpse of the girl I used to know. A wrinkle formed in her forehead, laden with regret. She waited for me to respond. Teardrops trickled down her cheeks.

"There you are," I sighed in relief, reaching out to touch her face.

She leaned away. "Don't," she whispered. "I'm not the same,

Archard. There is a malevolence inside me that I won't be able to keep caged much longer. The power is growing quicker than I can keep up with."

"Come with me," I begged, fisting my hands in the dirt at my knees as I tried to control the urge to touch her.

CHAPTER THIRTEEN

CONVERGENCE PART 2

"No, no, no!" I screamed, scrambling to get away, but my feet wouldn't budge. I stared into the flickering flames circling me, feeling like a caged animal getting ready to leave for the slaughter house.

They'd found me.

Why didn't I just run away from Archard? Why did I have to talk to him?

The ground trembled and fractured beside me. I gulped back my panic and stilled, refusing to let them see my weakness.

My eyes found the sheen of Archard's ocean irises in the unnaturally black night. He looked at me with such an adoration and a need to protect me that I wondered if I could ever go back to what I was before, but he didn't realize how far beyond his protection I had fallen.

He turned toward the Crucio demons spitting curses and threats at him in their evil language, priming for combat.

The slivers in the dirt next to me widened, and I knew they would be here soon. I wobbled and shook with the ground beneath my feet, struggling to keep my balance. Currents of red power snapped and crackled from within the wide crevice.

"Archard!" I screamed, leaning as far away from the hole as I could.

I felt my Ater's commanding presence before he even rose above the surface. His whispering mind spoke to the wickedness inside me, knowing that it would react and yearn to be under his control. I fought the darkness rattling my bones, swallowing the urge to let it free.

With a zap of forceful power, my dark angel flew from the broken land and soared over my head. His strong body fell to the ground, bound to Hell by a tether of blood. His master didn't allow him to stray too far from home. He must've been granted a temporary pardon to drag me back down.

Lucky me.

The moment he occupied the spot to my left, I couldn't deny his authority anymore. My eyes traced over the perilous, evil-polluted veins winding up his beautiful muscles.

As he stretched his powerful body and settled his strong raven wings, he slowly lifted his head, his black hair acting as a veil to the mysterious, empty face I'd grown to hate—and adore.

Oh, how my body missed him.

My insides warmed with the heated ferocity I carried within. He called out to the rage and lust fueling my inner beast. "Bron," I exhaled as I lost control of the bridled cloud of doom writhing inside my chest.

He turned his featureless head down toward me, and my thighs clenched to relieve the growing ache between my legs. I dropped to my knees, assuming my submissive position, and awaited his command.

Dammit. I thought I'd learned to deny his control. I'd done so well at denying him during our last encounters.

The world was silent. The rapid thrumming of my heart and the throb of superiority radiating from Bron was all I could focus on. I wanted nothing more than to please my dark angel.

The chill of his cold hand puckered my skin as he carefully slid his fingers under my chin. I tingled from the tips of my toes to the top of my head, my body begging for the return of his attention when he looked away from me. I held my breath, patiently yearning at his feet.

The muffled sound of my name resonated from outside our protective circle of flames, but I couldn't be bothered by it. Bron turned his head back to me, and I could breathe again.

Destroy him, Nevaeh, my dark angel's voice echoed against the walls of my mind.

I suddenly became aware of the being standing on the other side of the fire. Though I knew I should do what Bron asked, something in a hidden corner of my mind protested. I ignored the pesky notion, too eager to release my destruction, and raised off the ground.

As I stalked toward the Angel of Light, I pictured the endless ways I could bring him to his knees.

"Nevaeh," he said under his breath, watching me move toward him, desire and hope gleaming in his gaze. The need twisted around his strong body like clouds shifting into a storm.

I pressed myself into him and slid my hands up his chest, caressing his neck, then tracing my fingers up his jaw before stopping at his temples. His ocean-colored eyes closed, and he inhaled my venomous scent, drowning in the sweet danger I offered.

I licked my lips, thirsty for his demise, and stretched up, laying my mouth on his. I watched his face relax under my seduction and, when he opened his eyes, I let him see what I was capable of. I wanted him to know the ways I could tear him apart—the way I'd defeated countless others in their attempts to refuse The Dark and our ways.

He gasped as our lips parted for a moment, and I hungrily swallowed it, denying him any chance of escape.

Let me out, my beast begged. *I want to play with him!* A low, snarly giggle vibrated from under my ribs.

The pale angel gasped again, fighting for air under my smothering power. I released him from our kiss and rested my forehead against his, feeling excited by the despair in his glossy eyes.

"I told you to leave me alone. There is nothing you can do to save me," I whispered, knowing that the weak girl he searched for was buried deep in the shadows of the animal I was now.

I unleashed the wickedness thrashing inside my body. The cloud of darkness rushed to fill every space of my soul. In that instant, I felt a depravation beyond my control.

His rich oxygen flooded my lungs as I opened my mouth and inhaled his breath. It wasn't enough, though. I needed more—it needed more. I sucked in again, feeling the resistance of his body, his quivering beneath my hands. With another deep breath, I reached for something more satiating.

The intoxicating essence of his soul drew closer. I could taste it riding on the air I stole from his body. My heart raced, and my beast whimpered with anticipation of finally getting what it wanted.

I realized that I had the power to take the life force from my prey, not just their existence.

That's it, Nevaeh, Bron urged in my mind.

"Stop," Archard sputtered out, grabbing my hands.

Stop, a nagging voice screamed from her hiding spot in my thoughts.

A flickering moment of sympathy, familiarity, and sorrow for the angel broke my hold on him. Archard dropped to the ground, panting for the oxygen I'd thieved.

"Oh no! I'm so sorry," I pleaded with Archard, falling at his side. I rocked back and forth on my knees, digging my fingers into my thighs so hard I could feel the bruises already blooming. I had to get a grasp on my control. I couldn't let it overtake me. "I'm so sorry," I said, hoping I hadn't caused too much damage. Tears stung my eyes and slid down my cheeks while I waited for a response.

Archard looked over at me with relief in his glowing eyes. "There you are," he sighed. His hand reached out for me.

"Don't," I whispered, backing away from the touch I yearned to feel. I sensed Bron was closing in on us, his darkness slithering up my back. My body and emotions were already bracing for the pain that followed his impending punishment. I had to speak quickly.

"I'm not the same, Archard. There is a malevolence inside me that I won't be able to keep caged much longer. The power is growing quicker than I can keep up with."

"Come with me," he said. His features tightened, restraining the sadness and pleading I saw in his eyes.

As I gave in and lifted my hand to graze Archard's stubbly cheek, a shredding sensation stung my scalp. I screamed, squeezing my eyes shut. Bron hauled me through the dirt and grass, stealing me away from my Guardian. My nails dug into the hand he had fisted in my hair, but his grip on me didn't waver in his task to drag me back to Hell.

Don't forget who you belong to, little one. The snarl behind his thought made me shiver with fear.

"I'm sorry. I'm sorry!" I cried, prying at his iron fingers.

'Sorry' won't be good enough this time, my dear.

I opened my eyes, searching for a saving grace. Tears blurred my vision as I focused on Archard surrounded by Crucio demons. Each one taking turns swiping their weapons at him and teasing him with the illusion that he might be able to take them down.

I grunted through the sweet agony of the tell-tale blaze igniting in my body while Bron lugged me closer to the Hell-portal. Moments later, we were plummeting into darkness—the light above me shrinking and fading as I descended past the point of no return.

"You will learn your place," my Ater assured, his ethereal voice echoing in my skull. He pressed his naked body against mine from behind, sandwiching me between him and the onyx marble walls of my room—my prison. "I'll decide when you can cross realms. I'll decide who you see. As far as you're concerned, I'm the one who tells you when to eat, shit, and breathe." His steamy breath blew across my earlobe as I cried in silence with my cheek—and my bare chest—mashed into the cold wall.

This was who he really was. His true form no longer hid behind the empty mask of flesh that concealed his features.

I twisted and tugged on the restraints shackling my wrist at the middle of my back, my shoulders aching for relief from the tension. Every time I tried to stretch and loosen the strain wrenching my muscles, the cuffs pulled on the chain linked to the iron collar biting into my neck. Any effort to readjust my position led to me choking myself.

His foot kicked at the insides of my ankles, forcing my legs to part. A hiss of air and pain threaded through my gritted teeth. I would have fallen had he not had me pinned. He tangled his fingers in my sweaty hair and jerked my head back, extending my neck to an uncomfortable angle. His long, searing tongue licked my jawbone from chin to ear. My body shuddered with disgust while the beast inside me purred.

"Mm. You taste so good," he purred along my cheek.

"Please, let me go," I whimpered.

I couldn't do this anymore. I was losing myself, losing my will to be who I really wanted to be. Soon, I would become the monster they were making me, and there would be no chance of coming back.

He inhaled my scent of fear, desperation, and arousal deep into his lungs then slammed my face into the wall.

My vision blurred, and spots appeared before my eyes. I sucked in a loud breath from the sharp stabbing sensation radiating from my nose into my forehead and cheekbones.

"I didn't say you could speak, little cunt."

Dazed, I swallowed the warm blood trickling down my throat from my sinuses and focused on staying conscious.

His rough hands flipped me around to face him, then grabbed my throat, tightening around my windpipe until I was wheezing. His fingers slid under my chin and pushed up, forcing me to look at his face. "This is what you wanted all along, is it not? To see the face behind the mask?"

His bottomless eyes matched the walls, black and glossy, yet there were slim rings of vibrant blue in the center, the color of blue flame. Dark circles surrounded his eyes, looking very much like bruises, but they were likely due to the thinness of his skin. I could almost see the texture of each sharp bone sculpting his handsome, dangerous face.

The motion of him moving my head was dizzying. The pounding of my heart thumped in my ears like a drum.

Rigid, midnight wings stretched out behind his large frame, making him look bigger and more intimidating. "Give in to it, Nevaeh," Bron commanded. "Let it out, or I will destroy what's left of your precious George"

I choked out a cry but didn't dare say another word. I squeezed my eyes shut and wished I were somewhere else.

The salty taste of his long, thick tongue invaded my mouth, forcing my lips to open wider. I whimpered as he explored the roof of my mouth, my teeth, and nearly my throat with his vigorous probing. And, though my body betrayed me with reactions of arousal—tightened nipples, goosebumps crawling up my skin, and a sweet dampness between my thighs—I screamed in my head, anger boiling just below the surface.

My fists clenched behind me, trying to keep the growing rage inside caged. I knew he wanted me to let it out, but I couldn't. It was on the verge of consuming every bit of who I was.

Bron curled his arm around my back as I arched into his wicked kiss involuntarily. He grabbed the chain above my wrists and yanked as he took his mouth from mine and grinned.

I fell to the floor, screaming, as a ripping sensation tore through my right shoulder. The throbbing ache and loss of control told me it was dislocated.

Wincing and panting with pain, I rolled toward my left side to alleviate the pressure off my injured arm, but Bron shoved me onto my back with my upper extremities pinned beneath my weight. Another scream ripped from my mouth, pain surging into my chest and back.

The dark angel kneeled between my legs and leaned over, trapping me inside his muscled arms. He rubbed his soft cheek against my thigh then crawled up my body, skimming his face over my stomach, breasts, and neck. His long hair fell around my head as I stared up at the haunting face hovering above me.

How could something so wicked be so beautiful?

The quick ruffle of his wings caught my eye, and I braced myself for what was coming. His curved, white talons sunk into the muscle just above my collarbones restraining me from squirming away. I groaned and gritted my teeth.

A cold finger grazed my hip bone and slid down the front of my panties before hooking the crotch and tugging the fabric to the side. Without warning, Bron thrust himself into me.

I gasped from the shearing pressure in my pelvis. Fear, pleasure, agony, and rage stirred the dangerous cloud working its way up my chest. My ribs rattled as the beast billowed into my throat.

As Bron pounded himself against my helpless body, his talons dug into me, deepening as he rode. Malicious tendrils darkened my vision and swirled from my panting mouth. I opened my jaw wider, allowing the dark substance to burst from me like a volcano.

"That's it, my love," he cooed in my ear as I wrapped my legs around his waist and held on for dear life.

Archard

CHAPTER FOURTEEN

Not An Original

"Get off me you son of a bitch!" I slammed the demon holding the machete to the ground and looked back toward Nevaeh. My heart sank as I saw the fallen angel dragging her closer to the Hell-hole.

A loud clanking caught my attention. I turned, snapping my hand up to block the heavy, barbed chain flying toward me through the air like a whip. I clamped my fingers around the chain. Dozens of spikes bit into my flesh, burning my palm like the sting of a dozen hornets. The demon snorted then snatched the chain back, lodging the barbs deeper into my skin before shredding their way out of my hand. I roared in pain, cradling my injured hand at my chest.

I sidestepped in a slow circle, glaring at the bastards, and squared my shoulders, preparing for them to attack. Homing in on the steady patter of my blood dripping against the dirt, I forced my racing heart to attain the calmer rhythm. I watched the fiends lunge at me and then back away, testing my reflexes — and patience.

I glanced over my shoulder, clenching my jaw and balling my fists when I realized Nevaeh was gone.

"Fuck it," I said, deciding to make a run for the portal. A moment later, I jumped back, spinning away from the Crucio demon slicing its machete into the air only inches from my face.

My feet dug into the dirt. I rushed forward, tucking my wings close to my body, and sprinted across the backyard toward the glowing, red light sparking out of the crack in the earth.

The widened crevice began to close, the edges pulling together as if it were being sewn together by an invisible needle and thread. I extended my wings then leaped into the air, thrusting them out behind me for extra speed. As I lowered within a foot from the hole, cold metal wrapped around my neck where dozens of spikes punctured my flesh like teeth. I flopped backward to the ground with a gargled grunt.

My hands flew up to the metal band stuck in my throat, prying to break the hinge. A demon heaved the pole attached to my collar, skidding my body backward through the lavender and weeds. My heels banged against the ground while I twisted and turned, struggling to get loose. Beyond my feet, I watched the glowing sparks die and the crevice sealed shut with Nevaeh inside.

"Let him go, you shithead!" a male voice bellowed.

The collar slackened, and I fumbled back onto the ground, the tension suddenly released from the pole. A series of grunts and screeches filled the air, then a moment of silence was followed by flakes of ash and dust swirling on a breeze past my face.

I coughed and sputtered through the filth, tugging on the collar around my neck. I pushed myself off the dirt into a kneeling stance and squinted through the remains of demon floating through the atmosphere. When the sound of movement rustled behind me, I spun on my knees so quick I almost toppled over.

Malach and Arkin danced a slow, threatening dance, back to back, with the three demons left circling them.

"They're mine!" I rasped against the pain shooting through my pierced neck. My fingers groped around the collar in a race to find the opening spring. I stumbled to my feet, watching my brothers slice and hack at the demons, their swords gleaming under the emerging moonlight.

I tugged harder at the iron band only to push the spikes deeper into my flesh. "Son of a…" I yelped, clenching my jaw through the sting. I dropped my fists at my side and huffed an angry, deep breath before stampeding into the fight with a pole hanging down my back. The collar would have to stay on until I finished this.

My wings thrust up and down, lifting me into the air about fifteen feet before I soared over top of the demon with the sickle. I roared in my angelic voice, high and full of power, and slammed the monster to the ground, landing in a straddle over its torso. My steady hands wrapped around its head and twisted it in one quick motion.

The sound of leathery skin tearing and brittle bones snapping rang in my ears like the satisfying tune of a favorite song. My heart pounded in a frenzy of rage, desperation, and victory. My lungs filled with the ash puffing out of the demon's tattered neck.

In the background, Arkin grunted and cried out. I looked back over the crest of my wing and found him tangled in the barbed chain. Dark liquid trickled down his feathers, staining the white of his wings.

I grabbed the sickle laying by my knee and drew one of my wings back then dropped it down in a swift, forceful movement. My body lifted off the demon effortlessly and spun toward Arkin and his monster. I finished my vertical spiral through the air, pulling my arm back and swinging the sickle around until it connected with the head of the demon wielding the chain.

The putrefied body's arms ceased their task of tugging at the barbed chain and dropped to the fiend's sides. The form stood still for a moment before finally collapsing to the ground. As it hit the dirt, the top part of the fiend's head separated just above its dark, sunken eyes and flipped over, looking much like a bowl of shriveled, dried brains rolling to a stop at my feet.

My furious gaze shifted up, softening when I saw Arkin struggling to free himself from the chain. I stepped over the carcass and rushed to my brother. "I know the feeling," I assured Arkin and assisted him in untangling the metal spines from his wings.

"Uh, a little help over here would be nice," Malach called. I twisted around to see the Archangel swinging his sword out in front of him to block a swipe from a machete.

I glanced back at Arkin, asking permission to help without words. "Go, go!" he said, nodding his head as he removed the last few inches of chain from his bleeding shoulder.

I quickly approached the last demon from behind and raised the sickle up, but it spun on shuddering legs and swiped the machete at my stomach. The tip of the blade drew a quick, shallow line across my abs. Warm blood seeped from the laceration and dripped in thin lines traveling below my navel.

Malach swung his sword down over the demon's outstretched arm as it cut me, severing its hand at the wrist. The deafening, high-pitched screech assaulted my ears, and the monster lunged back away from our reach.

I crept forward as Malach moved behind the Crucio demon. He smiled at me over the demon's shoulder. The tip of a shiny blade emerged through the front of the demon's abdomen, glistening in the moonlight.

Malach slid his sword from the monster while I sliced the sickle through its right shoulder, sinking the curved blade down to its left hip bone. The resistance of ribs, lung, and vertebrae eased when I finally slashed it through the softer belly tissue.

The hell-bound creature silently buckled to the ground, a cloud of ash curling up between Malach and me as its body split into two pieces.

"Thanks," Malach said, winding his wrist and sword in two circles at his side then sheathing it in a leather frog on his hip.

"Thank you," I grumbled with a nod, grateful for his help but mad that I had to admit I needed it.

"What kinda shit-storm did you stir up this time?" Arkin chuckled, walking up behind me.

"Nevaeh was on the run, and I tracked her here, but they found her." The thought that I had once again delivered her to the hands of Hell made my heart ache. I hardened my stance, swallowing my sadness, and focused back on my brothers. "How did you find me?"

"With my help." A small frame left the shadows of the house and strolled across the backyard. "I know, I know. I'm that good. You don't have to keep telling me," Maggie said with a sly smile on her wine-red lips. She stopped at my side and stuck her tongue out playfully, her flaming hair barely reaching my shoulder level.

"Glad to see you're feeling better." I ruffled her spiky locks with my fingers as a gesture of appreciation, unable to afford another thank you, but knowing she would understand.

Maggie's heavily-lined, chocolate eyes flicked to Arkin as she smiled. "I am," she assured, dropping her gazed to her boots shyly.

I glared at Arkin with knowing eyes. He cocked an eyebrow and shrugged, a grin curling his lips.

"Wow, the mojo is crazy here," Maggie said, walking to the spot Nevaeh and I kissed.

"Yeah, tell me about it," I scoffed, remembering the power she held over me.

Maggie turned in a slow circle. Her left hand nervously picked a hole in her fishnet stockings just below the hem of her hot-pink mini skirt. She closed her eyes and raised her right hand to the crucifix hanging between her breasts, smoothing the metal with her fingers.

"What do you see?" I asked, stepping toward the slight figure soaking up the energy cast that my love and I left behind.

"I don't know." Her brow creased as she tried to sort through the remnants of our souls. "I've never experienced this before. I think my gift has progressed since the near-death thing at the club." Another moment of silence passed as she concentrated harder.

A gasp of sudden realization hissed past her lips. Her eyes flew open and widened, darting back in my direction.

143

"What is it, Maggie?" I closed the space between us and waited impatiently for her answer.

"I see her. I can see the shapes of your bodies in distinct molds of colored essence like smoke and vapors trapped in a clear shell. I can see everything you did. She kissed you, Archard." Her words rushed out as she stared up at me with unease in her sage eyes. "Her soul is darkening. There's less of her light swirling through, now. And..." She looked around us at the images only apparent to her then bowed her head.

"And what? Come on, Maggie, it's like pulling teeth with you. Just rip off the fucking band aid. What is going on with her?" I grabbed the sides of her head and urged her to look at me.

"The kiss. I can see her sucking out your soul. If you hadn't stopped her, Archard..." She wrapped her fingers around my wrists and guided my hands down from her face. I stepped back, anger barreling through my confused emotions.

"No, it can't be. That would mean..." I shook my head in disbelief. "Her demon side is taking over." I looked at Arkin as he slowly approached my side. I could tell by the concerned expression on his face that he understood the severity of such a thing. "Is she becoming an Animus? Is that what this means?" I asked my brother, hoping for the answer I knew he couldn't give me.

Behind Arkin, Malach raked his hands through his hair and clasped his fingers at his neck. Tension creased his face as he turned his back toward us, but kept his silence.

What took Hell centuries to achieve when transforming a soul, was only taking months to accomplish with Nevaeh. If she was fully demon, what would that mean for her victims or the poor souls that happen to fall under her power? Or anyone that The Devil deemed worthy to take? Every soul in the world was in danger if Nevaeh could harvest at will and portal jump whenever she felt necessary.

"There's no way," Arkin assured, squeezing my shoulder in a consoling gesture. "She can't be an Animus, right? She's the Clavis," he said with a hint of uncertainty in his voice as he failed to convince me that my love wasn't becoming what we hated most — the very thing we lived to kill.

I dropped to my knees, feeling helpless and defeated, and choked back a cry. "This is all my fault," I whispered.

I recalled the hunger in her eyes, in her kiss — that insatiable need that pulled at my soul. My bloody hand rose to my chest and folded into a tight fist as I remembered the suffocating sensation that came when she sucked whatever that was from me — but my soul? It couldn't have been. No, I refused to believe that she was harvesting me.

I rubbed my hands over my face, trying to wipe away the tension there, and huffed out an exhausted breath. My weary eyes settled on Maggie.

She had walked over by the shed and sat on the ground, her knees pulled to her chest with her arms folded on top. She pressed her mouth against her forearms, her brown eyes darting over to the spot where the Hell portal had opened and watching with curiosity. She picked her head up and pursed her lips. "He's an angel," Maggie said matter-of-factly.

"Yeah, a Fallen," I verified.

Her gaze switched to me. "He's the key to this somehow."

"What?" I asked confused, looking over at the singed grass where Nevaeh had disappeared.

"I can feel it in his cast. He's hiding something big. His energy is worn down."

She reached a pointed index finger out before her and drew squiggly lines in the air as she squeezed one eye shut. "There's too much residual light spinning in his darkness. He's not one of the Original Fallen. He didn't fall with Lucifer. It was much later." Her hand relaxed, her arm drooping over her knee. "He's not who she thinks he is."

CHAPTER FIFTEEN

Aftermath

"Fuck!" a rugged voice whispered harshly in my ear.

The clanking of metal sliding across the floor drew me awake. Someone shifted my limp body around.

I groaned through the aches and stings assaulting my bones and muscles with the movement. My swollen eyes wouldn't open. My thoughts were fuzzy as I tried to recall what happened before I passed out.

"That son of a bitch!" the voice spat.

Warmth surrounded my naked form when someone lifted my shoulders off the cold floor and cradled me in their arms.

"Nevach, please wake up." The whisper heated my ear. "Wake up for me."

The iron collar around my neck jostled, tugging the chain that extended to my wrist shackles. I screamed from the tearing sensation bolting through my dislocated shoulder. The tension quickly released, and a large hand smoothed the clumps of hair out of my face.

"I'm so sorry, Nev. *Shh, shh, shh.* I'm sorry, I'm sorry," he repeated with regret in his tone.

I pried my goopy eyes open to a slit. The bright flares of tiny orbs hanging overhead forced me to close my eyes again.

"Come on, Nevaeh. Open your eyes."

I obeyed reluctantly, my eyelids fluttering open and allowing the light to filter in as the blurry images became clearer.

"Gavyn," I said, my throat crackling around his name.

"Hey," he greeted with a smile that didn't reach his eyes.

I coughed on the blood and mucus that had oozed down my throat during Bron's days-long punishing session. Wincing, I adjusted my position in Gavyn's arms to alleviate my throbbing shoulder.

"I've been waiting for him to leave. Layla has kept me busy, but I kept coming back for you. I waited outside your door, Nevaeh. I could hear everything. I'm so sorry I couldn't save you—I couldn't get in." His sweaty forehead dropped down and rested on mine. "I don't even know how you're still alive."

"I'm fine. It's fine, Gavyn. Can you get me out of these lovely bracelets?" I asked sarcastically, my voice still scratchy and strained.

His head popped up. He raised his hand and jingled a key between us.

"Who did you have to kill to get that?"

"You forgot my gift. I swayed the Crucio outside the door." He scanned over my body, clearly unsure of where he could touch me or how to move me without causing too much agony. "Can you sit up?" he asked, appearing as uncomfortable with the idea of helping me as it would be for me if he did.

I nodded and took in a deep breath, blowing it out in one long exhale. I forced my abs to tighten and pulled myself upright. Sucking air through my clenched teeth, I waited for the shocks of pain to subside.

In the next moment, I heard metal grinding on metal then my shackles clicked open. My hands dropped beside my hips, the action stealing the breath from my lungs. I couldn't even scream through the discomfort of my arms returning to a more natural position because it hurt so badly.

I hiccupped a cry. Tears rolled down my bruised cheeks.

"What do you need me to do?" Gavyn asked eager to take the pain away.

"My shoulder. It's out of place. You'll have to pop it back in," I whimpered. My usable hand clumsily reached across my chest, applying slight pressure to the injured arm and holding it in place as I rolled up onto my knees.

Gavyn frowned and nodded, knowing it would cause more pain at first. He shifted to his knees and backed up a bit. Carefully, he gripped my drooping arm and massaged his thumb over the inside of my wrist a few times to comfort me. "You ready?"

I cleared my throat and inhaled a lung full of sulfur-laden air. Nodding once, I braced for the torture to come. In one smooth motion, he lifted my arm up in front of me then manipulated it out to my side, away from my body.

I bit my cracked lip, holding my breath until I heard the pop and felt the unbearable pressure of tense ligaments and muscles release. A strained yelp escaped my lips with the air as I slumped forward in relief, gulping back the need to cry.

"Are you okay?" Gavyn scooted closer, wrapping his arm around my waist to support my trembling body.

I waved him away, still leaning over and huffing through the diminishing ache radiating down my arm. "I'm okay. Just...just let me be."

As he sat next to me in silence, my downward gaze took stock of the damage Bron had caused to my body. Dried blood coated my inner thighs like red paint. My stomach and hands were covered in clotted cuts and scratches. Small, circular bruises dotted my skin all over, indicating the spots where he'd dug his rough fingers into me the hardest. Other areas showcased large splotches of purple, green, and yellow where he beat me into submission. And, as my thoughts became clearer, images of the horror I'd allowed my cloud of doom to create for the multiple random souls that he captured and dragged into my prison flashed in and out of my mind.

I blinked hard, trying to erase their terrified faces from my brain, but I couldn't deny the warm fuzzies I felt when the memories flickered before my eyes. The sweet sensation of poison flushing through my veins and the wild rumbling in my chest brought a wicked smile to my lips. I hung my head, regaining the strength I'd lost from my much-deserved punishment, and sifted through the images of torture I'd served with the same euphoria as thumbing through an old photo album of family photos.

I'd been a bad, bad girl.

"Nevaeh?" Gavyn called, interrupting my trance. He softly touched my cheeks and urged my eyes to look up at him. "Did you hear me?"

With my attention focused back on him, I shoved the malevolence back down.

"We have to get you out of here." He scrambled to my other side and guided my good arm around his neck.

I yanked my arm back. "I said I'm fine. I don't need your help." I heaved myself off the reflective floor while he sat on his feet watching, his lips pressing into a thin, frustrated line.

Sure, he got me out of my chains and was offering to help me break out of this forsaken place once again, but, as I stared up into his sunken, tormented eyes, I knew I couldn't trust him any more than I could trust myself; to some extent, he battled the same evil I did. Unfortunately, both of us would give in soon if we didn't find a way out of here.

"What are you planning to do?" His fist balled at his side; his monster wriggled deep beneath his strained expression.

"Can you get me past the guards?" I shuffled across the room and pulled out fresh clothes from the dresser then tossed them on the bed.

He nodded.

I poured stale water from a cracked ewer into a chipped porcelain bowl on the black-stained chest of drawers. I pulled out a rag and towel from another drawer and realized Gavyn was eyeing my every movement. I cocked an eyebrow at him disapprovingly. "Do you mind?" I asked, dipping the cloth into the cool water.

"Uh…oh. No," he sputtered, turning around to stare at the onyx wall behind him.

I proceeded to clean myself up as best I could with what I had.

"I'm going to steal George from The Devil." The words sounded ridiculous as they left my tightened lips, but I knew what I had to do. I winced through the discomfort of cleansing the evidence of my abuse from my body with only one picture coming to mind—the last time I kissed Archard.

Stunned by my statement, Gavyn jerked his head back to look at me then turned back around, remembering why I'd asked for privacy. "Are you crazy? Even if you could, what makes you think you would make it out of Hell with him alive," he questioned doubtfully.

I slowly dragged the wet rag between my bloody legs. My breath stammered through the stinging burn heightened by the swelling of my very sensitive parts. As slow tears trailed down my cheek, I bit into my upper lip, refusing to let Gavyn hear my weak reaction.

"Nev?" he whispered with concern in his raspy voice when I kept my silence for too long.

I cleared my throat and hardened my nerves. "They won't know I have him until it's too late." I glanced at Gavyn's back as I swirled the cloth around in the water, turning it red.

His head lowered, and his arms crossed over his thick chest. After an exasperated breath, he inquired, "How?"

I dabbed my towel over the droplets of water sprinkled along my skin then threw it on the floor next to the dresser and considered my answer carefully. I limped over to the bed, fighting the new stiffness settling in my legs, and started tugging on an old t-shirt and fresh jeans. "You can turn around now," I said, bending over to stuff my feet into a pair of boots. I laced the strings up, glancing at Gavyn through clumped locks of hair.

He spun around and took a couple strides toward me, waiting for a reply with expectation in his weary expression.

I gathered my messy hair into a ponytail and wrapped it with a rubber band from the dresser. "I just need you to help me get past the guards. Can I count on you to do that?"

I didn't feel comfortable telling Gavyn how I was going to steal George. My time was running out, and what I had to do to get him could potentially cross me over the line for good. Gavyn was still under Layla's thumb in one way or another. I wasn't sure of his loyalty to me anymore, so I couldn't trust him with the knowledge of my new power in case this was all a ruse set up by Bron and The Devil to thwart my attempts.

I stared at him from the other side of the bed. A hint of humiliation and sadness flickered across his face as if he knew what I was thinking. He rounded the end of the bed in two seconds flat and slid a hand around the back of my neck. Before I had time to protest, his lips were crashing against mine. He moaned into my mouth when I caressed his probing tongue with my tongue.

He reached his other hand up and clasped his fingers behind my neck while his thumbs rubbed soft lines over my jaw. My confused emotions jumped all over the place. He felt like the old Gavyn for a moment, like it was just me and him and none of this nightmare had ever happened; yet, the hunger in his kiss was too smothering for me to be fooled. The old Gavyn was more tender, thoughtful with his touches. He was holding onto me, now, as if I were the lifeboat that would save him from drowning at the bottom of a raging sea of sorrow and agony.

I gripped his wrists and slid his tremoring hands down from my neck.

He kept his eyes closed tight and pulled away from my mouth. "I would do anything for you, Nevaeh," he breathed.

Licking his taste from my lips, I felt a chink in the wall I was determined to keep up between us. His deep-green eyes opened and stared back at me with nothing but remorse and apologies.

"I just need you to help me get out," I whispered through fast, shallow breaths.

He nodded and slipped his fingers through mine, gently guiding me to my door of sinful etchings. Gavyn glanced back at me over his shoulder, and a tingling sensation ran the length of my spine. A deviant smirk curled along his lips as the air grew heavier, and the compulsion to surrender mingled with my will to focus and move forward.

He turned back toward the heavy, wooden door and yanked it open. A draft of heat rushed in, and suddenly the impulse to surrender vanished, the tingle gone.

He sucked in a quick breath of the polluted air and squeezed my hand.

"What do you think you're doing?" the sickly-sweet voice questioned from the other side of the threshold.

I stretched up on my tippy-toes to see over Gavyn's shoulder, but didn't really need to; I already knew who was there.

"Layla," Gavyn exhaled, squaring his shoulders in a protective stance.

Layla chanted the foreign language that always preceded a horde of Aether demons appearing. Wind kicked up in the stale atmosphere, whipping my hair against my shoulders.

Gavyn let go of my hand and clenched the edges of the doors so tightly his knuckles turned white. His muscles stiffened, preparing to fend off the impending attack.

The dim glow illuminating the dark tunnel beyond my room faded as the smoky figures gathered around Layla. Gavyn's breathing quickened and became more audible.

"Sway her," I yelled.

"I can't. Her necklace. It makes her immune to my powers."

My eyes landed on the gaudy, red stone nestled in her cleavage.

"I wonder if she's immune to mine," I mumbled, warming up to the unspoken challenge. It would be nothing for me to loosen the ropes and unleash my inner monster. I felt it rumbling inside me now at the mere thought of tasting freedom.

"No! You can't!" he commanded, peering back at me. His brow creased as he pleaded in silence.

I quickly sobered, realizing I was too eager to give my beast control. I glanced at the movement just behind Gavyn. "Look out!" I shouted, reaching out to grab his shirt and pull him into the room, but I wasn't fast enough.

He returned his focus to Layla in time to see her fury charging toward him.

I clenched the army-green fabric in my fists as the Aether demons darted through Gavyn and funneled around him, heaving him over the threshold. The fabric ripped. I fell backward. He kicked the door shut while they dragged him out of the room.

"Gavyn!" I yelled, throwing the swatch of torn t-shirt to the side. I scrambled off the floor and rushed to the door. My hand twisted and pulled on the knob relentlessly, but it wouldn't budge.

I stared at the horrific faces depicted on the door, suddenly aware that every set of eyes were now turned toward me—glowering at me with scrutiny.

I shivered and stepped back slowly, watching their heads and necks stretch out of the door to keep their sights on me as if they weren't made of wood at all. The back of my calves bumped into the bed, stopping my effort to evade the malicious little beings sending chills up my spine.

Slumping down to the floor, I folded my knees up and wondered what they would do to Gavyn, and how I was going to get out of here without him.

Archard

CHAPTER SIXTEEN

THE IN-BETWEEN

"Archard," Arkin pleaded. "You can't do this, man." He grabbed my bicep, intending to slow my path toward my room. "Your graces suffered last time. We don't know how much we have left."

I ignored his efforts to stop my plan and continued through the factory with my eyes fixed ahead.

"Come on, Archard," he yelled, stepping in front of me and stopping.

I came to a halt and clenched my jaw, irritated by his body blocking me. "What, Arkin? What am I supposed to do? What would you do, huh?" I glared back at him and waited for a response. "I would gladly give every last bit of grace lingering within my poor excuse of a soul if it meant I could save her." I looked into his eyes, knowing that he understood.

He lowered his gaze to the floor and placed his knuckles on his hips. "You don't even know if you'll find her," he said.

I raised my hand and rested it on his shoulder. "I know, but I have to try. Arianna could be the only person that can bring Nev back to us. I have to go, brother."

Arkin nodded reluctantly then shouldered past me, our cramped wings ruffling against each other in the narrow hallway. His footsteps stilled behind me.

"So, who's gonna save *you* if you can't save Nevaeh?" He sighed when I didn't reply. "You know it's a very real possibility she will destroy you. What if there is no saving her, Archard? All the grace in the Heavens may not be enough."

His footsteps began again then vanished when he exited the building.

Purgatory is a very subjective realm. One person might experience a glimpse of what they could become under certain circumstances in order to recognize where their heart and soul truly lies, as did Nevaeh. Another being might be thrown into the constant reminder of what precious gifts they left behind to live the selfish life they chose on Earth.

Take me for instance, even now as the flames singed my feathers and ate away my flesh, I could see a Heaven that was unattainable to me. The home I abandoned. A place that I've prayed would one day forgive me of my treason and accept me back into her bosom.

My heart longed to experience the love and happiness that lies at the foot of God. Memories of my station beneath His resplendent, sapphire chair taunted me, shaming me with visions of the angel I used to be. Oh,

I used to be so much more. My body yearned to be coddled by the indescribable holiness that once saturated every thread of my being.

In Purgatory, though, no matter what you experience, your soul was here to be purified — to be purged of the remnants of sin lingering in your heart. You were one of the blessed. A spirit that was too treasured to be damned to Hell. Yet, to enter Heaven, you must be cleansed, for the ordinary human is too tainted to kneel before the glorious, loving eyes of The Almighty.

A gut-wrenching roar escaped my mouth as I rolled into a ball on the floor of my room — the same place I crossed the line and showed Nevaeh the In-Between. This was the only place I had a sense of safety — an anchor to her love — to pull me back. It was too easy to fall into the cracks and allow the regret and guilt consume you in the In-Between.

I had to find my way through the endless domains of souls awaiting their ascension, including mine, and find Arianna.

The carnivorous fire finally snuffed out around me, the floor disappeared, and then the severance rendered me to a flightless soar into my domain. The cool breeze calmed the burn of fresh wounds covering my body. My wings fluttered against the updraft but couldn't control the drop.

"Lord, please take me to her. Please guide my heart and mind in the mission to reclaim what is truly yours and right the damage that was caused by my hand," I prayed, knowing that only He could help me now. Tears stung my eyes as I readied myself for the task of enduring the loneliness and misery of all manner of beings residing here.

The ground rushed up under my feet before I had a chance to realize how close I was to the bottom amid the dark atmosphere entering The In- between. I grunted as my knees buckled and I lunged forward catching myself on my hands, nearly colliding my face with the hard surface.

Feeling the overwhelming force of my own guilt and abandonment, I lowered my forehead to the ground and rested the weight of my body on my forearms. My body shivered with sobs exploding from my core. It was too heavy. I couldn't focus past the fog of sorrow swirling into my mind, begging for my penance.

The need to surrender to an eternity of contrition filled my pitiful heart. "I can't go on," I cried, suddenly not sure what it was I came here to do anymore.

A salty mixture of sweat and tears dripped from my face, spattering the ground for was seemed like ages. I stared at the pitch-black space within my forearms and concentrated on remembering. "Come on, Archard," I spat. "Get up and move."

I eased my head up to assess my surroundings, but instantly snapped my eyelids shut, shielding my sensitive senses. I forced my eyes to open a sliver and squinted into a small orb of light, floating inches above me. It waited patiently for me to acknowledge it. I pushed myself back on my feet and examined the radiant ball. It was the size of a melon and hovered in the blackness with a comfortable sense of belonging. It was meant to light the dark.

"Aaarchard." The light flared with the forced pronunciation of my name.

I gasped, surprised by the talking, glowing being. It ventured closer. I smiled, thankful to feel the warmth of its illumination bathing my face. I watched the light bounce around my head as if it were investigating me. I reached a hand out to touch it, but it jetted backward.

"Nnnope, nnope," it said in calm, drawn-out words.

When I settled my hand on my thigh, the ball drifted closer again. "What are you?" I whispered, squinting into the brightness. I sucked in a deep breath, noticing the faint outline of a face smiling back at me. Eyes of shining brilliance, a nose, and a perfect mouth were formed by glowing streaks of intense radiance.

"Vviiirtuue!" it answered proudly.

I nodded, now understanding. "The Shining Ones," I whispered, recognizing the being as an angel of miracles. Its kind reigned over the cycles of life and death. I lowered my gaze and shook my head, chuckling. Of all the different types of angels, it made sense that a Virtue was the Heavenly spirit guarding Purgatory.

So much power was rolled into that small ball of light. They had control over miracles, the seasons, stars, and even the moons. Time and atmosphere obeyed their command without refusal. Courage and Grace exuded from their very luminescence. Why not have them control a realm that was ever-changing upon the needs of the souls here?

"Uuppp," it demanded as it drifted away from me, beckoning me to follow.

Curious, I pushed myself off the ground, wiping my tears away on my upper arm, and settled my outstretched wings along my back. Following the light, I realized that the heartbreaking sorrow of my penance was less than when I first landed here. I assumed that the little ball of power controlled every feeling, every image, and every experience here.

We traveled in quiet darkness for what I estimated to be twenty minutes, but I knew better than to trust time in this place.

Suddenly, the darkness began to disappear from the atmosphere. Color and light bled through the air, dripping in giant globules like paint melting off a blank canvas. What was a vast, open, murky space was now walls of new scenery.

The light led me into someone else's domain. We were in the middle of a well-furnished living room. Sage-green throw pillows were scattered across a cream-colored sectional which took up most of the cozy room, and a large TV hung like a picture over a gray, stone fireplace that still had swirls of a smoldered fire wandering out of its firebox. The living room was connected to a pristine kitchen with white granite countertops and cherry cabinets.

As I rounded the dividing wall, my eyes were drawn to the couple arguing in slow motion next to the island.

Messy, black mascara lines marked the woman's eyes and cheeks where tears had fallen. Her arms wrapped tightly around her torso as if she were holding herself together. The man was backed into the corner of two adjoining counters with his hands spread out, palms up in front of him, pleading to the woman. His brows pulled together, and his red, swollen eyes begged for forgiveness from his partner.

"How could you hide this from me?" The woman squeezed herself tighter and stifled a sob as she spoke in slow, drawn out words.

"I don't know. I'm so sorry I lied." The man lowered his shameful gaze to a piece of unfolded paper resting on the island at the woman's side. "I was just so ashamed. I can't control it," he said in a whisper of regret.

"You wiped out our life-savings. You pissed it all away on horses," the woman accused.

The man bowed his head, a deluge of tears finally breaking his surface. "I know. I'm so, so sorry," he apologized with true remorse in his tone. "I didn't realize how bad it had gotten until it was too late."

Confusion twisted her features. She couldn't understand he had an addiction. The lines of his face were weighed down by sorrow and regret. He was truly sorry for the actions, though he didn't have the willpower to stop.

My eyes flicked to the Shining One drifting down a dark hallway next to the kitchen. I followed, leaving the sad sinner to his penance of reliving the pain and destruction he'd caused his family over and over again until his ascension came.

The wainscoted walls began to ooze and drip away as it morphed to yet another domain. We emerged into the dingy, studio apartment of a young girl selling herself in her own bed just to make ends meet—and to drown away an irreparable damage caused to her self-esteem years before. Echoes of silent prayers, begging forgiveness and salvation, lingered inside the walls of her home as she stared blankly out the window, waiting for the man on top of her to finish using her body.

The radiant orb, invisible to the young woman, hovered over her face and cast its light on her. The atoning soul inhaled a deep, cleansing breath as her tears ceased, and the man disappeared from between her thighs. Every tormented contour of her face smoothed.

I watched the interaction between the angel and the woman, amazed by the blooming love and respect transferring between them. Her eyes widened, and she smiled then opened her mouth. A single flame floated up past her soft lips, surrendering to the orb as a token of sin redeemed.

The Virtue's glow shrunk, pulling the flame into itself, and accepted her payment. Satisfied, the angel's radiance began to expand, reaching outward until every shadowy corner of the room was filled with a light too bright to look upon. When the blinding glow subsided, all that remained was me and the Shining One surrounded by night once again.

That domain was erased — that soul nonexistent in this realm anymore.

I ventured on after the orb, crossing into many other domains and waiting while souls either paid their tokens for forgiveness and were gratefully released into the Heavens, or were assessed while reenacting their sins repeatedly.

As we passed into the next soul's territory, a whirlwind of color and emotion painted the blackness we had journeyed through. Gray and red splatters stuck to the air, filling in the dark, empty spaces between.

The Virtue stopped floating and hovered a step in front of me. I paused, squinting into the whirlwind of disorder and melancholy, and waited for the disorienting domain to finish piecing itself together around me.

The illuminating ball stretched its perimeter bigger and bigger until it took up as much space as I did. My cheeks warmed when the glow reached my face, and I relished in the tranquility it brought. The Virtue brightened the smoky wind rushing around us, seeming to slow the gust as it expanded. My ruffling feathers and hair settled with the quieting wind.

When the last few swirls of red-tinged smoke cleared, I stared out over a wide, sweeping area of land with lush trees and waving fields of wildflowers. I peered down from the top of a small hill — one of many surrounding mounds, varying in size. White, cottony clouds drifted across a clear, blue sky. The more I examined the vast land, the more I noticed it was changing before my eyes. The changes were subtle but detectable.

Hills rolled at a snail's pace. Even the ground beneath me shifted seamlessly. I rode the large mound of land until it was a valley in the midst of small mountains reaching for the heavens.

"Where are we?" I asked the Shining One, curious as to why this domain was so much different than the others. The territories before were reproduced snippets of a soul's past or future. This soul's In-between felt more real — and more present.

The orb set into motion, leading me through the changing valley, but keeping to the base of any higher land. I peered up at the crystal sky, watching the clouds morph from white and fluffy to wispy hues of deep purples and pinks. The bright sun sailed in a straight line above us from left to right as fast as a minute hand ticking around a clock.

The sky began to darken moments before the sun lowered beyond the fluctuating horizon, and a blanket of strangely large stars coasted over us. Faint outlines of planets and moons that appeared as large as the mountains next to me became clearer, illuminating the night.

I hiked the undulating ground in awe of the beautifully unstable atmosphere of this domain.

A short time later, hints of light from the rising sun began to bleed into the sky at my left, forcing the magnificent evening into hiding so an amazing day could shine again.

Even with all the wonder of this realm though, my heart still detected a heaviness — a sorrow — that wasn't my own.

"Hhheere," the orb said, drifting over an eight-foot-high pile of petrified trees.

I stretched my wings out and thrust myself up and over the stack of logs, landing expertly on the other side. The orb was waiting for me at a small cave entrance surrounded by brush and ivy vines. The sliver of opening was barely six inches wide and no more than four feet tall.

I pursed my lips and scrunched my brow together, certain that my large frame couldn't make it through the opening.

The glowing ball of light darted into the hole and back out, twice, then hovered next to me.

"There's no way I'll fit in there," I scoffed.

"Gooo!" The Virtue demanded.

Raising my brows in shock, I gaped at the light. "You can see, right? You know how big I am?" I asked sarcastically.

The orb darted into the hole and didn't come back out. The light spilling from the crevice vanished as the orb traveled deeper into the crack.

I looked up at the fading day and growled in frustration before finally bending my knees enough to tuck at least some of myself into the opening. I pulled my wings tight to my body and slid my shoulder into the crevice. My wings and knees scraped along the rock as I shoved into the tiny space.

When I managed to wedge myself about half-way in, the walls began to reform around me as if they were trying to accommodate my size. I inched farther along the opening, leaning my weight toward the cave. "Just…a little…more," I grunted, pushing my hands against the mountain wall as if I could move it myself.

Clumsily, I tumbled out of the opening and fell into a small, dank room, slamming my hands and knees onto the rock floor. A steady plinking of water dripping onto stone echoed in the background as my vision adjusted to the intense brightness overtaking the little room.

I narrowed my eyes, scanning over the thick mound of blankets and pillows piled in a small, hollowed nook to my left. My gaze wandered along the smooth, stone walls, over to the three lanterns struggling to be seen amid the Virtue's glow, and then to a stack of old, wrinkled papers lying neatly on a boulder with a flat top.

I stood upright and turned my head away, quickly shielding my eyes as the Virtue zoomed to my side.

"It takes some getting used to, doesn't it?" a frail woman's voice spoke to my right. "Living in such a gloomy space? She's just too much for this little room." The woman chuckled.

Turning toward the voice, I lifted my wing and blocked the Shining One's intense glow so I could see. The outline of a slender frame kneeling at a slab of stone became clearer.

I took a step closer to her and watched as she raised a hand to her forehead, lowered it to her heart, and then moved it across each shoulder. When she finished making the sign of the cross, her shaky hand gripped the edge of the altar, assisting her in a struggled effort to stand.

I rushed to the woman's side and wrapped an arm around her waist with my other hand gently bracing her elbow.

"Thanks," she said.

Her gray eyes peered up at me, slight wrinkles creasing the corners. Long, dark hair shrouded her shoulders and back, matted in some places by years of neglect. She reached a hand up to rest on my cheek and smiled. "I thought you'd never make it."

As I stared down at her, I realized that there was no mistaking the similarities. "Well, here I am, Arianna," I assured, smirking at the glimmer of hope shining on our future.

CHAPTER SEVENTEEN

DIGGING FOR STRENGTH

A harsh light poured in through my doorway, forcing my heavy eyelids to flutter open. I swallowed back the taste of blood and ick that had drained into my mouth while I was asleep. Using the heel of my hand, I wiped away the string of drool that had dribbled on the red, satin pillow under my throbbing head. I winced at the lingering effects of Bron's punishment, cursing that the little bit of rest I'd gotten didn't help alleviate my headache.

A large shadow broke the streak of light spilling onto the crimson comforter piled at my feet. I quickly pushed up onto my hands and knees then backed myself to the head of the bed until my toes pressed into the wall behind me. My achy muscles tensed, readying for an attack.

The shaded figure entered my chamber with a cautious gait and stopped at the foot of my bed. I narrowed my eyes at the brightness behind it, wondering if I had enough strength to make a run for the open door.

A loud sigh broke the silence as the body folded its arms over its chest.

My muscles relaxed, and I rested back on my heels. The spiced, woodsy scent mixing in with the stale odor of blood and sex told me exactly who was standing before me. Subtle waves of need pulsed through me, tempting the beast inside to awaken.

I reached my shaking hands up to my temples and pressed in with my palms to soothe my pounding brain. My body began to rock as I tried to pull myself together and control my growing desire to forgive Bron and submit to his will.

"C'mon, Nev. You can do this," I whispered through gritted teeth, digging my fingernails into my scalp and squeezing my eyes shut. "You are strong enough," I told myself.

"You know, I wanted to do this the easy way, Nevaeh."

My eyes shot open at the sound of his velvety voice infiltrating my head.

The bed dipped as Bron kneeled on the edge of the mattress and inched closer to me in a slow crawl. The darkness inside me uncoiled and stretched its claws, digging into my ribs for leverage to explode out at the first chance.

I leaned my back into the wall and pulled my knees out from under me, tucking them into my chest. I prayed it was enough of a barrier to keep my dark lover's seductive body at bay — and enough reinforcement to keep the wickedness caged within me.

A large limb extended toward me. I jerked my head back as his hand opened next to my cheek and touched me.

"What's wrong? You don't love me anymore, my sweet little cunt?" His patronizing voice rumbled in my mind.

His energy pressed down on me, drowning me in a sea of lies and deceit. My own thoughts threatened to betray me and give in to the whisperings of beautiful promises filled with his lust and fire.

"I never loved you. I never will," I spat at the empty face staring back at me. I could almost sense him sneering at me as he wiped my spittle from his smooth, featureless skin.

His long fingers wrapped around my neck, pinning me to the wall in a movement too fast for me to anticipate. He shuffled closer on his knees, his muscular thighs closing in around my small body, eliminating any space left between us, then he sat back on his heels.

My eyes jerked toward the movement of his raven wings stretching out from behind him and settling in a cape around his broad shoulders.

My cautious stare flicked back to his featureless face. Somehow, I tightened the ball I was curled into a little more, fearing that I couldn't withstand his power if he penetrated my walls.

"I just wanted to love you. I just wanted to help you fulfill your destiny—a destiny given to you by God, mind you. Was it too much to ask to stand by your side as you took over the world?" he relayed into my mind with a hint of genuine sadness lacing the words.

His smooth cheek rubbed over my forehead then trailed down to my jawline, caressing my skin with his enticing touch.

Instinctively, I leaned into him, loosening my guard and inhaling his alluring scent deep into my nostrils.

"I knew I should have taken you at birth. Maybe then you would have been easier to tame."

I continued to nuzzle into his cheek and neck, drunk with the lust that always pulled me to him, and listened to the words echoing in my brain.

"You knew about me before I was born?" I asked with a giddy lilt and slurred words. I was falling deeper and deeper under his spell.

He pulled his head back from mine, holding his position only inches from my nose as he seemed to study me.

Glimpses of the man behind the mask flashed in my thoughts.

He leaned his jaw down to my ear, and a warm breath heated my neck. "I knew you before you were even conceived, and I knew exactly who you were the moment you crossed into Hell, Nevaeh. Who could mistake that irresistible yearning for evil buried deep in that soul of yours?"

My breath hitched, and my body shuddered.

His voice was no longer in my head. Each syllable heated my earlobe as he spoke. Goosebumps raised on my skin when something wet trailed down my neck.

I jerked my head back and took in the broad chin, thin but uniquely formed lips that curled into an arrogantly beautiful smirk, and strong nose with a slight downward tip that I now associated as my punisher's face. He made me want him as much as I detested him.

"I've shown myself to you twice now." My eyes raised and locked onto the mischievous gaze looking back at me. "Won't you follow me to greatness?" Bron's sharply angled brow raised expectantly.

Nearly black circles emphasized the lightning blue irises scrutinizing me. His harsh attributes made him appear more wicked, but his bare, devious beauty only increased the wetness between my thighs.

I raised my hand to his chin and traced my thumb over the soft lips I'd worshiped in my mind countless times—the same lips I'd tasted when he stole his fill from me.

He exhaled against my touch and slid his dangerous tongue out to lick the pad of my thumb. A moan escaped my salivating mouth.

I pressed my other hand flat against his bare chest and urged him backwards.

Bron followed my lead and lowered onto his back, his wings extending out past the edges of the bed. I crawled over his body and straddled his hips, keeping my gaze locked on the black and electric blue eyes watching my movements like an eagle. He tilted his hips up, rubbing the hardened flesh resting on his stomach into my crotch. He licked his parted lips, his gaze darkening with need.

I considered the beast eyeing me like I was dinner and smiled. He hungered to be inside me.

Leaning over, I raked my fingers up the ripples of muscle forming his stomach, chest, and neck.

"I won't follow you anywhere, asshole," I whispered sweetly next to his ear then bit into the tender flesh and tugged until it slid from between my lips with a pop.

He sucked in a quick breath through his teeth and dug his fingers into my hips, grinding me down against him.

I groaned as the incontestable heat ignited at the apex of my thighs. I slid my hand from Bron's enticing flesh to the glossy, midnight feathers splayed around his powerful body. My fingers smoothed over each black plume until it reached the crest curving just above the dark angel's shoulder.

My brain argued with my body as I gripped the bony structures supporting his feathers and clamped down with all my might.

Bron hollered, bucking beneath me as he grabbed my waist and threw me across the room.

I crashed into the marble wall, my head bouncing off the shiny surface before I plopped to the floor. A sharp gasp filled my lungs. I scrambled to my knees, holding the knot forming on my scalp, and hurried toward the door, fumbling to attain momentum.

As I reached the opening, a strong hand snagged the back of my shirt and lifted me upright. My bare feet slid against the slick floor. Bron slammed me into his chest, curling his massive arms around my midsection.

"You cannot escape me, bitch," he growled in my mind.

I looked over my shoulder at the nonexistent face I was accustomed to. Black, inky lines sped up the side of his neck like poisoned blood racing through his translucent veins.

"Fuck you," I squealed, wriggling and twisting in his arms. I kicked the empty air below, praying for a moment of weakness in his grip. My hands clawed and grabbed at his shoulders, reaching for the wings just beyond. He jerked me against him, tightening his hold around my chest.

I inhaled a staggered breath and expanded my ribs out against his forearms. Silky softness slid beneath my bloody fingertips. I pinched hard, latching onto the crest of Bron's wings.

My head nearly split with the piercing sound reverberating from the

169

Ater's monstrous yell. His grip faltered enough for me to tear from his arms. I dropped to the floor and ran like hell.

Everything was suddenly silent. No steady drip of water from the crevices in the wall, no rocks skipping across the floor under my feet, and no haunting screams echoing through the tunnels. My mind focused on eluding the dark angel, gauging his pursuit of me.

Thump...thump...thump, my heart beat in my chest, throbbed in my head, and pounded in my ears.

Heavy footsteps struck the dirt behind me almost synchronizing perfectly with my racing heart.

The anger and determination that always hid in the back of my mind when his spell captivated me finally sprung forward.

I couldn't let him take hold of me again.

I couldn't let anyone have that much control over me.

My bones rattled with the dreadful heat and ferocity lurking inside me. My chest throbbed with the building pressure clawing its way out.

"Get a grip," I commanded myself. I looked back to see Bron barreling toward me, his wounded wings scraping against the walls.

Zoning in on the destination ahead, I let the pounding in my ears drown out any distractions. Sour breaths rushed in and out of my lungs, spurring a slight haze amid my thoughts as I fought to concentrate.

I turned down the first tunnel and then the next, unsure if I was going the right direction, but eager to lose the dark angel gaining on me.

My feet struggled to keep up with the pace I was pushing. I stumbled over a large boulder jutting out into my path and bashed into the wall beyond it.

"Son of a bitch," I groaned, clenching my teeth in a vain attempt to keep my voice low. I slid along the wall, rubbing my hand feverishly over the injured shoulder, then propelled myself forward into a sprint again.

Peeking over my shoulder, I took note of the eerie darkness filling the silence behind me.

Please, tell me I lost the bastard.

I slowed a few yards later and ran my palm over the dirt next to me.

When my fingers curled around the edge of an opening in the wall, I squeezed into the small space and squatted down.

My eyes strained to see into the pitch-black of the tunnel. Stagnant air rushed in my mouth and blew out in hot puffs. I held onto a lungful of the air for a moment before releasing it, concentrating on slowing my ragged breaths and flittering pulse.

A tiny echo drifted down the corridor from several yards away. I cautiously shifted into a sprinter's position — hands and toes digging into the dirt — then ceased all movement.

I inhaled deeply and held it, waiting for the footsteps that were scuffing closer.

"I can feel you, Nevaeh. Can't you feel me?" Bron asked with sickening confidence.

He knew I could sense his heady energy swirling with mine. His alluring scent wafted into my nostrils, forcing me to breathe him in. Never mind the small voice stirring in the back of my mind, begging me to play his venomous game — to surrender to all he was.

The beast buried deep in my core purred, sensing his proximity. I squeezed my eyelids shut, clenched my jaw tight, and shook my head, fighting the urge to let my monster out. I fisted handfuls of dirt at my feet, pressing the granules of gravel and earth into my palms, praying that the pain would give me something to anchor to.

"That's it, my girl. I can smell the fire burning in you." The loud sniffing sound of Bron inhaling a deep breath reverberated off the rocky surroundings. "Just let it out. You would be so much happier. No more suffering. No more hiding the truth."

A forceful scuff across the ground startled me, and my eyes snapped open. A rock skipped along the floor, rolling to a stop in front of my foot.

He was so close.

I swallowed back the cloud of doom nearly billowing out of my throat.

I can't keep running. God, please help me get out of here. Just let me get to George.

I rocked back on my heels and gulped down the smothering sensation filling my mouth. My eyes watered from the sting of vicious tendrils threatening to blot out my vision. I dropped the dirt in my fists and lifted my arms out slowly, spreading my fingers against the slabs of rock on either side of me. Clumps of earth stuck to my sweaty palms and ground into the walls as I pushed out through my hands, hoping that I could hone my control and reign in the monster breaking my cage.

A form disturbed the air in front of the opening of my hiding spot. I stiffened.

Please, don't see me, I repeated over and over in my mind. Beads of perspiration trickled down my forehead, nose, and mouth, leaving salty remnants on my lips before dripping off my chin.

The familiar odor of burnt flesh suddenly filled the air, and a warm presence leaned in behind my body.

"Run," he whispered in a gruff voice.

Stunned by the unexpected command, I hesitated for a moment.

"Run!" he yelled in my ear, pressing an uncomfortably hot hand into the small of my back.

I burst out of the small opening and shouldered into Bron, pushing him off balance. The swift movement of his hand reaching to grab me sent a chill through the air and up my spine. I spun away from him and righted my footing as I set into a steady run down the tunnel.

In the darkness behind me, vibrations of growls and grunts bounced off the walls. Bron's attention was averted by another demon, one that seemed to show up at just the right times.

Kenet had saved me again.

I would have to thank him…if he made it through Bron's attack.

I raced through the undergrounds of Hell, trying to find my way back to George. My lungs burned from the acrid air rushing in and out. My legs felt heavy and tired. Beads of perspiration that had gathered on my skin from the humidity and my running suddenly began to evaporate. The atmosphere was growing drier. A bone-deep chill crept up my legs and spread to the rest of my body, letting me know I was getting close to Sinner Sea.

The dirt floor soon turned into cold slabs of frozen rock. I slowed to a cautious pace as horrid screams fought to travel through the corridor and reach me only to be absorbed by the tunnel. An eerie gray light flickered into sight some distance ahead, forcing me to stop at the edge of the next level of Hell and reconsider my determination to continue.

I teetered from one prickly foot to the other, afraid that if I stood still for too long my feet would freeze to the ground. Slow, white clouds of breath floated out from my mouth as I gathered the courage to enter the next section of damnation.

"You have to do this, Nev," I reminded myself. "For George. This has all been for George. You can't let him down now."

I inhaled a deep lungful of crystalized air and stepped forward.

CHAPTER EIGHTEEN

HISTORY LESSONS

I lay on my bed, feeling sore and drained from traveling back through the spirit realm's portal with Arianna. The journey was getting harder. This last time, I struggled to extract myself from the world that would graciously swallow me up and deal me my due penance.

I could feel the last sparks of Grace I contained sifting away like sand through my fingers. There wasn't much left. Another trip like that would cut the remainder of my angelic ties holding me to Heaven; a gossamer thread dangling to a home I haven't been able to reach in over a decade.

Chattering down the hall piqued my interest, and I listened for a moment to what sounded like Arianna and Arkin talking about me.

I reached my left hand over the edge of the mattress under me and clutched it as I rolled off my aching wings and sat upright. I sucked in cold air through my teeth, stifling a curse word from the ache shooting through my body. My weak hand found the knot in my neck and rubbed without relief.

I looked down at my bare chest, taking care not to breathe too deeply. A large purple-green bruise stretched from my right hip bone to the ribs under my left armpit. My eyes scanned over my bedroom, stopping on the small table which usually held my water pitcher. It was smashed into splintered wood planks, and the pitcher was cracked on the floor next to it.

Boggled memories of clambering into the room and turning to get a frazzled Arianna some water came to mind. I must've blacked out and landed on the table. Stretching my wings out around my shoulders, I watched a few feathers float down to the floor at my feet. I swiped them aside with my toes, then pushed myself up off the bed and stumbled toward the door.

Slamming into the doorjamb on the way out, I fumbled into the hall. My hands splayed against the walls to steady my gait, catching myself before I landed on my ass. I forced my feet to step one in front of the other. Finally gaining my equilibrium back after a few strides, I scuffled to the next open door.

Arkin's eyes darted from Arianna to the doorway and held the coffee cup that he was about to sip from, frozen, just shy of his lips. "Well, good morning, sunshine," he greeted with a slight smile, then slurped his drink.

Arianna's head turned, focusing her bright eyes on me from over her shoulder. Wavy, chestnut hair disappeared under the tan, wool blanket wrapped around her shoulders, forcing a pang in my chest to stir. The resemblance between her and Nevaeh was almost too much for me to handle.

She rose from her chair in front of Arkin and gathered the blanket closer to her meek body. "Hi there," she said, her mouth curving into a gratuitous smile as she moved closer to me.

"Hey," I returned with a nod. "What's going on in here?"

Arianna peeled my hand from the door frame and hooked it around her neck, then reached an arm around my waist and gently pulled forward. "We were just waiting on you to discuss what I know."

"How long have you been waiting?" I asked with a strained grunt. She helped me cross the room and assisted in lowering me into a third seat at the table next to Arkin.

Her gray eyes shifted to my brother's and then back to me. "Two days."

I gritted my teeth and sneered at Arkin, frustrated that he'd let me sleep for so long.

"I know, man, but you needed to heal. You keep doing this shit to yourself...you won't wake up next time." He took a loud sip from the brown liquid in his steaming mug.

"You got any for me?" I groaned, dismissing my aggravation with him. He was just looking out for me, and I couldn't stay mad at him for that.

He jumped out of the chair smiling and strolled over to a half-full coffee pot on the counter at the back of the office.

I examined the weathered woman sitting across from me. "How are you feeling?"

"Better than you, I'm sure," she answered, watching Arkin set a cup on the table before me.

He nudged the coffee pot out toward her, offering a refill. She placed a hand over her mug and shook her head. "No, thanks," she whispered, then looked back at me.

"You took quite a spill last night. Scared the piss out of me really." A soft humorless laugh escaped her lips. She picked up her cup and lifted it to her mouth, took a drink, and pulled it away to stare at the warm fluid. "I'd forgotten how good a crappy cup of coffee could be." Her eyes flickered between Arkin and me as she giggled.

I feigned a polite smile as another pang shocked my heart. Even certain inflections in her voice sounded like my Nev.

"I've got her all up to speed, Archard." Arkin took his seat, leaning forward and resting his elbows on the table, one wing on either side of the chair.

I nodded appreciatively. "So, now that I've gone through the trouble of getting you out of Purgatory...what can you do to help us save your daughter?" I asked, wincing as I shifted forward in my seat.

She shrugged, setting down her cup. "I can at least fill in some blanks." Her small hands slid across the table, one palm opened to me and one opened to Arkin.

"Let me show you a story," she said, her eyes asking our permission for something that didn't feel like she actually had to.

I glanced over at Arkin, my brow creasing with confusion. "Show us wha—"

A light touch on the back of my hand transferred me to another time and place.

"Hi there," Arianna's words echoed in my head.

It was dark, and I was outside. An evening chill skimmed over my skin as I waded through knee deep water. I looked down. Blue light from a full moon hanging low in the sky lit the smooth skin of a small body that was definitely not mine.

"It's okay. You can come out," I urged in a tender voice that belonged to a woman much younger than the Arianna I knew now. "Come on out, silly. I know you've been watching me."

I stepped onto dry land, scanning the area around me. A large pond spread out behind me. A lush tree line blocked my path ahead.

Water trickled down my naked skin, causing a pleasant shiver to radiate up my back.

"I've felt you for days now," I whispered under a heavy, excited breath.

Dry, browning leaves rustled just feet away. A shadow moved behind them.

"I've been here for far longer," a deep, low voice answered.

I leaned over, grabbing my dress from a nearby rock, searching the woods for movement. I tugged it over my head though the feeling radiating through my body begged to keep it off.

I toed closer to the pair of eyes watching me from the dark. The glint of moonlight reflected off the curious orbs causing them to shine like quicksilver.

"What's your name?" I took another step closer.

The tall figure pulled back a branch and stepped into the blue light. "Rhett," he said smirking as he drank me in.

Droplets of water soaked into the neckline of my dress while a dampness gathered at my thighs. I gasped as my eyes trailed over his long, black hair, strong chest, and broad white wings that surrounded nearly every inch of him.

He was the most beautiful creature I'd ever seen.

"What are you?" I asked, dropping to my knees in worship.

He traversed the last step separating us, held out his hand, and waited for me to accept it. "I'm your Guardian."

Keeping my hungry eyes on him, I raised my hand and placed it in his.

He pulled me up and held me in his arms. "There's no need to kneel, Arianna."

His burning lips crashed into mine, stealing the breath from my lungs. I knew it wasn't meant to be this way—whatever it was between us—but I couldn't deny it. It was like I was on a ride at a carnival too fast for me to stop.

The earth shifted under me.

A whirlwind of images swept around me like time speeding through the air. Nausea and dizziness forced me to shut my eyes and take slow, deep breaths.

I held out my arms and flexed my wings to steady my wavering balance. Opening my eyes, I saw a new scene unfold itself. The rushing storm of memories stilled on one.

Shelves of boxes and cans stood on either side of me. Florescent lights buzzed above. I was in a grocery store. My hand gripped the plastic- covered bar of a grocery cart.

Movement behind me triggered my keen alertness. I spun on my black high-heels. I threw up my hand and braced myself against a fist hurling toward my face. Ducking down, I kicked my foot out in a spinning ground sweep, my red mini-skirt bunching around my hips.

The short, lean man toppled to the floor, his head bouncing on the tiles and rendering him unconscious.

I jumped up and positioned myself to defend any further attacks. A woman glared at me from the end of the cereal section.

"Can't you guys just let me shop in peace?" I shouted at the Dark Celata through Arianna's mouth.

"If you wanted peace, you should have joined our side, bitch." She flicked her finger in my direction. A fiery bolt of light sparked from the fluorescent lights chained to the ceiling and zapped the air, surging straight for me.

It moved too quickly. I'd never be able to avoid the lash. I crossed my arms over my face and doubled over to guard my core.

The ground shook from the explosion inches from my toes. Boxes tumbled off shelves, bags burst open, and a shower of sugary flakes and spheres pattered against the floor.

I straightened, scoping the area for what took the brunt of the assault, since it hadn't targeted me like I'd expected.

Boots clacked down the aisle as the Dark woman ran out of sight. I slowed my panting and noticed a man laying at my feet. Black, shiny curls stuck out in a mess framing his boyishly good-looking features.

I kneeled, grabbed the lapel of his washed-out denim jacket, and threw it open. Resting my ear against his chest, I listened for any sign of life. His heartbeats were steady, and he was still breathing. I reached a hand up and gently slapped his cheek.

"Hey. Wake up!" I demanded, shaking his muscular shoulders.

His eyelids snapped open. I gasped a bit surprised by the vibrant bluish-purple eyes staring back at me.

"Hey," I greeted, sitting back on my heels.

"Hi," he replied in a gruff, baritone voice. His lips curled into a wide smile as he seemed to memorize every line on my face.

"Did you just save me?"

"I think I did." He slowly propped himself up on his elbows, wincing at the painful movements.

"Thanks," I said with an appreciative grin, holding my hand out to the stranger. "I'm Ari."

"Kenet." His large hand surrounded mine like a mitt and shook.

Our gazes stayed locked on one another. In the next moment, he yanked me down on top of his chest and hooked his fingers around the nape of my neck. Peering into his violet eyes, I allowed him to guide me to his lips.

I couldn't tell if the smoldering heat of his mouth was from our attraction or from something else entirely, but I didn't care. I knew within an instant that I was in danger of loving this man.

With a single kiss, I knew my future was laid out by his side.

My head spun with images again. I growled through the disorientating feeling of being stuck on a merry go 'round as the scene shifted.

Luxurious raven hair draped over my angel's wings. He sat in a small room, behind an old desk, writing feverishly in a book bound in red velvet. I walked across the creaking floorboards and stood behind him, waiting for him to acknowledge my presence.

"What are you writing, Rhett?" The words squeaked timidly from my mouth. My unnatural bond to the angel was there and never fleeting, but a deep fear was creeping into my heart now. I knew what I felt for him was a ruse, spawned by his selfish need to possess my heart.

He continued penning his story with the bloody feather he'd plucked from his own wings days ago.

I reached out my hand to touch his back. His sharp features turned to glare back at me. I jerked away.

"It's your miserable future that I'm forced to write."

My heart sank under the burden of doom he lay upon my shoulder. "What are you talking about?"

"God has shown me the result of your choices. He's told me what will happen if you continue your relationship with that demon."

I frowned and dropped my gaze to the floor. "And what of my relationship with the angel?" I whispered. "What does God tell you of *our* future, Rhett?"

The anger in his eyes dissipated and his snarled lips relaxed. "I don't know," he admitted, closing his tormented eyes.

"I'm doomed either way, you see? My fate with the angel that tricked me into loving him is sure to fall to pieces, and a life with a demon whose true love is promised to bring me troubles beyond my comprehension. What am I supposed to do, Rhett?"

The angel slid from the chair and settled onto his knees. He wrapped his arms around my waist, burying his face in my stomach, breathing in my scent like I was the only air that could satisfy his lungs.

"Please, Ari. Please, stay. You will learn to love me on your own. I can make you happy."

My hands rested on his silky tresses and smoothed downward. "I need something that's real. You can understand that, can't you?" I knew he never would. His blind love for me had overpowered his mind's ability to know right from wrong in recent weeks.

A chesty growl rumbled from his mouth as he shoved me backward. I collided with the floor, banging my elbows and rump against the wooden boards.

Rhett raised up, grabbed the velvet book and blood-tinged feather off the table, and turned to look at me one last time.

His once beautiful and inviting eyes held nothing but rage and judgment when he peered down at me. The angel disappeared from my sight, though I could still feel him there. This was his way of punishing me—denying me the privilege of being in the presence of his Graces.

My heart broke. I sucked in a deep, unfulfilling breath, and wept at the loss of a dear companion.

I pressed my fingers into my temples as visions of Arianna's memories featuring Kenet flooded my mind; happy memories of them building a life in hiding.

Kenet had pretended to maintain his position among the Dark Celatum as he plotted to leave that life behind for Arianna. The expression of love on his face when he saw her was genuine and undeniable, as was hers when she looked upon him. However, the toll he paid to uphold his charade seemed more noticeable every time I saw them meet. His cheeks a little more hollowed, his eyes a bit emptier, his skin a tad more fevered than before. The game he played was costing the soul he struggled so hard to replenish.

Arianna had bravely fought the demons and Dark Celatum creeping out of the corners of Hell — until she couldn't anymore.

The next scene slammed to a halt around me. My hand rested on a swollen belly. My cautious eyes darted around a dank, empty closet. A sliver of light touched my face as I peeked through a crack surrounding the door.

My breath hitched when my stomach and back muscles tensed so tightly I felt like an electric wire was shoved up my nether region and turned on. I gritted my teeth and bared down through the concentrated pain. Sweat trickled down my forehead. Moments later, the sensation subsided only to repeat again every ten minutes.

I prayed that Kenet would make it home soon. He'd been missing for days.

Outside the closet, the walls creaked and bent in the shadows of a setting sun filtering through the curtains, threatening to unleash the monsters of another dimension. Lately, they were getting more brazen and nearly succeeding at breaking through without a death to claim.

I wiped away the salty fluid dripping in my eyes with the back of my hand and hunkered down for another contraction.

"I can help you," a familiar voice spoke softly from the other side of the closet.

"Rhett," I exhaled.

"Just promise to stay with me, Ari," he begged. Angst and sorrow laced his words.

"I knew you were still with me. I never stopped feeling you."

He placed a gentle hand on my stomach and stared at it in amazement as if he could see through the flesh of my belly to the baby inside. I spread my hand over his and locked my fingers between his knuckles.

"Please help us. I need to get to my mother's. We'll be safe there," I grunted during another contraction.

The angel's dark silhouette nodded in agreement. "Wait here."

As I gasped in another deep breath to subdue the cramp in my abdomen, Rhett's hand reached for the door knob. He shoved the door open. I watched him muster his angelic powers and force the demon's penetrating the Hell portals forming on the walls back to where they belonged. High-pitched screeches and deep groans of power pierced the air in that little abandoned house I'd used for hiding.

He didn't bother repairing the cracks and broken floorboards left behind by the shift in our realm. He just thrust the demons back into the portals once they broke through, then ran his hand over the sparking membrane the demons had created, reversing the portals power with his Heavenly touch.

Rhett hurried to the closet and bent down on one knee, scooping me up in his arms. He raised me off the uncomfortable ground and carried me out of the rickety shack.

I held onto his shoulders and buried my face in his neck as he lifted me and my unborn child into the sky.

The comforting odor of spices and chocolate lingered in my nose while my surroundings shifted again like a movie on fast-forward. I watched as myself again, a bystander trailing through the corners of Arianna's mind while she played her memories for me.

Rhett and Arianna landed on the front porch of a white, two story Colonial house. I stepped forward, following the pair toward a front door I recognized from my own memories.

Rhett yanked on the screen door, propping it open with his elbow as he carried Arianna into Theora's home. I tailed them inside, surrendering to a pull that kept me close to the angel and his ward.

My gaze swept over the large sitting area to our right, then to the dining room at our left. I looked up the steep stairs but didn't see any movement on the second-floor landing.

"Mama?!" Arianna squealed during another excruciating contraction. Her voice trembled around the word. Her face was pale and sweaty. Scared.

Shuffling steps moved from the back of the house. A surprised face peeked around the arched entrance to the kitchen.

"Oh my heavens, Arianna!" Theora hurried down the hall, waving for Rhett to follow her into the dining room. "Lay her on the table," the older woman said, reaching into an ornately decorated hutch in the corner of the room. She pulled out piles of sky-blue linens and placed them on the table next to Arianna's legs. "Get the pillow off the couch," Theora ordered Rhett then disappeared into the hallway.

The angel rushed to the cream and pink floral sofa in the sitting room, picked up a pillow crocheted using the same colors as the upholstery, and nearly leaped the few feet back to Arianna. He gently lifted her head then settled it back on the cushion.

Her skewed face stared down at her full belly, ignoring the doting being beside her. Spittle flew from her gritted teeth as she bared down again.

"Mama! It's coming!" she cried when the tension started to release. She pressed her knees together, trying to slow the process.

"Don't worry, dear. I'm right here," Theora answered, emerging from the hall with a smile. She carried a pot of steaming water, scissors, and dishtowels with pictures of roosters on them to the table.

A piercing scream erupted from Arianna's clenched jaw, and her whole body shook. Rhett slowly backed away from the women, watching the two prepare for the baby's birth. His expression morphed to one of sadness, helplessness, and fear. Rhett's gaze fixed on Arianna's agonized face.

Theora tugged sopping jeans off her daughter's legs and threw them to the floor. "Alright, baby girl, you have to relax those legs," the older woman instructed, opening Arianna's knees with her hands.

Rhett stood on the other side of the room, a worry line wrinkling his forehead and his lips tightening into a thin line. Arianna reached out for him, inviting him to her side, but he shook his head.

"I can't," he whispered. "Ari, you have to give the baby to me. I can protect it." His fists balled against his thighs.

"What?" Arianna gasped between labor pains. "No!" Another scream breached her mouth, and she began drawing her legs back together.

"Ari, she's not supposed to be." He almost sounded like he was pleading with the young woman, trying to get her to understand that he knew something about this child that she did not. His eyes drifted over her swollen tummy. "The angels will not let her live, Ari." He frowned looking down to the floor. "The others will turn her into something they can use against us."

Arianna's brow furrowed, and her eyes narrowed from pain and confusion. "What are you saying, Rhett? What are you...," her breath hitched, "suggesting I do?" Fear laced the hard, tired plains of her face.

Rhett shook his head as if settling an argument in his own mind, then looked back at Arianna. "I don't know. I...I just know that He told me the child was powerful. She will be a force to be reckoned with. We can't let the Dark ones get her, Arianna."

Gritting her teeth for the onset of another intense contraction, Arianna spat her protest, "I'll keep it safe. I'll keep it hidden until Kenet comes home."

"No," Rhett shouted. "You're not listening. You can't keep it hidden from the angels. Maybe from the demons, but not from the angels." He forced his voice to lower at the last word. Regretting his harshness with his ward, he walked to her side and dropped to his knees.

The ends of his glorious wings spread over his lower legs and onto the floor like a cape of white magic. A twinge of jealousy sparked in my gut as my eyes drank in the pureness of his feathers, but I shook it off quickly.

Rhett's hand locked around Arianna's.

She scowled at her Guardian and jerked her fingers free from his grasp. "You're an angel. How do I know that you aren't here to take my baby from me? You hadn't said a word to me in months." She closed her eyes, sucked in a sharp breath, held it for a minute, and then released it, setting her narrowed eyes back on Rhett. "How do I know that you aren't just tryin' to get me to give up on Kenet? You never wanted me with him. Why should I believe you? Why should I even entertain the thought that God," Arianna glanced up to the ceiling with a sneer, "told you my baby is evil?"

Rhett's wings twitched, and his jaw tensed. He was holding back the anger I saw swirling in his eyes. "God did not say it was evil. But it could become evil if the child is not taken care of properly, Arianna," he growled. "You can't watch it every second of the day. They will come for you. They will get the baby."

Arianna's eyes glanced past her knees, searching her mother for some sign of guidance. Theora shook her head in a movement that was so slight, Arianna almost missed the action.

Her gaze returned to the tortured face pleading with her. She mulled over what he said for a moment. "What did He tell you would happen? How will my baby become evil?"

"I don't know," the angel responded, rubbing his hands over his weary features. "He still keeps the ending from me. I only get part of the picture, but the part I've seen is...it could be the end of us all."

"Let me read it. Show me what He's shown you. Maybe I can see a different meaning. A different future." Her expression softened as she asked to examine a very intimate part of Rhett's life.

"No," he barked, raising from his knees and taking a step backward.

"I can't keep us safe if I don't know what to keep us safe from, Rhett," Arianna cried, holding her hand out to receive the book she assumed he kept near. She stifled back another scream and kept her focus on his.

A moment of emotion-filled silence thickened the atmosphere between the two.

"It's mine to interpret. It's me that He speaks to. My riddle to unravel," the angel scoffed.

Arianna pulled her hand back to her chest, her fingers smoothing over a silver, circular pendant at her neck. "Then I can't have you around my child." She turned her head away from the angel to save herself from witnessing the hurt flaring across Rhett's face. "I don't want you to come near me or my baby again."

Rhett's body stiffened, his eyes widened in disbelief and fury. "You don't know what you ask," he said, stepping closer.

When his ward denied him eye contact, he stopped. He glanced at Arianna's belly once more, carefully measuring his next words.

"I will keep you safe, Ari. I'll prove my love to you. If that's what it will take for you to be mine. I'll guard your demon baby."

His shoulders broadened, flexing his great, white appendages behind him, then he directed his eyes toward the ceiling.

Suddenly, the walls began to shake. The floor rippled. China rattled in the cabinets lining the dining room. Nevaeh grunted as another wave of physical pain hit her.

"It'll be alright, sweetheart," Theora comforted, patting a knobby hand on Arianna's knee.

The dining room table skidded two inches to the right with Arianna on it as Rhett blasted through the watery opening whirling on the ceiling. Everything froze in the suspension of time that happens when angels seek passage across Heaven's gate. The portal swallowed Rhett quickly, closing as soon as his foot disappeared to the other side. The plaster mended on the ceiling, and the walls flattened.

The room started spinning around us, propelling me through Arianna's memory. The phantoms of moments past sped along her timeline, picking up the pace while I stood still, watching the scenes play out like a movie stuck in the fast-forward mode.

Theora coached Arianna through her labor so fast it was dizzying. What I knew had taken hours to occur happened within minutes.

The twirling room stopped on a dime. The illusions stilled. The air filled with a waving energy that radiated straight into my soul. My body tingled. My senses heightened.

The next slow beat of my heart felt like the first I'd ever experienced.

She was here, and like the day she was born, I could feel that connection clicking into place.

I flexed my wings and spread them out at my sides, steadying my body as it relived the bond being built between Nevaeh and me. Though this bridging was something that Arianna didn't witness, it happened regardless, and I could feel it in the atmosphere of her memory — an imprint entwined in the very fabric of Nevaeh's birth.

Arianna didn't remember me transporting from my position in the Heavens and coming to watch over my ward, but I could feel an earlier shadow of myself arriving in the very spot I stood now. It was an awkward feeling, like I was possessed by a ghost of myself.

The burden of protection and responsibility settled upon my shoulders. Love sparked inside my heart and blossomed into a link that could never truly be broken. A small, ethereal part of me drifted from my mouth and kissed Nevaeh's lips. It soaked into the breath she inhaled between weak cries.

That little bit of my soul made her mine forever.

After that moment, I went where she went. I hurt when she hurt. I grew to love her more than she could possibly know — more than I ever should have. Even during the years of separation, I could feel the piece of her that was mine like a phantom leg that had been amputated. There, but gone.

The memory began to play at a normal pace again, as if the moment of Nevaeh's birth had only been a stutter in the record.

Theora lifted a newly born Nevaeh from between Arianna's legs. She wiped the baby down with the rooster towels, careful to get all the blood off her face and out of her mouth, then laid her on Arianna's chest.

The tension in the room released. The young mother's slender, delicate fingers combed through the downy-fine curls dusting her baby's head.

Her proud face beamed at the little girl, but her sullen eyes spoke of fear. She knew what a sacrifice she'd just made. She had an idea of what troubles would follow. Her soul would be hunted by the slyest of demons. The angels would call her traitor. And it would all be for the sake of the part of her heart she now carried on the outside.

She focused on the chubby face working hard to stare back at her, memorizing every tiny detail. A slight smile pulled at her lips. It was an automatic reaction from her motherly love. "Nevaeh. That's your name," Arianna whispered, grinning in amazement and wonder.

Her eyes flooded with tears as she planted tender kisses all over the child's cheeks and forehead. She paid no attention to her mother while she cut the umbilical cord and cleaned the remnants of childbirth from her skin.

Until now, I had no idea what happened before Nevaeh's birth. The two women never spoke about Rhett while in Nevaeh's presence, and so

I was ignorant to what occurred.

The furniture began to fade around me, dissipating into the air like wind. Colors blended together, whirring around me as the memory moved on to another time. A place our memories coincided.

I was rocking on a white porch swing, peering out over a lush garden consisting of blooms representing every color of the rainbow. Tiny drops of dew still dampened the trees, sparkling in the sun like glass globes trapping each ray inside their walls.

The roof moaned under the weight of Arianna's slow movement back and forth. She sat next to me like this many times, oblivious that I was there, offering her what little comfort I could. It was my purpose to be her daughter's keeper, but I took pity on Arianna and extended my Grace to her when she felt alone and desperate.

Before now, I had never understood why her loneliness ran so deep. As Guardians, we commit to a life away from our brethren. We didn't see one another unless we willed it to happen, even if we were standing side by side. Most of us didn't present ourselves to other angels though. I'd always accepted the reasoning behind keeping our solitude and seclusion from other angels; in numbers, we could more easily influence the will of our charges, and that wasn't always a good thing. However, this theory often became a major downfall for our time in the human realm. It made it harder to help our wards in instances like this, when more information would benefit our humans versus harm them. If I could've spoken with her Guardian, maybe we could have found a way around his fear, around the future he thought would come to pass.

I closed my eyes and rested my head back against the cool metal swing. Wind rustled through the large oak shading us from the summer morning sun. The crooning of a southern blues singer and his guitar drifted through the screen door of Theora's old house, the birds chirping along with the songs.

My eyelids popped open with the sweet sound of giggling at my left foot. Her laugh made me tingle in delicious ways, filled me with a magic I didn't comprehend.

I peered down on the paint-chipped porch and found a small body stumbling bare-foot to the edge of the swing. She slammed a ragged doll onto the seat between her mother's leg and mine. I smiled, wishing I could play with the child for even a moment.

"What is it, baby girl? You wanna sit up here with me?" Arianna leaned over and lifted the toddler onto her lap. A grin spread across her face, hiding the dark emotions stirring in her eyes. "If only your daddy could see you now. He'd be so happy. Two years old and tryin' to take over the world with your busy feet already."

Nevaeh's tiny, plump hand reached up and fiddled with the pendant dangling from Arianna's neck. Arianna hugged her close and kissed the child's temple.

I reached out to brush through the brown curls mashed against her head, but stopped short, remembering it was pointless to touch her. She wouldn't feel it. Her big, violet eyes darted toward me and stared into the space I occupied.

I gasped. I'd forgotten that moment—how she'd seemed to know I was there.

Her stubby finger poked out, pointing at me.

"Man," she announced to her mother, looking back and forth from Arianna to me. "Man," she repeated in an eager, infantile voice, trying to get her mom's attention.

Arianna stopped rocking the swing. "Yes, baby. I see him." I held my breath in surprise.

They could see me?

I didn't remember Arianna ever knowing about me. I glanced up at the young mother, expecting to see her looking at me too, but she wasn't. Her steady gaze focused off into the distance, beyond the flowerbeds and bushes that decorated the immediate yard.

"Man," Nevaeh shouted giddily.

"Shh," Arianna demanded. A noticeable unease tightened her muscles.

I rose, stretching my pearl-white wings out behind me. My breath caught at the instant appreciation I felt seeing my feathers untainted for the first time in over a decade. It was all an illusion, but gratifying none the less.

I stepped toward the opposite end of the porch to get a better view of the figure treading through the pasture. "Theora," I yelled, knowing she wouldn't be able to hear me.

Something was wrong.

A vague recollection of this vision unraveled in my mind, and I didn't like what I remembered.

"Theora," I shouted again, extending my Grace out to her in hopes that it would reach her—warn her. She needed to take Nevaeh somewhere safe. "Take her inside, Arianna!"

"Mama!" Arianna called through the screen door as she raised off the swing and hurried across the creaking floor boards.

"What is it, dear?" Theora appeared at the door, wiping her wet hands over the red rose print of her apron. Her eyes followed Arianna's gaze to the man almost to the end of the pasture. Soon he would be at our front steps. "Give her to me." The springs on the screen door wined as Theora pushed it open. "Now, Arianna!"

Arianna nodded and handed the jabbering toddler over to her mother. "Hide her. I don't think there will be any trouble, but I don't wanna take the chance."

Without a word, Theora shuffled inside with Nevaeh, letting the storm door clap shut behind her. I stretched my wings, preparing to defend my ward and her family. It was pointless since I couldn't affect anything in this memory, but it was an instinctive reaction I couldn't control.

My chest tightened with disappointment when I caught a glimpse of my plum-tipped feathers from the corner of my eye. The illusion failed as my earlier self followed Nevaeh into the house. I'd felt almost whole for a moment, sitting next Arianna without the stain of my decision to abandon my world. Feeling the full extent of my Graces unfurling around her was a sensation I'd forgotten long ago.

The mystical leash tying me to Nevaeh tugged at me from inside the house as I assumed Theora was carrying my ward farther away from me. I remembered trailing them into a concealed closet used to hide soldiers of war ages ago. I ignored the call, knowing it was just the residual energy of that day.

The figure was walking between the two rows of peony bushes leading to our home. I glanced to my left and found Arianna focused on the being with her arms wrapped around her waist. She was guarding herself, but the release of a heavy breath and faint smile said she knew the stranger.

I studied the visitor's long, raven hair, confident shoulders, and brown trench coat.

"Rhett," she breathed.

"Arianna," he greeted, approaching the bare patch of dirt worn down at the bottom of the porch stairs from years of rain and traffic. "I've come for you." His voice cracked. Silver-gray eyes swept over Arianna, drinking her in like she was the only water in the world that could quench his thirst. His angelic features were full of anguish and yearning.

Rhett was different in this vision than in the previous one. The shine in his eyes a little duller, the color of his skin a little less vibrant, and his face showed signs of aging that were so minute a human wouldn't be able to tell; but I could tell. I'd seen those traits of an angel dimming every time I looked in a mirror.

Arianna lowered onto the top step, her arms still wrapped around her middle, holding her walls together. "You shouldn't be here," she said.

"I can keep you safe now. I will keep you both safe." His fingers reached out and brushed over her forearm.

She flinched and leaned away from his touch even though her eyes said she wanted to throw herself at the angel. "No, Rhett. If they find you here, it'll only draw more attention. You have no idea what I've had to deal with since you've been gone." Arianna took a deep breath and trapped her top lip between her teeth, holding back the tears I saw brimming her eyelids. "They just keep coming. I can't leave this property without having to fight for my life. Thank God this is consecrated land and my mother's shield holds up. It's the only place I can find peace — that I can keep Nevaeh away from the demons."

The muscle in Rhett's jaw ticked. "You made your choice," he reminded her. His gaze lowered to the ground as he composed the anger bubbling to his surface.

Arianna shook her head. "I'm not blaming you. I just...I can't let them find us. I can't leave, Rhett." Her arms unfolded, and she raised a hand to his cheek, caressing the strain from the angel's face.

"I can keep you safe," Rhett repeated with his eyes closed, leaning into his ward's touch.

"No, you can't. The demons will never stop, and if the angels find out about your prophecy, they will hunt us until she is dead. You will only draw them to us. I'm afraid there isn't a road that leads to freedom for us." Her words were soft and full of regret. She missed him.

"Fuck the prophecy," he spat. His eyes lifted to her face, darker than moments before. "He quit sending me visions when I left you that day." Rhett backed up two paces and grabbed the lapels of his coat in each hand. "I gave it all up though, Ari. I can't live without you anymore. I tried to keep my distance, but I need you." He peeled back the stiff fabric from his chest and shrugged it off his arms.

"What did you do?" Arianna cried, her hands rushing up to cover her mouth as she stared in disbelief.

I studied the wings that were once more pure than mine in their original state and recognized the change instantly. It was a transformation that stained more than our feathers when we abandoned our God — it scarred our souls.

Deep emerald stained the tips of his feathers, fading to a bright lime halfway up the plumes. Glints of bronze-colored quills sparkled throughout the rich color.

"They can't track me now. We can be together. We don't have to worry about the delusions of a god who plays us like pawns anymore." He reached behind his back and brought forth a book I was all too familiar with. His fingers clenched the red velvet binding as he shook it in the air. "This has caused me too much pain. We have both suffered from the ignorance I've had to scribe on its pages." He tossed it into the dirt at his feet, the half-filled book thudding against the bare earth. "I won't let this get in our way again. Please, Arianna. Please, come with me," he begged.

His ward's cheeks glistened from tears of confusion and hurt. Arianna's focus was pinned to the book as she slumped down on the top step, her legs too weak to hold her upright.

My heart ached from the grief and loss emanating from Arianna's energy, her emotions flowing outward in a river of pain and betrayal.

"What did you do?" she asked again on a shaky breath, skimming her gaze back over the green-tipped feathers sprawled around her angel's shoulders.

"We are equals now, my love." Rhett buckled, his knees hitting the dirt patch just below Arianna's perch. He searched the troubled features, trying to understand the bemused look on his charge's face. "I've surrendered my rights as an angel to be at your side."

A sob left Arianna's mouth. She slid her hands over her face, trying to hide in the darkness of her palms—from a reality that I sensed she knew was ill-fated. Her shoulders slouched, and gloom flared from her soul.

She shook her head, rocking back and forth on the porch step. "You shouldn't have done this. I never asked you to do this, Rhett."

Her face lifted from her hands, eyes wide from a sudden realization. "How long has my soul been without protection? That's what happens, right?" Another sob erupted from her chest.

"I did this *for* you, woman," he growled with his fists grinding into his thighs.

"How long?" Arianna yelled.

"After you denied my place in your life. The next day, I forfeited my Holiness. What good is it if I can't protect you? If I'm just a tool being used to enlighten the world about its end?"

Arianna stared down at the book laying on the ground. Its cover was open and pages flipped to a spot marked with the blood-tinged feather Rhett had used to scribe his visions. The feathery tip of the quill was stained with the color of his disloyalty as well—green as the greed he harbored for her love.

"God will never forgive you." Her eyes trailed up to the angel that used to be her Guardian.

"No more than he will forgive you for laying with a demon I suppose." His teeth ground behind his snarling lips.

She gasped. His words hit harder than any fist.

"Leave." Her hand reached up to the railing and gripped tightly, steading her weight as she rose from the step. "Leave, now," she demanded as her fingers hooked under her pant-leg and unfastened a dagger from her ankle strap in mere seconds.

Rhett's wings thrust forward, standing him upright. "What do you plan to do with that?" His gaze darkened. "Go ahead, Ari, pretend that you are more righteous. I know better. I know where your heart lies — in the thralls of a demon. One day, you'll remember how much you loved me — how much you wanted me — before that demon put his spell on you."

"It was you that tricked me into loving you, not him. He may have been a dark soul to begin with, but he sought out repentance in the end. You can't say that, anymore. Your heart is too tainted to see past your own selfishness. He will come back to me and replenish his faith. Where will you be?" Arianna stalked closer, hand raised, gleaming dagger poised to defend.

The Holy markings winding up the blade sung to me like a lullaby.

"Perhaps in Hell where I returned your demon lover. Don't count on him coming home anytime soon." Rhett smirked.

Arianna screamed, jumping over the three steps leading off the porch and landing on her feet as nimble as a cat. She lunged forward at the earth- bound angel. Rhett pushed his emerald-tipped wings forward, propelling himself away from the glistening blade. His features hardened, his fingers sliding over his chest. Grim eyes examined the blood smearing his fingertips then darted to the drop of crimson falling from Arianna's dagger. An enraged expression sharpened every angle of his beautiful face.

"You will regret this, Arianna," he spat.

"I only regret that I didn't stab it deeper," she snarled back.

The angel turned away from his former ward, took two large strides, and then leaped into the air, taking flight.

Arianna watched the creature rise higher and higher into the bright halo of sun until he wasn't visible any longer. The moment he was out of sight, her hand lowered to her side. Clamped fingers loosened from around the hilt of her weapon, and a thump marked the end of the blades descent to the ground.

The strong woman that stood before me only minutes before, collapsed to the dirt. She hunched over, rocking on her knees as she wept into bloodied hands. Guttural sobs were broken by suffocating gasps for air.

The aura of pain and sadness emitting from her core slammed into me with a wave of mangled emotions. I moved down the stairs and kneeled behind her, hoping to comfort some of her disquiet. I knew better though.

The screen door opened with a whine then clapped shut behind us. I looked over my shoulder to see Theora taking each step, one by one, on wobbly knees, then pausing at the bare patch of dirt. She bent over slowly and picked up the heap of pages lying at her feet. Compassion bloomed in her eyes when she considered her suffering daughter, but Nevaeh's call for her mother dragged Theora's attention back into the house, beyond the weathered netting of the screen door.

"Come child, she needs you," the older woman said, grabbing the rickety railing and climbing onto the porch.

The aura of unruly emotions clouding around Arianna receded. She inhaled deeply and steeled her walls again.

Though I wanted to follow and see Nevaeh as a sweet, innocent child one more time, I stayed behind. I'd seen what I was supposed to see from this scene.

The winds of change whirled in around me, and the image of a sunny day outside of Theora's house disappeared.

"Wake up, baby. Arianna, wake up for me." The affectionate words whispered through the air, coaxing me to open my eyes to a new time.

The shifting kaleidoscope of smoke began to settle on fresh imagery.

"Arianna, I'm here, baby. Please, wake up. We have to hurry." The male figure hunched over Arianna's bed, smoothing hair from her face. Late evening moonlight cast a navy glow over the small room, lighting it enough for me to see the deep shadows on his withered face and flecks of silver hiding in his dark hair.

The body under the blanket stirred and stretched. Sleepily she replied, "Kenet?"

"Yeah, sweets. We need to get our baby and leave." He gently dragged the covers back and pulled at her arm, helping her sit up.

Tears erupted from her eyes as she latched onto the man she thought she'd lost. "I can't believe you're here," she cried.

His body stiffened under her hug, but his hand rubbed circles on her back, keeping her close. "They tried to keep me captive, but I found a way out. They aren't far behind though. We have to leave, now." He unwound her arms from his neck and placed his shaky hands on either side of her face. "Go get our baby, and I'll throw some clothes in a bag for you."

"We can't leave, Kenet. This is the only place we can stay safe. Mama has a shield around the farm." She swung her legs off the side of the bed and stood up as Kenet steadied her by the elbow.

"They will get past the perimeters, Ari. The things that hunt me are stronger than the Dark Celatum. Darker than the usual demons. They won't stop until I'm back in Hell." His eyes glazed over for a moment, seeming to picture the torment he never wanted to experience again.

"If we aren't safe here, then we won't be safe anywhere. I can't subject Nevaeh to a life of running and hiding, Kenet. Besides, I have my own demons waiting for their chance to take me down." Her eyes lowered from his face in defeat.

"Nevaeh," Kenet released on a breath. His expression filled with joy.

Arianna offered him a smile. "Yes, that's her name. You have a daughter with eyes as wise and violet as yours, and soft, brown curls as unruly as mine."

A tear trailed down Kenet's high cheek bone. Arianna caught it with her thumb and wiped it away with a smile. "Would you like to see her?"

she asked.

Kenet sliced his head to the left once, his body tightening. "If I can't take her with me, I don't want to see her." He took Arianna's hands in his and smoothed his thumbs over hers, drooping his head. "They've won, haven't they?"

Arianna's shoulders shuddered as she tried to keep from crying. She nodded. "I don't see any other way. I don't even know how I'm going to keep her hidden for much longer. They lurk just outside the edges of our farm, waiting for me to surface. She'll have to start school soon, be a normal little girl. With my Guardian gone, the Darkness calls to me. It's getting harder to deny them, Kenet."

"Rhett is gone?"

She nodded. "He's gone rogue. Couldn't deal with my decision to choose you. And he claimed his prophecy predicted she could become…destructive." Her nostrils flared, and she pursed her lips. "He said the demons *and* the angels would both chase her when they found out about her."

"We have to draw the demons away from her, Ari. If I managed to get past the borders of your mother's power, they will find a way, too."

"What do you have in mind?" Her gray eyes searched Kenet's weary gaze as he thought for a moment.

"I have to go back."

"No. You just got here. You can't leave us again. I won't have it," she argued, gripping Kenet's forearms.

"It's the only way I can keep them away from you all."

"What about me? I attract them too. They'll still be around whether you're here or not. Stay. Please," Arianna begged.

"I can't. You know it's the right thing to do, sweets." The man slipped his hands around Arianna's waist and drew her closer to his body. His shoulders and ribs expanded, breathing in his love's scent when she rested her head against his chin. Her small hands slid up the ridges of his heaving chest and neck, fingers winding into the sweat-dampened waves of his hair.

"I'll go too, then," her meek voice agreed.

Kenet jerked Arianna away and stared into her startled face. "Absolutely not," he growled. "You'll stay here. Take care of our daughter." His hands squeezed her upper arms, emphasizing his disapproval.

"I'm putting her in just as much danger as you would, Kenet. I can't keep her safe if I stay either." Arianna's fingers mindlessly reached up to her silver locket and smoothed the polished treasure, considering her options. "Mama can watch over her. We can lead the bastards away, and mama can raise her until she comes into her gifts. If she can just stay under the radar for that long…then, we can come back to her."

Kenet let go of her and sat down on the edge of Arianna's bed. He raked his hair back and dragged his hands down his worried face, pondering his lover's proposal. She dropped down on the squeaking bed next to him, resting her head on his shoulder.

"Not with me. You can't follow me to Hell, Arianna. I won't allow it."

"Where then?" she asked, looking up at Kenet.

"Purgatory," he answered in a contrite tone. "I can open a gate." He searched Arianna's face for signs of her thoughts. Uncertainty hid beneath the feigned sternness of his jaw.

"Will I be able to see her?"

"No," he murmured.

Arianna nibbled on her top lip, weighing his words. "The demons will leave her alone?"

"I don't know, but I hope so."

"Okay. I guess I don't really have any other choice." She skimmed over the moonlit objects in her room, committing her childhood relics to memory. "I just need to tell her goodbye."

She rose from the bed, but Kenet caught her hand. "You can't risk it. You may not have a Guardian, but she does. They cannot know your plans. We can't trust the angels with her any more than the demons. We must cut the ties clean. Your mom will figure it out."

Arianna frowned, conceding to Kenet's words. She reached behind her head and unclasped the necklace hanging around her neck. The locket slipped onto her palm as she unthreaded the chain. Walking to a distressed jewelry box sitting atop her dresser, she carefully opened the lid and laid the chain inside. She rifled through the baubles at the bottom and retrieved another chain, shorter than the one she put in. She threaded the locket onto the new necklace, clasped it closed to keep the pendant from slipping off, and spread it out over her comforter. Her delicate fingers lifted to her mouth where she planted a kiss on the pads and then touched the gleaming locket once more.

"Okay," Arianna said, offering her hand to Kenet.

He accepted her hand and waved his fingers through the air as if he were wiping off a window. Particles in the atmosphere began to singe and crackle, forming a ring of fire in the middle of the small room. The ring grew. The singed air turned into orange-white flames that flickered violently against the calm background of Arianna's home.

Once the circle of flames was large enough, Kenet turned toward Arianna and peered down at her. "If she should fall, I will be waiting in the Underworld to bring her back."

Before Arianna could respond, his lips covered hers and moved relentlessly. She melted into his body as her fingers combed the waves of his hair, tugging and pulling him closer. They kissed as if it would be the last time they'd see one another. Flares of passion and longing swam outward from the two, reminding me of the kiss Nevaeh and I shared the night we entered the cathedral and she surrendered herself to the Devil.

I bowed my head, feeling the need to grant them privacy in such an intimate moment.

Minutes passed before they finally ended their goodbye. Sounds of panting from their intense kissing and rapid heartbeats from fear of their future lingered in the room. Without another word, Arianna smiled at Kenet then stepped into the ring of fire, accepting her fate in the world of the penitent.

CHAPTER NINETEEN

Giving In

It was easy to give up in the darkness—to just let go and stop fighting the force trying to mold you into something new.

This was the thought that ate at my resolve to continue.

I had forgone the neon-green torch to light my way as I entered the cavern, knowing it wouldn't do much good in the pitch black of Sinner Sea. When I approached the glossy waves, emotions of defeat and failure dove into my heart, settling into a seed there and digging in roots. I took my first step into the tar colored waters.

My toes wiggled over the strange, sentient substance meeting the shore. I waded forward, holding my breath for a moment, adjusting to the shattering chill raking up my bones and the fear wrapping its hands around my throat. Submerging my calves...knees...hips, I trudged through the thick stickiness while it wound greedy tentacles up my limbs. My fingers slid between the slithering forms of corruption swimming around me like sharks gathering around a meal.

Now submerged to my chest, I peered back over my shoulder and tried to gauge my progress by the tiny sparks of green fire spitting from the wells ashore. The claws of failure clamped down on me a little harder when I saw how close I still was to the flickering light.

"C'mon, Nev. You can do this," I goaded myself. My cautious eyes scanned the waking, ebony water in front of me again.

Slimy objects bumped into me and retracted when I swatted at them. Other more curious creatures jutted out from the fluid itself and latched onto any part of my body they could grasp. I jerked against them until they gave up and left me alone.

After what seemed like hours of blind trudging, the icy floor began to graduate upward. I shuffled quicker, eager to leave the deceitful waters.

The faint glow of green sparks bled into my vision, guiding me out of Sinner Sea. My chest cleared the tarry substance, and then my waist. I squeegeed the inky fluid from my arms, slinging it from my hands while I sloshed to the shallow end. The green halos radiating from the rock wells beckoned me; *You're almost there*, they seemed to whisper.

My knees emerged, and I toppled forward, bracing myself on outstretched hands. I'd been in the sludge for so long, and was so thoroughly numb, I'd become unaccustomed to the ease of movement outside of the viscous sea.

Behind me, the sea bayed for me to stay. The whispers that followed me along my trek grew to a deafening roar. I jerked my head around, watching as the relatively calm surface thrashed into a frenzy of storm waves, rising into long, spindle-like points that crashed with the force of a building collapsing.

I clawed at the stony floor, scrambling to stand on my unsteady legs. My feet pounded forward, only a few more yards to go until I reached frigid, dry ground.

In my peripheral, thin tangles of black webbing shot out of the inches of water and flung around me, trapping my body from neck to ankles. The tarry liquid receded from the shore, lugging me backward into deeper waters.

A scream exploded from my throat as the demonic substance dragged me under like chains linking me to a plunging cinder block. I slapped my hands and legs, searching for leverage, but I only sunk deeper.

A gulp of the liquefied ick splattered into my mouth, choking off another scream. It wriggled down my throat and into my stomach as I gasped for air.

A glassy, ebony form raised at my right then wrapped around me in a cocoon and slammed me under the surface.

My eyes stung as if a million prickly needles covered every particle of the tar water overcoming me. I squeezed them shut, but that only made the agony worse. It flooded my nostrils and ears, scraping my insides raw, working to invade every hole the substance could fit into. I gritted my teeth and sealed my lips tight.

Soon, the heaviness of a millennia's worth of iniquity, and the Poseidon of Sinner Sea, weighed me down at my core, weakening my resolve. The defiant spasms of my legs and arms ceased. My body relaxed into the tragic reverie.

I couldn't overthrow this monster.

George would be trapped forever. Gavyn would perish to his loss of control...and Layla.

The water-demon seethed around me, twisting and twirling me on the currents of hatred, exuding its wicked intentions on my weak soul.

My bones bent and compressed. The flesh around my skeleton rippled. I bared my teeth at the being commanding that I conform into a mushy vessel of defilement and take my place among the rest of what dwelled in this god-forsaken place.

My foggy mind wandered, thumbing through elusive images of happy memories, searching for a moment strong enough to keep me lucid. It was all fading quickly. Minutes from now, I wouldn't be able to name the reason I'd entered this level of Hell. Only a constant reel of my sins would replay in my head — and I'm not exactly sure what version of those would haunt me into eternity.

As my body quieted in acceptance, that restless part of me rattled its cage. It punched into my ribs, growling inside. My cloud of doom swirled and jetted into cramped cavities, fighting the evil tar cramming into me.

I convulsed and arched as the sticky thickness retracted from my orifices then clambered back into me, trying to stuff my cloud back down to a manageable size.

My monster wasn't having it.

Power bubbled into my veins, pushing out from the inside, attempting to revive my will to live. My monster raged, begging for release. I was at a loss. Either I would suffocate from the evil goo invading me from the outside, or I would lose myself to the wicked beast strangling me from my core.

It didn't take long to weigh the choices during their fight to take me over.

I surrendered to the intense pressure thrashing against the cage of my ribs. My mouth opened, unable to hold the seal any longer. Out billowed the fierce cloud I'd tried so hard to contain.

Blaring groans and creaks traveled the waves of Sinner Sea and reached my ears as the last of my smoky beast fled the canals there. It flowed from me, trailing a long vaporous tail past my lips, followed by the scream trapped in my depths from the moment the dark water took over.

My head bobbed above the surface. I gasped deeply for the first breath of air I'd been able to inhale for more than five minutes. Rigid, oozing corpses gathered around me, dragging my struggling body back into the dense material. Boney hands seized my legs and arms as I jerked through the choppy, oily waters, trying to right myself.

I breached the violently crashing surface again.

Another loud gasp.

A burning desire to destroy blasted through my being, strengthening my determination. Anger...the need to continue on...the will to live?

Whatever it was, I was driven to redeem my cowardice actions.

From here on, I would be the reckoning force.

I would be the thing that was feared by all—Heaven and Hell alike.

I found footing against the uneven bottom of the sea and held my dripping arms out over the undulating waters. My dark cloud hovered just above the sentient form that reigned over the horrid ocean of sinners, tangling with its wet whip-like limbs as they lashed at my beast.

Wading forward, I pushed through the souls sentenced to this terrible fate and approached my cloud of doom. It bifurcated to the side, spreading like arms inviting me into its fold. I entered the space, feeling reconnected with a vital part of myself.

It no longer wanted to control me; it wanted me to copilot.

Regardless of how amicable the beast was to me at that moment, it still whispered to something inside me like it had left a piece of itself behind for insurance. I was stupid to think I could overcome the violence of this power, but there was nothing I could do now except embrace it.

I settled on the decision, and for the first time, unleashed every bit of control I had on the monster.

An electric current shot through my flesh, vibrated along my bones, and sizzled as it leaped from my fingertips. The watery demon sparked and screeched, cowering from the jolt. It was too slow. The current spread out in beautiful, neon-purple bolts, widening and multiplying as it ventured farther away from my body, targeting the wickedness writhing up from the black waters.

The nerves branching out through me tingled with an energy that I'd never experienced before. I felt more alive than I ever knew was possible, my senses more attuned with my surroundings.

Then, there was the downfall. That poison I'd denied, even in my descent to Hell, crept into the veins and arteries of my heart, darkening every molecule of life-force and emotion it could find. I groaned as my body adjusted to the infernal element crawling under my skin—stretching out its metaphorical legs and arms, making itself comfortable in its new freedom.

A deep, satisfied growl rumbled from my throat. I extended my hands up into my cloud, grinning in admiration as electric-purple lightning zoomed from my fingers, zapping and igniting like sparklers in an evening storm. I pulled back my hands and, in doing that, my cloud retracted, readying to obey the movements I commanded.

The power was such a rush. Tangible. Engulfing.

The ebony form glistened under the amethyst flares popping through the atmosphere. It gathered more matter from the ocean and grew in size, rearing back in an attack position. As it arched into a liquid "C" shape, dripping globs of evil from a towering height over me, I thrust my hands forward, shoving every ounce of my energy in its direction. My cloud billowed toward it at jet speed, my lightning offering a sweet burn while it arced out of my arms and zigzagged through the pitch waters until it shocked the demon of Sinner Sea.

Deafening mutated screams echoed off the toothy, stone ceiling. Stalactites fractured from the high cavern and plummeted downward, splashing into the thick, gooey ocean. Splatters of the tarry fluid hit my face, but I waded on in a slow confident path to the shore as sharp shards of rock fell around me. Vibrations from the steady electrocution surging the writhing figure tickled my legs when I plodded by. I sneered, wobbling with the choppy waters caused by the demon's agonized shifting and crashing in and out of the surface.

My high-voltage monster hovered around me like a silent tempest tethered to my heart. The victory nourished my urge to destroy, spurring the need to do it again.

I approached the shore and sloughed off the remnants of tar-like sludge. My wet feet slapped against the icy rock, and I continued my journey deeper into Hell. The fire within me now burned too hot to be affected by the numbing cold of the mirrored cavern.

Not bothering with the torches, I entered the corridor leading away from Sinner Sea. I sprinted through the snaking tunnels, resolute in reaching my destination at the end. I knew exactly where I was going and what I was going to do to get George out of Hell.

I traveled the winding paths, crossing into the next level of tunnels when my feet stamped from a hard, stony surface to a soft, dusty ground. Dirt clumped between my sticky toes with each step, but I ignored the uncomfortable feeling and continued toward George.

I passed several crevices leading to some unknown place of torture deep in the bowels of Hell, then opted for the fourth on the right. The odd shaped boulder at the foot of the opening marked this sliver of space as the one the Crucio demons had guided me down. Soft screams and groans bounced off the walls like a rock skipping across a pond. I shook my head, trying to keep focus on getting to George.

That was still my plan, right? With this new power coursing in my body, I felt different, I recognized the danger it posed, but I was still me somewhere in here, wasn't I?

I was still in control. My thoughts were my own.

From the corner of my mind, I heard a playful purr, challenging me to test my theory.

I willed the smoky haze around me to thin for a better view. The amethyst electricity crackled at frequent beats inside my personal storm, offering enough light to guide my way. The ambient cries became silent as I moved forward.

Ahead, I saw the door. The iron gargoyles glared back at me, warning me to keep my distance, but I walked closer.

Digging my fingers into the dirt wall, I pried out the sharp, gold medallion next to the door. I gladly skimmed my fingertip over the edge. My skin sliced open, and I gasped a satisfied breath from the sweet pain. Once my blood siphoned along the recessed spaces etched into the gold piece, I slammed it into the receiving ring of the door. The etchings melted and shifted, morphing into what I assumed would become the raised reflection of my face like last time.

The swirls of gold wound and melted, building an exact miniature of my likeness. I crossed my arms and stared at it expectantly while it formed. The peak of my straight nose emerged, then my high cheekbones and small chin. Next, tiny versions of my almond-shaped eyes popped open and glowered back at me as if I'd just woken her from a deep sleep. My body stiffened in preparations for the door's hot, metal vines to reach out for me.

Nothing happened.

I scanned the decorative iron framing, smoothing my hands over the looping swirls and bends. The metal was warm, but unmoving.

My eyes darted back to the stern, gold face within the ring and noted its opening mouth. Small lips moved around unspoken words. I backed up a step and tried to decipher the message but couldn't understand any part of it. Suddenly, the tiny eyes seemed to plead with me frantically, then jerked to study the silent space behind me.

The atmosphere thickened in the tunnel and rushed into the small dugout area in front of the door, rolling around me in a dense smog. My dominant presence now felt cramped and inferior compared to whatever was approaching. I turned toward the tunnel and braced myself for the force of power approaching.

As quick, shallow breaths flooded my lungs, the sour odor of Hell intensified. A low baying sounded from the dark tunnel; a cross between a purring cat and a snake's rattle. I backed closer to the door with nowhere else to go. My fists balled anxiously at my sides then flicked open several times. Sparks popped from my fingertips. My skin prickled from the charge accumulating in my hands.

The ground vibrated beneath me in short, succinct intervals. Dust rattled from the ceiling with each beat.

That sinister matter of my soul stretched out and cooed, sensing the impending evil crowding the only exit. My ferocious cloud calmed and loomed close, intrigued by the pure wickedness calling out to me. I felt the need to obey and submit myself to its commands before I even saw the creature heading my way.

"Did you think I wouldn't figure out where you were going? Do you think I don't know everything you do?" A displeased voice boomed, forcing a shiver down my spine. "I had high hopes for you, Nevaeh." The words grew louder as the being neared the tunnel's opening.

"Sorry to disappoint," I muttered.

The hunched form squeezed out of the tunnel and stopped, planting its knuckles on the floor to brace its massive weight in a squatted position. My electric-purple glow highlighted its smooth, rubbery skin and the tight muscles bunching under the surface. Dragging giant black wings from the opening, the Father of Hell stretched upward, his body still too large to fit in the dugout. His red eyes burned with fury as they bore into me.

"I see you've learned a few new tricks since we spoke last," he snarled, assessing my flickering cloud.

I cinched my lips shut, refusing to answer, to give into his gravity and submit. The deviant side of me gladly wanted to bow down and relish under the scrutiny of the Master. It took everything I had not to drop to my knees.

"Doesn't it feel good?" His lips curled up, revealing glinting, sharp teeth. "We are so close, my child. Just let go of the last string. Cut that last tie, and we can assume our deserved positions among both worlds."

I shook my head. "What more do you want from me? I've already forfeited the last of my soul to this horrid place. You have me." I leaned into the iron between me and the door, praying it would come to life under the pressure of my body and take me to the other side.

He tsked, crouching down inches from my face. His curved horns trapped me against the metal framework, curling around me at either shoulder. "You haven't given in, not really." Puffs of hot breath wafted over my skin. "Your body cries out for me. Your soul begs for my attention. But, I can see it there in the back of your mind. Even now, staring into your eyes, I can see the glimpse of defiance buried inside that pretty head of yours. Until you release every bit of will over to me, we can't achieve the fate you are destined to fulfill."

I lowered my gaze to the immense chest heaving sulfuric breaths at me as he spoke.

Hadn't I released the darkness within?

My thoughts were mingling with the need to mindlessly do whatever the Devil wanted. My coherence was waning.

He was right. There *was* still a pea-sized piece of me that was gripping onto morality. I'd hoped to hang onto my humanity just long enough to get George out of Hell, then whatever happened, happened.

211

However, I'd lost my element of surprise. This was the Devil, and I couldn't escape his clutch anymore. The moment I severed myself from God, I agreed to be his slave. For whatever reason, he had tolerated my rebellion before. Everything I'd done up to this point was with his permission on some level. He had allowed me to feel like I'd gained footing during the few times I thought I had. Maybe, that was his plan — to ensure I developed my gifts. The domineering stare in his eyes told me he was done, though.

I couldn't save George. I couldn't save myself. All my attempts to do either had been in vain.

A searing pain radiated through the gunky fabric of my shirt and burned my back. I sucked air in through my teeth from the discomfort but didn't dare move. The sensation pulled my focus from the self-doubt snowballing in my mind and brought me back to reality. I raised my gaze, glaring at the crimson eyes watching me with a victorious smile.

The iron moved behind me, prodding my shoulder blades and spine, then slithered to new positions. I straightened my shoulders.

His hairless, hooded brow crinkled, suspicion becoming clear on his angled face.

How I still had some resemblance of control over my mischievous powers was beyond me, but I did. Somehow, I'd managed to release the monster in me, use my abilities, and still not give up on George or the hope that I could pull through this.

My will solidified.

His smug smile tightened into a sneer as I grinned back at him.

The iron rods burned red-hot when they finally unfolded and curved around my body, I cried out from the nerve-deadening agony, but kept my narrowed eyes on him.

"Don't for a second think you can get away from me, Nevaeh," the Devil said through gritted teeth. His ebony palm covered my torso and the cage of heated metal, attempting to pry me from the door. Sharp claws bit into my skin while the door secured me under the rods.

I grimaced through the tugging and squeezing, balled my fists against my thighs and thrust all my power outward. The moment my fingers extended, the calm cloud hovering above us rushed down and blanketed me in a shroud of blackness. Violent currents of amethyst lightning shot out from my hands, zapping the Devil.

His hand released me, yanking out of my cloud as if he'd laid it on a hot stove. Rage-filled curses echoed off the walls.

I ground my teeth through the pain of being pinned and scorched by the bars, unable to move or scream properly.

The door finally flipped end over end, my cloud sucked to the other side with me like it was vacuumed through an exhaust vent.

I dropped to the pavement, grunting from the impact on my limbs. I was in George's Hell, again. The single streetlamp shined on the slippery road, rain poured down from the moonless sky, and the far away dots of headlights broke into the dark terrain less than a mile from where I kneeled.

I pushed myself up, wiping my dirty palms on even dirtier pant legs. My cloud hovered close to my back, waiting for my next command. The rare flicker of amethyst current sparked in my peripheral every so often, perhaps slowing in syncopation with my own emotions, quieting in anticipation of stealing George.

Heavy rain drenched my hair and clothes, raising to a rushing flow over the ground. I stood silent, watching the events of George's wreck. I could almost recount the motions by second-hand, programmed to be the same every time it happened.

One-tick, two-tock, three-tick. George's headlights veer off the flooded highway.

Four, Five, Six. The boom of the crash cuts into the air, and the tall oak bends over the mutilated car.

Seven, eight, nine. George cries out for his dead wife, frantic and confused by the consequences of his mistake.

Ten, eleven, twelve. The banged-up spirit of the man I'd considered my father stumbles from the car, searching for a daughter he'd lost long before he found me.

As my eyes took in the commotion, my heart remained numb. There was no gut-wrenching empathy, or love, or even rage. I winced, understanding the meaning of my emotionless response. I was losing myself faster than I'd thought. Freeing George was not something I necessarily wanted to do anymore, but more a task that needed to be finished; a mere chore I had to check off my list before giving into my losing battle with humanity.

I picked up one foot and placed it in front of the other, treading through inches of water to get to George before the reenactment of his family's demise undid itself. Approaching the rear of the car, I found him rocking back and forth on the ground.

My dooming cloud was nearly too black for me to see against the background of the night, but I could feel it simmering with power. I opened my senses, surpassing my connection with the beast, and gathered the last of my will to help George before squatting down behind him.

Thunder boomed over the pounding rain. White lightning cast a swift glow on the area surrounding us. In that brief moment of sight, I spotted the hulking, ebony monster slinking around to my right. I pivoted on the balls of my feet and shielded George's soul.

"Ah. I see you are more cunning than I gave you credit for." A deep drone followed his words. "I will have you one way or another. You will see that I am the sole purpose you were born, Nevaeh." The Devil's growl rattled low in his massive chest. "You have no other choice. Don't prolong the inevitable, my child." His taloned hand smacked down against the wet pavement, creeping closer to me.

I glanced over my shoulder at a shuddering George, weeping for his losses. I knew I should be drowning in pain for him, but I just couldn't muster the emotion. What I felt was an urge to surrender to the Dark Master, to rip the world apart with the hate and anger churning in my gut. The evil circulating in my veins quickened at the thought of taking control of my power and using it to sculpt a human realm that would make the Father of Lies proud — and I could with so little effort.

I drew in a deep breath as the lightning flickered across the black, muscular form once more. "You can have my soul tomorrow, Devil," I hissed, willing my cloud to billow in around George and I, "Today, I'm getting what I came for."

The winged brute lunged forward as the last of my cloud surrounded us, thickening to an impenetrable shield. Purple electric zapped at a rapid pace, enhancing the barrier. My enemy wailed from outside my protective globe. He hammered his big fists against my shield while threatening to rip the world apart.

With each empty promise he made, and every unimaginable threat he barked, my armor cracked a little more. The heaviness of denying him pressed against my shoulders with a firm grip that would drill me into the ground if I didn't move quickly.

I lowered to my knees facing George and stared into his sobbing eyes. Images of his life's mistakes flashed along the inner wall of my cloud as all my victims' lives had done. My eyes flicked to each of his sins.

The sudden need to punish him began to boil in my body. I gasped, squeezing my eyes shut to block out the impulse. My fingers dug into my thighs, and I leaned forward. "I'm sorry if this doesn't work, George, but it's our last chance. I have to try."

I parted my lips and inhaled slowly, tasting the sweetness of George's soul graze over my tongue. An intense euphoria rushed through my body, and I nearly toppled to the ground. I swallowed the vaporous substance down. When I opened my eyes, George's soul was gone, yet I could feel him inside me.

I knew his thoughts, his emotions, his wishes and prayers.

I wasn't sure what to expect, but I suppose I had assumed my body would react like the Animus Demon's—eager to release the foreign being inside me. Instead, I felt calm. Even the yearning to punish had subsided. My darkness didn't hold any ill will toward George. It had already cast its judgment and deemed him worthy of love. What lingered now was a compulsion to carry him far away from here. He was not meant to spend his eternity in this horrid place, regardless of his past.

This was what I was made to do, not reign next to the Prince of Lies, wreaking havoc on the world.

I held my hand out at my side, allowing the thin membrane of Hell's air to swirl around my fingers. Picturing the city I had loved for so long, I drew the flickering bolts to my palm and concentrated them into a small ball of amethyst light. I winced at the sudden onset of scorching heat radiating through my fingers.

The scene of George's Hell began to peel away from the space in front of my hand and took flight on a gust of wind like a burning leaf. Inches from my skin, the window to an empty playground opened, quiet under a twilight sky. A low fog in the human realm whooshed in through the portal, tangling around my legs as I stepped out of Hell with the very thing I thought I might never save.

Archard

CHAPTER TWENTY

No More Keep-Away

After slamming back to my own reality, Arkin, Arianna, and I sat in silence for a few awkward minutes. My mind struggled to brake against Arianna's constant repeating memories overlapping my own.

I opened my eyes and grimaced at the meek face staring at me from the other side of the table. A slight line formed above the bridge of her nose, and she tugged her upper lip between her teeth like Nevaeh did when she was nervous or anxious.

My eyes snapped shut again, attempting to right the tornado of thoughts swirling in my head. The room was spinning at ninety miles an hour. I grabbed the back of the empty chair next to me and used it to hoist unsteady muscles into motion. Halfway up into a standing position, I toppled back down to my seat. An infuriated groan erupted from my throat.

My lids drew open, and I slowly slid my eyes toward Arkin. His forehead was resting on the edge of the table, heavy breaths heaving from his mouth. A string of drool dripped from his tightened lips and fell onto his bouncing knee. His palms pressed against his temples so hard I thought he might smash his skull at any minute.

"What the hell was that about, Arianna?" I slurred.

"That was a window into my life, my dear. I wanted to show you what we'd been through—what we had sacrificed and why." Arianna rose from her chair and approached my side.

My gaze flicked to the calculated movement of her hand reaching out to my shoulder. I jerked away from her touch, nearly vomiting from the action. "Don't," I yelled in a clumsy demand.

"I can soothe the disorientation effects."

She placed a hand on each of my shoulders from behind and traced her fingers upwards until she found my ears.

"Just hold still."

Her palms cupped my lobes, muffling Arkin's whines. A shrill tone pierced the muted background and resonated in my brain for a few beats. I grimaced, grinding my teeth together through the discomfort. When Arianna removed her hands, I scanned the room with perfect clarity. No more head-spinning, no more disrupted balance.

I slid my hands over my face, smoothing out the residual tension from before, while Arianna fixed Arkin.

She lifted her hands from my brother's ears, but he still clutched the edge of the table. His cautious gaze followed Arianna as she lowered into the seat in front of us.

Arkin's white-knuckled fingers finally let go of the table, and he slumped into the cushion of his wings, pinning them awkwardly to the chair back.

"What in the Hell was that about, Arianna?" I grumbled.

She folded her thin arms over her middle and shrugged a slender shoulder. "The past. A way to see who we were. Perhaps, the only way I knew how to tell you everything I know." Her shameful eyes lowered to her forearms as she picked at a stray thread on her sleeve. "I didn't want you to judge my disloyalty without knowing my reasons."

"Disloyalty to whom?" Arkin interrupted.

Arianna's eyes darted up to Arkin. "To God...my daughter?"

I leaned forward. "You sacrificed a life on Earth and the love of a family to damn yourself to a place filled with those constantly ascending to a Heaven you never got to experience." I chuckled in disbelief. "That in itself is a personal hell you didn't deserve. There is no disloyalty in doing what you felt was right for the care of others."

The sadness and regret in her eyes lessened an infinitesimal amount, and a smile graced her lips. "Thank you," she whispered.

"Now, what do you propose we do with this insight you've offered?"

"I spent many nights pouring over the Clavis, trying to decrypt its prophecy when Nevaeh was young, but I couldn't make sense of it. I settled on the fact that there seems to be hope that, even if she submits to the darkness within her, there is a chance she will pull through. I don't think it's up to us to figure out how it's used. We need to hand over the book," she said pointedly.

"Hand it to whom?" There wasn't anyone in the game that I trusted enough to hold the Clavis except for us.

"Nevaeh." The certainty in her voice indicated she'd thought this over for a very long time.

"And why is that?" I asked, shoving out of my chair to begin a slow pace around the room. "I've been told by more than one being that she shouldn't get her hands on it? Why should I risk what her evil side might unleash and put it straight into her hands?" I paused, awaiting her answer.

She raised up and leaned over the table, bracing herself on boney knuckles. With narrowed eyes, she spoke, "From what I read, she can't return to our side until she is pushed to her bottom. There was no option of never turning, only *returning*. She can't come back to us if we don't offer her a way out. Let's give her the book and hope that there is enough good in her to do the right thing."

A thunderous laugh poured from my chest. Positioning my restless fists on the table, I glared at Arianna. "Give her the book and *hope* there's enough good in her? Wow, that makes so much sense now. I don't know why we didn't think of giving the book to a woman with the power to open portals to Hell, and God knows what else, with that black cloud following her around."

"She is my daughter. Bred from my Celeta blood. She can do this. I have faith in her." Arianna forced her words through a clenched jaw, looking ready to pounce on me with any disagreement.

Arkin squirmed in his seat, shifting his gaze from me to her. "Ari, we know she can, but what if she doesn't want to? She was also bred from demon blood." His words were calm and genuine. "Freewill can be an unfortunate thing in some beings' hands," he reminded.

Her hard eyes stayed focused on mine. "God would not have given her these powers knowing that she would abandon us." She hesitated and took a deep breath. "Please, Archard. You know her better than anyone. You are her Guardian. Trust that she will choose to be the Celata God intended."

I relaxed my body and huffed out a conceding puff of air, settling back into my slow pace. "Even if we agreed to do this, how would we get it back to her? Kenet sure as shit won't help us. Would she even have the things she needed to fulfill the prophecy?"

Arianna crossed an arm over her chest, while her other hand fondled absently with her bottom lip, and she considered my concerns.

Arkin swiveled in his chair to face me. "Well, we have the book, what else do we need?"

"Original love's blood," Arianna whispered.

I stopped moving, pondering her words. "Yours and Rhett's?"

She shook her head. "What Rhett and I had was never love. It's likely Kenet's and mine."

"Okay, that gives us two of the pieces. What about the third and fourth? The key and the traitor's plume?" I asked, wearing a path in the floor. "I'm assuming the traitor's plume is one of Rhett's feathers."

"That's what I figured. More specifically, his writing plume. Mom kept it separate from the book after we came to that conclusion. Didn't want to make it too easy for anyone to get all of the tools, ya know?"

I nodded my head while rubbing my hand over the scruff of beard covering my chin. "So, we need to find the feather he used to write the prophecy. That should be easy. Where did Theora keep it?"

My eyes focused on Arianna as she dropped her gaze to the floor, the corners of her mouth turning down into a frown.

"I'm not sure. She didn't even tell me where she kept the book after I gave it back to her at the end of my study sessions. It was too dangerous for me to know…in case I was caught by the demons."

Arkin leaped up and smacked his hands together. "I know exactly where it is!"

Arianna and I watched a knowing grin curve his lips, his wings ruffling behind him with excitement.

"During the visions, I stayed close to Theora when she was around. We were glued together like the old days." His caramel eyes glistened at the happy thoughts of him being near his charge. "At night, she would shuffle the book and the quill around various hiding spots throughout the house. I remembered her doing this, but I never knew what the damn book was. She never opened it in front of me.

"That last night, before we ran with Nevaeh, Theora hid them in the most obvious place, hoping the demons would think we had them with us. She knew her shields on Nev's room would hold long enough for them to come after us and forget about the old house."

"You're killing me here, Arkin," I groaned impatiently.

"Brother, we're going back to the farm." His broad shoulders shook with a light chuckle. "The feather is in Nev's bed. Stuffed inside her baby pillow. I saw her wrapping the book in one of Nev's blankets a few nights before Arianna left. She stored it under some old pictures in her hope-chest, then she picked a loose seam in Nevaeh's pillow and tucked the feather inside."

"You didn't think that was important enough to tell me after we lost Nev?" My voice echoed against the walls as I stalked toward Arkin.

He held his hands out between us in a defensive stance, backing away

221

from me. "Hey, man, I honestly didn't remember the damn thing until mommy here blew our minds back in time. I didn't even realize that it was the book until today. You know how Theora liked to save her baubles. I thought it was just another history tome she'd collected. How was I supposed to know when they never discussed what was in it?"

Arianna's hand wrapped around my wrist without me even realizing she had advanced to my side. "He's right, Archard. There was no way he could have known. Even you didn't know. We figured our Guardians would be close and couldn't risk one of you finding out that the prophecy was real then telling the other angels. They would have hunted her like the demons."

My body relaxed under her touch and her words. She was right. The women had done well not to discuss anything in the open. And, just like I was oblivious to the bits and pieces of Arianna's and Theora's life outside of Nevaeh, I couldn't expect Arkin to know what was going on either.

"How did Theora know anything at all about the prophecy then?" I asked, feeling like I was missing a clue.

Arianna tapped an index finger to her temple. "We had our ways. It was the only way we could communicate safely after I found out I was pregnant with Nevaeh. We showed each other our thoughts for years before then…since I was a little girl really. We learned enough through our history as Celatum, and our exposure to the otherworld, to know we had to be careful—there were eyes everywhere. So, I implanted my thoughts into mom's head then kept an open path for me to listen in on hers in case she had something to tell me. She guarded us against those with similar abilities using her protection powers."

A low chuckle sounded from my left. "You are some sneaky little foxes," Arkin chortled, placing his hands on his hips.

I shook my head, dismissing my brother's amusement from Arianna's confession. "You think it's still there?"

Arianna nodded once. "It's a possibility." Her sapphire eyes slanted to the side, glossing over with unshed tears. "I just don't know what condition the farm is in now that mom's gone. The shield would've dissipated with her passing. There's no telling what the demons did after you guys left."

"Well, unfortunately, her powers didn't seem to help much in the end anyway," I reminded.

Arianna scowled at me. "The demons broke the barrier with help," she snapped, defending her mother's abilities. "Only someone that had a personal tie to one of us could've assisted in their crossing over the perimeter."

I thought in silence for a moment. If I didn't do it, and I was positive Arkin wouldn't have either, there was only one left. "Rhett," I snarled.

"Maybe." Arianna frowned. "I just don't know how he could have controlled the demons, let alone penetrate my mother's shield. I don't think he had the ability to create a breach in our wall, especially after giving up his Holiness." She shuffled over to her seat and slumped down, looking tired.

I followed her and planted my knuckles on the table, leaning down to study her reaction to my next proposal. "Alright, if not him, then what about Kenet?"

If her eyes could've shot bullets, I'd have quite the hole in my skull. The sharp lines on her forehead and flared nostrils told me she was not inclined to think Kenet could be part of such a plot against her family.

"He loved us. Why would he sacrifice me to a life in purgatory for the sake of keeping the demons away, just to lead them right to my baby?" "He does have the power to open portals, Ari. He's a demon. Kenet could have opened one inside the perimeters. That's probably how he got past your mom when he came to visit you. He might have been testing the limits. Sending you to the spirit realm could've been his plan to get you *away* from Nevaeh," Arkin pointed out.

The absolute refusal in Arianna's eyes shifted to the angel lingering behind me. "Kenet was trying to reverse his demonic change. I don't for a second think he had anything to do with this. He loved us." Her last words came out with a whimper as her gaze drifted to the table, reluctantly considering what Arkin had said.

"It's a valid argument. You have to admit that, Arianna," I urged softly.

A second later, her head shook, denying Kenet's involvement in silence.

Arkin inhaled a deep breath, flexing his indigo-stained wings out behind him then settling them back down against his back, his platinum feathers clanging into one another as he ruffled them into place.

"What's done is done. We can waste time arguing about who let the demons in later. Let's go to the farm and find that feather."

His strong hand gripped my shoulder, attempting to calm my agitated state. "If Ari is right, we need to spend our time figuring out how to get this stuff to Nev when we find it...and how to stop her if she doesn't see eye to eye with our plan."

I raised off my fists and gritted my teeth as I retracted the crests of my wings back into the pockets of muscle on my back, pulling them in tight. "I'll grab my coat. We'll go to the farm," I conceded, hesitant to return to Nev's home, "but there's someone we need to bring along."

"Who?" Arkin asked, grabbing his own duster from a corner chair and shrugging it on.

"Malach. If things don't go as planned, he's the only one I trust enough with the book. He'll do the right thing, no matter what." I tugged my duster over my wings and onto my arms then stilled. "Even if it means ending Nevaeh."

Arkin's eyes met mine, eyebrows raised in disbelief, perhaps to my faith in Malach, or maybe to my acknowledgment of what might have to occur to save the world.

"I don't know if I can hurt her. I love her too much."

A sharp pain pierced my heart with the realization of just how far I might let Nevaeh go if her powers consumed all the goodness she possessed. I may deliver the humans to her on a silver platter if it meant having her back in my arms.

Nevaeh

CHAPTER TWENTY-ONE

Evil In Every Corner

Twigs and branches splintered under my heavily pounding feet. Loud breaths raced in and out of my mouth, mingling with the eerie sounds made by the many creatures of the night. I glanced around, feeling curious eyes studying me from the shadows. Cicadas, owls, and coyotes chattered from unseen corners of the forest surrounding me, mimicking shrill screams and mischievous laughs that only added to my paranoia.

I zig-zagged around tall pines as if I was bouncing inside of a pin ball machine, leaping over fallen trunks and dodging low hanging brush.

The Hell portal had transported me to a playground, leaving me at a disadvantage with all the open space. It was far too easy for someone to see me.

The second I laid foot on this side's soil, I ran like...well, like the Devil was chasing me. I couldn't let them catch me before I put George somewhere safe. There would be no stopping until He was on his way to Heaven.

Unfortunately, my very human body still tired quickly. Fatigue and cramping had set into my muscles long before I left the demon world. Forming the portal and harboring another's soul within me, not to mention the constant physical and emotional wear and tear of my inner darkness, had me praying for a week of nothing but sleep.

That would have to wait.

I was slowly but steadily moving my way to somewhere more familiar. Flashes of George's memory popped in and out of my vision, guiding my way back to the inner city. His soul seemed well-aware of our location and knew which routes to take.

The vivid knowledge of George's soul, and the internal workings imprinted on it, threw me for a loop as I tried to accommodate his presence inside me while escaping from certain damnation. I wasn't sure how my body could house so many different...personalities? No. Essences? Whatever they were—my beast, the black seed rooted deep down in my core, George, and a very dimly lit part of myself—seemed docile, accepting their confinement within my small frame for the time being. I guess everyone was on the same page, knowing what would happen if I were captured, and didn't want to be the one to draw attention.

I grunted, stumbling over a crooked hunk of wood crossing my path, but I kept moving. The land began to slope upward into a slight hill. A persistent burning in my thighs increased with the higher terrain, and it felt as though I would never make it to the top. I surveyed the thick trees, barely able to see three feet away, but finally saw the first sign of the forest's edge when I climbed the incline. The yellow cast of a billion stars backlit the old pines, and beyond the thinning woods, artificial blue light radiated from a streetlight.

I tumbled out of the woods, landing on my hands and knees, panting. Welcoming the break, I leaned down and rested my forehead against the cool patch of grass framed between my thumbs. Salty sweat coated my lips as it dripped from my face and fell to the ground.

Just one minute. That's all I need, I thought to the others in my body.

An unexpected mutated howl resonated from the direction I'd come. My breath hitched. My head jerked up and stared into the tree line, waiting to hear the horrid call again. Chaos broke out inside me, my chest rattling with the panicked impatience of my monster. A slew of broken words flooded my mind, all in Georges voice.

"Go. Run aw…Hell houn…Now. Ru…"

I squinted, studying an open area in the woods about ten feet to my left. Two large, silvery reflections shined back at me. They skulked toward me, along the shadowy canopy created by the infinite number of pine needles over its head. It moved into the light of the street lamp, and I gasped.

A tiny figure stamped a bare foot onto the grassy area past the trees, and then the other, in shy, cautious movements. It ducked its small form under a low branch and stared at me. I stood up, surprised by the child studying me with its mercury eyes. Pale skin nearly glowed against the shadows framing him.

I took a step closer to the boy, scanning over the dirt smudged toes, bald head, and shredded bits of dingy clothing covering his scrawny body. *He couldn't be a threat; he was just a child*. My shoulders relaxed, and fear left my tense muscles.

"Hello," I greeted, inching toward the boy. Inside, George's voice clambered against my skull. My chest tightened under the pressure of my monster working its way up to my throat. I dug the heels of my palms into my temples, and squeezed my eyelids shut, trying to calm the chaos heightening within me.

When I opened my eyes, I jerked in surprise. The child was standing only a foot away now. There was no sound with his movements. A sense of dangerous mystery exuded from his silvery eyes.

I forced my hands down, though the calamity of George and my monster threatened to bring to my knees.

The boy tilted his head as if determining whether to trust me or not. His thin lips grinned awkwardly around a thin bracketing of metal fastened at the back of his head. It curved around to line his bony jaw like a well fitted piece of jewelry and disappeared into the corners of his mouth.

My eyes narrowed, focusing on the harsh, muzzle-like apparatus. Tiny locking mechanisms were popped open on either side of his head, just above his ears, making the bracket appear broken and incomplete. A vital part of it was missing on the front — the mouth cover.

Another gargled howl rang out from the depths of the forest. The boy's gaze darted toward the sound then returned to me. His youthful features transitioned at the blink of an eye.

Smooth brows angled deeply over his reflective eyes. A small button nose flared and pulled tight as the bones of his upper palate and cheeks shifted in a fluid motion. Two mouthfuls worth of teeth shifted, slanting forward and stretching out past his taunt lips until they were a nearly horizontal array of razor-sharp fangs. The boy's upper and lower jaws widened and elongated, tugging against the two wires hooking into his mouth. His lips and gums peeled back from the tension and revealed even more of his deadly teeth.

When the child's transformation finished, I looked into a disturbingly distorted human face with the extremely exaggerated snout of a rabid dog. I stumbled back, falling on my ass in the slick grass.

George shouted in my mind, "Ge...up. Run. Hell Hou..."

The child buckled his knees and bent over, resting his hands on the ground between his feet. Spittle sprayed onto my shins as he snarled and snapped his teeth at me. I shoved myself backward along the ground, but the child moved with me.

"Leave me alone," I commanded in a strained voice. My monster was clawing its way up without my permission. Considering the small being chasing me, I hesitated in granting my darkness freedom. Was it still a child on the inside? Could I kill a kid, even though it would clearly take me out at first chance?

Multiple bodies skittered about in my peripheral, stealing my attention from the boy at my feet. There were more of them, all adorned with the same harness that held back their faces to allot the extra inches of protruding maws jutting forward.

A sharp pain bit into the arch of my right foot and radiated up my leg. When the scream left my mouth, so did the dark cloud, but I didn't stop it. Blackness edged into my vision as its tendrils seeped out around my eyes. I widened my lips, encouraging it to leave my body so I could breathe again. My beast spewed forth in a rush, zapping amethyst bolts of lightning into the air.

The Devil's hounds were on me in a split second, totally unaffected by the power spilling into the space around us. Fangs pierced the flesh on my arms, shoulders, and thighs. Hot blood soaked into my shirt and pants.

I wrenched my arms away from the scavengers and thrust my hands toward the sky. My cloud mushroomed into a column above us, then crashed down with the flick of my finger. Bolts of electric-purple jumped out from the smoky substance, electrocuting each creature in synchronization.

Wolf-like yelps and whimpers tore into the atmosphere. They ripped their teeth out of my limbs and retreated to a safer distance but didn't venture too far.

I pushed off the ground, managing to prop myself upright on weak legs. Trails of crimson vined around my forearms and dripped from my shaking fingertips. I slowed my panting breaths, gathering the power I needed to finish these deceitful beings.

Their cautious gazes bounced between me and the black cloud hovering a few feet above. The hunger in their shiny eyes told me that they had no intention of surrendering. They understood the terms— death for them or death for me—and wouldn't stop until the deed was done.

Suddenly, one of the children was by my side. No warning. No crawling, walking, or skulking. It was just there. On instinct, I directed a bolt of energy to strike the small body. It flew backwards, thumping onto the ground, and convulsed for a moment. When it stilled, the extended teeth drew back, tucking neatly behind its slick lips. I stared at the child, quiet and motionless in the grass as if it were sleeping.

The next little creeper took its turn, popping up inches to my left. Another jolt arced through the air with the flick of my hand, hurling the hell hound onto its back five feet away, blood spurting form its mouth as it hit the soil.

Four more remained.

Two of them came at me at the same time. I wound my hands in circles, directing my cloud to divide and spin into twin cyclones. The whirling funnels engulfed the little demons and flung them back into the forest. Angry howls filled the distance until two loud thuds stopped their protest, followed by the sound of a tree cracking and falling.

Satisfied, I smiled and offered my attention to the last of the creatures standing. The hum of my power charged the air, awaiting my next demand. Feelings of sympathy for the devilish children had vanished rather quickly after freeing my over-exuberant beast.

One of the imps shifted its weight from foot to foot anxiously, mercury eyes zoned in on me. The child that had approached me before the others rested on its haunches with a calm expression on its canine face—as calm as it could appear anyway. It barked at the uneasy hound to its right. The restless demon cowered behind its leader, resisting the urge to pounce at me.

A fiery red bled into the leader's quick-silver eyes. Its shoulders hunched forward, arching its back. Three strained grunts exploded from its muzzle, sounding strangely similar to a cat coughing up a fur ball. With one quick motion, the creature's head whipped around one hundred eighty degrees. It looked up at the sky for a moment, then tipped its head backwards to face me from an inverted position, red-hot eyes boring into me.

My skin tingled under the evil gaze.

Its jaw cracked open slightly. Words began to flow from its unmoving mouth. "You can run as long as you want, Nevaeh, but in the end, you will be mine." The synchronized voices of the Devil's legion crawled up my spine and took root under my skin. "I have eyes and ears everywhere, my child. Don't ever doubt my ability to find you." A strangled wheeze expelled from the demon's throat.

I shivered and addressed the Devil. "Why don't you come get me yourself? I'm right here, asshole." My cloud started undulating a little quicker overhead, responding to my flighty emotions and fluttering nerves. I was drawn to the wickedness seeping from the boy, yet my own power refused to fall under the Hell King's spell.

The legion of voices growled in irritation. "I will have you. Whether it's me or one of my infinite soldiers, you will bow to me. Soon." The boy cackled, his small body shaking from the noise that was too grand for him to accommodate. "As for what you stole from me, I will create a special place for that soul. One that is far worse than anything you could ever imagine. I will throw him to the deepest level of Hell. To a maddening room that will have no key and no way to reach it."

"Over my dead body," I whispered, picturing the place he described. I would gladly die with George's soul stuck inside me before letting him go back to that.

"Oh no, my child. You will live to see every bit of it from afar, unable to help him in any way." Again, the child trembled with a cackle.

I thrust both of my hands out before me, forcing the black cloud and a steady vibration of electric toward the Hell hound. He continued to laugh as he watched my power blast through the distance between us. In an instant, the legion was silent. The child-hound, catching fire from the heat of my bolts, swooped up into the air and flew as far as my strength could hurl it. It disappeared into the night sky.

Opening my mouth, I called the tendrils of smoky substance and streaks of amethyst light back into the cage of my body. Seconds later, I swallowed hard and sealed the last of the cloud inside my fortress.

"Angel," George whispered in my mind.

I nodded, turned, and set foot on the sidewalk leading into the city.

It felt like years since I'd stood in front of Joe's. An eternity of life altering events in mere months can really mess up your perception of time—not to mention the stint I spent in the depths of Hell.

I examined the beautifully weathered building. A multitude of chipped bricks, the squeaking sign swinging above the red door, and four murky windows permitting me a distorted view of the empty café inside caused my heart to skip. I wanted to go back to that day. The one where I first looked up at Gavyn's home and business optimistic of a bright new future and a sense of well-being. If it were possible, I'd spit on the front step and run far away.

My lips twisted into a sneer.

Hindsight was a bitch.

I lifted my gaze to the second-floor window. A dim light spilled out into the misty morning air. Malach was my only chance at getting George to Heaven where he belonged, and this was the last place I saw him. I bit my top lip on the decision to push forward and hope for the best, ignoring the growing unease stirring the beings inside me.

Bending over, I reached for a clump of broken stone laying at the base of the steps then climbed up to the door. I palmed the knob and tried turning it, but the cold metal wouldn't budge.

"Okay. Time for plan B." I drew back my hand and smashed the jagged piece of stone into the warped glass beside the door. Dozens of thick shards tumbled down the brick façade and landed at my bare, mud- caked feet. Tiny red dots appeared on my skin where a few of the shards bit into my flesh on the way down.

I guided my hand past the broken teeth of glass in the window frame and hooked my arm around the wall. The rough bricks grated against my cheek as I stood on my tip-toes and pressed into the building, straining to achieve a longer reach. Blindly, I moved my fingers back and forth along the inside wall, finding light switches and the soft buttons of the alarm's keypad. I knew I didn't have to worry about setting off the alarm system since Gavyn had failed to get it hooked up when he bought the business. A moment later, the smooth, thin lever of a deadbolt came into range. I grinned when the pleasing click of its rotation unlocked the door.

I stepped into the old café and inhaled the welcoming odor of fruit and sandwiches ingrained in its surfaces. My eyes adjusted to the dark quickly as I walked in a straight path toward the back of the building.

"Don't go up," George whispered when I approached the stairway leading to Gavyn's apartment. "You can't go up," he repeated. A knot of panic coiled in my gut. I hesitated and wrapped my arms around my stomach, noting that the anxiety was not my own but his. Such a strange sensation to feel someone else's emotions.

"We have to. Malach is our only hope at getting you where you need to be." I lifted a foot and set it on the step in front of me, focusing on the closed door at the top. When I tried to lift my other foot, it wouldn't move. I could feel a cool tingling in my leg and knew it was there, but it wasn't obeying my brain's commands.

"Can't," George argued.

"George, I have to. Stop whatever you're doing, and let me go," I demanded. The hold he had on my leg continued. I grunted, tugging and shifting my weight to break free. Wrapping my fingers around the rail and holding tight, I gritted my teeth and struggled to keep my shit together. Regardless of who was up there, I had to at least see for myself. If it wasn't Malach, I would deal with it—deal with whoever it was—and move on to another plan.

"Not Ma…," George growled in my skull.

My beast began its restless pacing along my patience, stirring fury inside me that was becoming hard to ignore. Tingles of electric charged my fingertips, heating the metal railing in my hand to a dull orange glow.

"Not Malach. I get it, George. Let go before we're all in trouble." Wispy puffs of black cloud escaped my mouth on the breath forcing my words out. My chest and throat grew uncomfortable with the "too crowded" feeling I got just before the raging cloud erupted.

My foot released from the floor, and I lurched forward, catching myself on my hands and knocking my right knee into the next step up. The tightening in my torso loosened. I swallowed hard, gulping down escaping wisps of my beast.

"Good choice. I don't think I could have held it in much longer," I whispered to the now quiet soul.

Allowing my monster to have her freedom brought me new power, and though the purpose of the power was still unknown, I didn't regret it. The problem was that I had to assume some control over her, or the wickedness hiding in that shadowy corner of my soul, the demonic entity I figured I was born with, would ride its way out with her and never let me pull it back in. My actions and thoughts would be driven by an evil that would most certainly not agree to convert or surrender. I felt it in Sinner Sea, with the Hell hounds, and just now as an anger bubbled through my body. It wouldn't take much to flip my switch. I had to be careful to remember that, to choose my battles with my beast, to be sure the circumstances were right for letting her out.

Arguing with George over going into Gavyn's apartment was not the right circumstance to unleash my cloud of judgment and fury.

I took two steps at a time, climbing the stairs, then slowed at the top. The door was cracked, a sliver of light shining out from the table lamp in Gavyn's living room. I pressed my index finger into the door, urging it open. All was quiet.

"Malach?" I called, crossing the threshold. George was eerily silent, and my insides rolled with the thunder-like pressure my monster yielded. The hair on my arms and neck stood up.

Something was off.

"Malach." The floor creaked as I crept past the kitchenette and sitting area and moved toward the dim hallway leading to Gavyn's room.

At the end of the corridor, I noticed a lump huddled in the corner, rocking against the walls. A quiet mumbling mixed with the rough noise of the figure sliding back and forth across the flat surface. I flipped on the switch to my left, and the hall lit up, unveiling a lanky teenager curled up with his face hidden behind entwined shaking arms. Chunks of dirty- blonde hair stuck to the sweat dampening his neck.

"Hey there," I said, taking two slow steps towards the boy.

He stiffened at the sound of my voice and ceased movement. His pale face rose from the crooks of his elbows, showing me a youthful face experienced well beyond his years. Black eyes rimmed with red, inflamed flesh peered at me from over his arm.

"Hi," I tried again, inching down the hall. "What's your name?"

His swollen lips resumed the incoherent chant he'd stopped moments before. He tucked his head back into the cover of his arms and set into a steady rock.

"Dominic," a familiar voice answered. "His name is Dominic." Four feet of perfectly toned legs, topped by a sleek, pink skirt and black leather jacket strode into the corridor, positioning herself in front of the droning teen.

"Surprise!" she chimed sweetly—too sweetly. Her usual crystal-blue eyes looked fierce with the telltale crimson ring that encircled her irises when she was up to her deviant ways. The softness of her inviting features hardened when her small, feminine chin tipped down. She glared at me from under severely angled brows, undeniable chaos riling behind her stormy eyes.

"What are you doing here, Layla?"

Deep breath in.

Ribs too constricted.

Keep control.

My spit thickened, making it hard to swallow with the clenching sensation in my throat.

Layla's graceful arm reached out to her right, her hand disappearing into the bedroom. She jerked a body into the hallway. A stout man in his early fifties nearly toppled under her grasp. Course, black hair with just a hint of silver was plastered to the smear of dried blood on his forehead, clotting a three-inch gash.

He groaned at the mere movement of trying to keep himself upright.

My eyes focused on Layla, willing a hole to open between her eyes like the portals when I concentrated hard enough.

The man swayed beside her as she clutched his bicep. Layla shoved him, forcing his knees to buckle and hit the floor. A snide giggle echoed through the hallway.

I couldn't take my eyes off the weak, beaten man. Blood seeped from open cuts on his lips and nose. Bruises added hints of purple to his cheekbone and left eye. A strip of white fabric tucked haphazardly into the collar of his black shirt. He was a priest.

Why would Layla have anything to do with a priest?

"I figured it was time for a little motivation," Layla purred, reaching her fingers out to comb through the priest's thick, salt and pepper locks.

I narrowed my eyes at her ridiculous efforts to look like she cared.

"How do you plan to do that?"

"What do you think they'll do to a priest in Hell?"

"Cut the shit, Layla. I don't know this man. I don't care what happens to him." I did care—not because I was connected to him somehow, but because there was an inkling of humanity left in me that didn't want to see anyone hurt, but she didn't need to know that.

Her free hand raised and enfolded a jagged ruby hanging from her slender neck. "I know you don't know him, but it'll sure make me feel better to see him suffer," she whispered, lowering her eyes to the floor in a moment of...weakness? Sadness?

As far as I could piece together from Gavyn and the angels, that unpolished gem hanging from her person allowed her to travel through portals and stunted the powers of other Celatum.

"So this is a personal agenda you have going here? I thought you were just a puppet." I mocked.

My eyes darted back and forth between her, the man at her feet, and the clearly damaged boy rocking behind Layla. None of this was making sense.

"In a perfect world, none of this would have happened." She crooked an eyebrow, unwinding her fingers from the priest's hair and wiping the dampness off on the back of his shirt, her mouth twisting in disgust. "Why can't you just do what you're destined to do, Nevaeh? Let us all get on with our lives, instead of making us piss around for the sake of your precious free will."

"And what is it you think I'm destined to do?" I snorted.

"You are a puppet too," she answered, her eyes narrowing on mine. She paused in consideration. "You still don't know, do you?"

"All I know is that I'm some sort of Clavis, I have a power that is sure to consume everything good I have in me, and you bastards keep chasing after me like I'm going to just give up one day and bend to the Devil's will."

Her hand released the stone and rested on her narrow hip. She stared at me for a moment as if I were the most ignorant person she'd met, and then seconds later erupted into a ridiculous cackle. Through her tapering laughter, she managed to mutter, "You're not just 'some sort of Clavis,' Nevaeh. You are *his* Clavis. You are *his* key."

My mouth fell open. "What are you saying?"

She calmed herself, tsking at my stupidity. "The Master is tethered to Hell. You are his ticket out."

The soft clicking of puzzle pieces connecting echoed through my mind. More of the big picture revealed itself. My being half-demon, opening portals, and the wickedness that kept rearing its head inside me had a possible purpose.

Was I really meant to be the Devil's way to freedom?

George's saddened voice fluttered inside my skull like a butterfly trapped in a jar. "You are what you want to be, baby girl. Don't let them decide for you."

"If I refuse?" I asked Layla. My eyes drifted over the poor priest wavering at her feet and the insane boy behind her.

Layla closed her pink powdered eyelids and shook her head, then opened her red-ringed orbs again. A storm was brewing in her depths, perhaps more than I could handle. "You are making it very difficult to do my fucking job." Her full lips pressed into a thin line as she gaped at me with such hatred, I could feel it crawling over my skin. "I didn't want it to be like this, but we all have to make sacrifices. I have made more than my share: Gavyn, my soul, and my brother." Her hand opened and gestured toward Dominic. "Now it's your turn." The threat in her voice spurred the agitated beast inside me.

The chattering boy jerked his head toward Layla, then continued in his fit. I hadn't recognized it before, but the similarities were obvious. They shared the same elegantly angled features and caramel blonde hair.

"You *took* Gavyn. I had nothing to do with your soul, or your brother." My monster of doom was doing flips against my ribcage, struggling to get out and take this bitch down. A swelling charge sparked from my thumb, catching her attention. She smiled, and I could sense the challenge growing between us.

"The old Gavyn, not the mess of a man that you made. That you forced me to create."

I crossed my arms, tucking my hands under my elbows to restrain the lightning accumulating there. "Look, I don't have time for shoddy accusations. Nothing you say will make any difference to me in the end anyway."

Sleek, black stilettos tapped across the floorboards as she side-stepped around the priest and closed the distance between us. I threw my hands back down. My mouth tightened around heavy breaths, readying myself for the release of the combustible ferocity scratching under my skin.

Nose to nose, she peered into my eyes. We were so close I could feel her hot breath on my mouth, sharing my air supply. I noticed the thin streak of red outlining her blue irises shifting like she had her own electric current trapped in that tiny ring.

Maybe that was what the demons were attracted to, why they followed her orders. Perhaps that barely there, wiggling beam of glowing crimson was all the power she held. Maybe if I plucked her eyes out of her pretty little head, she'd be powerless.

"We all have our murky pasts. Do you think I chose this life willingly?" She paused, grinding her teeth together on a thought. "He promised to get my brother back from that filthy priest," Layla spat, her eyes never leaving mine. "Dominic was taken from our home when I left to scavenge for food one night. Our parents were dead, we were left on our own, and then I lost him too. The Dark Celatum guaranteed that they would get Dominic back from his kidnapper. All I had to do was follow him — the Master." She smirked. "My time for reward is here, but I assured him that you would come with me. It's your turn to pay one way or another."

I narrowed my eyes at her naïve willingness to surrender her soul. "Did you really think your 'master' would do anything for you? Surely, you understood the concept of good and evil. Heaven and Hell?"

Her sour laugh warmed my face, her eyebrows pulling up in shock. "Surely, you knew the difference when you made your choice too." She caught her lower lip between pearly teeth, judgment seeping from behind her red-ringed crystal-blues as they roamed over my guilty expression. "At least I follow through with my promises." Layla leaned back a few inches and crossed her confident arms over her stomach. "No matter. We made our choices — for whatever reason. I plan on redeeming my mistakes now, though. That's why you're coming with me. I will deliver you, if not for the sake of my brother's sanity, then for the mere fact that I hate your fucking guts."

My gaze dropped to the silent man slouched on his knees behind Layla.

"No."

She shrugged, swiping her tongue over her teeth in arrogance. "Fine, but I thought you might be a little less careless with your family."

"I have no family left, Layla. There's no one left to take from me." The words came out in a reluctant admittance. "You'll need more motivation than that."

Her apple-red lips turned up into a knowing smile as she looked over her shoulder at Dominic. The chanting halted. He raised his head, then nodded, confirming some unknown question Layla hadn't asked. She flicked her dangerous eyes back to me. "You see, my baby brother here has consulted with the demons, and the results are in, Nevaeh.

Kenet, that lying sack of shit who keeps helping you, is your father. Guess the pitiful, poisoned apple doesn't fall far from the tree after all."

Archard

CHAPTER TWENTY-TWO

Soul Bearer

It had been years since we stepped foot on this land. I couldn't bring myself to take Nev there, to show her where she came from. Besides the fact that we didn't really get the chance to explore much of her past before she was forced to decide her future, there was nothing left there for her. Her family was gone. The security of the farm shattered when the demons broke through Theora's powers; The supernatural safety of the consecrated grounds decimated by forces we still didn't know.

Shame from failing to keep her safe within my Graces haunted me every time I considered showing her where she started.

Memories of Nevaeh skipping through the fields of tall grass surrounding the farmland appeared before my eyes as if it were twenty years ago, and the world she knew was still innocent—when Nev was still innocent. Rays of warm sun touched her coffee-colored curls and rendered them a soft caramel hue while she bounced between the thin stalks of wheat. A twitchy feline tail stretched upward in front of her, provoking Nev to chase the mischievous cat. Laughing violet eyes glanced back at me over her shoulder then returned to the cat pouncing after a butterfly.

"Let's see if Theora left us a present," Arkin pressed, slapping me on the back. His broad chest rose on a deep breath, eyes homed in on Theora's turn of the century home. The shadow of sorrow darkening his gaze left little doubt that my brother was reliving his own painful memories of his beloved Theora.

Arianna walked ahead of us, her dark hair swaying in the light breeze, while the soft clinking of a sword against the brass studs of his leather skirt assured me that Malach was behind us.

We journeyed down the long, narrow path leading from the end of the property to the front porch, climbed the steps, and entered the creaking old colonial. The screen door was stuck open, its framing too warped to clear the rippled boards of the porch. We stopped just inside the foyer and took a silent moment to get reacquainted with the familiar smell of tea and maple syrup soaked into the bones of the musty old house.

"This way," Arianna whispered without looking back at us. I followed her while my brothers squeezed by her and preceded our ascent, searching for signs of trouble.

Arkin and Malach crowded the narrow landing at the top, giving me and Arianna just enough room to search the small room on the right. Nevaeh's room. I followed Arianna's wilted frame through the door and immediately my heart ached. Being here was a slap in the face, a jab to the ribs. A reminder of all that I should have given her. My fingers trailed along the soft, bubble-gum-hued blanket draped over the foot of Nev's bed. I skimmed the abundance of stuffed animals and pillows lining the twin bed pushed snugly against the wall.

Though it was much different now, more mature and wild, Nevaeh's fragrance saturated every inch of her room. My nostrils flared, breathing in as much of her lavender scent as I could.

I missed this little girl, but I yearned for the woman she had become.

A strained sob broke our silence, snapping me out of my own thoughts. Arianna sat across the small room, rocking in a chair next to the window. She clutched a doll to her chest as if it were Nevaeh.

Nev loved that doll, played with it most out of all her toys. I frowned at the mud staining its face and the single bare foot peeking out from under a tattered dress. She lost the doll's other leg when she was four, yanking it free from a tangle of rose vines that had snagged the toy as Nevaeh ran through the maze of shrubs in Theora's yard. The plastic leg was probably still out in the bushes today.

"If memory serves me right, Theora stashed the feather in that pillow there." Arkin leaned his shoulder against the door jamb and pointed to a small, lace trimmed square crammed at the corner of Nevaeh's bed.

I leaned over and picked up the pillow. Arianna stood from the chair, still holding the doll in one hand, and moved to my side. Her hand reached out to examine the age-stained lace hanging loose from the corner seam. She looked up at me with a glimmer of hope in her tired eyes.

I nodded and ripped the pale-pink satin. Puffs of yellowish stuffing spilled out onto Nevaeh's mattress, along with one silken black flight-feather.

Arianna gasped, her hands flying up to cover her mouth. "He's changed again," she muttered behind her fingers.

"Son of a bitch," Arkin said, he and Malach crowding around us.

"He's Fallen," I breathed, holding the feather up toward the window. Sunlight illuminated the dried rust-colored blood clumped at the scribing end of Rhett's feather.

Arianna slumped onto the bed. Her chest heaved as if she'd been kicked in the ribs. "I never would have thought..." She tightened her grip around Nevaeh's doll, searching for a grip on the realization that her once-Guardian had succumbed to the temptations of Hell.

"There's no telling what he's like now. If he knows who Nevaeh is and finds her, he will most likely take her out." My eyes fell to the mass of stuffing piled on the bed. "He'll have no conscience to hold him back."

"We'll have to find her first then," Malach insisted.

Arkin, Malach, and I stiffened and looked out the window at the same time.

"What is it?" Arianna asked, noticing our sudden alarm.

"We've got company," Arkin answered.

I hurried to the window and scanned over the farm. Just under the great oak marking the property's edge, a shaded figure with brown skin, peering back at us.

"Eyal?" Malach whispered, looking over my shoulder.

I nodded, sliding the feather into a hidden pocket on the inside of my jacket. "Let's see what he wants."

Shouldering past Arkin and Malach, I left the room and jogged down the stairs. An unease settled into my stomach, remembering the last time we saw each other, he tried to burn the book. When I gripped the door's handle, Malach's hand wrapped around my bicep, stopping me.

He stared at the end of the pathway, his focus on the Archangel waiting for us under the tree. "Be careful," he advised in a cautious tone. His eyes darted to mine. "I have a bad feeling about this, and you know I'm always right." There was no mistaking the cockiness behind his warning.

"Always," I responded, agreeing to be cautious.

He released my arm and directed his attention back to Eyal.

"Hey, I need you to hold these." I reached for the book I'd tucked into my pants before we left for the farm. The red velvet tickled my back as I tugged it free from the safety of my belt. "In case something happens to me." I held the book and feather out toward Malach.

"Do you think that's wise?" He hesitated in taking the book and plume. "I'm not exactly good at keeping track of important things."

"You are as trustworthy as any of us. Just...," I paused, thinking about all the things that could go wrong in trying to get Nevaeh to use the tools as we hoped, "just make sure she gets them if I can't." My gaze darted to the figure pacing restlessly at the end of the walkway. "I can't go out there with these in my possession."

Malach nodded with understanding, but his eyes veered up to the ceiling and his breath stilled.

"What is it?"

"Gavyn. I can sense him again. It's faint but...," his eyes narrowed on a crack in the ceiling as if he were getting his information from there, but I knew better. "He's in this realm." Peridot eyes turned to me, perhaps asking permission or forgiveness. "I have to go."

"Go," I encouraged. "Arkin will have my back."

"You know it," Arkin said from the bottom step with Arianna perched on the step above him, watching us over the sharp angle of Arkin's left wing.

With that, Malach opened the book to place the plume in its crease.

"Wait," I yelled, thrusting my hand onto the page he had open.

Malach's eyes opened wide. "Okay?" He obeyed, confusion clear in his expression.

I snatched the book from his hand. "Do you see this?" I asked Arkin, holding the pages up for him to see.

His jaw dropped open. "Yes."

My fingers traced over freshly written words. The effects of aging had changed the older writings to the color of cinnamon, but these were new — the letters bright red. "This passage wasn't here before."

Arianna slid by Arkin and snatched the book from my hand. Her fingers flipped back and forth between the pages we'd all read and the new passages that had appeared since then. "No. No, this wasn't here," she verified in a shrill, shocked voice.

"What does it say?" Arkin asked, leaning closer to Arianna for a better view.

"It's in a different handwriting." Her busy hands stopped, and she showed the scrolling to each one of us. "A different language all together. I can't read it." She held it out to whoever would take it, pleading in her eyes, hoping that one of us would be able to translate.

"It says, 'The child will leave the world of the damned only to bring

245

with it the Darkness and Prince of Lies.'" Malach continued to read in silence for a moment, then spoke again. "She's a Soul Bearer," he huffed. His eyes still wide in disbelief. "That can't be right. No human has ever been a Soul Bearer."

Arianna raised an eyebrow. "She's not exactly what you'd call human."

"What else does it say?" I growled at Malach.

"We can't let her finish her transformation, Archard." He pressed his lips together for a second as if not wanting to continue, then rubbed a hand on the back of his neck. "She will unleash Hell on Earth if she goes through with it."

"Archard," a calm voice called from outside. My eyes darted toward Eyal. His long legs were striding down the walkway leading to the front porch.

"You have to get her the book, Malach. There has to be a reason this just showed up now and that she is like no other."

"If she is truly a Bearer, she could extract any soul she wants…damn any soul she wants. With her under The Betrayer's influence right now, he might force her to hand over every human soul there is. He'll have as many demons as his black heart desires." His eyes lowered to the floor, darkening with worry. "It will be more than our army can handle."

"Archard, we have to talk, now." Eyal yelled from the foot of the porch, impatience harshening in his voice.

Malach closed the book and tucked it in the waist of his leather skirt. His eyes glazed over and grew distant like he was staring into some far-off land no one else could see.

Air shifted in the room, unsettled by the otherworldly portal breaking the ceiling open. My heart cried as the pool of water appeared above our heads, spinning into a large, silvery cyclone of Heavenly liquid.

"I have to go. Something is not right," he said, squeezing my shoulder before he launched upwards into the whirling water.

I glanced back at Arkin who stood at attention with Arianna hidden behind his broad torso. "Guard her. I'll see what this is about." I shrugged off my coat and threw it on a bench positioned against the foyer wall. Sharp pain cut into my back muscles when I freed the crests of my wings pocketed there, but soon disappeared with the relief of freeing the appendages. I gritted my teeth through the quick sting and looked at Arkin again. "Don't trust him for a second."

He nodded and drew a treacherous looking knife from his ankle harness. It had a jagged main blade that extended down from his hand and a secondary slicing blade which curled around his knuckles. Arkin smiled impishly when I took note of the Holy scrolling etched along the wide slat of metal. "What? No likey?"

"New weapon?" I tightened my jaw in disapproval, knowing that he had more than likely "procured" the doubled-bladed knife from an Arch somewhere in recent days. With a shake of my head, I turned and stepped outside.

Eyal's eyes followed me as I walked to the steps and placed one hand on each rail, stopping to scrutinize his rich, brown features. "Why are you here, Eyal?"

"I made a mistake. I should have never let you keep the book." His eyes, the hue of burnt coffee, bore into mine as if he was willing me to hand it over. I smirked at the arrogance Archs managed to carry. It's a wonder they can stand themselves sometimes.

"I don't think I really gave you a choice. It doesn't belong to you." I folded my arms across my chest, restraining the need to pound into his face. "It belongs to Nevaeh, not burned to ash."

"Oh, I agree." A sly grin curved his lips. "When I said I made a mistake, I meant that I made the mistake of putting my faith in a God that would allow such an abomination to be born. For centuries, I've herded the sheep and kept them safe, obeying his orders and rules while the wolves grew hungrier and took as they pleased. I figured it's time to join a more proactive side, to follow a Lord that will offer more power than we ever had with The Almighty."

The harsh white of his teeth gleamed behind the dark contrast of his widening smirk, full of victory and ire. Waxy, midnight wings pierced through the fabric of his navy blazer.

"Hand over the prophecy, Archard," he commanded, stretching out the raven wings that were now far more tainted than my own. "I'll make sure it gets to the right hands."

In my periphery, I caught sight of a teenage boy and a middle-aged woman approaching from opposite corners of Theora's house. They flanked Eyal on either side in silence.

"Sorry to disappoint you, Eyal, but I don't have the book anymore." I raised my own wings, anticipation prickling through the stems of my feathers. "Why don't you take me to Nevaeh, instead."

The dark angel shook his head once, focusing on the door behind me. "Not going to happen. However, rumor has it, there is something else you've acquired that could be of some use to me."

Keeping my sites on Eyal and the Dark Celatum backing him, I called out, "Arkin? You okay?"

The sound of wood splintering and furniture sliding along floorboards echoed from inside the house.

"Arkin!"

"Archard, help him," Arianna screamed.

A sudden, still image of Arkin slamming into Theora's old hutch flashed in my mind, disrupting my concentration. I grunted, clutching onto the banister beside me for balance.

"Arianna, run!" I shouted, shaking my head to rid the disorientation.

Footsteps pounded away from the front of the house, then the back door unlatched and slammed. Arkin grumbled, and more crashes and bangs rang from inside.

My eyes remained focused on the traitorous angel below me. Satisfaction and curiosity bled into Eyal's expression.

"Arianna? Well, that's unexpected. The Master will be pleased we didn't come back empty handed."

I tensed, ready to pounce on Eyal and take him out, but halted when I noticed the woman to his left hold up her hand, smiling as she waggled her fingers at me in a dainty wave. In the next instant, she was gone. Only a blurry mixture of color from her deep red shirt and blue jeans remained, but they soon faded too.

Run and hide. Don't stop until I come for you, I kept repeating in my mind, hoping Arianna could hear my message.

I lunged off the top step and tackled Eyal. We fell to the ground with a loud thud. Clouds of dirt puffed up around us, filling my mouth with an earthy taste. One of Eyal's black wings twisted around me, struggling to gain leverage under my weight, while mine jabbed at his ribs and face as if they were secondary arms throwing their own punches.

The dark angel kicked a leg around my thigh and shoved me over, trapping me on the bottom. Beneath me, the soil began to vibrate, increasing to tremors within seconds. A loud pop echoed into the air. Eyal's hand pressed against my cheek, turning my head toward the teenage boy whose face twitched with absolute concentration.

His legs stayed steady and sure on the quaking ground. His hands slowly lifted from hip level to just above his narrow shoulders. With the boy's movement, clumps of grass drudged upward, followed by more and more earth until the clumps were massive balls of dirt — as large as a car — hovering over Eyal and me.

I threw another punch at Eyal's jaw. Drops of his bloody spit spattered onto my face. He bashed my temple with the crest of his right wing. Stars swirled in my vision, but I refused to give up.

Eyal rolled off me, yelling, "Now, Jake," to the boy controlling the boulders of dirt. The truck-sized forms of earth swung through the air, jetting straight for me.

I thrusted my wings down against the ground and propelled myself towards Eyal. I groaned when the rough edge of one of the masses struck my ankle, barely avoiding the brunt of the impact. A thunderous crash rumbled behind me.

My hazy eyes landed on the reflective surface of a narrow, long blade in the dark angel's hand. He danced around me like a boxer awaiting his prime opportunity to attack.

"I see you have no qualms about keeping our weaponry, traitor," I spat, recognizing the angelic writing etched along the Sai.

"I think I've surrendered enough of my life in servitude to deserve it." His pink tongue swept across a drop of blood gathering on his split lip.

A window shattered, spraying shards onto the porch. Glimpses of a man with shaved blonde hair bobbed behind the broken window, then Arkin came into view, roaring as he wrapped his hands around the man's throat and yanked him deeper into the house.

I scowled at Eyal, keeping his lackey within the same line of sight. A dazed expression slackened Jake's face, then the ground shook again. Loud popping sounded from the end of the property. Eyal smirked as if he'd already won the battle.

My head snapped to the right in time to see Theora's oak tree hurling at us like a freight train, its speed ripping off bunches of leaves along the way.

Arkin barreled through the door and leaped down the steps in one jump. I latched onto Eyal's coat and held tight, pinning him on top of me like a shield. Arkin lunged into Jake, knocking the boy into the tree's path behind Eyal. The seconds that passed before the oak made it to us seemed like minutes, everything playing out in slow motion.

Jake cried out, knowing it was too late to escape the tree's aim or redirect it. The trunk slammed into Eyal, ripping him from my grip, then into Jake, quieting his yell instantly. Their bodies soared into the house with the tree until it finally met a force big enough to stop it. Theora's home buckled in around the giant oak, stray boards falling off the front of the crumbling structure.

Arkin shuffled to my side, offering a hand to help me up. Smeared blood covered his arms and stained the white of his t-shirt. Purple bruises were already forming on his cheekbone.

I clasped his hand and hoisted myself upright. "You okay?"

He nodded. "Yeah." His eyes took stock of the uprooted tree, imploded house, and enormous holes in the yard.

We both jerked when the woman who'd vanished from Eyal's side earlier reappeared behind us. Her eyes widened in shock as she scanned over the destruction. Anger hardened her feminine features. A limp body pressed against the flasher's left side, doubled over her forearm like a rag- doll. Long hair hung in tangles, veiling Arianna's unconscious face.

I lunged toward the Dark Celata, but before I completed my first step, she and Arianna were gone. No warning. No fight.

"What the fuck just happened?" Arkin asked in a high-pitched voice.

"I'm not sure, but we've got to get her back." I extended my dirt-dusted wings and boosted off the ground.

Arkin jumped into the air and threw out his blood-spattered wings to follow me. "Great. We'll just add her to the ever-growing list of things we have to find," he deadpanned.

CHAPTER TWENTY-THREE

Unexpected Rival

Layla's confession was surprising, but not as shocking as I would have thought. There was no stutter in my pulse, no quick intake of breath. My shoulders almost relaxed with relief at the admission.

I felt a strange connection to the man in the tunnels from the very beginning. His violet eyes told me that we were of the same cloth somehow. I just wasn't sure in what way. Hearing Layla say the words filled an empty void deep in my heart—a place that had refrained from filling over the years, since I believed that he was dead for so long.

A cough escaped the priest's dry lips. He toppled over, catching himself on outstretched arms. His weary gaze found mine.

As I thought about Kenet and all that he'd done to help me, I took in the man hunched on the floor, wondering what Layla had planned for him.

"It doesn't change anything, Layla. I'm not going with you."

"I guess it's time to improvise then." She wrapped the fingers of one hand around the gem at her neck and slipped the other hand along her right thigh until it disappeared under her skirt. When it reappeared, long fingernails gleamed against the pewter hilt of a thin dagger. "Dominic," Layla snapped, ordering him to act.

The young man continued rocking, his black eyes full of misery as they focused on his sister.

"Dominic, sweetie, show her," Layla patronized, moving around the priest to approach her brother.

"N...n...no," his rough voice rang out between nervous shivers.

On a dime, Layla spun and fisted the priest's hair, snatching his head back. His calm eyes locked on me, his mouth moving to form a single silent sentence.

Don't surrender.

Once he knew I understood, he closed his eyelids and began a rapid mumble of prayers in a foreign language.

"Now, Dom," Layla demanded, "or I'll slay your loving priest right here. I swear I will." Her hand trembled around the weapon. She didn't want to kill him; I could see that by the reluctant movement of her arm when she raised the blade to the priest's neck.

During our months together, Layla had manipulated demons to kill for her, but she never took a life with her own hands.

Dominic stopped rocking and slowly lifted his gaze to the priest.

In that short moment of hesitation, time stood still for us all.

Layla flicked her wrist, springing forth a bright-red stream of blood beneath the priest's jaw bone. He winced, but a speck of relief was clear in his eyes. The cut was just deep enough to hurt, but not enough to cause major blood loss.

Suddenly, the boy's bones cracked and ground against one another. He rose, pressing himself to the wall, then twisted so that he faced away from us. More cracking and crepitus echoed from his slight body, and he doubled over backwards in a back bend too extensive for the human body to tolerate. His torso drooped as far as his damaged spine would allow, and he set eyes on his sister. An insincere, smile formed on his tormented face.

Layla clutched her necklace, a glimpse of fear flickering over her features. Dominic swiveled his head upright at an impossible angle, measuring his sister's threat.

What power did she have in that stone?

I opened my mouth, releasing the internal lock on my beast's cage, and permitted it to come out and fight. Two evil gazes shot in my direction. Layla held out the gem from her neck, directing it toward me.

I coughed on the few tendrils of power slithering from my throat, but they soon dissipated into thin air, and my monster drew back as if it had a gun to its head. Stepping back, I forced an exhale out and widened my jaw, hoping it would encourage my monster to explode out and take Layla down. Layla inched closer, renewed confidence hardening her features as she watched me struggle to free my power.

Dominic's contorted body skittered around the priest and set a course toward me. There was no use backing away. Where would I go from here?

The young man stopped abruptly, two paces from my feet. His hollow eyes stared at me while he dropped to the floor, upside down on all fours with his chest bowed up to the ceiling like a scared cat. A wheezing gasp sucked in over his rigid lips, followed by an otherworldly mingle of voices that were not the boy's.

"Nevaeh, don't listen to them. Whatever you do, don't come here." A familiar tone laced the pleading words. My eyes darted to Layla.

Her mouth curled up into a smirk. "Daddy dearest just can't stop trying to save you, can he?"

I looked back down at Dominic's empty eyes questioningly.

"He can possess demons. Funny, isn't it? It's usually the other way around." Layla approached her brother's side and rested her hand on his chest as if he were an obeying pet.

The teen's mouth parted once more and let out a billowing yell. He was in pain. Or maybe, Kenet was in pain. I couldn't tell anymore. How did I even know that this wasn't all a trick? I didn't, but I couldn't lose two fathers.

"Let me speak to your master," I demanded the puppet before me. Dominic cocked his head to the side in silence, his expression blank for a moment.

When he opened his mouth again, the voice that had controlled so much of me, had wrapped me in the binds of Hell, spoke with a grittiness and superiority that made me want to fall to my knees. "Why must you be so difficult, Nevaeh?"

"Bron?" I exhaled, stunned that my Ater was the answering being.

"I've tried to do this the nice way. Must I keep taking from you to get you to fulfill your destiny? *Our* destiny together?" His tone was sultry and patient, like I was a child who just needed a stern talking to — my defiance was inconsequential; everything came with a consequence though, especially with this being.

"Why do you think I would do anything to help you?" I asked, gritting my teeth until my jaw hurt.

"We belong together, you and me. Two halves of a whole. We could be the one, true God, if you'd only offer yourself to me."

"If I do so, will you release Layla, Dominic, Kenet, and Gavyn from your bindings?"

"I will," he said without hesitation.

I narrowed my eyes, pondering his eager answer. "I mean that much to you?" He'd give up four very powerful souls, useful Dark Celatum, to have me in his fold. If I could just secure their safety, I could figure out how to get free later. Was I strong enough to do it? I'd broken free in Hell. Surely, I could do it again. "How do I know I can trust you?"

"If you do as I ask, you won't have to trust me. We'll be entwined on a level so deep, you'll be my equal," he promised.

In the confines of my mind, George shouted, *Don't listen to him, Nev. He'll tell you anything to dig his claws into your soul.*

I don't have much of a soul left, I thought back. *There won't be enough for him to hold onto.*

You'll be giving up more than you think, girl, George attested against my skull, and then backed away into some unknown part of my conscience, leaving me with a sense of disappointment.

The beast taking refuge behind my ribcage began writhing at the challenge. She would not let me fail. She had shown me that we could rely on each other.

"Come on, Nevaeh. We don't have all fuckin' day," Layla spat, squatting down and wiping her bloody blade on the quivering priest's shirt before replacing it in whatever holster she had fastened under her skirt. She straightened, eyeing me with pure disgust.

I was making a barter for her and her brother, yet she couldn't even pretend to be grateful?

My gaze fell back on the priest, then moved to the contorted, boyish form trembling between us. "I'll go," I whispered.

The moment the barely-spoken words crossed my lips, Dominic untwisted and stood upright, his bones shifting and grinding back into place. His empty eyes lightened in color and filled with a sorrow so deep that I knew he'd never find peace with himself again.

Wind kicked up in the room, flipping my hair. Layla's wild eyes flicked to the area behind me and narrowed.

I spun around, preparing for whatever enemy was trying to sneak up on me.

Malach stood in the doorway, smiling like he'd just caught my hand in the cookie jar.

"Nevaeh," he greeted, his deep voice bellowing over the roaring gusts as he dipped his head in a polite nod. His smile faded quickly when he took notice of the two Dark Celatum at my back.

Crackles and snaps prickled through the hallway, ending near my left arm. I glanced over my shoulder. Layla held her stone in one hand and flattened her other palm against the wall.

"Dominic!" she shrieked, her focus remaining on the tall warrior angel striding across the room.

"No, I don't want to. Please don't make me go," Dominic whimpered.

The priest scooted his body in front of Dominic, doing the best he could in his frail state to protect the son he'd taken care of for so long. "Leave him be, Demon," he shouted over the wind with a thick European accent.

The electric-red in Layla's eyes intensified, her womanly features angling to a fierce expression of dominance and determination. The hall filled with smoky shadows, undoubtedly, awaiting her command. "You won't be able to stop me if you're dead, will you, Father?"

Before the priest could respond, Layla unsheathed her blade again, approached him raising her hand to the ceiling, and slashed the knife across the man's neck. Purple-red liquid spurted out in thick globs, spraying Layla's skirt and puddling on the floor around her stilettos.

My eyes widened, taking in the amount of blood blending in with the priest's black shirt, dyeing the small white collar below the gash in his throat. Dominic choked back a gasp, the inevitable sob of loss and distress breaking free from his chest when he lowered his gaze to the man slumped forward at his feet.

I tried gagging, heaving, and yawning for fuck's sake, damn near vomiting to force my beast out. Nothing helped though, there was no way I could fight back with her wielding that fucking stone.

"Sorry, Dom, but you had to know I wouldn't let him go. There's no way I was leaving here without you."

Dominic howled as one of the phantoms pierced his stomach. Two of the demons swirled around him, repeating their assaults in turn, dragging him across the hallway to the gaping wall. He wailed one last time and passed out as the fiends carried him into the portal.

"Don't worry, you're next, bitch." Layla thrust a hand in my direction, willing the demons to home in on me. The ghostly forms melted into one and slithered around my neck like a noose. They squeezed tight, knocking me off my feet. I tumbled to the ground, gasping for what little air I could get.

An equally determined grip latched onto my left ankle and pulled in the opposite direction. My vision began to fill with black dots, but not before I saw Malach playing tug-of-war over my body.

I managed a strangled word as the demons shifted to strengthen their constricting hold on me. "George."

Malach's eyes jerked from Layla to me in surprise.

"I...have," I wheezed.

Understanding donned on his handsome face. The demons yanked on me, gaining a foot toward the portal. Layla screamed at the creatures in the background, encouraging them to work harder.

Malach roared, "Nevaeh. I've got you." His strong hands engulfed my calf. If he let go for even a second, he'd lose me.

Pain shot through my hip and knee with the torsion on my lower limb, but the lack of oxygen was the worse threat. I was fading in and out, regaining consciousness when the demons lost their solid composure only to see spots again moments later under their renewed strength. Layla held the stone out from her neck as if it were warding off the angel, her eyes frenzied with the red current.

My leg strained under the weight of a sudden, unexpected jerk, sliding me back toward Malach a few inches. His fingers dug into my thigh, one hand climbing higher on my body at a time. He gripped my hips, and slid himself up my length, weighing me down to the floor with his own body. The angel crawled up my torso, stopping when we lay facing each other, his intent eyes peering into mine.

The last bit of air had left my lungs nearly a minute before. I couldn't even hear Layla anymore. the world was disappearing around me, vanishing with the oxygen in my blood. I couldn't comprehend what Malach was saying. His lips moved urgently, yet none of his words made sense.

I...have...George, I mouthed weakly.

He nodded. "Brace yourself," he warned before bellowing out a cry to the heavens.

Orchestral vibrations wove through the air, reverberating off every surface of the apartment, every molecule in the atmosphere, every bone in my body. The faint sensation of warm liquid dripped from my ears.

He belted out another call. Layla's demons screeched, unwinding from my neck before scurrying into the shadows.

I sucked in air, replenishing what I'd lost.

When he finished, Malach's chest heaved against mine. He searched the ceiling frantically.

Nothing happened.

Layla was huddled against the corner, pressing her hands over her ears and groaning. My gaze drifted to my left and landed on the priest's dead eyes. A chill snaked up my spine. I quickly looked away, focusing back on Malach.

"I don't understand," he breathed, shaking his head with confusion. "He didn't come." A line formed between his brows.

"Who are you talking about?" I whispered, wriggling uncomfortably beneath him.

He pushed himself off me and sat back on his feet. "The Reaper," was all he said.

I propped myself up on an elbow and glanced over my shoulder at Layla who was gaining her wits again. Her blood-soaked hands lowered from her ears. Red streaked her blonde hair, adding to that little bit of danger that seemed to be constantly engrained in her. She reached for the dagger lying next to her spikey heel.

I swallowed, wincing through the pain of a raw throat, and scrambled to sit upright. "Uh, Malach?" I rasped, locking my eyes on Layla's movements.

"Yeah," he answered half-hearted, still lost in thought.

Layla raised the dagger above her head by the tip, intent on aiming it directly at I me.

"Malach!"

A loud bang rang in the air. My entire body jumped from the sound. Stunned, I glanced behind me toward the shot's origin. It took a moment for my brain to process what happened, but I put two and two together the moment I saw the man wielding the gun.

My gaze darted to a tiny red dot on Layla's forehead, then followed the trickle of blood oozing from the center of it down to where the thick liquid dripped off the tip of her nose. Her hand dropped from the gemstone around her neck, and she slouched against the wall, lifeless. A silence filled the room as the crackling ceased and the portal vanished.

The ruby-colored rock was now a dull midnight black.

"Gavyn?" Malach said before stepping between me and the gun pointed in our direction.

Nevaeh

CHAPTER TWENTY-FOUR

Bearing Souls

Gavyn traversed the hall, side-stepping us to loom over Layla's body. His shoulders slumped, and his head drooped with a heaviness that appeared to weigh every fiber of his being down to the ground. Malach slid around me, maintaining his protective stance in front of me as we watched Gavyn's back expand and contract with his steady breathing.

"What did you do?" I whispered, not really expecting an answer.

The hull of a man I used to know squatted down and picked up Layla's dagger from the floor. Blood had dried in the decorative grooves etched in the blade, emphasizing the angelic words holding the power there. "She never could figure out the boundaries of our relationship," he scoffed, then spun around and set his lost, suffering eyes on us.

"There's no coming back now, Gavyn," Malach said with sympathy in his deep voice. "You didn't have to kill her."

"Didn't I? Tell me, what would have happened if I hadn't?" Gavyn's gaze landed on me. "I couldn't let her hurt Nev anymore. That was the whole reason I went with her in the first fuckin' place. This," he waved his hands up and down at his sides, gesturing to the withering body that imprisoned his damaged soul, "would have been for nothing if I didn't do anything."

"I can't help you now." I couldn't see Malach's face, but I heard the shaking distress in his voice.

Ire hardened Gavyn's expression. "You weren't helping me much anyway, were you, Guardian?" He took a step forward. "I should have known better when you let them take George's soul. You don't do anything against the grain. You're just a soldier following orders. Everything by the book," he scoffed. "God forbid, you go out of your way to help others."

"Gavyn," I protested, "you know that's not true. You were the one that told me the rules of this game. You know how much chaos could have resulted in him crossing the portal." My tone sharpened. "Don't blame him for your descent. You let it swallow you up inside. You alone," I said, pointing my finger at him.

He nodded with reluctant agreement, lowering his eyes to the floor. "Yeah, but I wouldn't have all this power if I hadn't." His eyes peered out at us from under his brow, and his dry lips pulled to one side in a smirk.

Malach shoved upright in front of me and drew his sword from its sheath.

I tugged on the hem of his leather vest. "No, don't hurt him. He's not in control of himself."

The angel glanced down at me with wide eyes, then back at Gavyn. "It's not me. He's making me move, dammit."

A low chuckle began at the other end of the hall. Malach's body lurched forward, appearing as if he were knee-deep in a vat of honey, his movements forced and cumbersome.

"Nevaeh," the angel called, "you have to take them." His words were calm, but his tone was grave.

I shot up and reached for his arm.

"Don't," Gavyn shouted. "Don't stop me, or I swear I will kill you both." The look in his eyes told me that he was so far gone, he damn well might. The power illuminating his normally bleak, green eyes, set ablaze the yearning to submit to the wickedness lurking behind them.

The warrior angel opened his mouth while grimacing in a fight for control over his body. "You are the Soul Bearer now. You must take their souls. There is no one else." Malach struggled to gain his own footing with each forced step. Nearing Gavyn, he lifted his sword and held it out like a gift.

I had no idea what he was talking about, but I'd better figure it out soon. I had to do something. My eyes glanced down at Layla's corpse, then to the pendant hanging from her neck. I should be able to bypass his influence. The crystal seemed to have died with Layla, and Gavyn didn't know about the abilities I possessed now.

Gavyn gripped Malach's sword in one hand, and with the other, drew back the dagger then stabbed his Guardian.

Malach reared back, releasing a howl that echoed through the apartment. A sly smile tugged at Gavyn's mouth before his eyes zoned in on mine, sparking with a charge of dominance and...fear? He was in there somewhere, the man that I'd grown so fond of. I just needed to dig him out, and make him see that he didn't have to be this monster.

One deep inhalation was all it took to break free of the frayed strings still tethering my beast inside. I arched my body and thrust every bit of the strength and stormy, midnight rage I had toward Gavyn. His hands flew out in my direction, half redirecting his own curse, half bracing himself for the electric fury rocketing toward him.

The hall filled with my dense cloud of doom. Hot, purple bolts zapped along the walls, floor, and ceiling like the inside of a tesla sphere. A hard thud and a loud grunt resonated from the end of the hall where Gavyn was standing. I couldn't see him, but I hoped the impact of my beast had knocked him on his ass...and maybe unconscious.

My darkness parted under my order, like I was the oil in its water, opening a path that led toward the sound. I glided down the corridor, stopping when a boot covered foot came into view. I squatted down and swallowed every detail of the man sagging on the floor. His messy hair, his relaxed face, his thick chest rising and falling.

There he is, I thought to myself.

I reached out to touch his cheek, trailing a finger over his stubbled jaw. "I'm so sorry for all this," I whispered, recalling the kisses I shared with that mouth. "I'm sorry I ever came into your life. You were too good for this."

His eyelids popped open. We stared at each other for a moment. There was no anticipation of our next moves, no tension between us; we were two lost souls seeking a glimmer of hope and comfort in one another.

I didn't know if things would ever be what they were before. Who was I kidding? I knew better. Nothing would ever be the same, but maybe, one day, we wouldn't be quite so misplaced and could become something beyond the tortured beings we were today.

"I'm not sorry for one minute," he breathed. "I would become this monstrosity a thousand times over, if it meant keeping you safe." His expression softened. Glimmers of the righteousness he'd buried deep inside began to liven his empty eyes.

I smiled, thankful for his intentions. It didn't change anything though. "I'm not safe. I never have been. Never will be."

I lowered to my knees and placed one leg on either side of his lap, straddling him. His breath hitched as I leaned closer. All traces of anger and deviance drained from his face. The static in the air sparked, and a bolt of electric shot through my spine in the most delicious way. My beast couldn't wait to play.

I gently brushed his lips with mine. His hands clasped around the back of my neck and forced me closer. His kiss was hard, determined, and hungry. When he finally withdrew for a breath, I panted, "I'm sorry for this too."

My eyes bore into his, reaching for the soul I knew was damaged but there. My cloud swarmed around us, undulating in rapidly shifting billows of blackness and purple flashes. Oh, she was loving this.

Tears flooded my eyes. Translucent reenactments began to play all around us like projected movies of every wrongful thing Gavyn had done. He groaned, eyes wide and distant, as he recalled everything he'd tried to forget about himself. I knew the pain he latched onto. I was experiencing it with each second that passed. A sob burst from my throat. It was agonizing putting him through this, but he had to see. He had to remember who he was, and if it meant shoving it all back in his face, then I'd do it.

Gavyn's body convulsed beneath mine. They always did when it got to the worst of it. My heart ached with the truth of his sins, so much worse than I thought. The whites of his eyes became more visible as his pupils rolled back in his head. After a few more seconds of seeing his wrongs, he passed out.

The sequences began to slow when they neared the end. I gasped, suddenly seeing visions of my first days at Joe's. Peaceful emotions blended with the maddened ones, gradually taking over.

My tears dried. Gavyn's breathing calmed.

The way he looked at me. The feelings that developed more fiercely than I could have ever guessed. The depth of his love for me was overwhelming. My gaze roamed over the abundance of joyful images hanging in the air. I usually relished, along with my beast, in the heinous acts those souls had committed, but now, my monster and I basked in Gavyn's peace. These memories soothed our rage and disquiet like a healing balm.

A scene of our time in the very hall we were in now overshadowed all his other memories. I focused on the sensations of our bodies pressing together. The shivers running over his skin when I trailed my finger along his back. The intense need growing in the pit of his stomach from just being near me.

I squeezed my eyes shut, refusing to watch anymore. I couldn't bear it. Seeing that only made things more complicated.

I found the goodness I'd searched for. Now that I reached it, I hoped it would be enough. Breaking our connection, I rose off Gavyn's lap and rested my fists on my hips, waiting for the dizzying sensation of experiencing someone else's emotions and memories to pass. My wits returned, recovering from my link to Gavyn. My cloud, more sated than she'd ever been, hovered around me, synchronizing with my movements.

I turned, scanning the floor for Malach and found him laying a few feet away. I kneeled at the angel's head and lifted it onto my thighs, gently patting his face to revive him. My gaze drifted to the strong heartbeat pulsing under the skin on his neck.

"Malach," I said. "Malach, wake up, dammit."

A patch of crimson seeped through the slashed vest covering his chest. I planted my palm over the gash and pushed down, attempting to slow the bleeding.

A strained growl startled me. "Did you get them?" he asked in a weak voice.

"No. Not yet," I admitted, struggling to drag him higher into my lap so he could sit upright.

"What the hell are you waiting for?" His bloodshot eyes peered up at me.

"What the hell am I supposed to do?" I scoffed.

He grimaced as he leaned on his side and reached under his lower back then tugged an object from under his body. His fingers gripped a small book bound in red velvet. He slapped it against my chest before letting his hand drop against the floor like the effort to keep it up was too much. His face twisted in pain. "I have a feeling you know what I'm talking about."

"No," I whispered.

Yes, you do, Nev. This is your purpose. It has been all along, George's familiar voice chimed in my mind.

"No," I shouted at them both. "There's no way." I shook my head, refusing to believe that gathering souls was my part in all this shit.

"There is only one Soul Bearer at a time, Nev. He didn't come when I called, and he wasn't there when George was abducted by the Animus. I just assumed it was because the demon got to him first. I'm not sure how long he's been gone, but I'm betting it's been since your powers started to develop."

I let Malach's raspy words sink in.

"So, someone was supposed to come take George's soul other than you?" I fought back hot tears. "Is that why you were late getting to him?"

Malach's head nodded against my legs. "I would have come sooner, if I had known. I just figured God wanted this to happen for a reason. Someone must harvest the souls, though. That's how this works. The Animus demons scavenge the souls the reaper deems unworthy and leaves behind. If no one takes the souls, the Animus demons will find them, and they'll be no hope for the spirits waiting to enter of Heaven."

Memories of the fiend taking George flashed inside my thoughts, settling on the devastation that millions of people could experience if they didn't get released to…well, to anywhere other than Hell.

I studied the angel's agonized expression. "What happened to this Soul Bearer? What makes you think I'm the one who needs to pick up the slack?"

His eyelids fluttered back open, and he rolled his eyes at my stubbornness before huffing out a response. "Do you have George, or don't you?"

My defiant shoulders slouched. I nodded.

His gaze flicked to the book I still held against my chest. "The book belongs to you. It's about you. There is no one else who's even close to capable of what on those pages, not until you came along. The answers are not clear. The prophecy is not complete. But have no doubt that you are the Clavis. Use whatever is in that book and do what is right. You are the only being on Earth that can extract souls and move through portals."

"But I can only take them to Hell. I can't damn these people. I'm damned myself. What am I supposed to do with that?" I whined.

"I don't know why, but you are the only one. I have no idea what is happening in the Heavens that ensured your succession, but it's gotta be you. Have faith, Nev. It'll work out in the end."

I puffed out a breath, throwing my head back in exhaustion, confusion, and doubt. My eyes wandered over the quiet storm rippling above me. "Will you be okay?" I asked the angel braced against my legs, my focus remaining on my beast.

He half chuckled, half coughed with pain. "Yes. I'll be fine."

I straightened to see a confident smirk on his face; the growing circle of blood on his shirt made me skeptical though. I didn't have time to consider his sincerity. Gavyn would likely be awake soon, and I had a deal with the Devil to settle.

George? I thought.

You know what you gotta do, baby girl. Don't you worry about me.

I swallowed back the guilt. I'd intended to save him—to pull him from the bowels of Hell and set him free. Now that I had him, I didn't have one inkling of what the fuck to do, and to make it worse, I was considering carrying others along with him, inside of a ridiculously unpredictable cage with a seriously unpredictable beast straight into Hell.

Again.

Carefully, I slid Malach to the floor. I slapped my hands on my thighs, relying on the little faith I had and the will to fix the mess I'd made. My toes pressed into the floorboards, and I hoisted myself up. With my cloud anticipating my next movements, I tucked the book in the back of my jeans and approached the priest.

I knelt beside his left arm, reluctant to use my past method of soul extracting, but it was the only way I knew at this point. It was hard to tell if it'd work at all since he'd been dead for so long, and his was a more virtuous soul than I was used to dealing with.

Placing my hands on either side of his cold, stiff face, I stared into his murky eyes and leaned down close to his mouth. My beast quickened, filling the space around us in a tight bubble. I lightly slid my fingers down his cheeks and pried his jaw open. Exhaling, I released all notions to draw on his sins, then inhaled deeply.

Nothing.

I bent down, a little closer, and sucked the air between us deeper this time. His shoulders and head lifted off the floor as if an invisible cord pulled him to me. Our lips brushed before he slammed back to the floor, a whip of vaporous material expelling from his mouth. Again, I inhaled. His torso raised up to meet me, our mouths touching once more, and I slid my hand under his back to brace his chilled body. Tendrils of his essence swam into my mouth, showing me memories of sadness, loss, and a father's love. There were very few instances when the priest had committed a sin past the age of eighteen when he made his vow to The Church and God. Even then, the sins he'd acted on were slight and later atoned for. Slow moments passed as I witnessed a good life and pondered the terrible future this poor soul would undergo if I left it in its shell. One more breath in and the last wisps of his spirit disappeared somewhere within me.

I leaned back, lowering the corpse to the floor, then looked over my shoulder at Gavyn lying against the wall quietly with his eyes closed. My gaze roamed to the Dark Celatum three feet to his left. She lay awkwardly doubled over at her side, the crystal draping off her shoulder.

This oughta be fun, I thought with a frown.

Jumping up, I traveled the distance between me and her in seconds. No point in postponing, right?

I dropped to my knees, fisted her shirt, yanked her upright, and lifted her chin with my finger. There was no way I was going to take it easy on this soul. I tugged at the shroud of violent clouds riling above me, pulling it down upon us. I positioned my fingers at her temples and pried open her eyelids with my thumbs and forefingers.

With an audible gasp, I called her spirit forth. Instantly, her body arched out toward mine. Her essence snaked out performing a cunning dance, tempting me to do my worst. Image after image of treachery and hate fell from her dead mind, filling the air with a pretty little array of her sins. This…this was the familiar past I'd hungered for during my prior times of making my victims see their wrongs.

My beast reveled in the abundance of wrongs Layla carried, but a

271

small part of me searched for something else. A part of me wondered if there was a tiny seed of good in her, stuffed way down at her base, like Gavyn.

As the last of her soul disappeared down my throat, a glimpse of what I wasn't sure I'd find shone through her darkness. A moment of tranquility and love expanded into the atmosphere. The last image that appeared was one of her brother, Dominic, smiling back at her from the other side of a dinner table. A woman in her early forties sat on her left smiling at her with such adoration, it could only be her mother. To her right, a man leaned into the table, grinning with outstretched arms. Layla winked at a much younger Dominic, then placed one of her hands in her father's and one in her mother's. The young boy followed suit, rolling his eyes as he conceded to pray before dinner. They all bowed their heads and chanted together in a moment of faith and love for one another.

I severed my connection with Layla and sat back on my feet with a tear trailing down my cheek.

"Where did you go wrong?" I exhaled, viewing her with a sympathy I didn't have before. Bracing the side of her face in my palm, I carefully slid her back to the position I'd found her. I reached to the back of her neck and unclasped her necklace.

I draped the jewel over my palm. My body stiffened under the sudden power that surged through me, and the gem came to life, glowing a bright amethyst that matched the bolts crackling in my cloud of doom.

You feel it too, don't you, sister? Layla's voice cooed in my thoughts, startling me from my trance-like focus on the stone. I stumbled back, surprised to hear her. I was so stupid. How could I have overlooked that small detail...that she would be a part of me, just like George?

I squeezed my eyes closed and muddled about in my brain a bit.

Priest? I thought.

Yes, my dear. I'm here too, he answered.

"Son of a bitch," I spat, shaking my head. "What have I gotten myself into?" I looked around at the bodies surrounding me — two dead and two somewhat alive.

I stood and ambled to Malach's side, peering down at him. "I don't know why I let you talk me into this."

Malach's eyes opened a sliver. "It's done then?"

I nodded without a word, then spun and stomped over to Gavyn. My fingers worked to fasten the chain around his neck. The stone came to life with a pale green illumination, assuring me that he was alive and that the pendant was offering its power to him now. I grabbed two handfuls of his jacket and lugged him across the blood-stained floor.

Malach craned his head to watch me. "What are you doing?" A line formed between his brows. "Nevaeh," he called when I didn't answer right away.

After a few grunts, and a lot of elbow-grease, I stopped and looked over my shoulder. "What I have to," I panted. "We are all going back to Hell, and I'm going to end this." My eyes fell to Gavyn's limp body, unconscious at my feet. "The Devil needs to follow through with his part if he expects me to follow through with mine."

I slapped my hand to the wall, my fingers tingling with energy. The drywall split open and a red-orange, fiery glow spilled forth. Bending over, I hooked my arm under Gavyn's and pulled him upright, holding his back to my chest, then slid my hands around his torso. I glanced over at Malach one last time and smiled, quickly committing his angelic face to memory in case it was my last chance.

"May God be with you, Clavis," he prayed.

Smirking, I responded with, "I hope so. I'm gonna need Him." I stepped backwards and entered the portal, hefting Gavyn along with me, hoping that my energy and the pendant's gift would be enough to keep him safe during our travels.

The intense agony that takes over a body inside the portals slammed into Gavyn, forcing him to wake to a world of hurt. The portal swallowed our cries, sealing behind us as soon as his toes crossed the threshold.

CHAPTER TWENTY-FIVE

SAVING GRACE DURING HARD TIMES

"We've been calling him for hours," Arkin reminded from the chair across the room.

I swung my fist out, toppling candles and shattering the glasses on the table next to me. From the corner of my eye, I saw Maggie jump, and I knew I needed to calm down. It was so damn hard though. Nevaeh was still missing, Arianna was gone, and Malach was nowhere to be found; not to mention, my dumb ass had given him the book, which in turn, was lost now too.

I raked my fingers through my hair and puffed out an exasperated breath. "What do we do?" I whispered to anyone who could offer an answer.

Maggie's tiny hands curled around my shoulder, and she leaned in against my arm. "We'll find them. I know we will."

I looked down at her hopeful face and wondered how mankind could be so naïve, yet so full of faith and love. She almost had me convinced that she was right. I managed a forced smile, not wanting to upset her with the doubt engulfing my heart, and patted her hand. "I know."

"Uh...Archard?" Arkin hopped up from the chair, his eyes fixed on the doorway.

I turned to find Malach's haggard form braced against the doorjamb, panting. His disturbed gaze raised from the floor and locked on me.

"Where have you been?" I yelled two seconds before plowing into him and pinning his body against the wall on the other side of the hallway. "Everything went to shit in a hand-basket, and you were MIA."

I loosened my hold on him, but only enough to let his feet touch the ground.

"They have her. She made another deal."

I let go of him completely and took a staggered step backward. "What kind of deal?"

Malach shook his head and glued his eyes to some distant speck in the room behind me. "I'm not sure. I just know she went back to Hell bearing an interesting group of spirits."

I growled, jumping for him again, but instead of pounding my fist into his face, I used every muscle I could and planted my knuckles into the wall only inches from the Archangel's cheek. "And, you didn't stop her?"

"I couldn't." His features morphed into an expression of helplessness and regret. "Gavyn showed up. He's...he's changed. He swayed me to hand over my sword, then stabbed me with an angelic dagger. I lost my ward, Archard."

The plains of his arrogant face filled with worry and failure. He pushed off the wall and shouldered past me, pressing his hand to a bloody spot on his leather vest. "By the time I got there, the deal had been struck, and blood was shed. In the end, *she* made the choice to go. You of all beings should know, you can't *stop* Nevaeh from doing anything she's set on doing. I came here as soon as I healed enough to stand upright. I'm blessed to still be breathing."

Arkin stood in the doorway, guarding Maggie as she peeked around his elbow. "What exactly did you see?"

Malach recounted Father Varga's death, Gavyn going crazy and stabbing him, and then he told us about Nevaeh swallowing two souls, along with already having George's stuck inside her somewhere, and her return to the Underworld.

"Archard, I could probably still see her imprint if we go now." Maggie squeezed around Arkin.

"I don't know what good it would do," I answered, rubbing my hand over my face.

"I don't know either, but it's worth a try. I can see their energy and maybe get a read on Nevaeh's power or her intentions. Something," she pleaded while Arkin stepped to her side and grasped her hand in support.

"Her intentions were right where they needed to be," Malach interrupted. The expression on his face was one of pride and hope.

I fell to my knees and pounded my fists into the floor, beating the concrete until my hands were aching and my knuckles bloody, until the cement began to break apart under the relentless force. I leaned back, chest heaving, tears flowing down my cheeks.

"How do I get her back?" Silence answered my cry for help. My gaze scanned over the faces struggling to hide the pity they felt for me. I hoisted myself off my knees and straightened. "How do I get down there?" I asked, my eyes landing on Malach. He was the only one that knew the answer.

"Maybe I can help," someone said from behind the Arch. He turned around and stumbled toward us, putting distance between him and the being hiding behind his massive frame. A faint light emanated around the source, casting a glow on Malach's outline.

I shoved past him to see a face I thought I'd never see again.

"Who is it?" Arkin called in an anxious voice.

I glanced over my shoulder, somewhat dreading how this meeting would end, then stepped away from Malach, creating space between us.

Arkin's face screwed in disbelief, and he slowly raised his hand to his heart, while his other hand dislodged from Maggie's. "Theo?" he exhaled, a single tear rolling from his eye.

"Did you really think we'd never meet again, my love?" Her lips curled into a sweet smile.

Arkin stepped toward her, drinking in every detail of her face, struggling to work out the hows and whys of her visit, recalling the connection he hid in the depths of his heart so many years ago.

Last time we'd seen her lovely face, she'd been in her late sixties, but now her skin was smooth, unwrinkled, and bathed in a Heavenly light that would never extinguish. She was renewed in her second life, embodying what most humans strive for in the end—youth, happiness, love, and wisdom.

My brother reached out a trembling hand, and in response, so did Theora. Their fingers met before she collapsed into him, hugging him tight.

"Who's Theo?" a small voice asked from behind me.

"She was his ward," I answered, glancing back at the little pixie. "He was her Guardian."

Maggie peered around my arm at the reunited couple, her eyes full of curiosity and a twinge of jealousy.

"She died, and it appears she is now a saint," I chuckled, surprised but glad to see her fortune.

"Huh," Maggie huffed as if to say it was no big deal, but her attempt to hide the ache building in her heart was unsuccessful.

My focus returned to Theora holding Arkin's face in her hands as a mother would, not a lover. Time had changed them both, perhaps more than Arkin had realized.

"What are you doing here, Theora? How did you get here?" Arkin asked, fascination thick in his voice as he traced over the details of her face.

Her smile faded. She looked over Arkin's wing at me. "I've come to give you a gift." Her gaze shifted back to Arkin, offering him a small smile and a wink. Theora stepped around my brother, letting her hand sweep down his arm to squeeze his hand before leaving him to approach me. "I know what she is. I know what it will take to get you down there."

I scanned the other angels' expressions, noting the reflection of doubt in their faces matched my own. "What gift could you possibly give that will allow me to cross Hell's borders?" My eyes stung with tears of frustration and the need to consider even the most nonsensical possibilities.

"This," she explained, resting her palm on my chest.

A dizzying sensation rushed my thoughts. My chest heaved in a deep breath, then stilled for what felt like years. Time ceased to pass while her hand stayed glued to my body. I couldn't breathe. The aching heart that beat relentlessly under my ribs froze. In my peripheral, I noticed that Arkin and Malach were motionless—one peering over his shoulder at Theora and me with a longing in his eyes, the other braced against the wall, holding his hand over his wound. Maggie was too far behind me to see if she was trapped in the same timeless moment, but from the complete silence and lack of her freaking out, I assumed she was.

"What...are...you...doing to us?" I gritted out. I was at her mercy, and I feared the impending consequences of her "gift."

Her wispy, chestnut hair flittered around her head, not from a breeze or any disturbance in the air, but from the pure radiance shooting out from her hand. Her energy pulsated under my skin, mingling with the suspended blood swimming freely in my veins moments ago. The energy she pumped into me contained such power my insides threatened to explode.

I stood there, braced like a statue under her touch, until another sensation flooded my insides. It was familiar. Spectacular. Memories of my life before Nevaeh—before I became her Guardian—flashed before my eyes. My time guarding God himself. My happiness in utter servitude to the being that created me to carry his mighty throne in the Heavens. Memories of the magnificent, Holy body I inhabited during that time.

A groan rang from my throat. My skin stretched, sliding over the displacement of my bones. My wings thrust out around Theora and me. The deep-purple that I'd rued for so many years began to drip from my feathers like ink bleeding from a toppled ink well. The creamy white that I often found dingy, and a constant reminder of my sins, brightened to the color of freshly fallen snow and glistened like frost on a window.

I tried to suck in a breath, but my chest was still locked in place under Theora's hand.

I cried out when twin stabbing pain ignited on either side of my back just below my wings. Secondary feathery appendages ripped out of my left side, then my right, stretching out under my flight wings. They were just as beautiful as I remembered.

Another sharp pain forced me to groan again. The skin and ribs under my arms stretched and morphed into elongated protuberances like hands reaching out from inside my torso, then they snapped back into my chest.

"Oh, no," Theora whimpered under a shaky breath. "I don't have enough power."

My eyes focused on her saddened expression. Her lips pressed together in a tight, thin line as she concentrated harder.

The flesh on my face began to morph, sliding over the changing ridges of my skull. My head thrashed back and forth, jerking and stiffening at brief intervals.

A beak extended from my jaw, stretching into a fine point at the tip. I opened my new, rigid mouth and cawed. My eyes widened, becoming more rounded in my sockets, pupils more dilated. The details of the room were magnified, my vision keener. I could see the tiny dust particles hanging in the air, the specks of gold in Theora's bourbon-colored eyes, and the pores on Malach's face from at least ten feet away. I tilted my head with curiosity, my tiny ears homing in on the sound of a choir singing. The music hummed from the glory flowing out of Theora and into me. I hadn't noticed it before, but the beautiful notes were easily detectible with my eagle senses.

My head thrusted to the right then the left, shifting bones again. The sharp beak elongated, widened, then blunted at the end, mutating to the mouth of an ox. Large ears sprouted on top of my head, flicking about to pick up the hum I'd heard second ago. My feet stiffened, toes fusing together, then hardening into thick hooves. A gruff snort blew out from my muzzle.

The muscles of my face tensed once again. My mouth opened and closed tightly, stretching against the pull and push of another change. I jerked my head to the right as my eyes regained a hunter's precise vision. My nose and mouth shortened and twitched around razor sharp fangs that lengthened amidst my teeth. A rumble vibrated in my chest and forced its way up my throat, resulting in a deafening roar. I was the lion.

One more shake of my head and my skull rearranged to the human face I'd been given at creation. My feet softened and elongated into human feet. I stared down at Theora in disbelief.

How was she able to do this? How was she able to give me my Holiness back?

The radiance that illuminated our skin was fading. Her stern expression was weakening. She took in a deep breath and ground her teeth, expelling a shriek through the last of whatever power she held.

Warmth traveled from my heart to my right shoulder, then raced to my fingertips. Flames hissed to life, increasing in intensity as they wound up my forearm, swirling around my flesh like a fiery cyclone surrounding my hand and forearm. I welcomed the divine heat. I'd missed it.

Theora's beaming energy waned, her posture slouching from the straight confidence she'd portrayed at the beginning of all this. Her head dropped as she gathered her wits, and she leaned her body into me, shuddering and spent. "It's not everything you had before, but it should do, Cherubim," she whispered. Her sweet eyes raised up to take in all she had given me with pride.

I could see every line, every pore, of her face with such a clarity it was disturbing. I could hear the tiny whispers of her breath like it was a gust of wind wrapping around me in a hurricane. I'd forgotten the keenness of such angelic powers. It was going to take some time for me to get reacquainted with them.

Now able to move, I held up my flaming hand and examined it for a moment before closing my fist to extinguish the fire. Though I couldn't see it, the constant heat throbbing under my skin told me my weapon would be there, ready, the moment I beckoned it again.

"You were once the Guardian of God's glory. He made you the Clavis's Guardian for a reason, Archard. Something is happening among the ranks of Heaven. There's a rift in power. Many angels were killed by one of our own. There's chaos and doubt everywhere you look. And, then I found out she was the new Soul Bearer. Now, millions upon millions of souls are left stranded in rotting corpses. We've already lost so many good spirits that could have strengthened our army."

"So, that's why Nevaeh is developing the trait? Because they are tearing each other apart up there?"

"Not just up there. The destruction is making its way here as well."

"How long has this been going on?" I snarled. It had to have been for a while, if the prophecy had foretold of Nevaeh's birth. Why didn't anyone come to help us sooner?

"Since Rhett left us. He left behind a mass of bodies on his way down. He was the original Soul Bearer." Her eyes glossed over with sadness. "You have to help her overcome them. Without her, there may not be any way to save the humans. There is no one else."

My jaw twitched. "Wow, God really knows how to put all of his eggs in one basket, doesn't he?" I scoffed. My gaze traced over the faint scar on Arkin's eyebrow, and the pure white feathers behind Malach. I rested my hands on my hips, pondering God's reasoning for all this. It all started with Him. Surely, He could have stopped this, prevented it somehow.

"Why?" I asked. "Why did He even tell Rhett this prophecy if He knew what damage the angel would cause?"

Theora crossed her arms over her chest and pondered my question. Her mouth opened around a frown. "I believe he was trying to warn

Rhett. God knew what would become of him if he continued on the downward spiral he was traveling. I'd like to believe God created Nevaeh as a counter-reaction, knowing where Rhett's loyalties would land in the end."

"Why didn't He just remove Rhett Himself — before it got that far?"

Her dainty hand reached up and caressed my cheek. "You know that's not how He works."

I blew out a breath and bent over, bracing myself on my thighs while her words settled in my mind.

"So now, the only chance we have to fix everything — here and in Heaven — is in Hell, teetering the line between damaged and damned like a fucking tightrope walker."

When I peered up at her from under my brows, she nodded once. My eyes fell to my feet again. If I didn't have so much power soaring through my body right then, I might have had a panic attack.

Theora's hands cupped my cheeks and dragged my attention back to her. "That's why I came back. I planted the book, hoping Nevaeh would get it and use it to guide her decisions, but that didn't work out the way I anticipated. Then, I thought, what better way to get her back than give her Guardian back his Holiness so he can save her? I've given you what I could afford from my own," she said, nodding with certainty that it was the best she could do.

"But, if I cross a portal…the consequences. It will destroy the veil." I shook my head. "I can't do it."

"It's the only way. The demons are already roaming this world despite what the sacred laws say." She lifted her hands toward the ceiling. "Heaven is already in danger of being breached." Theora dropped her arms down then shrugged a shoulder. "Do what you have to do, Archard. Bring her back to the Light."

Within an instant, the influence of time commenced, Arkin and Malach blinked, and Theora was gone.

Arkin spun around, bewilderment and loss lining his expression. "Where is she? She was just here."

His eyes landed on my wings. All four of them. A choked sound came from his mouth like he wanted to say something, but the words were stuck in his throat. He held his hand out, reaching for the wall next to him.

"Your...your wings." He scrubbed his other hand over his face and swallowed hard. "How?"

I flexed the heavy appendages behind me, adjusting to the weight of having more than I was used to. "She gave me back my Holy Light...at least part of it."

"What's that mean?" Malach asked, his face alight with awe as he stepped toward me to examine my changes. Even he couldn't deny the majesty of what I was now, yet it wasn't nearly close to what I used to be. No matter though, I was grateful for the chance to taste Heaven again. I wasn't sure how long this would last, how far it would take me in this mess, and what abilities Theora had restored, but I would take whatever help I could get.

"It means we need to find a demon that can open a portal for me." I smirked when the two angels' eyes darted to my face, searching for some sign that I was joking with them. "I'm going to Hell," I stated matter-of-factly.

"No worries," a voice purred. "I can find you a demon with no problem." Maggie stepped out from behind me, eyes glued to my wings, her fingers smoothing over my feathers. She gasped. Her gaze trailed up the pure white plumes until they landed on my lips. Passion and restraint warred behind her emerald irises.

Arkin rushed to her side and tugged her away from me, dragging Maggie to a safer distance until I could get a better hold on my hyped Graces.

I cleared my throat, feeling a little like a circus show. I didn't have time to wait for them to accept what I was. "How soon, Maggie?"

She tucked into Arkin's side, probably feeling more comfortable with his hum of power than mine. "Now," she said, tearing her eyes from me and focusing on a spot of blood on the floor at Malach's feet.

"Alright, then. Let's go." I strolled over to Malach and grabbed the hand over his wound, lowering it to his side. He winced but didn't fight me. I splayed my fingers over the patch of blood oozing from his chest and prayed I had enough juice. Concentrating my energy, I willed it to spill into Malach. Thin streams of light broke free from my palm, saturating Malach's damaged body like miniature rays of healing sunlight.

A second later, the Archangel stretched upright and inhaled a deep breath, his chest completely mended. Relief crossed his face as he leaned in, clapping his hands around my head and pulling my forehead to meet his. "Thank you, brother."

"No thanks needed." I grinned and nodded. "Demon hunting time."

The grimy corners of the city felt a little grungier than normal tonight, somehow increasing the anxiety and urgency I felt in finding a way to Nevaeh. The danger of humans traipsing into the otherworldly cross- hairs was getting worse. What used to be a once-in-awhile meeting with Dark Celatum, was now a regular happening. Their numbers were rising far faster than I'd anticipated — another reason for me to find Nevaeh.

They shopped at the street-vendor stands, dined outdoors at restaurants, and lingered just seconds too long in the occasional parking lot before getting in their cars to move on to do their Devil's business. Their eyes instantly jetted to our wandering group of misfits as we roamed the sidewalks and side streets. We piqued their curiosity, but rarely was it enough to result in them approaching us.

When we passed by the frequent alley gathering though, there was no stopping us. We had to interfere, saving some poor soul from a beating...or something worse. We'd taken out a group of five along the way; their attention was too focused on making a child beg for mercy while telling her they would kill her parents if she didn't agree to do their bidding.

Even with the distractions, it didn't take us long to find the demon we were looking for. Maggie was amazing at reading auras and seemed to have excelled in her gift since the last time she used it.

"In there," she said, pointing to the old Victorian towering at the end of Spradly Street. Maggie flicked her cigarette then drew in another puff, releasing the smoke when she spoke. "I sensed her the moment we hit Ninth. I'd heard she was a bad woman. I knew for sure the first time I saw her pruning those roses over there." Her hand gestured to the climbing vines trellised up at the end of a rose garden across the lot. Maggie shook her hands and wiggled her fingers around her head to demonstrate the frenzy of the woman's aura. "She was blacker than midnight with streaks of garnet twisting around her like a snake." The spunky, redhead took a deep draw on her cigarette and exhaled, then snuffed out the burning stick on one of the hundreds of decorative wrought-iron bars separating us from the house. Her gaze shifting to a window on the second floor of the home.

A yellow path stretched from that window to the walkway leading to the front door. "She killed her husband a few years back." Maggie's hand lifted and wrapped around one of the iron bars towering over us. "I can see her evil looming just inside that window, like black ink swirling in a room of water." Her head jerked back to look at us over her shoulder. "You better hurry. They'll come soon." She glanced back up, staring beyond the sheer curtains. "She's fading fast."

Arkin and I made eye contact and nodded, knowing what to do next. We shed our coats, dropping them on the sidewalk, and stretched our wings out in a synchronized motion, releasing the parts of us that we held back too often.

I dug my heels into the earth and leaped into the air, thrusting all four of my wings downward to follow Arkin over the fence. He peered over at me, studying the Holiness glowing just beneath my skin as I landed.

"Are you sure about this?" he asked.

"Yes," I assured, gripping his shoulder and squeezing slightly to ease his worry.

He trailed me to the front door, then into the house, stopping only when I paused in the foyer.

I looked back at him, a sick feeling churning in my stomach. "Maybe you should stay here. I don't know how this is going to go down." I wouldn't be able to live with myself if something happened to him. Arkin had been my brother, my right-hand man, for so long; I wouldn't be able to live with the knowledge that he met a doomed fate because of me.

A low growl rumbled in his throat. "Don't you dare take this away from me. I'm just as much a part of this as you are. Anything I can do to help, I will. She is as much my family as you are, so I will continue on until I can continue no more." The angelic sheen of his narrowed eyes glinted in the shadowy first floor.

My gaze lifted to the ceiling, noting how quiet it was above. No matter what we encountered at the top of the stairs, I would find a way to Nevaeh.

The bottom step creaked under my weight, and I proceeded to climb toward my fate.

A distant chanting grew louder as we ascended the stairs; a shaky, aged voice babbled about the sins she'd committed over her long life. It became clearer the closer we got that she wasn't praying but reciting her iniquities like a list of deeds she'd accomplished in the name of love and loyalty.

Searing heat radiated into the hallway on the top level. I moved forward, cautious of the being inside the far room. Sweat beaded on my skin. I ignored the alarms sounding in my head and entered the doorway with Arkin guarding my back. Sparking red bolts zapped over the walls and leaped onto the furnishings. Hell-light leached from a torn piece of warped paneling in the far corner, casting a flickering glow over everything in the bedroom.

It was an odd sight. Doilies protected the modest 1950's night-tables on either side of a bed topped with an old lady's floral comforter. Frames hung scattered along the wall depicting a family without a father, as well as pictures of roses and birds. It was such a warm contrast to the haggard crone kneeling naked on the floor.

"Come get me. Take this old soul and do what you will, Master," she begged, offering her dripping wrists out toward an Animus demon slinking closer to her. "I have done what you asked, lover. Rid me of this rotting body, and use my soul as you deem fit." Her frail body trembled as the demon inched in. Puddles of blood gathered at her sides, growing as the life gushed from her fileted flesh.

"Well, that's convenient," Arkin whispered behind me. I shot him a disapproving glance. This poor woman had no idea what she'd wasted her life for. She had no clue to the eternal suffering she'd surrendered herself to.

I stepped forward, capturing the demon's attention. It raised off its claws, stretching upright, nearly reaching the ceiling with its tall frame. The demon tilted its mutated head and flexed lean arms out to its sides, flashing black claws like weapons, readying for an attack.

The woman's body arched backward, her eyes examining me upside- down with an expression of disgust and hate. Her bleeding arms reached over her head, bowing her chest toward the ceiling even farther. Her fragile spine grated and bent unnaturally.

A blaring shriek erupted from her toothless mouth as the Animus demon stabbed its talons under her rib cage. The monster glared at me, waiting for me to react. Her soul was damned no matter what I did to save her. She'd chosen her destiny as I'd chosen mine, and I couldn't stop what would happen to her in the end.

The demon dangled her limp body in the air, siphoning her soul from the multiple openings it had created in her chest. She continued to stare at me as the dim spark of life left her body and filled the fiend's skeletal nose. Within seconds, the harvest was finished, and the crone's body slammed against the wall like she was nothing more than a peanut shell being disposed of once the demon got what it came for.

The mass of burnt skin and atrophying muscle barreled toward me. I rushed forward to meet it, hooking my arms around its torso. We thrashed around, banging each other into the bed posts, dresser, and walls. I panted, breathing in the sulfuric odor seeping from its pores, as we struggled with each other's strength.

"I gotcha," Arkin grunted, clasping his hands around the monster's waist.

I punched its gruesome, mouthless face again and again while Arkin held it down.

Soon, the monster was too weak to fight.

I backed up a few paces and stared at the fiend, focusing every ounce of rage on the decomposing being slumped over in Arkin's arms. I roared, uncurling my fingers from tight fists. Fire spewed from my right hand, flames blazing up my forearm with purpose. I reared back my arm and slashed through the air. The demon's head thudded against the beige carpet and rolled twice, leaving a trail of ash in its wake.

Arkin's wide eyes watched my right arm as the flames retreated and fizzled out. "Well, that's new," he joked. His gaze jumped to the portal behind me. "Archard. It's time to go."

The orange glow was dimming, giving way to the pale pastels that had filled the room before. It wouldn't be long before the wall began to mend itself, closing my opportunity to cross realms. I looked one final time at Arkin and smiled. "I love you, brother."

"And I you, brother," Arkin returned with a wink.

I tucked my wings against me tight and took two quick strides across the room before diving into the receding crack. The wall gave like I was pushing through a vat of gel, then hardened behind me, serving me to a world of pure evil.

CHAPTER TWENTY-SIX

The Devil Always Has A Plan

My eyes strained to see the path ahead of me as I moved through a rocky tunnel too small for me to stand straight in, but big enough for me to hunch over and move onward.

"Gavyn?" I whispered. "Gavyn?" He didn't answer.

Somewhere, during our short, agonizing travels into Hell, I lost my grip on the captive I'd lugged with me. Gavyn passed out rather quickly after he awoke to the pain of portal jumping. I didn't know whether to be happy about that, or mad that he didn't have to suffer it like I had.

My hands skimmed lightly over the rough surfaces around me. I gasped, jerking my hand away when I came upon a bump that felt like a nose and mouth. My chest tightened with surprise and fear. I reached my fingers back into the darkness. The soft pads of my skin smoothed over the wall again, trying to see as a blind man would without sight.

A protruding ridge poked a couple of inches out of the stone, feeling too pliable to be rock. Below the ridge was a small hole. My thumb fell into the opening, and the gap closed around it. A slight suckling sensation tugged on my thumb, followed by a fleshy tongue swiveling its way along my finger. Teeth grazed my skin, then clamped into me. I yanked my hand away, holding back a yelp from the stinging at the base of my thumb.

I couldn't make it through this place with no light. There was no telling what dangers lurked in this black tunnel, especially with the walls trying to eat me.

I inhaled a deep breath, then relaxed my chest, releasing the air along with the slightest bit of my beast. The entity hovered in front of my face, occupying an area the size of a soccer ball, while discharging tiny flashes of violet into the air. I smiled graciously at the control it allowed me, and how well-behaved the beast was. Maybe there was hope for me after all.

The bright streaks zapped into the tunnel, streaking the atmosphere with light that spread out in a web-like pattern yards ahead of me. My smile fell, and I wrapped my arms around my middle as tight as possible.

Hundreds of faces grimaced, grinned, and sneered back at me. They jutted out from the sharp shards of rock, locked in a never-ending display of suffering and disdain. Their skin was as soot-black as the air filling the pathway, only distinguishable when my light illuminated their twisted features.

Their dead eyes chased me, boring into me as I did my best to avoid bumping into them. I pressed forward with creepy tongues unfolding and stretching out to taste bits of my flesh when I passed. I dreaded each step but continued deeper into Hell.

The rocky surface beneath me soon softened, becoming a soppy mess under my feet. It was like walking in loose, wet sand. Sucking sounds filled the tight space each time I pulled my foot up. I stumbled along the corridor, smashing faces when I threw my hand out to brace myself from falling, and nearly lost my right ring finger.

There's still time to turn around, a scared female voice urged in my head.

I squinted, clapping my hands over my ears, and slipped on the wet ground. My shoulder pounded into the wall of faces, grazing a sharp tooth. I hissed and righted myself quickly.

We can go back now. Trust me. You don't want to see what's waiting, Nevaeh. Layla's high-pitched begging rang against my eardrums.

"Stop," I commanded, gritting my teeth. "You were the one who wanted me to do this all along."

I know, she thought, regret lacing her essence. My eyelids relaxed, and I blinked a few times, relieved that she'd found her inside-voice in my head. *I had lost so much before...I still had so much to lose. Helping you will be the last good thing I can do before you send me to my eternity. I'm begging you, please don't go to him.*

"I have too much to lose too," I responded. "I guess we really aren't that different, are we?" I took a step forward and noticed that the wall I gauged to be around thirty feet ahead had moved, creating a dead-end only ten feet away. The faces scattered along the wall to my right began to peel apart in a straight line, separating like a seam in a zipper from ceiling to floor. Agonized groans fled the ebony, salivating mouths. Cold, meaty tongues split in two. Oily liquid poured from their wounds and dripped to the ground. The soppy material under my feet made perfect sense after witnessing that nasty mess.

I inspected the new corridor to my right with a knot forming in my gut.

He's leading you to him. He knows you're here, a heavily accented man added.

Follow your heart, baby girl. You can't live in fear of yourself anymore. I know who you are, and you have the strength to make it through this. Don't worry about saving everyone else...save yourself. George's words bleated out the other souls in my head and took precedence over my own doubtful feelings.

He was right. I had to save myself. I had to have faith in what I'd been given and my ability to tell the difference between the good and the evil inside me.

I straightened my spine as much as possible in the low tunnel and gathered my confidence, taking the opening to the right.

My cloud guided me through the dark until, finally, I entered a cavernous, dome-shaped room. I grudgingly slid my feet into the space, my eyes studying the disturbing surfaces surrounding me.

Thousands upon thousands of skins were nailed to the curved chamber with rusted ten-penny nails much like hides on a teepee. This was infinitely worse though. These were human skins of all colors and sizes. How many women and men had been subjected to the skinning process to make a collection this big?

I reached out a hand and dragged a finger over one of the skins. It was surprisingly warm as if blood still flowed beneath the surface. The flesh quivered under my touch and goose bumps raised to meet the pads of my fingers. It reacted to me. I gaped in disbelief as my gaze roamed over each malicious nail and stitch.

They are alive, I thought, swallowing the lump building in my throat.

"Beautiful, aren't they?" A deep timber spoke behind me. "These poor bastards sold their bodies for sex without remorse. Displayed their flesh for all to see and use like it were nothing more than a garbage can to lay their waste in. Some of these lustful bitches even did it for free."

Turning slowly, I curled my hands into white-knuckled fists, calling my small undulating shroud tight to me. The rest of my beast coiled in the confines of my ribs, anxious to burst out at my will.

"Bron," I grated, tensing my body and using it as a shield to protect my fragile spirit. Memories of how easily I lost my confidence when he was near floated into my mind. He was a master at manipulating. A master of me. Regardless of how much stronger I'd become after my escape, I could still feel my body leaning a minute amount toward him, yearning to surrender.

His waist-length, raven hair draped over his shoulders, shining under the yellow glow of the torches as he crossed the expanse separating us. His featureless beauty called to me like a siren in the darkest of nights. I shook my head, blocking the delicious shiver riding up my spine, and focused.

My Ater's midnight wings hung lazily behind him, dragging along the dirt as he moved. The dim light gleamed off the talons protruding just above his shoulders, spurring a memory of the way they felt when he pierced my skin. I swore the sting never left the scars he gave me.

"You've got me here, so let's get this over with."

I recoiled when he brushed the back of his hand against my cheek. His cocked his head to the side, his face pristine and deceitfully smooth. I knew what lay beneath that disguise, and I didn't, for one second, believe he was anything other than the monster he was. Evil to the core.

"Why do you shy away if you have already agreed to accept my proposal?"

I laughed without humor, resisting the urge to punch him, and leaned in close enough for my lips to graze his ear. "I think we negotiated some other issues you've yet to make good on."

Bron's chest vibrated with a chuckle that bounced off the slabs of flesh pinned around us. "You are correct, my child."

He turned and raised a hand, gesturing to a doorway on the other side of the skin cave. "She wants to get straight to business. No point in dragging it out."

Brace yourself, hon, Layla warned sympathetically. I squinted at the shaded silhouettes wavering in the opening. Torch light spilled onto their heads when they entered the space. Bron rubbed his hands together, his wings twitched excitedly, while he watched his guests arrive.

I swallowed a lump of anxiety and stepped to his side. My body stilled. I held my breath afraid to give away too much emotion.

First, Kenet stumbled through, streaks of blood dried all over his face and body like crimson tiger stripes. Blue and yellow circles rimmed his eyes, which locked onto mine the moment he noticed me standing next to Bron. A colossal Crucio demon stammered behind him, forcing Kenet to the side, steering him by the iron manacles securing his hands at his back.

When the next prisoner entered, the breath I held came out in an exhale of desperation. I felt like I'd been punched in the gut. My tearing eyes traced over a much older version of the woman I saw in the mirror every day. No amount of time away from her could wipe out the memory of how she made me feel, what she looked like, and the sound of her voice.

My mother shuffled forward, grunting and mumbling curse words at the Crucio demon appointed to her.

My throat was raw from choking back. The emptiness that had hollowed out the part of my heart saved for my parents ached and thumped to life.

George? I thought. *After all this time...I...I thought I'd never see them again.*

I focused my attention between the violet-blue eyes staring at me with pride and regret, and the frail beauty that shared my bone structure, hair color, and hidden power.

I know, girl. I prayed so many nights that you'd have this day, but now that it's here, I wish we were somewhere else. I fear they'll be yer downfall, George answered, sorrow lacing his tone.

Kenet's demon pulled his chains upward until he was doubled over with his arms wound backwards nearly above his head. He dropped to the ground, grunting from the pain of having his shoulders on the brink of dislocation.

My mother's demon reared back his hand and slammed a thick, metal pipe into the back of her knees.

I gasped, then relaxed with relief when the small razor blades fixed at the end of the pipe missed her flesh. She thudded forward on the dirt, toppling over until her head smacked against the ground. A curt whimper crossed her lips as she fought to hold back a scream. She rolled onto her shoulder and shoved herself upright, kneeling at Bron's feet.

My chest pulsed with electric power, eager to get revenge.

Bron turned to face me, waiting patiently for a half-cocked response.

At that moment, I would do anything to get them out of Hell. I opened my mouth to cry out my devotion, but a distant chant of prayers began filtering into my mind. I couldn't understand the language, but the priest's effort was comforting nonetheless. His words calmed my nerves to a functional level. I closed my eyes, inhaled a slow, deep breath, then opened them with renewed resolve, and exhaled.

"It's time to let them go," I said, scowling at the dark angel. "That was the deal."

He stroked his chin with one hand, considering our bargain. "I don't think that our previous arrangements are going to work for me, Nevaeh." He spoke my name like it was a curse to his very existence.

Purple-neon sparks ignited above me, reacting to the rage building within me. My eyes narrowed, and I struggled to keep control of myself.

Maybe that was what he wanted. Maybe he wasn't counting on the strength I've gained since we last met.

"How about we take this up the ranks. I believe it was the Devil himself that wanted me at his side. I'm done playing with a lesser Hell-Angel. Does he know what you are doing—trying to hoard me all to yourself?" I sneered.

Nevaeh! Layla shrieked through my brain, the rest of her words falling short under the breakout of thunderous laughter echoing through the cave.

I cupped my hands over my ears and lowered my head.

"Rhett?" my mother gasped in disbelief as the booming laughter subsided. My head whipped up, expecting to see another angel joining us. Instead, Arianna's gaze slid over the sharp eyes forming on Bron's face, then to the distinguished nose, and onto the sly grin curling his lips. I looked back and forth between the two, wondering why she thought Bron was Rhett.

From the corner of my eye, I noted Kenet struggling for a way to escape the demons and his cuffs. His jaw clenched, and his face reddened as recognition donned on him as well. Arianna's demon drew back its elbow, and the sound of a blade stabbing a hard, fleshy surface sounded in my ears.

I watched the fiend tear the razored end of its pipe from Kenet's back. His features twisted in intense pain. A horrifying roar erupted from his mouth.

I extended my spine, pushing my shoulders back, and opened my mouth as wide as possible. Fine streaks of current dashed up my arms, tingling along my skin in a mission to charge me with.

A large hand wrapped around my throat and clamped my airway shut. I wheezed and gargled.

"You might want to think twice, child," the Ater advised. "You let that monster go before I approve, and I'll make sure your precious mother suffers for all eternity."

Nevaeh, can you hear me? Arianna's voice filtered into my crowded mind.

I wiggled my finger, hoping she would see me and understand it as confirmation.

Destroy him. You can do it. Don't you dare miss your chance just to save us.

I wiggled my finger again, my gaze locked on the ruthless eyes glowering into my soul.

My slowing pulse pounded in my ears. Every vein above his hand felt like it was under extreme pressure, especially behind my eyeballs. It wouldn't be much longer before I blacked out. I clenched my hands around the forearm squeezing the life from me. My toes curled, my body stiffened, and I gave him everything I had. Jolts of power arced from me to him, lighting up the veins beneath his skin. He howled through the pulsating surge but didn't loosen his hold on me in the slightest.

"You wanna meet the Devil, darling?" His skewed features relaxed into a grin, and he pulled me into his broad, heaving chest. "I'll show you the Devil," his tone deepened as he spoke and splintered into a multitude of voices. The raven locks of hair cloaking his back and shoulders hardened, then flattened against his skin, creating an exoskeleton. The shell material spread over his torso, covering every inch of tan skin. The poisonous, black veins I'd trace with my fingers so many times before raced up his limbs like wildfire, melding with the slick mask of hair. Muscles rippled and doubled in size. Bones cracked and lengthened. His wings reached toward the walls, growing in proportion with his morphing body.

Seconds later, I hung in the air, nose to nose with the towering monster I'd met on two occasions. Once in the tunnel that led me away from my fantasy room my first time through the portal, and the other, when I stole George's soul from Hell.

All this time, I was The Devil's slave. I thought I had a grip on who I was. I was only kidding myself though. How Rhett had become the King of Hell I wasn't sure, and at this point, it really didn't matter, but somehow it happened, and I played his fool the entire time.

The gigantic monster snorted, the breath leaving his nostrils dampening my face and hair. His fiery red eyes swirled like rolling lava as he read my defeated expression and smiled. His free hand reached around my back and pulled out the small book I'd stuffed in my belt.

He dropped me from a height of at least fifteen feet. I crashed against the ground, the impact causing my knees to buckle at awkward angles under my weight. I cried out, rolling on my back and tucking my legs to my chest until some of the aching pain subsided.

"It started with this book," the multitude of voices explained, "and it will end with it." The ground quaked as he turned to address my mother. "You hid from me. You hid her from me. I thought you loved me." Wrath bunched his muscles. He was a cannon ready to fire.

"I never loved you," she spat. "I loved the angel that watched over me and offered me companionship—the majestic being that inhabited your body before you traded your Holiness for this Evil." Pure disgust bled from her expression. She wasn't afraid of him.

I gritted my teeth and propped myself up on my knees, then gulped down the pain-induced urge to vomit. Shifting one leg forward to push against my knee, I managed to stand myself up. My heart pounded in my chest. The voices in my head were quiet, but I could feel them there, rattling around behind my own thoughts. Fear emanated from them all.

Tilting back my head and opening my mouth wide, I exhaled, invoking all the power I held within me. Nothing happened. No sparks tingling in my fingers. No suffocating mass crowding my throat. Nothing.

My eyes darted to Kenet and Arianna. Kenet's swollen eyes opened a sliver and peered up at me, defeat clear in his gaze. Arianna lifted her chin in defiance and sneered at the Devil trudging toward her.

I shook my hands, then thrust them out in front of me.

Still, nothing.

The demon king chuckled, the sound vibrating my bones. "What's the matter, child? Your gifts from God not working quite how you planned?" He didn't even look back at me when he spoke. He wasn't worried about what I could do at all.

Why isn't it working? I closed my eyes and concentrated. My beast was anxious, riling to get out, but she was stuck.

There's something hindering you. A talisman or something like the Hell-stone I had, Layla whispered in my mind.

"Of course," I deadpanned. *What the fuck am I supposed to do now?*

I scanned my surroundings, finding zilch to help me take out a giant, winged, horned devil.

Rhett-slash-Bron-slash-The Devil bent over and lifted my mother from the ground, draping her over his large palm before surrounding her fragile body in his long, clawed fingers. Her face reddened, veins bulging, as he squeezed tightly around her lungs. He raised her to his face. Red eyes rolled to the back of his head as he inhaled her scent. A shudder ran down his spine.

"Oh, how I've missed you, my love," he cooed. The tip of his thick, pointed tongue peeked past his sharp teeth and slithered up my mother's cheek, tasting her as he'd done to me in the fantasies Bron planted in my head.

I shivered at the realization of how much I hated, yet needed, the affection he showed me. He usually followed it up with a stern punishment for not willingly conforming to his ways.

Now, Nevaeh. Get the weapons from the demons. My mother's voice whirled through my mind.

I lifted one foot, then the other, inching toward the demons that jealously watched their king taste the flesh of a Light Celata. My eyes jumped from the Devil to the demons to Kenet repeatedly. Kenet's body lay in a motionless heap on the ground. He peered up at me through narrowed eyelids, careful not to move and draw the demon's attention away from the Devil reminiscing with my mother.

A guttural snarl resonated around me. I stopped in my tracks, holding back a gasp.

"You think I don't know what you are doing?" The Devil slowly craned his neck toward me. "Don't, for a second, think you can best me, bitch."

He took two long strides in my direction, then dropped Arianna to my right. Her body slumped over, kneeling on the ground, audibly sucking in air. The giant scooped up Kenet and slammed him on the ground to my left. Kenet groaned, rolling on the dirt next to me, pieces of gravel sticking to the drying blood on this face.

"You will do what I ask," he commanded. "You will help me leave this place." The Devil's lips curled back over shiny, obsidian teeth. He tossed the velvet book at my feet. A coal-hued feather escaped the pages and drifted to the soil beside the book. "Pick it up," he snorted angrily.

"No," I shouted. I would not let him use me as a tool to fulfill his evil intentions.

The monster pounded his fists into the ground and leaned in toward my face. His blistering breath burned my skin like a bad sunburn. "Pick up the fucking book and feather, Nevaeh. Believe me when I say I have no problem forcing your hand."

I stared into the swirling pools of liquid fire that were his eyes. They were not empty as I would have thought. He carried the sorrow, fury, and torment of every soul ever condemned. Or maybe they were reflecting my own judgments and wrongs. Either way, I was drawn to the pain emanating from his depths. Why, I didn't know.

A piercing scream broke me from my trance. My gaze jerked to my right. Arianna was dangling in the air, impaled by the Devil's taloned wing. When I looked to my left, Kenet grimaced back at me, also floating with a talon jammed in his back.

"Don't," Kenet gurgled.

My eyes flicked back to the woman I'd lost so long ago. This was the only thing I could do. I just prayed I'd be strong enough to get us out of it.

I squatted down, gathering the book and feather, then waited for my next order.

"That's right, child. Open the book."

I did as I was told, finding some pages with words on them and some without. I flipped to a section with words on my left and a blank page to the right. My gaze skimmed over handwriting that shimmered against the vellum. It hummed to me, calling me to examine it closer, to explore the sentences with my fingers.

"Once the Clavis awakens its key with original love's blood and the traitor's plume, it will possess the power to unlock doors to the gates of realms beyond its own and travel at will," The Dark Prince recited with a smile.

Kenet and Arianna's bodies swung within reach of me, both staring at me with expressions of misery and sympathy on their faces. They knew what the Devil was talking about, and it didn't sound good.

"Take the feather and slit their throats," the Demon King directed in a low, satisfied blend of many voices. His perilous eyes gleamed with the anticipation of what he asked.

"Never," I squeaked out with a sob. There was no way I could kill my parents. My heart ached at the thought of it.

"Do it," he boomed, thrusting his captives closer to me.

"I will not!" Tears poured down my cheeks, blurring the distraught faces looking back at me.

It's okay, Nevaeh. Do what you must. Save yourself, my sweet girl. My mother's voice echoed amid my racing thoughts, warming me to the core.

It's not okay, I argued. *I just got you back.*

I jerked when my parents suddenly dropped to the ground. The cavernous space filled with roars of pain. The devil's large form tumbled backwards, liquid the color of wine spewing behind him like a geyser. He flailed around, grabbing at the gaping wounds on his back. My eyes widened, darting to the two appendages splayed across the dirt. Blood leaked from the torn flesh at their attachment points.

Another piercing groan rang in my ears. The Devil's body arched backwards, then he dropped to his knees.

My eyes locked onto the Heavenly being standing behind the giant, his right hand molded into a blade up to his elbow, razor sharp edges gleaming under the blazing whirlwind coiled around it.

Archard's gaze found me, and a relieved smile graced his beautiful face.

He was different now. There was a glow about him, and he had four wings—pure as snow. His chest expanded as he inhaled and tightened his face. He drew his sword up over his head, shifting his focus to the Devil's neck, revealing his intentions to behead him.

Seconds passed as I waited for my savior to end this nightmare.

The end never came.

"What are you waiting for?" I cried.

"He's waiting on me." Footsteps scuffled along the wall behind me.

I cringed at the sound of his voice. I should have known.

I searched the cave for Gavyn. He was standing just beyond the two Crucio corpses piled on the ground. His hands were fisted in the air, pointing in Archard's direction, holding him in position as if there were strings attached to my angel that only he could control.

"I can't let you leave here without fulfilling the prophecy, Nev." His troubled gaze flicked from Archard to me. There was anguish in his soul that I'd never be able to soothe, even if I was willing to stay with him and burn in the Hell fires.

"Why, Gavyn?" I whimpered. "We can end this now and leave." I took stock of his rigid posture, his tormented face, and the stone burning a bright emerald between his collarbones. I put Layla's necklace around his neck so he'd make it through the portal, and it was biting me in the ass.

"Forgiveness isn't an option for us, Nev. We can't go back." His voice cracked, betraying his grief and regret. "You have to fulfill the prophecy. It's the only way." Gavyn considered the feather in my one hand and the book in my other. "Even if we kill him now, another will take his place. That's the way of it. The universe requires a balance. Good cannot be good without evil to contrast and define the difference. If I have to be the bad guy to maintain the balance, so be it."

He pointed a hand out toward me, and I was suddenly immobile, my body submitting to Gavyn's reins. I tried one last time to call my beast to the surface, but my power was pushed down by the stone's authority demanding it to stay put.

A congregation of prayers in English, and Latin I assumed, flooded my head. The voices of three people repeated calls to God, begging for help, synching their chants to a distracting pace and volume.

I scrunched my face up and willed my limbs to move, but it was no use. Archard groaned from some distance away, but I couldn't turn my head to see what was going on.

Gavyn lowered the hand directed at me and dragged it in a line toward my parents. My muscles sprang to life and moved as he commanded, stopping when I was an arm's length away from them. I strained to look down at them. A fresh ache bloomed in my chest as I recognized the despair in their faces.

"Gavyn, don't do this!" I pleaded.

With this view, Archard was easier to see. His arms slowly lowered a few inches before yanking back up again.

"You made your own sacrifices. This is mine." Gavyn motioned for my hand to lift the feather in the air. "I'm sacrificing my soul for yours, Nev. I will waste away in this damned place, if it means you will become the saving grace the world needs."

He swiped his hand downward, forcing mine to slash at the thin skin below my mother's chin.

I sucked in a deep breath, my eyes darting to the blood dripping from the quill tip of the feather.

One more quick diagonal swipe of my hand, and crimson gushed from a fatal laceration in my father's neck.

Gavyn released his hold on me. I fell forward, landing on my knees, my palms flattened over the cursed pages of The Clavis. My shoulders quaked around useless prayers begging God for this to be a horrible nightmare. Tears spilled from my eyes and dripped to the vellum, mixing with the blood on my fingers.

Two rivers of red pooled together and blended in a single puddle, soaking the velvet-covered prophecy beneath my hands. Strained gurgles drew my attention from the book. My mother's fading eyes fixed on me, her lips pulling into a smile.

How could she possibly be smiling right now? I've killed her.

This is your destiny, daughter. Remember the goodness in your soul, because you will need it for what comes next. I forgive you, so forgive yourself.

"No," I shouted as the light dimmed in her eyes. "You can't leave me!"

I scrambled forward, planting my hands in the wet stickiness around her head, and placed my mouth on hers. I inhaled deeply. Her lips relaxed when I exhaled. I inhaled again, and nothing but the bitter scent of blood pulled forth. I pounded my hand against the ground and gnashed my teeth together to keep from screaming.

"Nev...it's okay," Kenet garbled in a barely audible absolution.

I sat back on my feet, twisting my crimson-stained hands in my shirt, wishing I could crawl in a hole and forget everything.

"The book," he rasped. "Evoke...the book." The fire in his eyes fizzled out with one last breath.

My body shuddered, ripping apart from a violent wrath and torment so shattering, I'd never be able to piece myself back together again.

An intense light beamed from the center of the room, momentarily blinding me. The influx of energy flung me backward, slamming me into the skin-wall. Moments later, when the light softened and my vision returned, I saw Archard barreling toward Gavyn.

The two crashed into each other, grabbing and punching any chance they got. Archard reached for the stone and received a jab in his side. His glow was fading. His head tilted back, shadows of an eagle's face dancing under his skin. He cawed and shook his head. The outline of a lion's head morphed from the eagle. He opened his jaw and clamped razor-sharp fangs into Gavyn's shoulder.

Gavyn recoiled, pressing his hand over the wound. "What the hell are you?" he breathed, examining Archard with a stunned expression.

"The Cherubim that will be your end," Archard promised. He jerked his head again, and horns sprung from his scalp then wavered, regressing back into hair. He snorted, and the horns returned.

You gotta move, baby girl. Get the book, George coaxed.

I sniffled and wiped away my tears with the back of my hands. Crawling forward, I found the book I'd kneed aside trying to save my mom. I breathed in a stammered breath and dragged the book onto my lap, the saturated binding leaving a cold moisture that soaked through my pants and chilled my skin.

The feather. Use it to prick your finger, Layla said.

No, you can't listen to her, the priest shouted in my head.

But it was too late.

Droplets of blood rolled from my index finger and splattered onto an empty page. Violet lightning arched from my finger to the page, zapping the wet, red dot. The rust-colored scrolling came to life and transformed into radiant gold, each letter gleaming with power. It slithered around the edges of vellum like a snake searching for a meal, swirling through the drops of blood and creating words that weren't there before. They shifted so fast I couldn't comprehend them.

Pressure built in my chest, and my throat filled with the suffocating substance I'd tried to set free at the beginning of all this misery.

"That's it, girl," the Devil's voice purred, his ill intentions weighing me down in a blanket of evil.

I choked on the power clawing its way out of me. My fingers tingled. My skin puckered with the need for release.

I glanced back down at the book, seeking guidance. I'd killed my parents and appeared to be doing exactly what the Devil wanted me to do all along.

Hiccupping a thick puff of my vicious cloud, I watched the lettering melt like metal in a kiln. The pages bubbled then liquefied into a milky substance, dripping between my fingers. I cupped my hands to contain the melting book. The velvet binding and blood dissolved, a few rogue drops spilling over the sides of my palms.

Tiny rivulets of white, red, and gold scuttled out of my hands, defying gravity as they spiraled up my wrists and forearms like tiny overflowing streams until my palms were dry. Sharp needle-pricking pain stabbed my skin. I rubbed my arms, trying to stop the discomfort, but it only made the stinging worse. The book's pages and words seeped into my pores and spread through my body, riding my veins and arteries.

I searched for Archard. I needed to see him alive. I needed him to save me.

My Guardian stood over Gavyn, pinning him to the ground, his sword tip aimed at Gavyn's heart. One push downward and the man who introduced me to this world, who sacrificed his faith for me, would die.

Archard trained his focus on me. His eyes widened, concern softening his fierce expression when he noticed the reddish-gold ribbons glowing under my skin.

Gavyn smiled, then peered up at Archard. "Do it. I'm damned either way."

The angel's eyes hardened, pausing for a moment as he considered Gavyn's words. He slowly leaned forward, slipping his burning hand into the Dark Celata's heart. Beside Archard's blazing arm, the emerald light of Layla's stone dimmed, mimicking the life-force draining from Gavyn's body.

A sob escaped my mouth. My cloud of doom followed the sound, tearing out of my body in a hurricane of grief. Electric currents whipped into the air, flickering amid the storm brewing above my head. Blood raced through my body, thrumming with a new power offered by the prophecy pumping in my veins.

I pushed myself off the ground and took one deliberate step after another until I stared down into the Devil's fiery eyes. Archard approached him from the other side, the flames swirling around his metallic arm flickering in and out from my gale-strength winds.

"Kill me, child. This body is just a vessel. My spirit will find another," he said, soaking in the bath of his own wicked blood.

I smiled and lowered to my knees next to his head. My hand caressed his hollowed cheek. His rubbery, midnight skin lightened to a pale-tan under my touch. The harsh ridges of his devilish face smoothed and recessed, vanishing to portray the featureless face I'd grown to care for in some demented way—the face of my Ater.

"That's the being I yearned for." I said approvingly, threading my fingers through his long hair before skimming my hands along the curves of horns. "How could I kill you, my dark angel?" I glanced up at Archard, then back to Bron. "You were the one who showed me what I could be. Thank you for that. Thank you for forcing me to develop my gifts so I could become the person I am now." I slipped my hand over the hard ripples of his chest, grazing the many dips and rises of his stomach. Leaning in close to his ear, I whispered, "Thank you for making this so damned easy."

The scent of fear drifted into the air as my fingers slipped upward, stopping over his heart. A stream of white, liquid electric poured from my fingers into the Dark Prince's body, arcing and scorching the air between us. He convulsed, arching his back up then slamming into the ground. His poisonous veins lit up from my surging power like a flashing road map under his skin.

My cloud churned violently, lowering around us to cast judgment over my victim.

I ripped my hand from Bron's chest and leaned back reveling in the high I felt.

"Nevaeh. Nevaeh, what's going on?" Archard shouted over the whirring storm, sounding distant—scared.

In my need for revenge, I didn't think to exclude him from my wrath. Images of a thousand suffering, agonized souls swirled around us, and he was likely seeing and feeling them as well. I glanced back down at Bron, making sure he was still breathing, that he was getting his fill of punishment. I had no idea what I'd do with him afterwards, but I knew he deserved to feel a little of his own medicine for shattering my world the way he had.

Through the storm of lightning and judgment, I caught sight of

Archard's hand moving in an arch downward toward Bron's neck. Flames billowed around his skin, meshing with my own fiery lightning.

"No," I cried out as Bron's head separated from his body.

In that instant, my life shifted once again.

My head reared back without permission, mouth opening to receive the stream of pitch black essence flowing from the corpse I'd only meant to torture. I screamed as the thick, bitter vapor stuffed itself into my body, purring happily as it dove in, pushing the other trapped souls I carried aside. My mouth snapped shut, gagging on the putrid taste of the Devil's spirit.

This was what Rhett had foreseen but gravely misinterpreted—what God had tried to warn us about. The unhappy ending to an unrequited love, a greedy heart, and a lack of faith.

This was what the Devil wanted all along. I would be his new vessel, and unless I stayed in Hell for all eternity, I would be his way out of here.

This is my body now, girl. There is no staying here, he roared in my thoughts.

THE END

BOOKS BY HAVEN

The Faltering Souls Series

Falter

Nevaeh Richards thinks she has found a chance to leave her homeless life behind. When the spirit of the only father she knows is wrongfully taken to Hell, Nevaeh is hurled into a world haunted by monstrous demons, rogue Guardian angels, love that is beyond her control, and a soul-threatening choice between the inherent evil inside her and the faltering faith she is struggling to grasp.

Severance

Nevaeh has to face the overpowering gravity of her choice to save those she loves while striving for strength to fight her greatest threat—herself.

Contrition

Trial after trial, Nevaeh's loved-ones have struggled to save her from a dark destiny. The time has finally come for her to return home and join the Earth-bound angels in a war threatening to destroy the Human race. Is it really Nev who's walking the Earthly plane, though?

The Perilously Pretty Series

The Perilously Pretty Series is a compilation of wicked romance novels about badass women from all eras and walks of life.

Craving Love & Death

Most women in the '50s dream of a perfect life, pleasing their bread-winning husbands and raising happy families. Vivienne…well…she dreams of a life in which she doesn't succumb to the need to murder the men she sleeps with.

Coveting Love & Revenge

1871, high-society Savannah, Georgia.

Penniless and jaded governess, Synthia James, is trapped with her employer. When he bids their young housemaid to kill a man who threatens his business, Synthia's maternal instincts take over, and she commits the heinous deed herself.

ABOUT HAVEN CAGE

Haven Cage lives in the Carolinas with her husband and son. After many years of dabbling with drawing, painting, and working night shift in the medical field, she decided to try her hand at writing. Unfortunately, her love for books came later in life and proved to add a healthy challenging during her writing journey.

Determined to hone her craft, though, she soaks up as much information as she can, spends her free time tapping away in her favorite local coffee shop, and keeps a good book in hand whenever possible.

What began as a hobby has grown into a way of escape and the yearning to take her journey farther, her love for writing and reading deepening along the way.

Haven loves to socialize and hear from her fans. Connect with her at the following links:

Facebook.com/HavenCage/
Instagram: Haven Cage
Pinterest: Author Haven Cage
Twitter: @HavenCage

Look for Haven on Goodreads.com and add her to your bookshelf!

You can, also, visit her website at www.authorhavencage.com. While you're there, join Haven's Groupies to receive updates, exclusive sales info, and play Haven's Puzzlers for chances to win prizes.

If you enjoyed this book, please leave a review as it is how authors succeed in the publishing world. Without the reader's love, we would be nowhere.